I0636401

SHADOWS OF
THE FALLEN

By Corey McCullough

Rust on the Allegheny: A Novel

THE FALLEN ODYSSEY SERIES

The Fallen Odyssey
The Fallen Aeneid
Shadows of the Fallen
Children of the Fallen
The Cycle of Aurym

ROGUES' GALAXY SERIES

A Knife in the Dark
A Knife in the Dark: Alloyheart

SHADOWS OF THE FALLEN

COREY MCCULLOUGH

SHADOWS OF THE FALLEN

2nd Paperback Edition

Copyright © 2024 by Corey McCullough

All rights reserved. No part of this book may be reproduced in any form.

ISBN: 978-1-964478-02-9

First paperback edition © 2018 by Corey McCullough

First printed in the United States of America in 2018

9 8 7 6 5 4 3 2 1

AUTHOR'S NOTE TO THE SECOND EDITION

I have a confession to make. *The Fallen Odyssey* series was supposed to be a trilogy.

Spoiler alert: It isn't.

Believe me when I tell you, I *tried*. I did my best to fit this story into three books, I really did! Right from the start, I knew how the story would end, and I envisioned it as a three-act structure. But as I set out to write that final act, something was bothering me that I couldn't quite put my finger on.

After a lot of false starts on writing Book III of the series, I came to realize that several key things had to happen between the events at the conclusion of *The Fallen Aeneid* and the events that logically marked the beginning of the final act.

To remedy this, I conceived of a Book III in which a significant passage of time had occurred since Book II. Some details would have to be thrown in here and there, possibly in the form of a few flashbacks, to show the reader what had happened off-stage during the interim. It seemed like a doable solution. Problem solved, right? Well, not so much.

I'm sure that the gap-in-time approach *could* have been made to work. But in execution, I found myself unsatisfied with it. It felt forced and hamfisted. Like trying to hammer down a bent nail. And, bottom line, it just wasn't much fun to be repeatedly taken out of the present narrative to get reminded of how the characters got where they were and to account for the gap in time. Consequently, this plan (and all the associated writing I did in support of it) was scrapped.

My next attempt at a solution was to write a short story that would bridge the gap in time. That would do it! So, I started writing.

Short story. Yeah, right.

Before I knew it, my short story was not so short. But I did not despair. Because the longer the story got, the clearer the vision became, and the more smoothly it flowed. It was coming fast now. And when the work flows fast and feels easy, like you're riding your bike down the steepest street in the neighborhood, you don't turn around and start peddling uphill. You don't question it. You hold on tight, let the wind take your hair, and see what happens. Besides, I figured the worst-case scenario was that my "short story" became a "novella" instead. Semantics.

The working title for this rapidly expanding story was *Shadows of the Fallen*, which started out as a private joke to myself: a reference to *Star Wars: Shadows of the Empire*, the 1996 novel by author Steve Perry (not the guy from Journey) that covered the events between *The Empire Strikes Back* and *Return of the Jedi*. It was kind of like Part 2.5 of George Lucas's Original Trilogy. To my surprise, my joke title ended up fitting the story better than I could have anticipated, so the name stuck.

It was when my "Part 2.5 novella" surpassed the 100,000-word mark and I still hadn't even reached the story's finale that I had to own up to the fact that what I had on my hands was a full-fledged, full-length novel, and an integral part of the series as a whole. The manuscript became Book III officially, and the final length of my fantasy series became . . . questionable.

Shadows of the Fallen, in spite of the improvisational nature of its writing and the uncertainty surrounding its production, was one of my favorite books to write. It busted me out of my longest stretch of writer's block to date, and I have fond, vivid memories of the process of sitting down and pounding out the words you're about to read, especially the parts told from Hook's perspective. Plus, there's just something about the story structure of three point-of-view characters in three storylines running parallel to one another that feels like sinking into a warm bath. It's probably not a coincidence that I have revisited this structure multiple times since.

If you enjoy this book half as much as I enjoyed writing it, you're in for a fun read. Thanks for reading, and watch out for sea monsters.

Justin's training culminated in Cyaxares casting doubts on Zechariah's motives. When Avagad himself arrived with an army of demons, Justin helped a portion of the Ru'Onorath escape, but at a great price: Ahlund sacrificed himself by running his own blade through his body to attack Avagad, giving Justin a chance to escape.

Now, with Ahlund lost and the future uncertain, Justin is left with more questions than answers. And, hundreds of miles away, Leah, now the queen of Nolia, must decide whether to prepare for the next demon attack or mobilize her forces and invade Avagad's seat of power in ERUM, half a world away. . . .

PART I

THE

KNIFE EDGE

CHAPTER 1

His ears rang from the volume of his own screams as the contraption was removed from his head. Even in the middle of it all, Hook found himself thinking back to something he remembered seeing as a young boy. Not that long ago, really.

He'd been standing on a waist-high wooden fence, flanked by a couple of his childhood friends, all barefoot and dirty-faced like himself. The morning's games had been interrupted by the chance to watch one of the local ranchers branding one of his newest calves.

To this day, Hook could feel the unfinished planks of the fence beam against the skin of his heels as he watched the little old man heat up his branding device: an iron rod bearing the ranch's symbol. The rancher had placed the rod's end in a bed of hot coals until it had glowed red. He'd confidently approached the animal from behind while the calf had stood there, none the wiser. Then he had pressed the red-hot brand against the calf's hindquarters, hard and fast.

Hook remembered how the calf had let out a startled bay and kicked once from the shock of the pain. Then it had shuffled off with a huff of annoyance, the new symbol of ownership burned into its rear. It had all happened so quickly, and the animal seemed to forget about the incident altogether after a moment.

But this device, the one they had used to brand Hook, was quite different.

As soon as he'd been pushed into this tiny room in the dungeons below the city of Ephixes, his eyes had been drawn to the small furnace in the corner, and the long metal rod resting in a bed of hot coals. The three men had forced him into a chair bolted to the stone floor, and metal shackles had been fitted around his wrists to keep him in place. Hook had known what was coming, and the memory of the branded cattle had naturally come rushing to the forefront of his mind. But nothing could have prepared him for the reality.

A contraption had been affixed to his head—an unremarkable little thing almost elegant in its simplicity. The business end was a simple one-inch-thick bar of cold metal hammered into a semicircle, which could be fastened about the back of one's head by way of an adjustable leather strap. There were several different sizes hanging from hooks on the wall, and the first one they'd tried had been too big for Hook. So the round-bellied, apron-wearing man in charge had switched it out for a smaller apparatus that had fit more snugly around the curvature of his skull.

The metal rod had been allowed to continue heating while his captors tightened the headgear, a half-halo of metal secured to his forehead midway between his brow and hairline. He'd tried to pull away, but the three men were too strong, and the leather belt was ratcheted tight. Only then did the biggest of the men retrieve the metal rod from the furnace.

While the other two men held Hook down, the rod's blunt, red-hot end had been applied not to Hook's skin, but to the cold metal band.

Over the course of several long seconds, the heat of the rod had slowly warmed the metal band. And the metal band had gone from cold to warm to searing hot against his skin.

The night before, curled up on the floor of a cell of bare stone and iron bars, Hook had promised himself that no matter his fate, no matter what they did to him, he would not ask for mercy, he would not beg, and he would not cry out.

He did not ask for mercy. He did not beg. But he did cry out.

He screamed, in fact. The headgear remained in place no matter how he thrashed, burning his skin. It felt bone-deep—felt like the soft matter between his temples was boiling. And the sounds that came from his throat were louder and far more humiliating than the baying of any branded calf. Even after the man lowered the heated rod, the agony did not stop; the metal band took much longer to cool down than it had to heat up. By the time the men finally loosened the leather belt, the room stunk like roasted ham.

Hook's screams did not sound like his own as the contraption was removed from his head. He felt an odd tugging sensation as strings of flesh peeled away with it, trailing from the edges of the branding device. Fluid trickled over his eyebrows.

The brander was tossed into a nearby pail of water with a sharp hiss, and Hook was still crying out in agony when the biggest man ducked down to look him in the eye. The man made a long face. He seemed perplexed, and maybe a little impressed, as if he were examining a type of carpentry joint he'd never seen before.

"Blimey," he said. "He's still awake."

Although Hook could not stop the noises coming from his mouth, he managed to force his jaw closed until his teeth were clamped shut. His cries did not end but took on a new cadence as he reformed them into words.

"I'll get you for this," he said, half snarling and half wailing through his clenched teeth. "All of you."

The three men ignored his oath. "This happen often?" one of them asked.

"Sometimes," said the big man in the apron. He returned to the wall with the hooks and fetched another tool. "Most of them pass out as soon as the brander heats up. Don't wake up again until the healer's seen to them. I feel sorry for the ones who manage to stay awake for this part. Hold his head, please."

Two sets of hands grabbed Hook's head. A thumb brushed against his freshly burned skin, and his vision went blurry with the pain. Hook growled and flailed, trying to throw himself free of their grip, but it was no use.

"What is he? A foreigner?" asked one of the men holding him.

"Hard to rightly tell," said the big man. "Manifest says he's half-islander."

"He seems young for this sort of sentence," said the other one. "Barely a man. What'd you do, kid?"

"I wouldn't make it a habit of conversing with them," the big man advised his coworker without turning around.

The big man approached the chair. In one hand, he held a triangular wedge of wood that looked like a doorstop. In his other hand was a pair of fireside tongs. He looked at Hook. But not at him, really. It was more like he was seeing through him.

"Open, please," the big man said.

"You will pay for this," Hook spat. "I'll be back for you. All of you. By everything holy, I swear it—!"

The rest of his words were cut off as the man pushed the triangular wedge of wood into Hook's mouth.

With a practiced hand, the big man turned the wedge sideways, so that the fat side pried open Hook's mouth and held it there. His jaw was forced open nearly as wide as it would go, his molars resting in a row of notches—tooth-shaped ridges worn into the wood through previous applications. He tried to spit it out, tried to push it out with his tongue, tried again to pull away from the hands holding him in place, and failed on all counts.

The open tongs were inserted into Hook's mouth. Metal claws pinched down on his tongue, one on the top and one on the bottom, so hard that they nearly punched through it.

"I used to talk to them sometimes," the big man said, a note of regret in his voice. "Used to ask them if they had any last words, as a courtesy. But I soon ended the practice. I found that it only further frightened the poor things, which is cruel."

The big man drew back on the tongs, pulling on Hook's tongue so hard that the narrow sliver of skin that anchored it to the bottom of his mouth felt like it would split.

A flash of orange light—the glow of the furnace's bed of coals reflected on the face of a blade in the big man's hand. It was not a knife but a small handsaw lined with overlapping teeth. The kind used for pruning branches.

As the big man in the apron raised the handsaw, Hook was still trying to yell through his open mouth. Trying to tell them they'd never make him beg. They'd never break him. He'd be back for them. Every one of them. They'd all pay for this.

But he forgot all of this the instant he felt the overlapping metal teeth come to rest against his tongue, and for the first time in his life, he couldn't think.

The big man locked eyes with him. And again, he seemed to be looking *through* Hook, not at him. As if he weren't really there. Only now did Hook realize that he was not getting out of this. This was really about to happen. He heard himself make an involuntary noise that sounded like a desperate plea. Then the man flexed his fingers to draw a tighter grip on the saw handle, and with one swift pull—

C H A P T E R   2

Hook woke up, sitting up sharply and clamping his mouth shut to stifle the scream about to erupt from his throat, biting his lip in the process.

He looked around. The barracks of the Palace of Cervice were dark. The sleeping figures in the cots surrounding him were illuminated only dimly by the coals of a dying fire in the big hearth at the far end of the room. Sword belts and boots rested on the brick floor at the foot of every bed. Some of the soldiers had blankets. Those who didn't used their second sets of clothing, or whatever else they could find, as cover from the winter chill.

Hook raised a trembling finger to his mouth and probed at the place where he'd bitten his lip. His finger came away dotted red in the firelight, but it wasn't bad. He seemed to bite himself like this every time he had that dream. Probably because he woke still trying to bite down to free himself before he could be silenced. Forever.

He pushed the pile of spare clothes off his body. City-wide rationing had imposed strict daily limits on allotted kindling, and the hearth was so ineffectual at this distance that it may as well have been empty. He could see his breath in the stale air as he stood from the cot, and he could hardly feel the cold of the floor beneath his stocking feet. Yet, despite the partial numbness in his extremities, he found himself covered in a layer of sweat. When the chill finally overrode his nerves, his sweat would become a freezing second skin that would sap his body heat. Best to dry off before that happened.

He raised his hand to touch the strip of cloth he wore around his forehead. Even it was wet with sweat. Beneath it, the half-halo of scar tissue that ran above his brow, in a perfectly straight band from temple to temple, ached. It always ached. It hadn't healed properly, and it hurt every moment of every day. Ever since a big man in an apron had given it to him all those years ago.

The details of that recurring nightmare were always starker than his actual memory of the event. In reality, he didn't remember the reflection of the furnace coals in the blade of the handsaw. He didn't remember feeling strings of flesh peel away from his skull. Nor did he remember the feeling of the individual teeth of the saw resting against his tongue just before the cut was made. These elements, and variations of other horrors, were inventions of his imagination that changed and evolved over time. The narrative never deviated. Nor did the outcome. But his subconscious seemed determined to find imaginative new ways to enhance the terror of the experience every time he relived it.

There was, however, one thing about that day that he would never forget, and that was the phrasing of his last words. They were, after all, the final words he had ever spoken and would ever speak in this life.

"You will pay for this," he had said. "I'll be back for you. All of you. By everything holy, I swear it."

Hook slipped his boots on and fastened his sword belt, trying not to notice the way his hands trembled as he buckled it. He moved silently down the rows of cots lining the cave-like interior of the barracks, filled with men and women of varying races and nationalities. There were Nolians, Endens, Mythaeans, Raeqlu, Cru, and others whose origins were less than obvious to Hook. Even some Darvellians—soldiers who had been part of a large-scale assault against the city just a couple of days before—had pledged their allegiance to Queen Leah and the Athacean League. All these disparate groups, brought together in an alliance of necessity against the demons, were now sleeping under one roof, without enough blankets to go around.

Not even enough fuel to keep a proper fire going through a winter's night, he thought.

Quietly, Hook took the single remaining log left beside the stone hearth, the last rationed piece of fuel for the night, and placed it atop the low-burning coals in the fireplace. As he held his hands out over the tiny flames that climbed up the split log, his gaze dropped to the glowing coals beneath it. His mind wandered back to a furnace in a dungeon beneath the Mythaean city of Ephixes, far from here. The place where he had uttered his last words.

You will pay for this. I'll be back for you. All of you. By everything holy, I swear it.

Something like fifteen years had passed since he'd made that oath. Fifteen years since the captain of the *Manticore* had selected him, freshly branded, from a lineup of fellow convicted criminals and assigned him to a seat in the trireme's underbelly. After that, with the exception of daily "constitutionals," forced marches around the ship to prevent slaves' leg muscles from atrophying, plus weekly douses of seawater to cut down on the body odor and haircuts and shaves once a year, Hook had spent almost every hour of every day seated in one spot. For years, he had eaten there, slept there, and labored there. And, during moments of respite, when there had been no labor to be done, he had waited there, thinking only about his oath.

You will pay for this. I'll be back for you.

A footstep behind him.

Hook turned. He was impressed. Even in a nearly silent room, Adonica Lor had managed to make it almost halfway to the hearth before Hook had heard her, and his ears were sharp. Like him, she was fully dressed and wore her sword belt. In a way, he was relieved to see that he wasn't the only one who no longer felt comfortable unless he was armed, even in the middle of a peaceful night.

Adonica approached the other side of the hearth and leaned casually against the stone with her arms crossed and one foot up against it.

"Wouldn't you know it?" she whispered, staring off into the room of soldiers in cots. "Weeks spent sleeping in a cellar in Hartla, days cooped up at sea, and the first decent bed I get, I'm stuck beside an Enden who snores like a shug-monkey with a head cold."

She turned to look at Hook, waiting for him to say something. Hook regarded her silently, then used the toe of his boot to adjust the log in the fire. He'd first met this Mythaean soldier two days prior, during the siege of the city. He'd managed to catch her when she'd fallen from the side of the burning wreck of the *Gryphon II*. Since then, their shifts on guard or reporting to Leah had not overlapped, and he'd only caught a few glimpses of her here and there. She hadn't thanked him yet, and he didn't expect her to; she didn't seem the type to express gratitude in the form of words, and he wasn't the type to crave it just for doing his duty.

"Can't sleep?" asked Adonica.

Hook shook his head.

Adonica seemed to suppress a shiver. "Ever since Hartla fell, it's only exhaustion that allows me any rest. Seeing my little brother cut down by Yordar's men was bad enough. But add to that what the demons did. . . ." As her eyes scanned the bodies in the cots throughout the room, she added, so low that Hook had to lean in to hear her clearly, "If these people had seen what I've seen—knew how close we were to the same thing happening here—there's no way they'd be sleeping. Their nights would be as sleepless as mine."

Adonica waited for a moment, then cocked one of her blonde eyebrows at Hook.

"You don't talk much," she said.

Hook nodded in agreement.

She shrugged. "Nothing wrong with that. This world might be half-hospitable if more people knew when to keep their mouths shut. Myself included."

She doesn't know, thought Hook.

Apparently, no one had yet explained to this young Hartlan city guardsman why the dark-haired, dark-eyed man named Hook Bard wore a strip of cloth over his forehead. Or why he never spoke. The Mythaean Thalassocracy, the same sea-empire that this woman fought for, had branded Hook, cut out his tongue, and condemned him to row in the guts of a ship until the day he died. Just like a hundred thousand other condemned souls before him.

And a hundred thousand more after me, thought Hook, watching the fire.

"A walk along the city walls might clear my head," said Adonica. "Seeing as I can trust you not to ruin it with conversation, why don't you join me?"

Hook continued staring into the glow of the hearth. Try as he might, he couldn't unsee the shape of a long metal rod resting in the coals. Without looking up, he slowly shook his head.

Adonica was silent for a moment, then unfolded her arms and ceased to lean against the hearth. "Hope you get some rest, General," she said flatly. Then she strode quietly back down the row of cots.

Hook waited until he heard the door on the opposite end of the barracks open and then close again. Waited until the encroaching breeze of the winter cold passed through the room and pushed at the flames in the fireplace. Then he reached up and untied the strip of cloth he wore around his forehead to keep his lifeslave's brand hidden.

Silently, he examined the strip of cloth in the firelight, noticing the dirt and sweat stains that had accumulated around its edges. Attached to his sword belt was a small waterskin that still contained a few drops from the day before. He undid the stopper and tilted it, allowing the water to run over the fabric. He massaged it with his hands, then rubbed it gently against the surface of a hearthstone. The grayish water ran over the stone's surface and dripped down to the edge of the fireplace, where it hissed and bubbled.

Hook squeezed the remaining water from the cloth, then held it out over the fireplace with both hands to dry, rhythmically caressing the fabric between his forefinger and thumb.

CHAPTER 3

The sun was only just cresting the plains east of Cervice as Leah swung her sword to swat at her opponent's incoming blade. The lunge, aimed straight for her chest, was redirected to her left, and she simultaneously hopped a step to her right.

She kept her eyes on the blade rather than the opponent himself. The shortsword coming after her was keen on both sides, while her saber sported a single cutting edge. With one hand, she raised it back to the proper defensive posture in front of her, just as the double-edged blade came at her again, this time with a slash aimed at her upper thigh.

Again, Leah swung her sword, batting the blade one way as she simultaneously stepped in the opposite direction. Attempting to block an attack with a saber like hers was never prudent; steel was not infallible, and when two blades met with the full force of their wielders behind them, they were known to bend or break. Far wiser to redirect an attack or swat it aside than to attempt to stop it altogether.

But her opponent was not thrown off-balance by the redirection, as she might have hoped. Instead, he maintained steady footing and pivoted in place to follow her movements.

Leah sucked in a breath of winter air and let it out slowly through her nostrils, sending a puff of vapor into the air. With her saber once again raised to the defensive position she had been taught, she stared over the tip of the extended blade, into the eyes of her opponent. In the dim light of a cold Nolian dawn, Marcus Worth stared right back at her. She noted, with some satisfaction, the sweat clinging to the reddish chinstrap of facial hair on his jaw, the steady heave of his chest as he panted.

The Enden captain shifted his shortsword to his off hand for a moment, seemed to reconsider, and then tossed it back into his good hand again. He raised the tip of the blade to point it at her neck.

"I find Nolian swordsmanship odd," Marcus said. "In Endenholm, we train our soldiers to end a fight quickly and by whatever means necessary."

"Nolian soldiers are taught no differently," Leah said. "But I have had no such training."

She had barely finished the comment when Marcus shot forward with another lunge at her. Leah, aware of her surroundings—a narrow walkway atop the fortifications of Cervice proper—knew she didn't have the room for a sidestep this time. Kicking off with her front foot, she jumped backward and landed surely on the ball of her back foot, slapping the advancing blade aside yet again as she did. But again, Marcus maintained his balance and left no opening.

He grumbled in annoyance. A drop of sweat fell from his red beard to the stone beneath their feet.

"You have had *some* sort of training, clearly," he complained.

"Clearly," agreed Leah, keeping her sword raised in the proper position.

Thus far, Leah had relied purely on defense. She had not launched a single attack, except for a quick counter early on, just to send the message that his feint hadn't fooled anyone.

Enden combat was all about shields and lances, phalanxes and heavy assaults. Olorus and Hook, likewise, were men of shields and spears, though still quite capable when forced to resort to their thick-bladed, single-edged swords, which were meant for hacking and slashing. Leah, however, had been trained in the art of courtly dueling, a purely one-on-one exhibition.

Such skills were, admittedly, less than useful in practical warfare. In a skirmish between clashing armies, Marcus's techniques would have been preferable. You couldn't rightly rely on the graceful defensive forms of courtly dueling in the midst of a real battle. Any fool who tried would be killed by the enemy who came at them from behind, unceremoniously cut down by a clumsy hatchet strike to the back of the head or something.

Other than some lessons on basic troop formations, Leah's training in war had been devoted mostly to history and political theory. But her unexpected and unasked-for position as a commander in the Athacean League had taught her the vital difference between a war and a duel. Waging war, she now understood, was about creating opportunities. But dueling was about waiting for them.

Leah adjusted her stance, shifting the saber to a high position over her own head, tip pointed down. Her off hand, she curled into a fist and rested against the small of her back. Rapiers were generally the weapon of choice in courtly dueling, but her saber did the trick just as well.

Marcus regarded her stance curiously for a moment, then adjusted his grip on his sword and came in high with a two-handed, overhand chop. But he advertised the move too far in advance. Clearly another feint.

Leah waited, prepared to slap the attack away if she had to, knowing that she wouldn't.

Marcus brought the blade down at her but, at the last moment, let go with his offhand and threw his body weight sideways. With his good hand, he swung his sword down and under in a raking upward slice. And with that, Leah had found her opening.

One hand still behind her back, she shifted her weight to her back foot and brought her saber down to redirect the oncoming stab so that it passed a few inches by her shoulder. As she sidestepped Marcus, she delivered the killing blow.

CHAPTER 4

Leah flipped the saber over in her hand, then brought the dull edge down to slap the back of Marcus's neck.

He made a noise in his throat. To his credit, he was not thrown off balance by the blow, but he couldn't resist rubbing at the stinging spot as he dropped his sword to the stones with a clatter.

"I am bested," he said as he bowed graciously in defeat.

"You did not hold back out of respect for my station, I hope," Leah said as she slid the saber home in the scabbard at her belt.

"I wouldn't insult you," said Marcus. He huffed for breath and wiped the sweat from his brow. "You are the better swordsman, Queen Anavion."

"In a very specific form of swordsmanship, perhaps," said Leah.

In accordance with tradition, she retrieved Marcus's sword from the ground and offered it to him. However, and also in accordance with tradition, the winner offered the weapon to the loser blade-first, a not-so-subtle reminder of the outcome of the duel. No reason to tell him that she could have finished him several times at the start of the duel.

"I wouldn't have guessed," said Marcus, sheathing the shortsword. "Shame on me, I suppose."

"I learned from my father," Leah said.

"Then the king taught you well," Marcus offered. "He must have been quite skilled with a blade."

Leah looked down at the hilt of her saber. King Darius Anavion had been called one of the best duelists of his generation. It was difficult to say whether this claim was true or if it was rhetoric meant to flatter the king, but she had certainly never seen him lose.

"My father had a thin scar on his face," she muttered, "gained from a duel in his younger years. It ran from his brow to his temple. Duelists refer to such scars as smites, and they wear them with pride. He called it a badge of honor."

Leah turned her gaze over the outlying districts of Cervice, across the river, and up the hills east of the city, where a bank of slowly swirling fog diffused the light of dawn. Darius Anavion had always been a man of honor. "Right is right," he had once told her. "If you can remember that, you have all you need to lead."

"Was it a favorite pastime of the king's?" asked Marcus. "Dueling, I mean."

"Quite," said Leah. "The only duelist I ever witnessed who came close to besting my father was Cimon Endrus."

"The captain of the High Guard?" asked Marcus.

Leah nodded.

The image flashed before her eyes. The same image that had prevented her from sleeping this night *and* the night before. The look on Cimon Endrus's face as the light left his eyes. The twin red floods flowing from the two places where his arms should have been. And the man who had called himself Innocen, doused in the blood of Endrus and a dozen or more other humans, snapping his teeth playfully at her.

In the end, thought Leah, *for all their skills and honors, Endrus was murdered by a monster, and my father met his end at an assassin's blade while he slept.*

Leah stared at the distant fog across the river, thinking about how the cruelest of ironies made for some of the most sobering of lessons.

"My Queen?" said Marcus from behind her. "Are you all right?"

Leah turned to face him, putting on her practiced diplomatic smile. "Thank you, Captain," she said. "This was a welcome distraction. More welcome than you know."

Marcus shrugged, looking almost bashful as he said, "I should be thanking you. I couldn't sleep either." He rubbed at the back of his neck again. "And it's never a bad thing to be . . . thoroughly humbled once in a while."

Leah snorted a laugh.

The sound of approaching footsteps drew Leah's attention toward the stone stairs not far from her position.

General Olorus Antony came up the steps dressed uncharacteristically in casual, informal clothing. His steps were hurried, and beneath his thick, gray-streaked auburn beard, his mouth was a thin, worried line.

"What is it?" asked Leah, forgoing a greeting.

Olorus scratched at his beard a moment and sighed before proceeding. "Three urgent pieces of news to report, My Lady," he stated. "With your permission."

"Speak plainly, Olorus," said Leah. "What's happened now?"

"It's Zechariah," said Olorus. "I've received a report from some of the watchmen. The old man left in the middle of the night. He told the watchmen that he was being sent on an errand personally by Her Majesty the Queen."

Leah felt her jaw clench. She forced it open and ran her tongue over the inside of her teeth to try to calm herself before responding. "I gave no such order."

"As I suspected," said Olorus.

The old man returns to us, thought Leah, *only to leave again on dubious terms. True to form, he causes no end of frustrations.*

How could he leave at a time like this, so shortly after proposing a plan to empty all of Cervice and leave the city behind? The demons had failed in their first attack against the city, thanks to the timely intervention of Raeqlund's massive army with Zechariah leading the way, but they would be back.

The walls of Cervice, no matter how strong, would not stand forever. But even if they could, what good did that do them? Demons swarmed the entire Oikoumene, under the command of an overlord named Avagad, who was rumored to reside on the other side of the world. Even Innocen had noted the precariousness of their situation; if the demons weren't defeated, then surviving here only meant they would live long enough to be the last ones to die. That was why, rather than digging in at Cervice, Zechariah wanted to mobilize the League and invade Avagad's lands.

Leah saw the merit in some aspects of Zechariah's plan. But as far as transforming her city and her people into one large, mobilized army, to march them unprotected across the face of the world. . . .

Leah shook her head. Now was not the time to think about that.

"What is item number two?" she asked Olorus.

"Gunnar completed his allocated workload," said Olorus. "The palace gardens, as you have requested, are full to bursting with freshly grown crops, thanks to his peculiar talents. However, he, Borris, and Pool then proceeded to infuriate many of the Nolian citizens by raiding the palace wine stores and drinking themselves into a stupor on several vintages dating from before the reign of your great-grandfather."

Leah closed her eyes, feeling her jaw clench again.

Gunnar had always been prone to indulging in the odd drink, but he had kept himself in an almost constant state of inebriation since her coronation, following their victory of repelling the demons from Cervice. The city was in low supply of almost everything, but spirits were the one thing they had plenty of. And Gunnar seemed hell-bent on burning through those stockpiles, too.

This was troublesome for multiple reasons, for Gunnar was integral to the survival of the city. His plant-growing powers were vital to cultivating the city's gardens. Without his aurym abilities to grow crops out of season and at a supernatural rate, the people of Cervice would have already had to start making some difficult decisions. Now, even the firewood was beginning to run short. Gunnar's plant-growing powers would soon need to be used to that end as well.

Of course, aurym powers were not limitless. In the same way that healing wounds with aurym took a toll on Leah, Gunnar could only grow so many plants so quickly before he became physically and mentally drained. The process exhausted him daily, which was how he justified his excessive recuperation. What Gunnar considered "recuperation," however, was what Leah considered debauchery. It was a daily challenge to rouse him from bed to assume his duties, which he normally tended to in a foggy-minded state of recovery.

Everything and nothing has changed, Leah thought. *Still the same fool of a fisherman from Lonn. Did I really expect him to change just because he put on a different hat?*

"And item number three?" she asked, declining to comment on Gunnar's antics.

"It's Asher," said Olorus.

"The former prime minister?" said Marcus from behind Leah.

Olorus nodded. His eyes met Leah's. "He requests an audience with you, My Lady. He says it's about your father. And what happened the night he died."

CHAPTER 5

The dungeons beneath the palace of Cervice were a remnant of darker days. In the modern age, lawbreakers were kept in the prison complex at Panum. These dungeons were rarely used to keep prisoners. Until recently.

Olorus led the way, and Leah followed close behind, both with lit torches in their hands. It had not occurred to Leah until now to wonder what had happened to the prisoners housed at Panum. Like most of Nolia's western cities, Panum had been evacuated on Asher's orders in the wake of demon attacks, and its people had been taken to Nolia's eastern cities. Whether the prisoners had been included in that mass migration, she did not know.

Olorus paused at a large, wooden door, removed a skeleton key from his belt, and unlocked the ancient mechanism with a loud *clang*. He pushed the door inward on stiff, unoiled hinges, and led her further into the dungeons.

Leah could remember these dungeons sometimes being used to temporarily hold offenders awaiting sentencing, but during her lifetime, they were mostly utilized as storage. She lamented the fact that with the entire city of Cervice functioning as a military fortress, the dungeons were once again being utilized as they had been by her ancestors. Presently, only two prisoners were housed here. One was a Darvellian ambassador who had attempted to kill Leah. The other was Illander Asher, the former prime minister of Nolia, who had colluded with the Darvellian government in a plot that had led to the assassination of King Darius and the entire Anavion family—with the exception of the king's only daughter.

Thoughts of Panum, Asher, and his forced population movements were reminders of how much Leah still did not know about the state of her homeland. Captain Endrus had told her that Nolia's eastern cities were reportedly overpopulated and undermaintained. She had sent messengers to those cities upon her return to Nolia, informing them that Anavion blood once again ruled the kingdom. She had received some responses from city officials swearing fealty to the restored crown. But one city had replied that it had signed a treaty with Darvelle, agreeing to be annexed by Nolia's rival right out from under Leah's nose. In other cases, she had received no reply at all. Did this mean that those cities had abandoned Nolia, too?

Or do they lie in ruins, like the cities of Endenholm? wondered Leah. *Overrun by demon hordes?*

Olorus and Leah turned a corner, entering a large chamber lit by several burning braziers on the walls. A soldier of the city guard stood before them. His position, at attention, indicated that he had heard their approach. Beside him were a chair and table with an open book on it. Other than that, the chamber bore no furnishings or indications of comfort. A row of iron-barred cells was built into the far wall. The place smelled of oil, moisture, and body odor.

"Your Highness," greeted the guard.

Leah nodded curtly. "Where is he?"

"On the far end," the guard replied, pointing.

"Death to tyrants," spat a voice from a cell closer by.

The guard took a threatening step toward the cell. "Shut up!" he barked.

Through the bars, Leah could just make out the silhouette of the Darvellian ambassador and would-be assassin who had attempted to kill her with a poisoned dagger. Olorus had intervened, only to receive a dose of the poison himself and nearly die from it.

"Wait outside, soldier," Olorus ordered in a measured voice.

The guard responded with a hasty "Yes, sir," before exiting the chamber the way Olorus and Leah had entered.

Before proceeding to the far end of the row of cells as indicated, Olorus approached the cell of the assassin. There, he drew his sword and stood, staring through the bars for a moment, deadly silent.

Leah saw the silhouette of the Darvellian ambassador shrink back into a corner of the cell. Only then did Olorus walk away, allowing the tip of his sword to tap against each bar of the cell in succession as he walked, like a child idly running a stick along a picket fence. The sound echoed through the chamber with a *ping, ping, ping.*

Leah gazed into the shadowed cells as she passed them, forcing herself to imagine the souls that must have perished in this place. She was well aware that she had grown up in an age of relative peace and civility. But in the ages when barbarian invaders and aggressive outlying kingdoms had regularly threatened Nolian life, less-civilized methods had been necessary.

Now that the world is falling into chaos, thought Leah, *will you revive such methods? Two of your dungeon cells are already filled, after all, Queen Anavion.*

They were several steps away from the cell at the far end of the chamber when ten long, knobby-knuckled fingers emerged from the darkness and closed tenderly around the bars of the cell door.

"Your Highness," hissed an aged, regal voice from the shadows. "What an unexpected pleasure."

CHAPTER 6

Leah did not shy away from the iron bars but was careful to remain out of reach. Inside the cell, Illander Asher's eyes squinted against the light of her torch. His face was more deeply lined than she remembered, and his gnarled old hands were white as pulp. He favored her with a tiny bow of his hairless, liver-spotted head. She suspected that the words "unexpected pleasure" had been meant to elicit a reaction from her, but she would give him no such satisfaction.

"Whatever you want, speak quickly and plainly," said Leah.

"I would not dare waste your time, My Queen," Asher said. "Not when the fate of our nation hangs by such a thin thread."

Again, Leah refused to take the bait. She stared into his red-rimmed eyes and said nothing. Olorus, meanwhile, still had his sword drawn.

"I am prepared to sign a confession to my crimes against the crown," Asher announced, carefully enunciating every word. "The enemy state of Darvelle blackmailed me, and I regret to say that I made a terrible mistake." He paused to sigh dramatically. "I was under the impression that their ambitions were purely economic, and I unwisely divulged state secrets in an attempt to pursue the greater good—and, admittedly, the safety of myself and my family. But they tricked me, and I unknowingly exposed my king to great danger. I had no idea that Darvelle would use the information I had provided to attack the royal family. After that, I was left with no choice but to do what I felt was right for our nation. We were leaderless. You were gone. Someone had to take the reins.

"I have always acted out of deep-seated patriotism and love for Nolia above all, but I am aware that my actions warrant swift and merciless punishment. Were I still in an advisory position, I would recommend public execution for such crimes.

"I humbly beg your mercy, My Queen. I plead for a stay of execution. In exchange for such a kindness, I can provide a detailed account of the events that led to your family's demise—everything leading up to that dreadful night, and everything that happened since. For what I have done, I do not deserve your mercy. But I can still be of use to you. I have learned much about Darvelle. Without my help, I assure you, *you* will be at *their* mercy."

By now, Asher's voice had begun to rattle, and he had to take a moment to clear the phlegm from his throat. Leah suspected he would have continued orating for several more minutes if she did not intervene.

"You seem to forget that Darvelle delivered you to me in chains," said Leah. "As a peace offering."

"And do you trust such a peace offering?" Asher demanded, so quickly that it was clear he had prepared for this question. "From a nation whose foreign policy is assassination and sabotage—?"

"If they intended to continue hostilities against us," said Leah, "why would they deliver to me an individual who could contribute to their downfall? I could easily use you against them, as you suggest. They know that. In fact, I see their decision to deliver you *alive* as a vote of trust in me. They no longer want war."

Asher smiled and shook his head. This man had not only been her father's closest advisor; he'd been like a surrogate grandfather to Leah, and this pitying shake of his head reminded her of the sort of expression he had given her whenever she'd made a mistake in her studies. Despite her resolve, she suddenly felt like that little girl all over again. Quickly, she set her jaw and banished the thought.

"You have grown into a strong, capable leader," Asher said gently. "But you still have so much to learn." He sighed. "These are treacherous waters. You have no reason to trust me. I have lost that right. I only ask that you give me the chance to regain it. If you truly believe a nation capable of reversing an era of strife for the sake of peace and reconciliation, then surely you must believe an old man capable of righting the wrongs that haunt him. Use the tools that have been given to you. Let me serve as your navigator."

For a few long moments, silence reigned in the dungeons beneath Cervice as Leah contemplated the old man's words. Illander Asher only watched her with sad eyes.

Serve as my navigator, thought Leah. *Just as you navigated my father.*

Leah turned and walked away. A moment later, Olorus sheathed his sword and followed. She expected a final word to be called to her from the cell—one last gambit from the old man. But no words came. Like the most gifted orators, Asher knew when to be silent as well as when to speak.

When they reached the outer chamber, Leah finally let her guard down. She leaned heavily against the stone wall, staring at the floor for a moment. Olorus waited patiently, saying nothing, then rested a comforting hand on her shoulder.

Leah looked up at him. "Where do you think Justin is right now?" she asked.

Olorus made a face. "Wherever he is, he is with Sir Ahlund, so he is in good hands. With any luck, they are on their way here even as we speak. With a fallen angel guarding our gates, this city will be the safest place in the entire Oikoumene."

Leah forced a smile. It was a nice thought. But somehow, she felt certain that such a thing would never come to pass.

CHAPTER 7

"Justin," said a voice.

For a few seconds, a half-remembered dream clung to Justin like slimy tentacles from the deep, weighing down his mind, requiring great effort to break the surface of his consciousness. He felt his muscles trembling and twitching. He felt weak, dehydrated, and above all, scared. For a moment, he felt like a frightened child waking from a nightmare, chin quivering involuntarily from some unremembered terror.

He lay on his back. Above him was a sea of stars. But the image that haunted him was the expression that had been on Ahlund's face, with his head clutched in the grip of the cythraul as daemyn power turned his flesh to black demonic non-flesh. His chestnut-brown hair falling from his scalp in smoking clumps.

Not a dream, realized Justin. *A memory. But no less of a nightmare.*

He sat up and rubbed the sleep from his eyes, realizing that tears clung to his cheeks. He was on a white sand beach, and he lay atop his toga-like cloak, which had been spread out to form a makeshift bed in the sand. Around him, the surviving members of the Ru'Onorath, the Guardians of the Oikoumene, slept on nests made of clothing and various scraps of cloth.

Justin looked out over the waters. The ocean did not roar but was strangely quiet, as the waves were quite gentle on this island—gentle enough to create a double image of the starscape and the twin moons over the sea. Gentle enough that, just a few hours ago, it had been quite easy to push the canoe bearing Ahlund's body out past the breakers.

Justin raised a quivering hand and ran his fingers through his hair. It felt like a long time had passed since that seaside funeral, but he had only been sleeping for a couple of hours. Turning his attention up the beach, he realized he was not the only one awake. Cyaxares, the leader of the Ru'Onorath, sat cross-legged and straight-backed at the edge of a grove of tall palms. The hood of her dark cloak was drawn over her head. She appeared to be gazing down at something in her lap.

Justin thought back to the voice that had awakened him. It hadn't been Cyaxares; he was certain it had been a male voice. Or had it been part of the nightmare?

He scratched at the thin fuzz of facial hair on his cheeks. Other than his boots and cloak, he had fallen asleep fully clothed. He was exhausted but restless after waking from that nightmare. Far too restless to fall back asleep. So he forced himself up onto his knees and tried to stifle a groan as multiple injuries jockeyed for position at the forefront of his perception. Each one was a stark reminder of the events of the day before. He had taken several hard hits from Avagad in the Treasury. He'd fallen down a waterfall—jumped, actually. He'd been pummeled by stones and pieces of broken buildings during the cythraul's attack at the crater of Esthean. And he'd been knocked unconscious when his skull had collided with bedrock.

Standing up wasn't pleasant, but he managed it. He groaned again at the dull pains in his legs and the sharper ones in his head and spine. In the sand beside his cloak were his boots. And beside them, Ahlund's broken sword.

Justin kneeled down and picked up the stump of the weapon. The longsword's blade had been snapped off about six inches from the hilt.

Ahlund had once told him that while some aurym warriors kept their aurstones in rings or necklaces, or even implanted them into their own bodies to ensure that they would never be without them, the Guardians of the Oikoumene did no such thing. They believed that a warrior who could be physically disarmed of his or her weapon did not deserve the metaphysical advantage of aurym power. That was why Ru'Onorath forged their aurstones into their weapons. It was a matter of honor.

Justin had been disarmed during his fight with Avagad, and his claymore sword had been lost. But to the very end, neither man nor demon had been able to disarm Ahlund Sims. His sword had remained firmly in his grasp. He hadn't dropped it, even after he'd used it on himself—running the blade through his own body all the way up to the hilt in order to unleash a final attack against Avagad standing behind him. He had done it simply to give Justin a chance to escape.

Ahlund Sims. The man had been inscrutable and duplicitous, sometimes cruel—and occasionally, nearly intolerable.

And now, he was dead. Avagad and his demons had killed him.

He sacrificed his life, thought Justin, staring at the broken sword in his grasp. *For me.*

"Justin," whispered a male voice.

This time, he knew he hadn't imagined it. And this was no dream.

Justin looked around. Kallorn, the lightning-wielding aurym warrior who had trained him in Esthean, lay sleeping not far away. Ezon, one of the Ru'Onorath's council of elders, was also close by, along with several other members of the Guardians. But none seemed to be awake, let alone to have said Justin's name.

The voice had sounded so close, and it sounded very much like the voice that had woken him from his dream. Justin turned to look up the beach toward Cyaxares. She had turned her head now and seemed to be watching him.

Justin slipped Ahlund's sword into his belt. Then he stooped and gathered up his cloak, shook it free of sand, and put it on the way Kallorn had taught him. He started up the beach toward Cyaxares—

"Justin," the male voice whispered again.

Justin froze mid-step. He looked around. Nobody. But the voice had come from behind him. Down the beach.

It was coming from the water.

CHAPTER 8

Justin turned away from Cyaxares and walked toward the gently lapping waters of the Raedittean Sea.

He limped badly and was surprised to discover that his left knee was unwilling to bend properly. It was like trying to walk with a splinted leg. He hoped that, whatever internal structure had been compromised, it had only been strained or sprained, not torn or separated. He rubbed at his sore jaw and grimaced. Using his tongue to push at the backs of his teeth, he found a molar that wiggled when he prodded it. Ezon had healed most of his serious wounds, but there had been other people to attend to, and the little old man had been exhausted by the time they'd turned in for the night. Minor injuries would have to wait until morning.

Justin stopped for a moment, still several steps away from the water's reach. Hours ago, he had stood at this very spot and watched the flaming canoe float away, taking Ahlund with it.

He looked up at the two moons and wiggled his bare toes in the soft, white sand. It made him feel like a child, and he found himself wishing he still was one. Wishing he could return to a time when the dreams ahead of him had outnumbered the nightmares behind. Dreams like college basketball, which had always been his plan. He'd been the leading scorer during his junior year of high school, and a scholarship had been a real possibility. He'd thought he would major in History in college, his favorite subject, but he was open to other options. Maybe something he'd never even heard of before would spark his interest.

The possibilities led him down rabbit holes; a single decision could change so much. Where would he go to school? What would he learn? Who would he meet? Where would he live after he graduated, and what kind of career would he have? He liked to be alone, so maybe he'd be a writer or an artist or something. But he also liked to help people and wanted to make a difference in the world in a tangible sort of way—do something altruistic and important.

The more he thought about it, the more he thought maybe he wouldn't play basketball at all. He had quit the high school team, after all. And besides—just because he was good at something, did that mean he was obligated to pursue it? Maybe he would go the opposite direction and turn his attention toward technology. Maybe he'd design apps or video games or something. He had always wanted to try playing the guitar. Maybe that was something he'd turn out to be good at. Who knew? He might get really into music, maybe be in a band and play the local bars. Maybe even freak his dad out a little and get a full-sleeve tattoo.

Justin's gaze wandered down from the twin moons in the sky to his left arm. His demon arm. The one that was too narrow for his body—as thin as bone without any of the surrounding muscles or supporting tissues. In both color and structure, it resembled a burnt stick, yet it was as strong and impenetrable as a shield. This dead bone armor fed on the dark energy of daemyn, and it diminished and languished without it.

And suddenly, Justin realized that he would never be in a band.

He would never get really into music. He would never design apps or video games. He would never major in History or anything else. And he would never play college ball because he was never going to go to college. He was never going to graduate high school or meet other young people who also wanted to try new things, start bands, or freak out their parents by getting tattoos. Justin didn't know if he *really* wanted to do any of those things. But he'd wanted to, if he'd wanted to. And he had grown up assuming that the options would be there for him when he was ready. But now—

"Justin."

This time, the voice was so loud and sudden that it made him jump. It was very close. And it sounded like Ahlund.

Justin turned to look back up the beach. Cyaxares was still watching him, but she didn't seem to have moved and did not appear to have heard the voice.

Did anyone else hear it? he wondered. *Did I really hear it?*

But he knew he had.

Slowly, he took a few steps forward. His toes and then his feet touched the waves lapping the sand. The water was so calm and tepid that one might have mistaken it for a shallow pond warmed by the afternoon sun. As he stepped further out, the tropical seawater crept up to his knees. The edges of his toga-like cloak floated around him. The moons were so bright that he could see straight down through the water to his feet, even in the dead of night. Several creatures in large, swirled shells retreated over the sandy bottom to flee his encroaching strides. And at Justin's side, tucked in his belt, Ahlund's broken half-sword began to glow.

CHAPTER 9

Justin stared at the sword. It was not his imagination. The blade was glowing red, seemingly of its own accord, just as it had done whenever Ahlund had called on aurym to bring it to life. Bubbles formed on the submerged portion of the blade, then detached and floated to the surface in a low boil.

"Ahlund?" Justin whispered, squinting out across the water.

Then the bubbles ceased, and Ahlund's blade faded back to plain steel again.

Justin squeezed his hands into fists as the weight of it all came down on him. The weight of everything he'd been through and everything he had become. This person he was, was not the sort of person he had ever thought he would be. Not by a long shot. Once, his future had seemed wide open and limitless—a trail unblazed, a story waiting to be told. But those days of vast potential, and the dreams of what life would or could or should be like, were gone. Instead, *this* life was his life, and it was the only one he would ever have. A life of running and fighting.

But running and fighting for how long? wondered Justin. *And to what end?*

Until his luck ran out, he supposed. Until he could run and fight no more. Perhaps he would die a painful yet possibly glorious death like Ahlund. Or he would be taken alive and turned into a cythraul. Or would it end for him as it had for his father?

Benjamin Holmes, if Cyaxares was to be believed, had come to the Oikoumene as a fallen angel five thousand years ago. He'd defeated the demons only to pay the ultimate price—being corrupted by the very power he'd used to win the battle. He'd installed himself as humanity's overlord and had ruled as a tyrant over all the Oikoumene. Or at least, that was the story the way Cyaxares told it.

Justin hung his head. Even if the story was true—even if he could do the impossible and defeat the demons the way his father had—that wouldn't be the end of it. The Nameless One would live on. The immortal god-king of the demons, if he truly existed, was somewhere out beyond the Oikoumene. And if history was any indication, defeat was only a temporary setback for him. Even if Justin defeated the Nameless One, he would rebuild his strength and, hundreds or perhaps thousands of years from now, mount another attack.

The cycle would continue. The war would never stop. Not until the Nameless One succeeded in wiping out all aurym—and, by extension, all natural life. Only that which was fueled by daemyn, which could hardly be considered living to begin with, would remain. Justin found himself wondering if the hopelessness of this cause was what had driven his father to do what he had done. Or had it been for some other reason?

He looked back at Cyaxares again. Avagad was a deceiver, but he and Cyaxares had both agreed on one thing: Zechariah, Justin's first and closest mentor in this world, was not who he claimed to be.

Cyaxares claimed not to know who Zechariah was, despite the fact that he was supposedly a fellow member of the immortal Brethren. And Avagad had claimed that Zechariah was his ally and had been working with him all along. Was it true? Or was it a fabrication meant to manipulate Justin—to make him further question everything he believed? And what about Cyaxares's story about what Justin's father had done? What assurance did he have that *any* of it was true?

"There's only one person," he whispered to himself, "in this world or in any other, who knows the truth."

Justin exhaled long and slow through his nostrils, realizing what he had to do.

He reached into his shirt and took out a small stone. This seemingly unremarkable pebble had several names. Gauge stone. Y'thri'ra. Keystone.

Justin calmed his mind and fed his aurym power into the stone.

CHAPTER 10

A powerful green glow radiated from within Justin's hand. Within seconds, it became so bright that he could hardly look at it.

"Justin!" Cyaxares cried.

Turning, he saw her standing up.

"Stop!" she shouted as she ran toward him, her long robes trailing behind her.

Justin turned away from her to face the ocean.

As he fed more aurym power into the keystone, pushing it to its second form, the glowing pebble lifted from his hand and began to levitate several inches above his palm. Its center became a burning, swirling white light within a jade halo, which expanded to encapsulate his entire body. The sparks at the periphery formed emerald constellations around him that twisted and swirled, obscuring his physical surroundings until all he could see was a green nebula of pure energy.

The light became everything, and soon, he could no longer feel the warm water around his knees or the ocean breeze.

For a long time, Justin could see nothing in the bright light. The air became cold and dry and still. An acrid smell stung his sinuses, and he quickly recognized the aroma. It was the old-fashioned coal furnace used by one of the neighbors up the street. As a child, he'd always hated that smell. But the older he got, the more he liked it, for some reason. He heard the white noise of nearby traffic and the hum of more contemporary heating systems.

When Justin's eyes finally adjusted to the light, he was greeted by one of those rare winter days in Pennsylvania when the sky was clear blue and cloudless instead of cloaked in its usual gray pall. He squinted against the piercing sunlight reflecting off hard-packed snow. It was briskly cold, but for a few seconds, he did not feel chilled. It was as if he had brought with him an insulating layer of the otherworldly atmosphere. A strange mist rose within his vision, and he realized it was coming from his body—the warm moisture of a tropical sea turning rapidly to visible vapor in the cold, hanging like a cloud of smoke around him.

The snow at his feet was not deep. Only about an inch and a half lay on the driveway where he had played so many games of one-on-one with his father. And in front of him was the little house on Main Street Extension that had been his home all his life. His gaze went automatically to his bedroom window upstairs, and he smiled.

Justin threw back his cloak and slipped the gauge into the inner pocket of the shirt he wore beneath. Ahlund's broken sword was still clutched in his left hand. He tightened his grip on the hilt and felt the by now familiar tug of flesh against non-flesh as the skin of his wrist pulled against the scaly, chitinous material of his demon arm. That part of him didn't feel the cold. It felt nothing at all, in fact, and yet—

A shrill metallic clatter jarred Justin from his thoughts, and he glanced toward the sound. On the other side of the wooden fence that separated the Holmeses' property from that of the next-door neighbors, the driveway was half-cleared. Standing in the middle of it, dressed in a heavy coat and stocking cap, was a man with a short black beard and fogged glasses. A metal shovel lay on the blacktop where Jeff Emerson had dropped it. Justin's high school science teacher stood stock-still, knees slightly bent, gawking at Justin.

Justin adjusted his cloak and sheathed Ahlund's sword. "Cold one today," said Justin.

"*Tch*—" said Jeff.

A moment passed, and Jeff said no more. He didn't move except to quickly wipe some of the fog from his glasses with one gloved finger.

Justin nodded to Jeff. "Well, have a good one." And he walked to the front door.

The door was unlocked, as it usually was, so Justin let himself in. The record player that his mother had bought for his father a couple of years before was playing and turned up loud, currently spinning one of those prog rock albums from his dad's collection. Justin recognized the long intro of a ten-minute epic about a journey to a forbidden city and a search for immortality. For the life of him, he had never understood his father's taste in music.

He took a few steps toward the living room, then paused to turn and look at his mother's green jacket, still hanging on the coat rack, unmoved since the accident, as if waiting for her to return to fetch it.

"Hey, pal."

Justin hadn't heard the wheelchair's approach over the record player's screeching guitars and booming drums, but he turned to find Benjamin Holmes in the kitchen doorway, sitting perched forward slightly with his elbows on his knees. His glasses, with the chipped right lens, were partway down the bridge of his rather large nose—a rather large nose that Justin had inherited. He was smiling. Grinning, really. He always seemed to be grinning as if he knew something that everyone else didn't. Only now did it occur to Justin that maybe it was because he really did.

Justin grinned back. "Hey, Dad," he said.

PART II

THE HEART
OF THE SUNRISE

CHAPTER 11

Hook woke to the sound of muffled footfalls. Looking around, he realized that a source of light had entered the otherwise darkened slaves' quarters. The row-master—a round-bellied, beardless man who kept himself immaculately clean—stepped in. A lit candle was in his hand, a coiled whip at his belt. His name was Cadmus.

Hook continued to breathe slowly and rhythmically, so that he would appear to still be sleeping like the rest of the slaves. He didn't bother trying to measure time anymore, but it had been at least six months since his last haircut and shave. His beard was long, and his straight black hair, stringy with sweat, hung about his face like a curtain. Covertly, he peered out through his hair at Cadmus as he strode down the aisle separating the two rows of benches. Each bench was occupied by three men seated before the long handle of an oar.

In the more than two years since Hook had been brought down into these quarters, he had never once seen the paddle of the oar at which he labored. It was located on the other side of the hull, outside the ship, which was a place that, in all likelihood, Hook would never see again in his life.

Cadmus stopped walking. His gaze scanned the hunched, scarred, sweat-coated backs of the hundred-plus galley slaves chained to their seats within the guts of the *Manticore*. Then Cadmus's gaze landed on the empty seat—the only unoccupied rower position in the trireme. It was the aisle position, situated directly across from where Hook sat.

Hook's eyes shifted to study the empty bench seat as well, barely a foot and a half from where he sat. Until a few days ago, that seat had been occupied by an old man whom Cadmus had referred to as "Toad" or sometimes "Toadstool." He gave all his rowers names like that.

Toad had been in that seat on Hook's first day at the oars and had offered Hook a look of condolence as he'd been led in and chained in place. Toad had even shared pain-saving advice in the form of a silent, admonishing shake of his head when Hook had almost done the unthinkable by flagging down the row-master when one of his benchmates had passed out from exhaustion.

Hook continued to feign sleep, staring at Toad's empty seat. The previous morning, Toad had been found slumped forward in his seat, his arms draped over the oar. The row-master had given Toad's back three hard lashes to attempt to rouse him. Though the coral-studded leather had split the flesh of the old man's back, no blood had flowed from the lacerations.

Cadmus and the crew had wasted no time. Toad's lifeless body had been unshackled and carried up on deck. A few moments later, Hook had heard the splash.

The *Manticore* was currently somewhere in the southern Raedittean, and Hook found himself wondering how far Toad had been from home. He wondered if anyone from Toad's former life still remembered him and would have mourned his passing. He wondered what Toad's dreams had been, and how long ago he'd given up on them. And he wondered how old *he* would be when his own body was finally dropped, nameless and forgotten, into the Raedittean.

Not all of the slaves aboard the *Manticore* faced such grim destinies. Some were serving sentences of just one, five, or ten years of hard labor at the oars—the Mythaean method of paying off the "debt" owed to the crown for one's crimes. Lifeslaves, on the other hand—like Toad and Hook—were offered no such chance of repayment. Lifeslaves were criminals who had been convicted of crimes labeled "heinous" or "unforgivable." In other parts of the world, such crimes might have been punished by hanging or beheading. But the Mythaeans' chosen form of punishment was a life of servitude, a half-halo burn scar to brand the criminal forevermore, and, in some but not all cases, the removal of the tongue to silence them forever.

Hook's gaze drifted down to the shackles around his ankles and the chain bolted to the floor. Had his crime been heinous? No. Unforgivable? Possibly. He'd barely been a man when he'd done what he did. But that didn't change anything.

Hook hazarded a look at Cadmus, still standing silent and motionless in the candlelit bowels of the ship. Still staring at the empty seat. Now that Toad was gone, the *Manticore* would probably not have a replacement until it came to port or until a new slave was transferred to the ship. In dire circumstances, a marine might need to work among the slaves, but such things rarely happened. In the meantime, Toad's benchmates would be expected to pick up the slack for him.

Cadmus sighed. At the tail end of the sigh, he muttered, low and even, "Good morning, Dark-eyes."

Hook looked up at Cadmus. Cadmus's eyes locked with his.

Hook glared darkly. Cadmus smiled cordially.

Cadmus walked forward, past the empty seat, and continued to survey his workforce. Hook glared into Cadmus's back as he walked.

Cadmus stopped at the front of the ship, then rapped his knuckles twice against the pacer's drum to produce a pair of hollow bangs. His voice was strong and clear as he said, "Up, please."

One by one, the hunched, sweat-coated backs shifted or twitched as they woke. The ever-present smells of body odor and stale urine were stirred up by their movements, souring the air.

"Prepare arms," Cadmus said in a businesslike tone of voice.

A murmur went up among the oarsmen. Even Hook's brow furrowed a bit. Slaves were always kept fed, if not well. Every morning began with a breakfast of thick porridge, sometimes with a squeeze of lime or diced fruit to fight the scurvy. Rarely were they commanded to prepare arms before their morning meal.

"*Now*, please," said Cadmus.

With the sound of many rattling chains, the hundred-plus galley slaves took up their oars.

Hook raised his hands to grip the worn-smooth handholds of the oar before him. Hook's two bench-mates were lifeslaves like him. Currently manning the position closest to the rowlock was a small, middle-aged man. He had gray, curly hair, and a beard that was equally curly yet white as a trout's belly. Cadmus called him Curly. Although the rowlocks were slightly above water level and kept as water-tight as possible through regular applications of wax, the man in the rowlock position was the most prone to getting wet when high waves battered the hull.

Seated immediately to Hook's right, in the middle position of their bench, was a man who might have been only a few years older than himself. Fine, golden-blond hair coated his face, his arms, his chest, his stomach—everywhere *but* his head, which was bare and smooth as a river stone except for a clamshell pattern remaining at the back of his scalp. The only other parts of his body that were hairless were the raised whip scars lining his back. Cadmus called him Haystack.

Hook—or Dark-eyes, as Cadmus called him—sat in the aisle seat. Here, he had a bit of elbow room, as there was no one seated to his left. The downside was that he was within arm's reach of anyone walking up or down the aisle, and therefore most prone to drawing the ire of the row-master or passing marines, whether he deserved it or not.

While Haystack was a relatively new addition to the crew, Curly had been on the ship longer than Hook. Haystack was barrel-chested and cast an intimidating figure, but he was prone to crying at night. Curly, on the other hand, had had any tears beaten out of him long ago. His expression rarely deviated from a dour, tight-lipped scowl. Hook often wondered what their real names were and what they had done. He also knew that he would never know.

A second candle entered the quarters. Without so much as a look at the slaves, Pacer Hil sat down at the drum and lifted the mallets.

"Pacer Hil," said the row-master. "Begin, please."

The pacer brought his mallet down.

Boom.

CHAPTER 12

A pounding thump shook Hook from his dream. He leaned forward and realized he was seated, propped against the stone of a hearth.

Gradually, he remembered that he was not chained to a bench below the decks of a Mythaean trireme somewhere in the Raedittean Archipelago. He was in the barracks of the royal palace of Cervice. Sleep had eluded him for the second night in a row, and he had decided to sit by the fire for a while. Apparently, he'd fallen asleep seated with his back against the hearth.

Even after all these years, thought Hook, *I still sleep better sitting up.*

Looking around, he realized that the sound that had awoken him—the beat of the mallet against the drum in his dream—had, in reality, been the bang of the door at the far end of the barracks, closing behind Adonica. She crossed the room quietly, passing the many sleeping forms of soldiers, some in cots and others lying on the floor, and took up a position standing on the other side of the hearth. She did not look at Hook, but instead gazed into the low-burning fire.

She crossed her arms. "Couldn't sleep again, huh?" she said.

Hook shook his head.

Adonica chewed on the inside of her cheek for what might have been a full minute.

"You know," she finally said in a whisper, "not that long ago, I was on a sinking ship. A literal sinking ship. Not to be dramatic, but the atmosphere in this city doesn't feel a whole lot better."

It was a fair enough assessment. The city's future was uncertain, and many were beginning to question Leah's leadership. It was even whispered that she had met with Illander Asher, the former Prime Minister of Nolia accused of masterminding the assassination of the royal family, in his prison cell beneath the palace. This had sparked a rumor that Asher was instructing Leah on how to run the city and, by extension, the Athacean League. It was all nonsense, of course, but Leah wasn't doing herself any favors by staying quiet. Sooner or later, she would have to decide on a course of action for the people of this city and the kingdom of Nolia as a whole. Otherwise, if tensions ran much higher, someone else might try to seize power and decide for her.

"Speaking of sinking ships," said Adonica.

She didn't finish the thought. When Hook glanced up at her, he realized that she was looking at his forehead.

Somebody finally told her, he thought.

Hook raised one hand, gripped the strip of cloth tied around his forehead, and pulled it up to reveal the lifeslave's brand beneath.

"So it is true," she said.

Hook nodded, then replaced the headband over the scar. He didn't expect any further thoughts from the likes of Adonica Lor on this matter. She was, after all, a Mythaean. The revelation that he was a lifeslave was more likely to arouse suspicion from a Mythaean than to evoke any

sympathy. In fact, her current expression was one of such forthright in-
dignation that he wondered if the very idea of serving alongside a
convicted lifeslave offended her.

Adonica looked him up and down. Then she made a sour, disgusted
face. "Whoever did that to you," she said, "ought to be gelded and
strung up for coblyns."

Hook cocked an eyebrow.

Adonica gave a dismissive wave. "Or keelhauled through shallow water—I don't know. Gunnar could probably think of something more
creative. At any rate, to hell with whoever did it." She scratched at the
back of her neck. "And, look, my mouth runs free of my head sometimes when I'm not paying attention, so if I've said anything stupid in
your presence, just know that nobody saw fit to inform me that you
were a freed slave."

Hook nodded. If Adonica had been familiar with hand signs, he
might have seen fit to correct her—to explain that he hadn't been freed
at all. Far from it.

The door on the opposite end of the barracks swung open again. It
thudded against the back wall, and a few soldiers stirred in their cots as
a broad-shouldered form stepped in.

Major Lycon Belesys walked with the measured step of a man who
prided himself in military formality, but Hook did not miss the slight
limp or the way he favored one side as he moved. It was a miracle that
Lycon had survived plummeting from the walls of Cervice. Or perhaps
the miracle was that the man who had kicked him over the side—if Innocen *was* a man—hadn't torn Lycon's head off instead.

Upon spotting Hook and Adonica by the fireside, Lycon quickened
his pace toward them. Hook stood and brushed himself off as Lycon
came to a halt, clicking his heels together before him.

"General Bard," Lycon said with a salute. He made no effort to lower
his deep, booming voice, and even more of the sleeping soldiers in the
room began to stir. Hook decided to give the man the satisfaction of
saluting him back.

"Something up, Major?" asked Adonica.

"We have need of you at the gates, General Bard," said Lycon, a nervous look in his eye. "Immediately, Sir."

CHAPTER 13

Leah looked down from the walls of Cervice with a furrowed brow. The crown of Nolia rested atop her head, and her blood-red cloak flew behind her like a banner in the morning breeze. She had decided to stop wearing her mother's powder blue cloak, opting instead for this dark red one. She intended it to be a statement to those around her, an acknowledgment of the perilous times in which she ruled.

Her mother's cloak was a garment better suited for times of peace. Someday, she hoped to wear it again.

The sun was rising over the plains south of the city—illuminating a mob of strangers standing outside the gates of her city. There were about a hundred of them, on foot, and they had approached without weapons drawn.

"My Queen?"

Leah turned to face Marcus Worth, standing dutifully behind her.

"Is everything all right?" asked Marcus quietly.

"Everything is not all right, no," she said. "But thank you for asking."

The people at the city gates were her most immediate concern but not the most pressing. It was not the first time it had happened. In the weeks since her return to Nolia, the arrival of refugees had become commonplace. And as rumors spread that the city had withstood the onslaught of a demon advance, she imagined more and more people would seek to emigrate to Cervice. What had her concerned at the moment was what had happened in the middle of the night.

She'd gone from fast asleep to wide awake in an instant. There had been a flash of light before her eyes and a ringing in her ears—pure sensory overload. For several seconds, she had been unable to move, paralyzed by the sensation, watching greenish-white flashes of light dance across her vision. Pure aurym power. She would have recognized the source anywhere. Justin.

She had felt power like that before, on the night he'd left Hartla. She had felt it again when he'd returned to the Oikoumene. What did it mean to feel it again, now?

Gunnar had informed her that Ahlund and Justin were on their way to a place called Esthean, where Justin could train in the ways of the

Ru'Onorath—the Guardians of the Oikoumene. Leah hoped that wherever they were, Ahlund was keeping Justin safe. But she'd had an uneasy feeling about the whole thing.

That feeling of power, she thought. *Does it mean he's left the Oikoumene again?*

"Hey, you can't just—!" Leah heard a guard cry out from the stairs below.

"Watch me," replied a female voice.

Leah turned toward the stairs that led up to the walls. Marcus put a hand on his sword's hilt and positioned himself between Leah and the stairs, but Leah placed a hand on his shoulder to put him at ease. Adonica Lor mounted the stairs, taking them two at a time, with a member of the High Nolian Guard chasing after her.

"It's all right," Leah said. "Let her through."

Adonica shot an antagonistic salute to the guard in response, then crossed the top of the wall to join Leah.

"Nothing against your soldiers," said Adonica, wiping her nose, "but every time I think I've proven myself, they try to pull rank."

"The High Guard has a spotty record," said Leah. "They're just trying to prevent another mistake."

Adonica nodded to Marcus. "Lycon rushed Hook off to the gates, but he wouldn't tell me anything. Where do you need me?"

"Time will tell," said Leah.

Adonica cast a look down at the crowd assembled outside the gates. "More new arrivals?"

"It looks that way."

"No outward signs of aggression," Marcus spoke up. "Sif thought they might be Eeth."

"Eeth?" said Adonica.

"Tribal peoples that live in the deserts of northern Otunmer," he explained. "If so, they're a long way from home."

"So far, we haven't found anyone in the city who speaks the language," said Leah. "But there is one among them with a long, thin scar across her forehead."

CHAPTER 14

"A scar like Hook's," said Adonica. "I see. A brand."

"Maybe," said Leah. "Probably a long shot. But it's worth a try."

If Zechariah were here, she thought, *he might be able to speak directly to them.*

But the old man was still nowhere to be found. Zechariah seemed to do as he pleased, without feeling any obligation to explain himself. The last time he'd disappeared, he'd been gone for months. Leah could only hope it would not be quite so long this time. It seemed that with each passing day, there were fewer people in her life whom she could rely on. They kept dying. Or leaving.

Justin, she thought. *I don't believe you would leave us to do this alone. I don't believe you would leave . . . me.*

"General Bard's returning from the gate," said Marcus.

Leah moved forward to stand at the top of the stairs to wait for Hook. He and Lycon were passing through the guards to climb up to her position.

At the top of the stairs, Hook strode toward Leah with Lycon close behind him. His face was unreadable, but that was not unusual. He had removed the strip of cloth from his head, revealing his slave's brand. He was currently tying it back on to hold his long, black hair in place.

"My Queen," signed Hook.

"My friend," Leah signed back. She was not as dexterous with the signs, but she had attempted to learn as many of them as possible. *"Any news?"*

"Your guess was right," signed Hook. *"The woman with the scar was a lifeslave on a Mythaean ship. Like me. She speaks using a variation of the same system of signs."*

"Very lucky," signed Leah. *"What does she say?"*

"Their people are," began Hook. He paused and communicated the name phonetically, using signs that represented sounds rather than words. He had to repeat it twice before Leah got it.

"Rorrdvuuk?" she said aloud.

Hook nodded.

"Rorrdvuuk!" said Marcus. "Then they are tribal peoples after all, but they're much farther from home than the Eeth!"

"Demons from the south drove them from their homelands," signed Hook. *"They numbered in the thousands when they started north. Now, there are only a few hundred. They had hoped to find refuge in the capital city of Pheodops, in Raeqlund. Apparently, there are some ancient ties between the two peoples. But the Raeqlu turned them away."*

Leah bit her lip. Many Raeqlu were present in Cervice—a whole army, in fact, led to Nolia by Zechariah himself. She didn't know as much about Raeqlu culture as she would have liked, but she knew about their people's emphasis on social classes—of which the non-citizen was the lowest of the low. The Raeqlu were highly compassionate toward their own citizens and toward the citizens of nations whom they recognized as allies. But non-citizens held no rights within their system of government. Outsiders were treated as undesirables and sometimes, unfortunately, were scorned outright.

"Despite being turned away," continued Hook, *"they learned that a Raeqlu army was on its way to a fortified city in Nolia, and they decided to journey north to find it. They are requesting refuge. They say they are prepared to work or fight to earn their keep."*

"Do you trust them, Hook?" asked Leah, verbally.

"I trust the words of the former slave with whom I spoke," said Hook. *"There is no way to be sure about the rest of them. But they appear desperate."*

Leah nodded. "Take me down there with you, please. With you as my interpreter."

"Do you mean to let them in, then?" asked Marcus.

"I will propose my terms and welcome them in *if* they are willing to accept." She turned to Lycon. "Major Belesys, please remain here with Marcus and Adonica. At the first sign of trouble, raise the alarm and bring the whole city to arms."

"Yes, Queen Anavion," said Lycon with a bow of his head.

As Leah and Hook started down the stairway, Hook held his hands low to keep his signs hidden.

"I respect your decisions," he signed.

"Thank you," she signed back, bracing herself for whatever was coming next.

"But you must know that this city can only be a temporary refuge," he continued. *"This will not last. It cannot last. The people need to know where you stand. And where we are going."*

Leah let out a long breath. *"I know,"* she replied.

CHAPTER 15

Only now, standing toe to toe with the Rorrdvuuk, did Leah gain a true appreciation for their size.

They were broad-shouldered and exceptionally tall. They had some of the whitest skin of any people Leah had ever seen, and almost every one of them had his or her face decorated with tattooed patterns of interlocking circles and triangles. Most had hair that was either light red, almost orange, or gray like smoke. All wore white and brown furs, and every one of them—men and women alike—had long spears or javelins either clutched in their hands or leaning at their sides. The blades of these weapons appeared to be made of reflective hunks of volcanic rock—sharp as glass, yet strong as iron. Some of them had steeds, but most were on foot.

Leah found herself marveling at the wide-reaching effects of the demons' invasion. To her knowledge, the Rorrdvuuk lived in the ice-packed regions of the deep south, where all the maps she had ever seen faded away into unknown, uncharted lands. What were conditions like in the south to drive these people so far north? And to erode their numbers from the thousands to mere hundreds?

Sometimes, thought Leah, *it feels like our world is falling apart.*

Leah stepped forward, her hand resting intentionally on the hilt of her sword. To one side stood Hook Bard. At her other side was Sif of the Cru. The three of them were out here alone, as she had ordered the rest of her forces to draw back as a show of good faith. She knew from experience what Hook and Sif would look like as they flanked her: one wearing a perpetual glare, the other wearing a perpetual grin, both ready to fly into action at a moment's notice if necessary.

A large, elderly Rorrdvuuk man stood front and center. His thin white hair had perhaps once been red-orange like the others but had lost its color with age. Like the rest of the Rorrdvuuk, he had a rounded, hairy jaw and a flat, wide nose. The blue-inked tattoos running up his cheeks and across his forehead appeared faded with time. Upon his wizened head was the symbol of his authority: a helmet made from what appeared to be the skull of a great lion. Two long fangs extended downward from the skull's jaw, hanging out over the man's forehead, and two volcanic rocks had been set in the eye sockets. From the back of the headdress hung a long cape of white fur. The lion's fur? Possibly. Leah had never seen a white lion before, not even in books at the Academy, but who knew what sort of creatures roamed the deep south? The Rorrdvuuk's furs may have come from animals she'd never seen or heard of before.

Beside the man with the lion headdress was a broad-shouldered woman who would have easily stood eye to eye with Justin, who was over six feet tall. Her red-orange hair was shorn short, and she was clothed in white and brown furs like the rest of them. She had facial features similar to the others, including blue, geometric facial tattoos, but unlike any of the others, a perfectly straight band of scar tissue ran horizontally across her forehead.

There could be no mistake. It was a brand. And it was identical to Hook's.

"I am Queen Leah Anavion of Nolia," Leah said, addressing the man in the lion headdress. At barely over five feet tall, she was used to looking up at people. She no longer let things like physical stature intimidate her. "Welcome to our capital city of Cervice."

She waited for Hook to sign her words. The woman with the scar watched Hook before leaning toward the man in the lion headdress. She, in turn, related the message by signing to him, a copper gauntlet on her left arm flashing in the morning sun as her hands moved. Although Leah had a passing knowledge of Hook's signs, she had difficulty following the ones used by this woman. Leah was able to recognize the female pronoun when the woman referred to her, as well as the sign that meant, roughly, "Welcome," but clearly there were regional variations in the sign language. Some of the signs must have been purely phonetic, for she was unable to follow them.

After the woman had communicated the message, the big Rorrdvuuk man looked down at her and spoke.

"Leah," he said.

Leah nodded to confirm that he had said it correctly.

Then the man with the headdress began to speak.

CHAPTER 16

The Rorrdvuuk language had an up-and-down cadence and seemed to utilize an almost sing-song quality. Perhaps, like some languages Leah had read about, the meaning of words or phrases could change depending on inflection or tonal variations.

When the man in the lion headdress was done speaking, the female interpreter began to sign to Hook. Leah tried to follow her signs at first, but the combination of known and unknown signs confused her enough that she decided to wait for Hook to relay the message rather than risk a misunderstanding.

"This is Folgruuth, King of Dvuuk-land," signed Hook, using phonetic-based signs to communicate the sounds of the names. *"I think the literal translation of his name is something like Trailblazer or Path-Mapper. The translator is called Megara, which means Lantern-Bearer."*

Leah bowed to the king. "Folgruuth," she said, then she turned to face the translator and said, "Megara."

Both returned her bow. Then Megara, unprompted by Folgruuth, signed something else. Hook gave a rare look of surprise in response.

"What is it?" asked Leah.

"She says she can understand your words," signed Hook.

Leah turned toward the woman. "You know the Waelik language?"

Folgruuth cleared his throat, and Leah recognized it as the interjection of a man attempting to assert his role. Megara responded with a deferential bow.

"We have traveled far," said Folgruuth, his words relayed to Leah through hand signs. *"Ancient evils drove us from Dvuuk-land. Our mighty people have been reduced to a band of nomads trying to survive. We have no place to go. We heard that your city takes in people who are in need."*

"How many of you are there?" asked Leah.

"We set out from Dvuuk-land ten thousand strong," said Folgruuth. *"Now, there are less than two thousand of us."*

Leah shot a glance at Hook. "I thought you said there were only a few hundred."

Hook appeared to be at a loss. Then Folgruuth elaborated. *"This is my entourage. The rest of my people have made camp in the forest, west of here."*

Leah hoped the hesitancy did not show on her face. She didn't want to turn these people away, but supplies in Cervice were dwindling as it was. Another two thousand people added to the mix would complicate matters significantly.

She knew that any hint of indecision or lack of confidence would cast her in a poor light—not only in the eyes of the Rorrdvuuk but in the minds of her own people as well.

We'll have to make it work.

"Nolia does not turn away people in need," replied Leah, "so long as those people pledge an oath of peace to this country and to the military alliance to which we belong: the Athacean League."

Leah paused to allow the two translators to catch up, then continued.

"I must warn you that Raeqlund counts itself as one of the members of our League. I would not fault your people for bearing bad feelings for the Raeqlu, but I warn you: I cannot tolerate conflict within my city. Within our walls, your people must submit to my authority." She paused again to let this thought be translated before adding, "If we hope to survive in these times, we must all make compromises."

A few moments passed, and Folgruuth stroked his furry jaw as he looked down at her appraisingly. The volcanic rocks in the eyes of the lion's skull almost seemed to be peering down at her, too—along with every other Rorrdvuuk man and woman assembled here. Folgruuth opened his mouth to speak—

A loud, long wail of a horn cut through the early-morning air. Leah's head snapped toward the sound. It was coming from atop the city walls.

Hook stepped forward, placing himself between Leah and Folgruuth. Leah backed away, fearing some sort of trap. But Folgruuth seemed just as baffled as Leah.

The alarm horn rang out again. Up on the walls stood Marcus, Lycon, and Adonica. Lycon was blowing the horn while Adonica gestured frantically eastward—the direction from which Darvelle had attacked Cervice not long ago. Not far from the command post, a member of the city guard had both arms raised, bearing two lit torches. It was the signal of an enemy attack.

Leah's guts felt cold and hollow.

Not again.

CHAPTER 17

Leah opened her mouth to explain the situation to Folgruuth, but the large man beat her to it, singing out several syllables in quick succession. Megara relayed the message to Hook, who quickly signed it to Leah.

"We will return to our people. If there is danger, we must be there to defend them."

Leah nodded. "Do not come to the city until you are certain it is safe."

Folgruuth agreed, and the Rorrdvuuk set out on foot, hurrying westward.

A detachment of the High Nolian Guard was already coming to meet Leah as she, Hook, and Sif hurried back to the walls of the city. The horn continued to blow, and everywhere, the city was coming alive in response to the call to arms. Soldiers rushed to their posts, preparing to defend the city.

Within moments, Leah had reached the eastern command post atop the walls. From here, she could look out over the outer districts of Cervice. Makeshift walls, cobbled together by the forces of Cervice, surrounded the outer districts. Most of the walls were still in decent shape, but some sections had been damaged during the demon army's attack or even utterly destroyed by the daemyn blasts of cythraul.

Outside the city, the river wended its way over the plains and into the Borderwoods. All but one of the bridges had been collapsed to defend against possible invasion, and the last remaining bridge had been outfitted with makeshift fortifications. The city guards atop those fortifications were also blowing alarm horns, rousing soldiers to take up positions in preparation for the attack.

Lycon, Adonica, and Marcus were waiting for Leah when she, Hook, and Sif arrived.

"Report, Major," ordered Leah.

"No sign of the enemy yet," said Lycon, "but the alarm was sounded due to a relay all the way from the edge of the Gravelands."

Leah stood straight-backed and solemn atop the walls, aware of the many eyes watching her—knowing that at any given moment, something as simple as her posture or her expression could inspire confidence, or cause a lack thereof.

From the Gravelands, thought Leah. *The same demon army attacking again? Or a new one? Either way, how can we withstand a second demon attack? We can't. Not a full-scale one, anyway.*

"My Queen!" a gruff voice called out from behind them.

Leah turned to find Olorus addressing her, bowing. He then greeted the others one at a time: "General Bard. Elder Sif. Major Belesys. Captain Worth. Private Lor."

As the males returned his greeting, Leah heard Adonica mutter something under her breath about deserving a promotion.

"Olorus," said Leah. "Your response time is impressive."

"I thank you for the time you have allowed me to spend with Mother," said Olorus, "but I will not neglect my duties."

Hook, a spyglass raised to his eye, suddenly leaned forward. Leah could tell from his body language that he had spotted something. Adonica held another spyglass out to her, and she took it.

It took Leah a moment to find it through the scope, but it was impossible to miss. There was movement. Something coming fast through the trees.

Two riders on steedback burst forth from the forest, both pushing their steeds to the limit, galloping. The rider in the lead rode with his cloak and long beard billowing in the wind.

"Zechariah," said Leah.

She didn't recognize the other rider.

A tap on her shoulder. She turned to look at Hook and saw that he was pointing—not at Zechariah or the other rider, but at the woods behind them.

Leah shifted her spyglass, and her breath caught in her throat. It was as if a great, collective shadow were moving through the trees, darkening the entire forest like a bank of black fog.

As Zechariah and the second rider raced toward Cervice, a flood of coblyn bodies burst forth from the trees. They moved like a single entity: a herd of galloping, loping, child-sized demon bodies. A thousand of them, at least. Chasing just two human riders.

"Open the gates!" Leah shouted. "Two riders coming through! All hands to battle stations! Archers—be at the ready!"

Olorus repeated the order, and Leah heard it being echoed up and down the streets, relayed to the soldiers at the outer walls.

"Queen Anavion!" someone shouted.

Leah turned. A member of the High Nolian Guard had rushed to the command post.

"My Lady," said the guard, raising a finger to point out over the walls. "A rider!"

Leah opened her mouth, about to make a snide comment that she could already see that. But then she noticed where the guardsman was pointing—not toward Zechariah's position in the east, but to the south.

Leah turned to look. Sure enough, past the southern reaches of the city, a lone rider was racing across the plains. The rider was moving not toward the city, but away from it. For a moment, she thought one of her soldiers had broken ranks. Then Hook lowered his spyglass and signed, *"Megara."*

CHAPTER 18

"The Rorrdvuuk translator?" said Sif.

"What?" said Adonica. "What's she *doing*?"

The hairs on Leah's neck stood up as she wondered if the Rorrdvuuk really had been laying a trap. It wouldn't be the first time that humans had allied themselves with demons. She'd been told after the fact that there had been humans fighting alongside the demon army during the attack on Cervice. And people like Lisaac and his raiders—devotees of the rumored overlord Avagad—had willingly pledged themselves to fight with coblyns as their comrades in arms.

But, scanning the city outskirts and the country beyond, Leah could see no sign of the rest of the Rorrdvuuk. They seemed to have departed to rejoin the bulk of their people. It was only Megara, the female Rorrdvuuk with the slave's brand like Hook, who was racing out as if to intercept Zechariah's path to the city.

"Shall we stop her?" asked Marcus.

"I'm not sure we could reach her in time to stop whatever she's planning," said Olorus.

"Sif," said Leah. "Are your riders ready?"

"Ready, My Queen," he said.

"I agree with Olorus," said Leah. "I don't think there's enough time to intercept her, but if anybody can come close, it's your Cru riders. Lead them out, please."

Sif nodded once, then hurried down the stairs toward the gates below.

Leah turned to Hook. *"Any idea what she is doing?"* she signed.

No knowledge of signs was required to translate Hook's response: a shrug.

Down below, Zechariah and the second rider were nearing the outskirts of the city, but both steeds were visibly weary, and the coblyn horde was quickly gaining on them. A thousand coblyns wouldn't present a significant threat to the city itself but would be more than sufficient to tear Zechariah and the second rider limb from limb.

"She's not heading toward Zechariah," Adonica suddenly said. "She's moving *toward* the coblyns."

Leah trained her spyglass on Megara. Before she could confirm Adonica's theory, a glint of bright light in the spyglass made Leah close her eyes involuntarily. A reflection of sunlight caught in the lens, probably. But when she looked back, she realized the bright gleam of light was still there—so bright that she could hardly keep her eye open. And instead of remaining in place, the light appeared to be moving. It was following Megara's form as she rode.

"What is that?" said Olorus.

Leah lowered the spyglass. The bright gleam of light following Megara was visible from here, even with the naked eye. The light was like a star moving along with her as she rode, so bright that Leah couldn't tell if it floated over her, if she held it in her hand, or if it *was* her. Whatever it was, it was moving straight toward the coblyns as if to cover Zechariah's escape.

And it may have been Leah's imagination, but the coblyns' advance seemed to be slowing down.

"Aurym," Leah realized aloud.

No sooner had she spoken the word than the light erupted brighter than ever, eliciting gasps from the onlookers.

A sweeping beam of light swung across the front lines of the coblyns. Even from here, Leah had to close her eyes. It was like trying to look at the sun. When she opened her eyes again, the beam of light was gone, and a cloud of smoke was rising from the front of the coblyn horde. The front lines appeared to have come to an almost complete stop. Some were falling to the ground, while those in the back were still attempting to push forward.

The beam of light shot out from Megara's position again. Flames jumped from the coblyn lines. Smoke rose in tiny jets. The light was burning the demons alive.

By now, Sif and his Cru riders had rushed out to Zechariah and his fellow rider and were escorting them toward the city's outer walls. Megara adjusted her course and began to swing back toward the city.

A few moments later, Zechariah and the Cru passed through the gates of the outer walls. The gates began to close, but Zechariah leaped from his tired steed and could be seen gesturing wildly. The guards manning the gate winches stopped and kept the gates open a while longer as Megara raced toward them.

Leah could now see dead coblyns littering the plains, surrounded by scorch marks in the grass. The rest were chasing after Megara on all fours. She shot another beam of light into them as she fled, and her steed made it through the gates just as the coblyns came within range of the archers. The archers began unleashing their arrows, and lines of coblyns fell.

As the gates closed shut, Leah breathed a sigh of relief. The archers at the walls could handle the coblyns, as long as there wasn't a cythraul nearby.

CHAPTER 19

While the archers along the walls finished off the last of the coblyns, Leah was not surprised to find Zechariah speaking to Megara in fluent Rorrdvuuk. His fellow rider appeared to be a young Raeqlu man whom Leah did not recognize.

Leah approached Megara first.

"Thank you," signed Leah.

Megara only nodded.

Then Leah turned to face Zechariah. She decided to forgo the pleasantries, leading instead with her gut reaction.

"Where the hell have you been?" she said.

The old man was unfazed. "My house," he said with a grin.

Leah squinted at him. "In Deen? You left and crossed the Gravelands without telling me—?"

"It was more important that I went discretely, and alone," Zechariah responded, cutting her off. He then gestured to the Raeqlu man beside him. "Well, almost alone. I was hoping we would be back before you even noticed we were gone. Ran into a bit of trouble at the end. But otherwise, the trip was uneventful."

As if on cue, coblyns could be heard slamming against the gates not far from their position. The twangs of the archers continued rhythmically from above.

"I won't apologize for my actions," said Zechariah.

"Indeed, why start now?" said Leah.

Zechariah's grin did not falter. "I think you will soon agree that the journey was worth it. There was something I needed to retrieve from my library."

Zechariah reached to his side and used his hook—a long, curved spike where his right hand had once been—to snare a small satchel.

The old man paused. Leah knew he was waiting for her to ask what was in the bag, but she refused to take the bait. She wasn't in the mood. She looked instead at the Raeqlu man. He only smiled.

Finally, Zechariah shrugged and said, "Suit yourself," and he and the Raeqlu man began to walk away.

Leah shot a look at Olorus and Hook. Hook sighed, Olorus rolled his eyes, and Leah gritted her teeth.

"All right, what is it then?" she finally asked.

Zechariah stopped and looked back over his shoulder. "Follow me, and I'll show you."

CHAPTER 20

Long after Leah departed with Zechariah, Hook remained behind to help the guards fight off the last of the coblyns. This turned out to be an even easier task than anticipated, especially after the Rorrdvuuk woman called Megara climbed the fortifications and began shining burning beams of light down into the ranks of the creatures. At closer proximity, Hook could now see that the light originated from a tiny glass-like stone set in the copper-plated gauntlet mounted on her left arm.

An hour later, members of the High Nolian Guard and an entourage of Cru were escorting an assemblage of two thousand Rorrdvuuk in through the city's western gates. At the front of the procession, Folgruuth led his people into the city, accompanied by Lycon, Sif, and Olorus, who would show them to the empty granaries that would serve as their temporary quarters.

Hook, meanwhile, rode on steedback at the rear of the procession, keeping a watchful eye on the Rorrdvuuk people. He did not anticipate trouble. Their body language told him they had seen enough of that and had no desire for more. There were very few steeds among the group, and Hook found himself wondering if they had walked on foot all this way from the deep south.

Hook's gaze wandered to the Rorrdvuuk riders escorting the last of the people through the gate. There was Megara. The big, broad-shouldered woman with the face tattoos, the short-cropped orange hair, the gauntlet on her arm . . . and the band of scar tissue across her forehead.

Hook waited for Megara to ride up beside him. He looked at her, and she looked at him. Wordlessly, the two fell in line, riding alongside one another.

Only after Hook heard the gate doors thud shut behind them did he turn and sign to her, *"I have never seen such aurym. Is it fire?"*

Megara gestured upward, then signed, *"Sun."*

The two continued riding in silence, Megara taking in the architecture of Cervice, gazing at the towering minarets of the palace, and Hook observing the interactions between the city people and the Rorrdvuuk. He noted a fair share of suspicious glances, but he also saw people coming forward to greet the newcomers—an old man shaking hands and offering kind words of welcome to anyone he could reach, and a little girl and her mother handing out pieces of fruit to the Rorrdvuuk who passed them. Some of these fruits were far out of season and were met with astonished looks. When one of the Rorrdvuuk tossed a fig to Megara, she looked at it doubtfully, then shot a look at Hook.

"Aurym," signed Hook. *"There is a man here who can grow plants."*

Megara gave an appraising look at the fig, then took a juicy bite. After it was gone, she gestured to the strip of cloth tied around Hook's head. *"What ship?"* she asked.

Hook signed, *"The Manticore. You?"*

Megara thumbed her chest and signed, *"The Lion of the Sky."*

Hook only nodded, but inside, he had to suppress the urge to flood this woman with questions. Not once in the years since he'd escaped from the Mythaeans had Hook encountered a fellow lifeslave—let alone a free one. There was so much he wanted to ask, most of which would have to wait for a more opportune time. But there was one question he could not resist asking right away.

"The language of the hand signs," he said. *"Who taught you?"*

Megara seemed to consider the question for a moment. *"The lifeslaves aboard the Lion of the Sky practiced it in secret. They taught me when I was brought aboard. It was a small ship—difficult to keep it hidden from the row-master."*

"We, too, had to keep the signs hidden," replied Hook. *"We failed, in the end. . . . We learned from a slave who was transferred to our ship. She brought the signs with her. She taught them to us."*

"What was her name?" asked Megara.

Hook signed it phonetically, but Megara shook her head. The meaning was clear. She didn't know the name.

"I should warn you," signed Hook, *"there are Mythaeans here."*

Megara looked sharply at him. *"This city keeps slaves?"*

"No," signed Hook. *"But there are many Mythaeans here. And the military alliance the Queen spoke of—Mythaeans make up a large portion of the League."*

Again, Megara gazed at the strip of cloth tied around Hook's forehead. This time, she looked at it with disgust. *"And you wear that thing to hide who you are?"*

Hook's gaze darkened. *"I hide nothing."*

"How can you be allies with such people?" asked Megara.

Hook looked away, checking for any sign of onlookers. He lowered his hands so as not to be seen as he signed, *"I swore to repay the injustices done to me. And I still intend to."* He turned his dark-eyed gaze forward again, toward the city of Cervice, and added, *"Perhaps sooner than they realize."*

CHAPTER 21

The council chambers of the palace of Cervice had once served as the meeting place for representatives from across the kingdom of Nolia. Here was where laws were made, where votes were taken on issues ranging from taxes to foreign policy. But today, the chambers' many chairs were empty, and the floors and desks already showed the dust of disuse.

The chamber door was closed, with Marcus Worth standing guard outside, leaving Queen Leah Anavion alone with the old man she knew only as Zechariah.

Leah crossed the chambers and pulled back the curtain from the lone glass window to let in the morning sunlight. It shone in visible rays through the cloud of dust that rose from the curtain.

Leah turned back to face Zechariah. He sat with his unopened leather satchel on the table in front of him. She decided to refrain from speaking first. Instead, she leaned back against the wall with her arms crossed.

"Well," said Zechariah. "How are things in the city?"

You would know if you'd been here, thought Leah. "Not very good, thank you for asking. And how was Deen?"

"Mostly destroyed."

Leah grimaced, almost wishing she hadn't asked. Deen was the little town where Ahlund had taken her to escape the political instability of Nolia after the assassination of the rest of the royal family. It was also where Nolian soldiers, under the orders of the former Prime Minister Illander Asher, had abducted her from Ahlund's care.

"A demon attack?" she asked.

"It certainly looked that way," Zechariah said, and did not elaborate further.

Leah, arms still crossed, drummed her fingers against her bicep. Finally, she said, "Your business is your own, and far be it from me to pry. You are, after all, no subject of mine. In the future, however—and with all due respect to your status and your abilities as an advisor and as a leader—I would thank you to at least let me know *when* you plan to disappear."

"Disappearing is a trick best done without making an announcement beforehand," said Zechariah. "But I shall take your gratitude into consideration in the future, and I will assess my options accordingly."

Leah sneered a little at having her rhetoric so adroitly countered. "You clearly felt that *someone* was worthy of such an explanation. That Raeqlu man you took with you."

Zechariah cleared his throat. But instead of offering an explanation, he changed the subject.

"Two weeks ago," he said, "we all met in these chambers, and I submitted a proposal for your consideration. Have you given the matter any thought?"

Leah drummed her fingers on her arm again. The proposal he referred to was his plan to mobilize the forces of Cervice.

Leah had given this matter a great deal of thought. Zechariah had argued that fighting a defensive war against the demons would be an exercise in futility. At best, it would lead to a slow, prolonged defeat as their forces were gradually beaten down by demon hordes. Their only chance at true victory, he had argued, was to fight the war on their own terms. To attack rather than defend. In fact, he had gone so far as to suggest that the entire Athacean League—the alliance forged between Nolians, Mythaeans, and other nations and lands to fight the demons—be made mobile and leave their homelands behind. This plan involved combining the League's military might into a single invasion force and marching across the face of the world to invade the far-eastern continent of Erum, the demons' rumored seat of power.

Leah couldn't argue with the old man's logic. But mobilizing so many people. . . .

To request a course of action of an army was one thing. But what about the civilians? The children, the elderly, and the sick? The slim hope of victory that Zechariah was proposing came at a steep price.

Anytime a leader ordered troops into battle, it meant she was sending people to their deaths. A full-scale invasion would mean condemning soldiers, perhaps thousands or perhaps even tens of thousands, to die violently and painfully, far from home. And mobilizing citizens meant condemning those same soldiers' families to similarly grim destinies.

A chance of victory, perhaps. But at what cost? How could a leader ask her people to take such risks? And who would willingly follow such a leader?

"I am considering it," said Leah.

"Indeed," said Zechariah.

Something about the way he said it annoyed Leah—as if he didn't believe her. But instead of explaining himself, Zechariah began to open up the leather satchel on the table before him. From the satchel, he pulled out a scroll of parchment bound by a length of string.

"First reactions speak volumes, my dear," said Zechariah. "I could tell what you thought of my plan the moment I shared it with you. Based on your initial reaction, I knew my plan of action would not be adopted—at least, not as I originally envisioned it."

"I didn't say I had rejected the idea," said Leah.

Zechariah shook his head. "It's not a matter of accepting the idea or rejecting it. As the leader of these people, any proposed course of action will require that *you* be its most ardent evangelist. It's not enough that you be convinced of a plan's viability. You won't be able to convince others to follow you if they sense reluctance or half-heartedness. Not with so many lives at stake." He paused, leaning forward a bit. "But we must do this. Because it is the only hope we have."

"What about Justin?" Leah asked, surprised to find that her throat was a bit dry.

Zechariah's face hardened. "I'm sure you felt it, too."

She did not need to ask what he was referring to. "Was it him?" She had to pause for a moment before she could work up the courage to ask the next question. "Do you think he left us?"

"I do not know," said Zechariah. "But I have felt nothing of his presence since then—no indication whatsoever that he is still in our world. The aurym powers of an ethoul can change everything in a moment. But we must face facts. Justin may be gone. We may never see him again. At any rate, we must operate under the assumption that no one is coming to save us. We are our only hope. Or, more accurately, *you* are."

Leah turned away. Looking out the window of the council chambers, to the city streets outside the palace, she let out a long, slow breath. She wasn't sure why, exactly, but she felt as if something inside her had suddenly died.

"I 'disappeared,' as you put it," Zechariah continued, "in search of an alternative plan."

Leah turned back around to find Zechariah untying the string around the scroll of parchment one-handedly. He then used his hook-hand to unroll it. She crossed the chambers to get a better look.

On the interior of the scroll was a hand-drawn map of the continent of Athacea. But, leaning in closer, Leah realized that its coastlines were slightly different than any map of Athacea she had ever seen. There were cities in places where, to her knowledge, no cities existed. And the language used to label these cities was an old form of the Waelik alphabet that appeared to follow a different set of lettering rules, with unfamiliar symbols interspersed throughout the words.

"This is why you went to Deen?" said Leah. "To get a map?"

"I went to get many things," said Zechariah. "Unfortunately, circumstances as they were, *this* is all I was able to come back with. But this is not just any map. This map leads home."

CHAPTER 22

Zechariah used his good hand to place a finger on the map, near the middle portion of the continent of Athacea, slightly off-center.

"This is where your capital stands today," he said. "At the time when this map was drawn, nothing existed here. Nolia did not yet exist, but there were other kingdoms on this continent. Other bastions of power."

He slid his finger north of that location, across a river, through an area labeled with paintings of trees. Then he dragged his finger east until it came to rest on a large, semicircular range of mountains. On the map, they were labeled *Thucymoroi*. Leah knew them better as the Shifting Mountains.

Leah's brow furrowed. On the map, at the center of the mountains, an image of a stairway had been drawn. To one side of the staircase, the cartographer had sketched a series of vertical, feather-shaped objects; on the other side was the outline of a ram's skull.

"This map," said Zechariah, "shows the entrance to an underground citadel beneath the Shifting Mountains. A realm lost to time. A city once occupied by the Ancients, presumably long abandoned. A place where the elderly, the sick, the children, and anyone else who so desires might—and I do mean *might*—find shelter and safety. For a time, at least."

Leah felt an involuntary grin tug at her lips. "That . . . could work."

"It *will* work," said Zechariah. "Depending on the state of the place, of course. While our armies march to war, our civilians can remain behind, hidden beneath the mountains." As he spoke, he deliberately rolled up the map and re-tied the string into place. "And now that you have this map, you can announce where you will be taking your people—a place where noncombatants can remain safe while you and your armies take the fight to the enemy."

Leah held out her hand to accept the map. But then she hesitated.

"You must have predicted this complication," she said. "Did you have this in mind all along?"

Zechariah's expression darkened. "*No one* can know that." He pressed the map into her waiting hand. "Understand?"

Leah accepted it but shook her head. "No. I don't."

"I proposed my plan to you publicly, in front of your advisors," said Zechariah, "because it was important that you be seen carefully considering my proposed course of action—before you came up with *your own*, more effective version." With the tip of his hook, he tapped the map she now held in her hand.

"You want me to lie and take credit for the idea as my own," said Leah. It was not a question.

"The stability of this League and its subsidiaries is weakened by its reliance on multiple leaders wielding equal power," said Zechariah. "For there to be any chance of its survival, we need to establish centralized rule beneath a singular authority."

Leah blinked. It took a moment for the implication of his words to dawn on her.

"Me," she said.

And again, it was not a question.

Zechariah nodded. "You, Leah."

"Centralized rule," Leah said, shaking her head. "The League is supposed to be a military alliance, not an empire. Wulder Von Morix—and others like him—will become wary if a single individual starts to become too powerful. If I take too many liberties in my position, they'll fear that I have ambitions not just to lead the League, but to rule over Athacea. Maybe they'll even think I mean to one day rule over Mythaean territory."

"If we don't win this war," said Zechariah, "they'll be nothing left to rule over. That is of secondary concern. And besides, I can assure you that someone like Von Morix is already positioning himself to benefit handily from this arrangement. If the war is ever won, he will have his own plans on how to come out on the other side more powerful than ever. We don't need him. And anyway, if you *were* to rule over all those territories, would it be such a bad thing?"

Leah swallowed hard. She was barely able to believe what he was proposing. If certain ears were to hear words like this, the charge would be treason.

"You can cross that bridge when you come to it," said Zechariah. "When the time comes, you'll know what to do. For now, all you need to remember is that *I* did not find this. For this to work, you must be the one to have found it."

Leah squinted at the old man. "Why?"

"Because that underground city is not just *any* city. It is the ancestral 'Home' of the Cru people. Their creation mythology says that they emerged from underground. Their eyes grew so accustomed to the sun that they could not find their way back. They became trapped above ground, and ever since, they have been searching for the way Home.

"The two sketches on the map, the feather-shaped columns and the ram's skull, are rock formations that flank the hidden entrance to the place where the Cru's ancestors truly did emerge from below the ground—from a city of the Ancients deep in the heart of the mountains. Their people, an offshoot of the Elleneans who once ruled this part of the world, are one of the few groups who survived the first demon invasions. Those are the true origins of the Cru, and the true story of their Home."

"And you knew that the whole time," said Leah.

"To tell the truth, I probably could lead you there myself by memory," said Zechariah with a sigh. "But if the Cru knew that—knew that, at any time, I could have pointed them in the direction of their ancestral Home—well, one can imagine the seeds of distrust that would sow. They would resent me and almost certainly you, too, through association. But if you were to have stumbled upon this map, say, while studying your family's oldest records, while you were trying to decide your next course of action. And if you were to then take this map to the elders of the Cru, asking for insights, and allow them to come to the conclusion themselves, then they might be so grateful that they would allow your civilians to weather the storm of this war alongside them in their Home."

"That would mean the deliberate, deceitful manipulation of an entire culture of people."

Zechariah did not react visibly. Instead, he simply said, "Can you stomach the manipulation of a few in order to save many?"

CHAPTER 23

Benjamin did not seem surprised. His grin didn't falter. In fact, he didn't so much as blink at Justin or his otherworldly attire. But when his eyes wandered to Justin's left arm, any hint of a smile vanished.

"Your arm," he said.

"Yeah," said Justin. He ran his hand over the bone armor, then gestured at Benjamin. "And your legs. Right?"

Benjamin's face became flat and expressionless. "Yeah."

A moment passed in which neither said a word.

There was so much to say that Justin didn't know where to start. Too much to tell. Too much to ask. And the telling and the asking suddenly felt like very awkward endeavors. Justin was not the same boy he had been when he'd accidentally left home. And yet, in other ways, he was. Benjamin, likewise, was the same person he had always been. And yet, now that Justin knew the truth, he realized that he barely knew this man.

Justin considered the quiet despondency of his father. The night terrors he sometimes heard coming from his father's room in the year since the car accident. The haunted look in his eye when he would stare off into the distance as if looking straight through the wall. In the past, Justin had put all these things down to him losing his wife so violently and suddenly. But now, Justin saw it all in a different light. Maybe the despondency had a different source. Maybe the night terrors were him reliving other, even darker memories. And maybe the haunted looks were not so different from the look on Justin's face now, as he thought back to his arm being turned into a demon arm within the grip of a cythraul.

Benjamin pushed himself forward into the kitchen/entryway. He approached Justin, stopped a foot away from him, applied the brakes on his chair, and reached out.

And that was all. He just reached out.

At the sight of his father's open arms, a deep-seated instinct took over. Justin lowered himself to his knees, until he was at eye level with his father. Then, without looking at him, he leaned forward into the embrace, and his father held him.

"It's all right, pal," said Benjamin. "You are okay."

Pal, thought Justin.

It was a throwback to another time. The nickname his father had called him when he'd been a small child. Even in his early teenage years, when Justin was practically a man, Benjamin still sometimes called him by the name he'd used when Justin had spilled his juice or fallen off his bike. To hear it now, while still nursing the wounds of a super-powered battle from another world, felt strange to Justin. Yet it carried undeniable comfort. And as his father patted him on the back, he felt his tense shoulders loosen.

He let his guard down. He slumped forward, letting his father hold him up, like he used to. One last time.

Several moments passed. When Justin finally pulled away, his father clapped him on the back.

"It's damn good to see you," said Benjamin.

"Don't be mad," said Justin. "But I lost my inhaler."

Benjamin laughed. It was loud and unrestrained. The way he used to laugh. With the prog rock record playing in the background, it was almost as if, for a second at least, things were close to normal again.

"We have to talk," said Justin. "I have a lot of questions but not a lot of time."

"Do you have a keystone?" asked Benjamin.

Justin reached into his shirt and pulled the gauge from his shirt pocket. He held it out to Benjamin, who took it. He grinned, running his thumb over its surface. Then he casually flipped it up as if it were a coin and snatched it out of the air. There was a gleam in his eye as he said, "With this, we've got all the time in the world."

"All the time. . . ?" said Justin.

"You'll see," said Benjamin. "We're gonna take a short trip. But before we go, there's something you'll wish you had done later if you don't do it now."

"What?" asked Justin.

Benjamin pointed to the stairs. "Take five minutes. Shave and take a shower."

Justin cocked an eyebrow. "But the time difference. Won't it—?"

"There are a few things that I assure you are not overrated, and a shower and shave are two of them. Trust me. If you don't take the opportunity while you have the chance, you'll wish you had. Besides, the time difference isn't an exact science. So you can either waste more time thinking about it, or you can take it from somebody who's been there, and just do it."

Justin thought about this for all of half a second, then ran up the stairs, taking them two at a time.

CHAPTER 24

"I like it," said Benjamin a few minutes later, looking up the stairs.

After the cleanest shave and the most magnificent shower of his life, Justin stood at the top of the stairs, wearing comfortable jeans, basketball shoes—his game shoes, in fact—and a hooded red sweatshirt. He held Ahlund's sword at his side. A simple draw-string backpack hung from his shoulders, containing his otherworldly clothes and a few other things. He knew he would need the tunic, cloak, and boots when he returned to the Oikoumene, but for now, his old, clean clothes felt like heaven. It was a shame, in a way, that he didn't have time to run the otherworldly clothes through the washing machine. But, then again, a Samsung high-efficiency unit and tumble dryer may have been too much for a hessian tunic and a hand-spun cloak.

Justin hurried down the stairs. He'd refused to be frivolous with his time; he had stopped by his room only long enough to find the clothes he wanted and to grab a couple of small, incidental items. In the bathroom, he'd glanced at himself in the mirror only for a second. To waste any further time would have been foolish. His scraggly, unkempt hair had been longer than he was used to, so he'd chopped at it with a Bic safety razor until it looked slightly more masculine, albeit no less scraggly.

"You ready? There's nothing you want to pick up before we leave?" asked Benjamin as Justin reached the bottom of the stairs.

Justin thought about it. "A gun?"

Benjamin tilted his head appraisingly. "Not a bad idea, but I'm guessing that in your hands, *that* is more useful." He gestured toward Ahlund's sword, clutched at Justin's side.

Justin took a deep breath and coughed a little. He had been joking earlier about his inhaler, but he suddenly realized that his lungs did feel a bit deflated. For the first time in a long time, he had the urge to use it. Something about Earth's air, maybe.

"So we're going back?" he said. "Together?"

"Not quite," said Benjamin. "Stand here by me and just do as I say."

Benjamin held the gauge stone out to Justin, who accepted it.

"First," he said, grasping Justin by the arm, "the keystone's first form."

"All right, here it goes," said Justin.

He fed a tiny sliver of aurym power into the gauge in his hand, making it glow with a green light. This was the elementary application of the gauge, used by people in the Oikoumene to determine whether someone possessed aurym power—hence the term "gauge." Aurym-wielders also utilized the simple light-up function to serve as torches. Justin, however, had discovered that he could push the stone to a second stage and use it to travel from the Oikoumene to Earth and back again.

"Good," said Benjamin, the stone's green light reflecting in his eyes. "Now, we're going to do something a little different. Instead of pushing it to its second form by *increasing* the power, we're going to sidestep it, to an alternate form."

"Huh?" said Justin.

"Think of it like a crossover to juke a defender," said Benjamin. "You're not pressing forward but making a sidelong shift. Not hard, just different."

Benjamin kept one hand on Justin's and moved the other hand sideways, slowly and deliberately, palm upturned. Justin mimicked the move.

"Right," said Benjamin. "But increase the power—only slightly—and spread it out."

Justin pushed more aurym into the gauge. As it had done before, it began to levitate above his palm, and the aura of a green glow expanded, encapsulating himself and his father.

"Stop," said Benjamin. "Perfect. Right there, no more than that. Now, shift sideways." He made the move again with his hand.

Justin focused on the stone, then moved the hand suspending the gauge stone from right to left—

He blinked in surprise. While his hand moved, the stone did not come with it. Instead, it remained suspended in its original location, floating in the air above the place where his hand had been a moment ago.

"Do it again," said Benjamin, "and this time, take some of the power with it. Remember, you're not creating it. It's always there. You are the lens through which the light passes. All you have to do is adjust the lens."

Justin focused on the stone. Again, he moved his hand to the side, trying to change the course of aurym's flow as he did. In response, the circular aura of green that surrounded Justin and Benjamin moved, too. It bent with the movement of his hand, morphing from a circle into something more like an oblong spheroid that crackled along the edges.

"Perfect!" Benjamin said, raising his voice a bit to be heard above the rush and roar and crackle of the energy. A photo hanging from the living room wall was swaying back and forth from its mount, and a pile of papers on the kitchen table blew onto the floor and swirled as if caught in a whirlwind. "Now, increase the power like you normally would!"

Justin did as he was told. In the past, the light would become everything, and the world around him would be sucked into it. But this time, the view of the house around him, with its swaying photo on the wall and his mother's green coat on the coat rack, seemed to bend and distort as if he were viewing the scene through a spoon.

Then the oblong spheroid of green light folded in on itself like one massive, blinking eye, and everything disappeared. Not into the light of day. Not into the dark of night. But into gray.

PART III

THE EDGE

OF TWILIGHT

CHAPTER 25

As the row-master, Cadmus, clipped the metal cuffs around the woman's ankles, every head within the guts of the ship was turned in her direction. She was in Toad's old seat. Directly across the aisle from Hook.

A female slave was not unheard of, but a female rower—that was a rarity.

As Cadmus finished locking the woman in and hefted his girth out of the way, Hook was afforded a better look at her. She wasn't a lifeslave. The lack of a scar ringing her forehead was proof of that. She wore the same sack-like trousers as the rest of the rowers chained down here, but she, unlike any of the others, had been afforded the dignity of a ragged shirt to cover her upper body. Though she looked no older than Hook, possibly even younger, her hair was a striking silver color. It appeared to have been cut short recently, forming a hacked bob that hung just below her ears.

For a moment, Hook wondered if Captain Gelon was so desperate for a rower to replace Toad that he was pulling slaves from other duties to fill in. But the woman's clothes were work-worn and sweat-stained, and she positioned herself at the oar in a way that bespoke familiarity. New rowers didn't sit like that. Not at first, anyway. After a while, everyone adopted the same hunched, bent-backed posture. And, like all experienced rowers, her biceps were like stretched cords, and her shoulders were tight balls of muscle. Hook craned his neck slightly, trying to get a view of her hands, wondering if they were as calloused as his. Wondering if they had labored at the oars of some other vessel and for how long.

"Our new team member comes highly recommended," Cadmus said in his typically genial and strangely soft-spoken tone of voice. "Captain

Gelon has expressed some concern that she might prove to be a distraction to you boys. Let's all prove him wrong, please, and continue to live up to the high standards I know you're all capable of."

Cadmus turned. His gaze fell heavily on the young woman. His hand rested on the coiled whip at his belt. There was a look in his eye that made Hook's skin crawl.

When Hook had first been brought aboard the *Manticore*, he'd been surprised to discover that the row-master was not the monster he'd been expecting—not outwardly, anyway. Before long, he'd come to realize that the row-master's job was not to inflict horrors on his slaves; his job was to make them work, and horrified slaves made for poor workers. It was all about results, and there were better means of motivation than fear. Usually, he was polite to them. He even praised them. Sometimes, he gave them rewards for a job well done.

In short, Cadmus attained obedience not by beating the slaves into submission but by cultivating a carefully crafted sort of hypnosis. It was not uncommon for some of them, in a sick sort of way, to begin to actively seek the approval of their row-master. Over time, there were those who came to love him like a father.

Hook saw it play out in every new arrival. The expectation of a living hell, contrasted by the row-master's congenial attitude, had a way of tricking the slaves into believing that their row-master only treated them badly when they deserved it. Horror and violence could break a man. But manipulation and misdirection could do better than break a man; they could brainwash him into a sort of fearful respect. Even admiration. Like beaten, starved dogs, they loved the very hand that abused them.

The game hadn't worked on Hook. When Hook looked at Cadmus, he saw the monster beneath the surface.

And when Cadmus looked at Hook, a hateful, murderous glare was what looked back at him. And Cadmus would just smile.

That was why Cadmus called him Dark-eyes. Because Hook knew. And Cadmus *knew* that Hook knew.

That is why they cut out our tongues, thought Hook. *Stealing our voices is essential to depriving us of our humanity.*

It brought Hook great satisfaction to see that as Cadmus looked down at the new arrival before him, she stared back at him, unblinking, unafraid. Neither her expression nor her posture faltered beneath his gaze.

Finally, Cadmus turned to walk to the front of the ship.

"All hands," he said.

Every rower raised his—or her—hands to grip the oars. Only Hook hesitated, watching the woman across the aisle from him.

The head atop the woman's long, lean neck turned to face Hook. Her eyes were big and strikingly blue, but the look on her face spoke volumes. Inexperienced rowers sometimes wore an air of defiance, as if trying to tell everyone around them that they would never be broken. Other times, they looked despondent—knowing they were about to be broken and fearful of the inevitable agony that was to come. But weathered, experienced rowers like this woman had a different sort of look in their eyes. A look that said, *If I am broken, so be it.*

Haystack, Hook's bench-mate seated immediately to his right, jabbed Hook with a blond-haired forearm. Hook broke off his gaze and quickly took up his position. He heard the sloshing of water against the hull outside and felt their vessel being pushed off from wherever it had docked. A moment later, an order was shouted down from above.

"Aye, aye," replied Cadmus. "Pacer Hil. Begin, please."

The pacer brought his mallet down on the large drum before him. *Boom.*

CHAPTER 26

Hook woke with a start, this time in his cot in the barracks.

For a moment, he found it difficult to breathe—as if his lungs were paralyzed. His upper body, he realized, was tense. His muscles were flexed in the much-practiced position of readying himself to move the oar. He had to force his shoulders to relax before his lungs started working again, taking in quick, labored breaths.

Angrily, he threw the blanket off him and began to dress.

Damn the dreams, he thought, pulling on his sword belt. *Damn the sleepless nights and the memories, and damn waking up like a child fighting terrors.*

Yesterday, when Lycon had approached him to share the news of a woman with a lifeslave's scar on her forehead, there'd been a part of him that had hoped it would be her. A foolish, misplaced hope, of course.

Hook sat on the edge of the cot, staring at the floor. The burn scar on his head ached. He rubbed at it.

No one had been more surprised than Hook to learn that Megara knew the same system of signs he had been taught. No one aboard the *Manticore* had known the sign system until Jocasta had been brought aboard to replace Toad.

Jocasta. The woman who had given him a voice again. From the very first day, Cadmus had called her Fawn.

Communicating with Megara—a fellow escaped slave—hadn't been as comforting as he might have expected. Instead, it had been unnerving. A reminder of the past, dredging up memories of horrors and abuse and a life sentence he had so narrowly escaped. As much as he wanted to deny it, Megara's accusation that he had allied himself with the very people who'd committed those atrocities had shaken him. But not all Mythaeans were guilty of those crimes; not all Mythaean city-states kept slaves.

But some do, thought Hook as he crossed the barracks. *Some of the members of the League. People you call allies, Hook Bard.*

Hook looked around at the tiny, cramped barracks. The low ceiling. The windowless walls. The two rows of cots with an aisle separating them down the middle. Suddenly, it was hard to breathe again.

He stood from his cot, walked down the aisle to the door, and exited the barracks.

A cold wind cut into Hook as he burst out into the night. There were no stars visible tonight. The only light was the meager glow of a watchman's lantern a few dozen yards away. The watchman turned to face Hook at the sound of the door closing, but soon looked away again to continue his patrol.

Hook stood outside the door, savoring deep gasps of the bracingly cold air, feeling his heart pounding in his chest. A thin layer of snow covered the ground, pushed into meandering pathways by the wind like a knife spreading butter. For some reason, he found himself grateful for the cold. Maybe just because it wasn't a subtropical sea that had greeted him when he'd opened the door.

Suddenly, he spotted someone moving through the snow, coming toward him. Not the watchman. A lone wanderer who carried no torch or lantern, coming slowly and silently toward Hook through the darkness. For a moment, the superstitions of Hook's islander mother were stirred up in him, and he thought of revenants stalking the night.

The figure stepped forward through the snow, a long white beard fluttering in the breeze. He stopped a few feet away from Hook and regarded him quietly for a moment.

"Do you believe in signs and portents?" Zechariah asked.

Hook raised one hand and signed, *"Sometimes."*

Zechariah nodded, then raised his good hand to give the sign that meant *"Same."*

Then he said verbally, "Come with me."

CHAPTER 27

The door was unlocked, but Zechariah kicked it in anyway. Cold wind whipped in, followed shortly by the old man in the lead and Hook close behind him.

Hook was familiar with this part of town. And so, as the kicked-in door swung wildly on its hinges and slammed against the wall, he was not surprised to find himself on the threshold of a tavern. What did surprise him, however, was that the interior was warm and fully lit. A fire blazed in the hearth—a hearth *piled* with burning logs, with no regard, he noticed, for the rationing that was being observed by the soldiers who shivered in the barracks across town.

Captain Pool—once a fisherman from Lonn, now a Mythaean ship captain—stood on top of the tavern's bar, bare-chested and playing a wooden flute, his ample, hairy belly bouncing in time with the tune. Zechariah and Hook's violent intrusion momentarily interrupted Pool's playing, but he was so drunk he didn't seem particularly surprised. Captain Borris, on the other hand—likewise a fisherman from Lonn, and likewise the recipient of a questionable promotion—was so surprised by Zechariah kicking the door open that he missed a dance step, lost his grip on the hand of the barefooted Raeqlu woman he was dancing with, and toppled over backward to land sprawled on the tavern floor. This halted Pool's song entirely. The little man nearly dropped his flute as he bent over, snorting peals of laughter.

In the center of the room, at a table beneath a fully lit chandelier, two more Raeqlu women sat in the lap of Admiral Gunnar Erix Nimbus. At the sight of Zechariah and Hook, he raised both hands in joyous welcome.

"Well, dip me in butter and call me an oyster," Gunnar called out. "Two more of my best-good friends! Could this night get any better? Get in here and have a drink! You're way behind—and you'll have to work for it if you hope to keep up with these girls."

Gunnar's hair, normally tucked neatly beneath either a Mythaean admiral's cap or a bandana, was unfurled and hanging in curly black locks. His long mustache had been carefully greased into place, but the rest of his face was uncharacteristically unshaven. A dozen or more empty bottles lay on the table before him, and his pipe, still lit and smoking, sat tipped on its side.

"Ladies," he said, slurring as he spoke, "these guys here, they're good guys. Can't really vouch for their character. To be honest, I don't really know them that well—but take it from me, you get in a fight, you want these two on your side. Especially the one with the headband thing. He doesn't talk much, but he's all right in my book. I'd take a long walk off a short pier before I crossed him."

Without a word, Zechariah stepped forward through the tavern. Hook followed him through the room, still not sure why the old man had wanted him to come here with him in the first place. If nothing else, it was proving to be a welcome distraction.

Zechariah stopped before Gunnar's table and looked down at him. Across the room, Pool had resumed playing his flute, and Borris was trying and failing to pull himself up off the floor.

Hook regarded the women in Gunnar's lap. Even for a warm tavern, their choice of wardrobe seemed far from prudent. One of them batted her eyes at him. Another raised her knee toward Zechariah. The old man was silent as a tomb.

Gunnar looked up at Zechariah. His lone eye was red and glossy. The patch where the other eye should have been was slightly askew. "Ale or—liquor? Which'll put the wind in your sails, old man?" Before

Zechariah could answer, Gunnar leaned in toward one of the women and said, "He's right-ancient, it's true, but you never know. Even after the fire goes out, you can sometimes still stoke the coals—"

Without warning, Zechariah swung his right arm over his head and brought it violently downward. There was a crash and a thud as his steel hook buried itself into the surface of the table, sending splinters into the air and knocking bottles off the table to shatter against the floor.

"*Out!*" roared Zechariah. "Now!"

The Raeqlu women shrieked. Both jumped up from Gunnar's lap and bolted, nearly forgetting to grab their clothes from the next table before making a break for the door. The one who'd been dancing with Borris did the same. Borris, still on the floor, reached brokenheartedly toward one of her ankles as she scampered away. Pool, still atop the bar, was so badly startled by Zechariah's outburst that he dropped his flute and took an unsteady step backward in surprise. There was a high-pitched squeal as he skidded in a puddle of spilled drink, and his foot slipped out from under him. The round-bellied little man didn't even have the presence of mind to cry out as he fell headlong behind the bar, which made for a strangely silent descent as he dropped out of sight, punctuated by the noise of crashing crockery.

CHAPTER 28

Within seconds, the three Raeqlu women were gone. The tavern was silent but for the occasional stirring of the broken crockery behind the bar, which indicated that Pool was, at the very least, still moving.

Gunnar looked from Zechariah's hook, still lodged in the tabletop, to the closed door where the women had disappeared. His gaze lingered there for a few seconds. Then he puffed out his cheeks and blew an exasperated raspberry.

"They're nice girls, you know," said Gunnar, and Hook noticed that his speech suddenly did not seem slurred whatsoever. "All you had to do was ask them politely to leave. Would that have been so hard?"

"No," admitted Zechariah. "I guess not."

"What about us?" Borris asked from the floor, arching his back to look upside-down at Zechariah. He spoke in his distinctive lisp, caused by a badly healed scar across the corner of his lips. "Ya want us to— leave, too?"

Zechariah looked down at him. In a good-natured tone that could not have been more unlike his previous outburst, he said, "I do not care in the slightest."

"Good," said Borris, then loudly decreed, "Blow us another tune, Pool!"

From behind the bar, Pool responded by blowing a plaintive, single-noted tune without the aid of any instrument. Borris threw back his head to laugh but instead bumped his head against the floorboards and groaned.

"So, to what do I owe the displeasure of having a perfectly good evening diverted mid-escapade?" Gunnar asked.

Zechariah opened his mouth to answer, but when he attempted to raise his hooked hand to make a point, he found it stuck fast in the wood of the table.

Gunnar tilted his head to give the stuck hook an exaggerated appraisal. "Problem?"

Zechariah glared at his hook, tugged on it, muttered "Damn it," and wiggled it back and forth, but it wouldn't come loose.

"Tsk, tsk," said Gunnar. "Looks like you could use a—"

"Don't say it," Zechariah warned.

Zechariah used his good hand to pull back the sleeve of his opposite arm. There, he undid a metal clasp and loosened the leather straps holding the rig of the prosthesis to the stump of his forearm. He pulled his arm away from the table, leaving the metal hook stuck there. Hook then stepped forward, grabbed the base of it, and pulled it free of the table's surface.

"There's a fun play on words," said Gunnar.

Hook had to think about that one for a second. Then Zechariah took the hook from Hook.

"Leah tells me you've been hard at work growing crops during your waking hours," said Zechariah. "I see you've found no shortage of distractions to occupy your mind and your stomach during your downtime."

"I had most of the major organs covered, true," said Gunnar.

"*But*," Zechariah cut in before Gunnar could say more, "the fun is over."

"I guessed as much, judging by the nature of your entrance," said Gunnar with a sigh. "What is it this time? Another riverboat excursion? It turned out so well last time, why not do it again?"

Gunnar had meant the comment in jest, of course, but a strange look crossed the man's face as if his own words had shaken him. He swallowed hard, leaned forward, grabbed a cup from the table in one hand and one of the less-empty bottles in another, and started to pour the liquor into the vessel. Hook's eyes narrowed. The bottle was dinging repeatedly against the lip of the cup.

Gunnar's hand was shaking. Badly.

Gunnar's lone eye snapped up, catching Hook staring at his hand. Without warning, he slammed the bottle down on the table.

"You're even quieter than usual," Gunnar snapped at Hook. "What're you, the old man's silent enforcer now?" He raised the cup to gulp it down.

The cup was halfway to his mouth when Hook plucked it from his hand.

Gunnar looked up, a sneer on his face. Hook waited long enough to give Gunnar ample opportunity to protest. In the end, Gunnar did not rise to the challenge. He ran his tongue over his teeth and said nothing.

Hook took a casual sip from the cup, then set it down on the next table, unfinished. He noticed the fingers of Gunnar's empty hand twitch. Gunnar quickly closed his hand into a fist to make them stop.

"I didn't come here tonight purely to spoil your good time," said Zechariah. "Rather, I have a task for you." He glanced sidelong at Hook. "Both of you."

Hook arched an eyebrow.

Before Zechariah could say more, Pool finally managed to stand up from behind the bar.

"We're flattered," Pool said. Then he hiccuped. "But me and Borris are—*hic*—pretty busy at the moment."

Borris snickered uncontrollably from the floor.

"By the seas, I love you boys," sighed Gunnar.

Zechariah looked at them. "I've changed my mind," he said. "Get out."

CHAPTER 29

A few minutes later, Pool and Borris were gone, and Hook, Zechariah, and Gunnar sat around the table, which had been cleared of most of its empty bottles.

Gunnar took a puff on his pipe, then passed it to Hook. Hook accepted it, drew in an inhale of the smoke, and let it out through his nostrils. Then it was Zechariah's turn.

"I recently returned from a journey to the Gravelands," said Zechariah, smoke riding his words. "I had intended to retrieve a few personal effects from my former home. Things I was forced to leave behind in the haste of my previous departure."

"Your favorite beard comb?" said Gunnar.

Zechariah ignored him. "One of the items I was most keen to retrieve was a small chest I keep in my cellar. Inside that chest was a treasure accumulated over a lifetime. A collection of hundreds of aurstones of dozens of different varieties."

Gunnar nodded. "I had a collection like that once," he said. "Only, my collection was one of seeds. Trees. Herbs. Grasses. Flowers. Many kinds for many uses and occasions. Lost them all when the first *Gryphon* went down in the Greenspring."

"Then you can sympathize," said Zechariah, "for my collection was lost as well. Stolen, it seems. I did not tell Leah this, but when I returned to my home, I found the place ransacked. That chest, along with many other things that were precious to me, was gone.

"It took me centuries to collect those aurstones. I had intended, once Justin came into his power, to use that collection to test his aurym to find a stone that matched his abilities. If I had known, when we left Deen that day to ride north, that the course of events that followed would take me away from my home for a matter of weeks and eventually months . . . then I never would have left them there. At the very least, I'd have taken *some* of them with me. Now, they're lost, and several lifetimes' worth of work is gone."

Zechariah turned his gaze intently on Gunnar's good eye. "You are part of the reason I went back for those stones."

"Me?" said Gunnar.

"I took a Raeqlu man with me on my journey," said Zechariah. "He is called Alcaeus Leo. The son of an acquaintance of mine. He can use the godsbreath stone."

Gunnar leaned forward with sudden interest. "He can grow plants like I can?"

"So he claims," said Zechariah. "He says he did so back in Pheodops, but the stones he used were the property of the crown, and they were not permitted to leave the capital. He doesn't own one himself. But imagine if he did. Imagine if we found *multiple* individuals who can do what you do. You would no longer be trapped here as the queen's resident gardener."

Zechariah allowed this to sink in for a moment, and Hook saw that it had the intended effect; Gunnar was puffing thoughtfully on his pipe, staring at the tabletop.

"Furthermore," said Zechariah, "imagine if even one in one hundred of the people in this city proved capable of wielding aurym abilities."

Hook considered. For so long, they had been fighting the demons with blades and arrows, aided only occasionally by lone aurym-users such as Ahlund or Gunnar, and supported by aurym-healers like Leah and Lycon. But what might their battles be like with a dozen Gunnars? A hundred Ahlunds? A legion of Leahs and Lycons to save the dying before they slipped away?

And Megara. The strange power she wielded had halted an entire horde of coblyns. What if they had a hundred of her, too?

"Is that possible?" signed Hook.

"Very few people ever realize their aurym potential," said Zechariah. "For one thing, certain individuals can only use certain stones, and the odds of finding the correct stone and using it in the correct way are slim—even *if* one is actively seeking it. And, to tell the truth, few people can even comprehend *what* aurym is, let alone how to use it. Most do not have the benefit of a dedicated teacher to show them the way.

"My hope—my intention—was to bring my collection of stones here and invite everyone, from the lowliest to the highest, to step forward and be tested for spirit abilities and, potentially, training in the use of aurym powers. With a collection of aurstones, I could help the individuals we have assembled here discover and unlock latent aurym abilities, which would change everything for us. Hence my frustration in finding that my aurstones had been stolen."

Zechariah paused for a moment, using his hook to scratch absentmindedly at the tabletop. "And there's one other thing.... I had, among my collection, a hydstone. Just one. They are exceedingly rare. It was the only one I've ever come across in my lifetime. I had hoped that someone, *anyone*, among our people would be able to use it."

"Hydstone?" said Gunnar.

Zechariah looked hard at him. "The kind of aurstone used by the one who called himself Innocen."

CHAPTER 30

Hook saw the pipe in Gunnar's mouth abruptly straighten as he clenched his teeth.

"Ragny," Gunnar said.

"The use of hydstones dates back thousands of years," said Zechariah. "It is a rare aurym ability that gives the user unnatural strength and speed. Uncanny physical power. Its most noteworthy practitioner was a man called Xanthicles, who was so devoted to developing his powers and passing them on that he undertook the pursuit of training a series of apprentices in the use of hydstones. Legends say that Xanthicles would come in the night to promising aurym users and offer them a bargain. He would allow them to try to use a hydstone. If they succeeded in willing aurym through the stone, he would train them in its ways. If they failed, he would consume them."

"Consume them?" signed Hook.

"Xanthicles was a daemyn worshipper," said Zechariah. "As you know, coblyns derive sustenance by feasting upon the living internal organs of their prey to consume aurym energy. There were many daemyn-worshipping cults in Xanthicles's time—and there still are, in some parts of the world, operating in shadow. Some of them believe that humans can consume aurym the same way a coblyn can."

Hook saw a slight shudder sweep over Gunnar.

"The Cult of the Hyd," said Zechariah, "which developed out of Xanthicles's twisted belief system, has endured through the ages. Their *religion*, if it can be called that, includes the pursuit of a sort of spiritual purity through the denouncement of earthly luxuries. They often drift from place to place, living as hermits. They use no weapons, only their bare hands. And because of their beliefs regarding the consumption of aurym energy, their ambitions often involve . . . *hunting* human beings. Particularly aurym-users. After hearing Leah and Lycon's accounts, I believe that Innocen, the man who assumed the false identity of 'Ragny' to infiltrate the city and attack Leah, was a devotee of the Cult of the Hyd.

"The use of these stones is very rare, but the nature of their powers makes hydstone-users exceedingly difficult to defend against. Over the years, I have sought ways to kill one, in the event that I ever encountered one myself. With Innocen, we got lucky."

"Lucky?" Gunnar blurted. "Do you know how many people he killed?"

"Yes," said Zechariah. "And I still count it lucky. Not only did he fail to accomplish his mission, but he was injured in the attempt. That injury is all that saved us. Hyd members believe that the physical consumption of aurym, feasting upon living entrails, provides natural healing powers to the body. They also see pain as a rite of passage. As a result, they are forbidden from seeking out the services of an aurym healer. Or so I have heard, anyway. Therefore, it is fortunate that Innocen was injured because it buys us a little time while he heals. It certainly does not remove the danger he poses, but it does lessen it. Or at least, it delays it."

"Have you found anything that can defend against these powers?" asked Hook.

Zechariah hesitated. "Short of having an ethoul like Justin by your side, I have found only one solution."

"Which is?"

"Fight fire with fire, so to speak," said Zechariah. "I had planned to have every last one of our people attempt to use the single hydstone in my collection, in the hope that someone could channel their aurym through it."

Gunnar cleared his throat. To Hook, it seemed as if he were forcing himself to relax. "In other words," he said, "you want us to help you look for your lost box of rocks."

"Oh, don't delude yourself," said Zechariah. "My aurstone collection is gone. There's no way to know who took that chest, when it was taken, or where the thief has gone. But there is an alternative. South of the Gravelands, in the ruins of a palace along the coast, is the tomb of an old Ellenean king. In life, his royal raiment included a headdress tipped with sixteen precious stones—specimens of every type of aurstone known to their culture. I happen to know that it was buried with him. Perhaps it is still there. And perhaps, with such a collection, we could identify individuals among our numbers who could help us fight the demons."

"And maybe find someone who can use a hydstone," said Gunnar.

"Maybe," agreed Zechariah.

"Will just sixteen aurstones really make such a difference?" signed Hook.

"Depending on the size of a stone, it can be cut to create more," said Zechariah. "Even so, yes. Sixteen potential aurym warriors could make all the difference."

"Enough for me to risk my life for it?" asked Gunnar.

"I'd go myself, but I'm needed elsewhere," said Zechariah. "And you're right. It will involve great risk. A large group would draw too much attention. This is a two- or three-person operation, at the most. I need people I can trust, and I need someone who knows aurym." He leveled a meaningful gaze at Gunnar before adding, "And I think it's clear to everyone that *you* need to get out of this blasted city for a while and clear your head."

Hook saw Gunnar's fingers shaking again.

For a moment, Hook considered the old man's words. In the not so distant past, Gunnar had fled a life of political responsibility, abandoning his birthright to run away and start a new life, apparently with no intention of ever returning. It was Hook who had revealed Gunnar's true identity, forcing him back into his role as a Mythaean Royal Admiral. If he hadn't, it was possible that Gunnar may never have taken up his former mantle again.

Perhaps, by providing Gunnar with an opportunity to escape now—for a time, at least—Zechariah was trying to mitigate the chance that he would flee permanently.

"What about growing crops for the city?" said Gunnar.

"My friend Alcaeus can see to that," said Zechariah. He extended his good hand across the table, palm up. "All he needs is to borrow your stone."

Gunnar stared at Zechariah's hand. For a moment, Hook thought he was going to tell Zechariah to shove off. Instead, he tapped his pipe, emptying the spent ashes onto the floor, and said, "I'll sleep on it."

Zechariah turned to Hook. "And you?"

"Why am I needed in this?" Hook signed.

"A feeling," said Zechariah.

"Signs and portents?" asked Hook.

"Something like that."

CHAPTER 31

Looks could be deceiving. Leah knew that all too well. In fact, she remembered a time when Zechariah had claimed to be over twelve centuries old, thanks to an aurym ability that effectively stopped the aging process. By all appearances, he was not much older than her grandfather had been when he'd died, yet he moved like a man in the prime of life.

Thid, on the other hand, the head elder of the Cru people, had no such spiritual boon to alter the effects of time on his body. At least, none that Leah was aware of. As she sat on the floor across from him, she found herself wondering just how old he was. Maybe over a century. His skin looked papery thin on his arms and hands, and his face was lined with deep wrinkles. One of his eyes did not seem to be able to open, and the other was clouded a glaucous gray. It dawned on Leah now that the only times she had ever communicated with him, he had been seated. It was possible he was no longer mobile.

They were alone, both seated cross-legged on a blanket that had been spread across the hard stone floor. When she had offered up the palace's tower suites, Thid and the other Cru elders had insisted on being closer to the earth, closer to their animals. And so they had taken up residence in one of the guardhouses near the stables, within close range of the pastures where their herds of bison grazed outside the city walls, able to be rounded up and ushered through the gates to safety at a moment's notice.

He sat with his hands in his lap. His beard was so long that it lay draped over his legs. To Leah, the position looked horribly uncomfortable, but it seemed to be the natural posture of his body—like a deep, gnarled root, set in place and unlikely to change without great time and effort. He looked so frail, so close to death. But looks could be deceiving.

Thid's open eye glanced up at her, and although she did not know if he was seeing her properly, the coherence and wisdom in his gaze were clear. Zechariah's map of Athacea lay unfurled on the floor between them.

"Describe the symbols to me again," said Thid with a voice like rustling autumn leaves.

Leah pointed to the shapes on the map. "One of them looks like a ram's skull," she said. "On the other side is a cluster of what I think are arrows or maybe feathers standing upright. Seven of them. Between the two symbols is a set of stairs."

Thid said nothing for a moment. Didn't move. Hardly seemed to breathe.

"Where did you find this map, Elder Leah?" he finally asked. In the Cru meaning of the term, "Elder" was a title of leadership; it did not carry implications of age, but, rather, of authority.

"I have been worried about our people," said Leah evenly. "I have been tasked to fight a war, yet I often lay awake at night, dreading the pain that will come to those who are not soldiers. Those who cannot fight. And so I have been seeking answers, trying to find a path forward that will keep our people safe. When I first saw this map, and its symbols marking what appears to be a descent underground, my first thought was that no such place exists. At least, not to my knowledge. It occurred to me that if anyone would know what it meant, it would be you."

Thid sucked his gums once. "I say again, child. Where did you find this map?"

Leah took a breath.

"It was given to me," she said. "By Zechariah."

Thid said nothing.

"He told me that these symbols mark the location of a place your people greatly wish to find," said Leah. "He gave me this map and instructed me to bring it to you. He also instructed me not to tell you that he had given it to me."

"Indeed," said Thid. Leah could not tell if it was a question, an appraisal, or something else.

"His intention, I think, was that my *discovery* would ingratiate me with you, to the extent that you would allow the people of Cervice to take refuge in your Home. There, they could be safe from the demons while our armies marched east to invade enemy lands."

"He told you to deceive me," said Thid.

"Yes, Elder Thid," said Leah.

Thid didn't move.

Leah reached down, rolled up the map, and re-tied the string around it to secure it. "Zechariah calls himself a scholar and scribe, but he is more like a diplomat. Like me, he seeks an answer to the problem of bringing our peoples together and keeping our civilians safe, while also winning a war. My alliance with the Mythaeans, and others, came as a result of necessity. Through political maneuvering, Zechariah went on to leverage those circumstances to turn an informal alliance into the Athacean League, whose forces now number in the tens of thousands. He led Raeqlund's vast army here, but I still don't know the details of whatever deal he brokered with them in order to make that happen. I fear that I may not like the terms when at last I hear them, but I cannot deny that their arrival saved my city. He is a man who has no qualms about making compromises and sacrifices, so long as it serves what he feels is a greater purpose. When he perceived that I would not be willing to uproot my people and take them on the warpath, he gave me this map and advised me to use the knowledge it contained as leverage against you."

"But you did not," said Thid.

"Zechariah has his way of doing things," said Leah. "His ways are not my ways. My father taught me that the ends cannot justify the means. Because in the end, what we do is all we are. I believe it is preferable to lose a war than to lose oneself in it."

Leah held the map out to Thid. She wasn't sure how well he could see, but judging by the shift of his open eye, he must have at least sensed the movement.

"This map belongs to you, Elder," she said. "And you alone."

There was a sound like dry, creaking leather, and Thid's arm lifted from his lap. With no little difficulty, he reached out and took the map in his bent, knob-knuckled fingers.

"Is this a gambit?" he asked. "That by your act of generosity, you would sway me to achieve the same ends that your advisor had planned?"

"No," said Leah. "I would count it as a blessing if your people and mine could have a shared future together. But we have very different legacies, and I will respect and honor whatever path you choose. Zechariah has mistaken my reluctance for indecision. He thinks I am unwilling to lead my people on the warpath because of the hardships it will inflict on them, so he has attempted to prod me in the right direction." She sighed. "I am only reluctant because I know what I *have* to do. I do not want to take these people to war, but I will. And I, for having made the decision, will bear the full weight of the blame for the consequences. Many will die, which is why I will not force anyone to go. But *I* am going. And, I suppose, deep in my heart, I don't expect to ever return. Maybe *none* of those who choose to follow me will."

She left that final thought hanging in the air, and for a long time, neither she nor Thid said a word. The map in his old hand shook slightly.

"I shall discuss this matter with the rest of the A'cru'u'ol elders," said Thid.

"Then with your blessing," said Leah, "I will take my leave."

"You have it," said Thid.

Leah stood and bowed. She was partway to the door of the guardhouse when Thid added, "No matter what happens, thank you for this."

Leah turned back to face him. "I have heard your people say that each man—or woman—sees the world from the summit of her own central mountain. I hope that you and your elders are blessed with a clear view, Elder Thid."

CHAPTER 32

For a moment, Justin could see nothing but gray. It was like a roller coaster he had once been on that had caused him to black out on a steep, banked curve; he had been conscious and aware, but his vision had succumbed to a bubble of black. But in this case, instead of black, it was gray. His vision steadily gained clarity, and he blinked in surprise. He hadn't known where his father was taking him, and he wasn't sure what he'd been expecting. But this wasn't it.

Justin stood on a rocky embankment. Benjamin was seated in his wheelchair beside him, still holding on to Justin's arm. The soil beneath their feet was a dull, muddled gray, like too many watercolors mixed on a canvas. The embankment fell away before them into what appeared to be a thick forest of trees, all drooping, either dead or dying, and all the same unnatural gray color as the soil. The surrounding hills were gray, too—an entire wilderness of it. Looking up, Justin realized even the sky was gray. Not clouded. Simply gray. There was enough light to see by, yet there appeared to be no sun in the sky. His body cast no shadows upon the ground, making him wonder where the meager light was even coming from. Everything he could see in this autumnal world had a pallor of perpetual twilight beneath a cloudless sky the color of ash.

Benjamin tapped him on the arm. Justin looked down to see his father holding the gauge stone, which had been hovering in the air when they'd taken the "sidestep" to enter this place. Apparently, the stone had fallen out of the air, and Benjamin had caught it.

Justin took the stone back and tucked it into the pocket of his jeans. "What is this place?" he asked.

"It's called the Kharon," said Benjamin.

Justin's brow furrowed.

The Kharon. It was the name Cyaxares had given him for the realm used by Avagad to communicate with him over vast distances through strangely realistic dreams.

"The Kharon?" said Justin. "So, we're not really here, are we? Our bodies are still back on Earth."

"No, we're here," said Benjamin. "Mentally, physically—we're all the way here."

"But I thought the Kharon was, I don't know, some sort of dream-world or something."

"It can be used for that purpose as well," said Benjamin. "I've spent a long time in this place, and I still don't have all the answers. I sometimes used it as a sort of base camp."

Benjamin gestured over his shoulder, and Justin turned to see a cave-like rock shelter behind them. The entrance was mostly hidden by a stand of trees, gray and drooping. Justin walked to the trees and pulled back a gray branch. Behind it, he saw several bags and quite modern-looking hiking backpacks on the cave floor, along with an ancient chest with a bronze lock where a skeleton key would have fit. Several sets of garments, cloaks, and other articles of clothing lay draped over the various odds and ends. And in one corner of the rock shelter, dozens if not hundreds of books sat stacked in piles.

Justin turned back to his father with many questions on his lips, but he abruptly forgot all words. Because at that moment, his father was doing something he had not seen him do in a long time. Benjamin Holmes was standing.

Benjamin was shorter than Justin remembered; it had been so long since he'd seen him standing that he'd almost forgotten that he was taller than his dad by four or five inches.

Benjamin tested his weight on his legs, groaning with the effort as he squatted to stretch a bit.

Justin couldn't contain his smile. "You—you can stand?"

"There's not a whole lot of daemyn here," said Benjamin. He began bouncing back and forth on the balls of his feet, almost playfully, like a boxer in a neutral corner. "But there's enough, at least, to breathe life back into these old legs."

Suddenly, Benjamin snapped one leg backward, slamming a mule-kick into his wheelchair. It flew off the ground, flipped violently, crashed against the gray soil, and then went rolling end-over-end down the rocky embankment, dinging and pinging with impacts.

When the wheelchair finally came to a stop, at the bottom of the hill at the edge of a gray forest, Benjamin looked down at it and said, "Ah, hell. Probably shouldn't have done that, but I'm so sick of that thing. Hope I didn't break it." He turned to face Justin. "Now. What was it you wanted to discuss?"

Justin tried to gather his thoughts. "Can we really talk here? What about the time difference?"

Benjamin shook his head. "Not an issue. Time doesn't pass in the Kharon."

"Time *doesn't pass*?"

"Nope. We could spend ten years here—a hundred, even—and when we returned to Earth, we would arrive the very instant we left. You might even catch a glimpse of yourself fading out of reality."

"But how can time just stop?" asked Justin, squinting.

"I wouldn't say that time *stops*, per se," said Benjamin. "More like it doesn't exist. Even its effects on your body, to a certain extent, are negated. Your heart still beats, and your blood still pumps in your veins, yet you don't have to sleep or eat. Not sure how that's possible, but the life cycle of the cells in your body must become drastically extended here, because you don't even age."

The implication suddenly struck Justin.

Immune to the effects of time. The ability to live, unchanged, for an eternity. No need to sleep.

"This is how they did it, isn't it?" said Justin. "The Brethren. The immortal men."

"You've heard of us, I see," said Benjamin. "Yes, it's something like that."

"*Us?*" said Justin.

Benjamin chuckled. "The daemyn ability that grants everlasting life involves tapping into the Kharon and channeling a part of it through the bridge between worlds."

A jolt of concern shot through Justin. "Did you say it's a daemyn ability?"

"You have a lot to learn, I guess," said Benjamin. "Yes. It's a daemyn ability. How are the Brethren, anyway? It's been a long time."

Justin lowered his gaze to the gray ground. "Dad, there's a lot I have to tell you. Not just about the Brethren. About everything."

"Right," said Benjamin. "Take your time. Here, there's no rush. Like, literally." Then he sat down on a log outside the entrance to his rock shelter and crossed his legs. "Tell me everything."

Justin sighed long and deep. Where did he start? So much had happened. How could he possibly tell him everything?

But then, he did.

CHAPTER 33

Leah ran her hand over the armrest of the great chair, a throne of polished wood and cut stone, upholstered with fine fabric. It was set upon a raised dais built of a single piece of black basalt from the Orlia Flats on the coast to the northeast, with a long, blood-red carpet stretched from the doors at the far end of the room to the throne's base.

Outfitted in traveling clothes with a set of chain mail underneath—the hood of a cloak pulled tight over her head and her saber sheathed at her side—Leah ran her fingernails over the fabric of the throne. Back when she'd been a little girl, the seat had seemed so enormous and magnificent. It still seemed big—too big for a woman of her smaller-than-average stature—but somehow, not very magnificent.

Leah stood from the throne and walked down the carpet toward the doors. In the satchel at her side were the usual provisions, bandages, and healer's herbs. But packed in with them was also the crown of Nolia. She wasn't particularly attached to the symbol of authority and didn't particularly relish wearing it, but after her coronation, she had vowed, in honor of her father, to never let the crown leave her side.

She turned to take one last look at the throne, trying to remember the way King Darius Anavion had looked seated upon it. A figure that inspired courage. Confidence. Unity.

"Permission to approach the throne?" said a voice from the doors behind her.

Leah turned. Zechariah stood at the far end of the blood-red carpet.

"Permission granted," said Leah.

The old man approached with a regal stride. Even clothed in ragged robes, even with his long white beard hanging uncombed and untrimmed, he carried himself with an air that said he belonged before the thrones of queens and kings.

"Ready to go?" he asked.

"The others are waiting for me at the north gates," she said.

She offered no explanation as to why she had come here, to the throne room, before leaving. In fact, she wasn't even sure she knew exactly why. Maybe because she was afraid she would never see it again. Maybe because she knew it was possible that this would be the last time in history that Anavion blood would be in this room.

"I have heard that Sif and Lycon are going with you," said Zechariah. "Any others joining your entourage?"

"Marcus Worth and two of my personal guard. Sif is bringing five Cru warriors hand-chosen by their council of elders. And, per your request, the Rorrdvuuk woman, Megara, has agreed to come as well. I still wonder, however, if it might be better for her to stay here to help protect the city, given her abilities."

"Given her abilities," replied Zechariah, "there is no one else you'll want more in the dark underground beneath the Thucymoroi."

An image flashed through Leah's mind of giant scorpion-spiders emerging from tiny holes in cave walls, swarming and attacking a steed. The striking of stinger barbs. The sounds of snipping pincers at work.

"Perhaps you are right," she said.

"Do you feel confident, taking so few?" he asked.

"It is wiser," she replied. "Easier to avoid being spotted while we travel."

Zechariah let a few moments pass before he spoke again. "I would be remiss if I did not point out that there is no reason for the queen of Nolia—the highest-ranking member of the Athacean League present in this city and one of its most indispensable leaders—to go stomping off into the wilderness on a scouting expedition. You have people for that."

"If I can be candid with you," said Leah, "I'm not sure a scout's report would be enough for me. There's so much at stake that I don't think I could bring myself to act on it unless I have seen it with my own eyes. And if a scout reported that they *hadn't* found anything, I would feel the need to go looking for it myself, anyway."

Zechariah crossed his arms. "You need to learn how to delegate, young lady. And while we're being *candid* with one another, I can't help but feel a bit betrayed."

Leah had been waiting for this. "Because I told Thid that you gave me the map," she said. "Because I revealed your intent to use it as leverage against them."

Zechariah unfolded his arms and began to pick idly at the nails of his good hand with the tip of his hook. "Yes. That."

"Your strategy was sound," said Leah, "but I had to do it my way. I'm sorry if it has damaged your relations with the Cru."

"My ego is, I suppose, of secondary concern compared to the bigger picture. The important thing is that it worked. . . . It *did* work, didn't it?"

"The Cru council of elders will decide how to proceed based on what we find."

Zechariah tilted his head. "Quite a gamble."

"I know," said Leah. "Either way, our days in this city are numbered. For all of us. Most of the people in Cervice are already refugees. It won't be difficult for them to pick up and get moving on short notice. Olorus has been briefed on overseeing some of the initial preparations, although we'll be keeping this as quiet as possible until I can confirm our destination. You and Olorus are in charge here while we're gone. Please carefully oversee things with the Rorrdvuuk and Raeqlund. Olorus can handle the Nolians, Mythaeans, Endens, Lundens, Darvellians, and the Cru."

So many people to keep track of, thought Leah. *Am I forgetting anyone?*

"I'll also see to the Holy Army," Zechariah offered, as if reading her thoughts.

Leah closed her eyes in frustration. "Yes. Yes, of course. The Holy Army."

The Holy Army. The band of zealots whom Gunnar had brought to Nolia from Castydociana—reinforcements to help her defend the city when Wulder Von Morix had refused to send her any of his troops.

How could I have forgotten about them? she wondered. *The vehicle by which that creature, Innocen, infiltrated our city.*

"Olorus staying behind to play the role of the diplomat?" Zechariah made a thoughtful sound in his throat. "I can scarcely remember a time when at least one of your two devoted bodyguards wasn't at your side—at least, not when it was within their capacity to be so."

"I *was* planning to ask Hook to join me," said Leah. "But then I learned of the assignment you gave him and Gunnar. I need not remind you that Gunnar is integral to keeping this city fed."

"Ah, yes," said Zechariah. He reached into his robes and pulled out a small stone. It was almost perfectly spherical, reflective as glass, and solid black as the night sky. The old man tossed it playfully into the air and caught it. "All taken care of, My Lady."

Leah hesitated for a moment. She found herself staring at the floor.

Nothing more to do, thought Leah. *Everyone has their duties to attend to.*

"I think it's time," said Zechariah.

Leah nodded. "It is."

She resumed her march down the blood-red carpet toward the doors, away from the throne, feeling the weight of the Nolian crown in the satchel at her side. She did not look back.

PART IV

STAGNATION

CHAPTER 34

Over the course of untold hours, Justin told his father everything.

He spoke of all that had happened to him since storming out of the house on Christmas Day and waking up in the Oikoumene, including the people he had met. Occasionally during the telling, his father would interrupt to ask him a question that would lead to many other questions, branching out into long tangents about specific subjects or certain people. But thanks to the time-altering effects of the Kharon, Justin did not grow weary of speaking.

He told Benjamin about meeting Zechariah and about helping Ahlund rescue Leah. He told of fleeing the pursuit of cythraul, how he, Leah, and Zechariah had escaped into the Shifting Mountains, and how Ahlund had been lost and presumed dead. He told of meeting Olorus and Hook in the wilderness, of the Cru village, of being forced to journey underground deep into the caves beneath the Thucymoroi. He told of meeting Gunnar. And he told of being captured by Lisaac, one of Avagad's lieutenants.

With the exception of his questions, Benjamin listened silently and attentively. Each time Justin told of a moment when he had been wounded or placed in danger or nearly killed, Benjamin looked sick. Never was this truer than when Justin told of being repeatedly beaten at the hands of Lisaac's men and ultimately having his arm transformed by the cythraul's daemyn touch.

The sick look on Benjamin's face did not dissipate when Justin related calling on aurym power for the first time to kill Lisaac and then the cythraul, unknowingly turning the tide of a battle being waged miles away.

As Justin shared the story of the victory celebrations at Hartla, Benjamin only looked sad. Justin got the impression that the more

Benjamin learned, the more guilty he began to feel about what his son had been through. He did, however, noticeably furrow his brow when Justin told him about calling his sword to his hand.

As Justin continued the telling, he revealed how he'd repeatedly encountered Avagad by falling unconscious and being dragged into the dreamworld of the Kharon. He explained that he had finally learned the secret of the gauge's power to transport him home after reading about it in a book. Here, Benjamin interrupted him to confirm what Justin had already suspected.

"Bet you never pegged your old man for an author," he said.

"Then it really was you who wrote it," said Justin.

"The original version, anyway. It's possible that this Avagad, whoever he is, had a copy, perhaps painstakingly replicated by hand. I wrote those words in a journal I kept, at a time when I was quite confused about my situation. Hopeless, really. I certainly never intended my little diary to become a religious relic."

Justin went on to explain how Hartla had been destroyed by the demons during his brief absence, and how, upon returning, he'd been blindsided by the incommensurate passage of time. Benjamin made a strange face yet again when Justin mentioned calling his sword to his hand, but when Justin paused, expecting him to ask about this, he only urged Justin to continue. So he told how, after he'd escaped Hartla, Ahlund had taken him to Esthean to be trained by Cyaxares and her Ru'Onorath.

Cyaxares. One of the Brethren whom Benjamin had referred to as his friends.

Revealing the Brethren's fate was one of Justin's most unpleasant tasks during the telling of his tale. As far as Justin knew, Cyaxares, Avagad, and Zechariah were the last living Brethren. The rest had been killed when Avagad betrayed them to the demons. Benjamin was struck dumb by this news and visibly devastated. When he finally managed a response, he commented that he didn't remember an Avagad or a Zechariah being a part of the Brethren. But then again, Benjamin had been gone a long time. He surmised that both had been brought into the fold long after he'd left the Oikoumene.

"I'm relieved to hear that Cyaxares survived the breaking of the Brethren," said Benjamin. "Very relieved. But Amphidemus. I just can't believe it."

"Were you friends with him?" asked Justin.

"I owe my life to him. He became like a father to me. Or maybe more like a grandfather, really. But I'll explain all that later. First, I want to hear the rest of your side of the story."

Justin did as he was asked and kept going. He told of his training with Cyaxares, Ahlund, and Kallorn. Of his experience with the blue tiger in the wilderness. Of his encounter with Avagad in the Treasury. And of how Esthean had been attacked by a demon army at Avagad's command. Last of all, he told of how Ahlund had sacrificed his own life just to give Justin a chance to escape.

"I tried to call my sword to my hand," said Justin, "the way I had done in the past. But that time, it wouldn't come." He bent down to pick up Ahlund's broken sword from where he'd placed it on the ground. "This is all that's left of him. I carried him all the way to the boats, but he. . . . He passed away as we were paddling out." Justin ran his thumb over the flat surface of Ahlund's blade. "Later, we buried him at sea by setting him adrift on a burning boat. With salt to flavor the meat of his game and coin for future hunts. I guess it's a Ru'Ono-rath tradition."

Benjamin nodded solemnly. "That's an Othical tradition, actually— Cyaxares's native land. She probably adapted the practice for her Ru'Onorath warriors. I'm very sorry, Justin."

In spite of his resolve, Justin found himself blinking back tears, but he refused to let them fall. He swallowed hard against a lump in his throat, then placed Ahlund's sword back on the ground beside his folded tunic and cloak.

"So," said Justin. "After all that, I was there with the rest of the Guardians on that island. No one seemed sure what to do next, not even Cyaxares. I had so many questions. So I just thought. . . . No, I *decided* that I had to know what was really going on. I had to find out if the things about you were true, and what really happened in the past. So I came home." He shrugged. "And here we are."

"And here we are," agreed Benjamin.

Benjamin seemed to consider it all for a second. Then he raised his arms above his head and groaned as he performed an exaggerated stretch, as if he'd just woken up from a long nap.

"Guess I ought to count myself lucky," he said. "Most dads can't get their teenage sons to talk to them for five minutes, let alone—well, however long we've been talking." He made a face at Justin. "Remember what you used to say when I'd ask you, 'What happened at school today'?"

"Nothing," said Justin.

"Every time," said Benjamin. "Every single day of your life, nothing happened. It was a phenomenon."

A few seconds passed. Finally, Justin broke the silence.

"Dad," said Justin. "What *really* happened when you were in the Oikoumene?"

"Oh, nothing," said Benjamin with a grin.

But Justin did not laugh.

His father's grin went away. His gaze went distant, and all at once, all the playfulness left in him evaporated.

"Lots of things happened," said Benjamin. "Bad things. Very, very bad things."

C H A P T E R　3 5

"Did you send me there?" asked Justin.

Benjamin blinked. "How?"

"I don't know, you tell me," said Justin defensively. "One minute, I'm walking out the front door, and the next—"

"Oh," said Benjamin. "I guess I see your point. No. I had nothing to do with you going to the Oikoumene. Not as far as I know, anyway. After we argued, I heard you storm out of the house. I went after you to try to stop you, but before I could even get to the front door, I felt this sudden surge of aurym. I knew right away what must have happened, but I didn't want to believe it. I felt sick. It never occurred to me that what happened to me might someday happen to you, too. If it had, I might have warned you, or, I don't know, tried to protect you from it somehow." He paused to sigh and close his eyes as if fighting a bad headache. "I went through the motions of having Grandpa and Uncle Paul over for Christmas Dinner, as planned, and I told them the truth—or a version of the truth, anyway. That we'd had an argument, that you'd stormed out of the house, and that I hoped you would come back soon. When I saw you through the kitchen window later that night, I knew you were safe, but the look on your face told me you were going back. To my surprise, instead of my initial instinct to rush out the door after you, I found myself feeling proud. Because at that moment, I knew."

"Knew what?" said Justin.

"That you were a better man than your father."

"*What*? Dad. . . ."

Benjamin looked away. For a long time, he said nothing.

Justin felt the urge to say something, anything, but he didn't know what to say. Never, in all his life, had he seen his outgoing, fun-loving father this way.

"The night of the accident," said Benjamin, in a voice that was almost a whisper, "the night your mother died, I was thrown through the windshield of the car. But I didn't land on a country road, or in a ditch, or down at the bottom of that embankment where I told the police I woke up hours later. I landed in broad daylight, in the middle of a forest clearing, at a different time of day, in a different season of the year. I was confused, almost certainly suffering from a concussion, and bleeding from a hundred cuts, but I crawled through that clearing, desperately looking for you and Mom. I yelled for you. I searched for our car. But at some point, I realized that the fallen leaves beneath my hands belonged to a kind of tree I had never seen before. I looked around and noticed that the plants were species not native to our corner of Earth, and the air carried a thick, heady smell. I couldn't have known it at the time, but I was in a deep forest in southern Darsida, in the Oikoumene.

"It's a miracle that I made it through my first day there—alone, injured, confused, wandering through the woods and shouting for help like a fool. Like you, I didn't know where I was or what had happened. I remembered the car ride leading up to the accident and the impact when the other car hit us, but I didn't know what had happened after that. I started to wonder if I was actually unconscious and this was where your mind went when your body lingered over the precipice of death. I didn't know what to think. And I certainly didn't know that there were demons everywhere, or that my arrival had unleashed a powerful aurym blast felt by everyone and everything within a thousand miles. If the coblyns had found me first, I would have been eaten alive on the spot. Instead, it was a cythraul."

A shiver ran down Justin's good arm. He tried to imagine how he'd have felt if the first thing he'd seen in the Oikoumene had been one of those hulking black giants with their fleshless, skull-like heads.

Benjamin continued. "The cythraul apparently did not think a puny thing like me capable of being the source of the aurym blast that had drawn it to the area. It mistakenly assumed me to be a runaway slave."

"A runaway slave?" said Justin.

"The cythraul took me to the nearest demon city and 'returned' me to the enslaved human population there. There were many other humans, but I did not speak their language." He paused to clear his throat. "I cannot describe to you the horrors of a demon city in the prime of their domination over the Oikoumene. The world was overrun with demons at that time, and all of humankind was enslaved to them. The coblyns were like commoners, and the cythraul were the nobility. Humans were both their slaves and their cattle. We labored under their whips. We raised and cared for livestock to feed their hunger. And, during the great feasts, some of us were selected to be eaten alive in creative, satisfying ways. I labored and languished in the dungeons beneath that demon city for months."

"*Months*?" said Justin.

Benjamin nodded. "More than long enough to become sufficiently convinced that the car accident had been the end of my life, and that this was hell. Literal hell.

"Then, one night, the doors of the dungeons were thrown open, and a group of humans entered. They quietly slew the cythraul guards using strange powers the likes of which I had never seen, and they freed us all. We managed to slip away into the wilderness, but by now, I was more confused than ever. If this wasn't hell, then what was it?

"Days and weeks passed, and I did my best to survive alongside these strange people. We were on the run from pursuing demons, and there were many near-disasters. I got to see these spirit-warriors use their powers to fight off coblyns and cythraul. I did what I could to contribute, and I learned a bit of their language. Gradually, as I befriended them while eking out a living in hiding, I learned enough to communicate some of my story.

"Something about my tale struck a chord with the spirit-warriors, and it was decided that I needed to be taken to a faraway place. I was to be presented to one of the oldest among them. Their leader. I had learned that an ancient culture known as the Elleneans had ruled the Oikoumene prior to the demon invasions. The people I'd been enslaved with, as well as the warriors who'd freed us, were their descendants. But this man whom I was being taken to, Amphidemus, claimed to have been a commander in the Ellenean army in the time before the invasions. Before the fall of mankind, at least a thousand years before. People claimed that Amphidemus was immortal and had somehow survived for all those generations. He was the leader of the sole surviving group of free humans. I was brought before him."

"Amphidemus?" said Justin. "As in, the leader of the Brethren?"

"Eventually, yes," said Benjamin. "But at that time, he was the one and only immortal man. The last of the true Ancients. When I told him my story, he claimed that there had been another like me, many years before, who had been called 'ethoul.' He claimed that this ethoul had been a powerful warrior who had come from another world. And he said he sensed the same power in me."

CHAPTER 36

"From then on," continued Benjamin, "I was trained in the ways of aurym. I learned how to use it to fight, and I became every bit as powerful as Amphidemus had predicted I would be. He was grooming me to be the spearhead of a war against the demons. With my powers, he said, we could liberate humanity and drive the demons out of the Oikoumene forever.

"In truth, all I wanted was to go home. Now that I knew this was another world, and that I had been transported here somehow during the accident, I longed to find a way back. Before that, I'd had no hope to cling to. But maybe there was hope after all. Maybe it was possible for me to see you and your mother again. And yet, I didn't have any way of knowing what had happened to you that night. Were you alive and wondering what had happened to me? Or was I the only survivor of the crash? Or had the same thing that happened to me happened to the two of you, too, and were you somewhere out in this strange world, lost and alone like me. . . ? It took my mind to some very dark places, but it also gave me a reason to fight.

"With the help of Amphidemus, I became a warrior. We assembled a powerful fighting force, and we set out on the warpath, straight into the heart of the darkness."

Benjamin sighed. A few moments passed. His hands were clenched into fists at his sides.

"I do not have the effort, even here in the Kharon, to tell you everything that happened during the years I was at war."

"*Years?*" said Justin.

"Years," said Benjamin. "Amphidemus and I led the charge, driving through demon territory, reclaiming lands as we went, and flying our banner in all the liberated cities: a flag bearing two white wings, symbolic of the 'fallen angel' who had come to the Oikoumene to save humanity. I suppose you'd call it propaganda. It wasn't my idea, and I certainly didn't mean to manipulate anyone. But it worked. Belief in the fallen angel became something almost like a religion, and it emboldened others to join us in our fight. We lost many good people, and I saw things that will stay with me as long as I live. But finally, we reached the demons' last bastion of strength. It was a fortressed city on the shores of Erum. And it turned out to be a trap.

"By the time we realized our mistake, it was too late. A cythraul got its hands on me. It managed to turn my legs with its touch before Amphidemus saved me. Everything was going to hell. To escape, I was forced to. . . . I had to blow up the city. The whole city. Everything and everyone in it was turned to dust, including many of our own soldiers. People who were my friends. That was how we finally won the war, if you can call *that* a win."

Benjamin looked away, a haunted expression on his face.

"I'm sure you didn't have a choice," said Justin. "The demons would have—"

"No. I had a choice," said Benjamin flatly. "I thought, at the time, that it was the right choice."

He left any other thoughts on the matter unspoken, and Justin decided not to pursue it further. For now, at least.

"At the end of the war," said Benjamin, "I discovered the way to go home. The Keys of the Ancients, otherwise known as keystones."

"Or gauges," said Justin.

"That's right. I reappeared at the scene of the car accident. The car had been towed away, but I could still see pieces of glass and bits of taillights on the road, which seemed very odd to me. I didn't realize at the time that only a matter of hours had passed on Earth in all the time I'd been gone. It was the middle of the night, and no one was on the road, so I walked all the way home, hoping I would find you and Mom there. But when I got to the house, that's when I realized that everything I'd been through in the Oikoumene had occurred within one night on Earth. And I realized that if you and Mom weren't at the house, then maybe you were at the hospital.

"I couldn't exactly drive myself there. How would I explain that? So I changed out of my Oikoumene clothes, and I went back to the accident site. I was already bloodied and bruised from my recent battles. All I did was muddy up my clothes and lie down on the side of the road. Around dawn, a woman in a pick-up truck saw me and pulled over. I told her I'd woken up at the bottom of the embankment on the side of the road and had crawled up the hill. I found out later that you and your mother had both been unresponsive when first responders arrived. They did an initial search for the driver of our vehicle, but they hadn't been able to find me."

Benjamin looked hard at Justin.

"I never wanted you to know this," he said, "but ever since that night, the police keep checking in on me, keep asking me to repeat my story. People don't just go missing from accident sites and reappear. The authorities don't seem to be buying the version of events I tried to sell them." He paused here and cleared his throat. "I'm sure there's an open investigation into the matter. They're probably building up their case against me."

"A case against you?" said Justin. "For what?"

"To any outside observer, the situation would appear suspicious, at the very least. If they can find a hole in my story, or a motive. . . ."

CHAPTER 37

Justin's guts felt cold and hollow.

"*What*?" he breathed. "You mean they think you set it up somehow—that you tried to hurt us *on purpose*? That's crazy."

"Crazier than the truth?" said Benjamin. "Another thing I had going against me is that I refused treatment at the hospital. I couldn't have them examining me, for obvious reasons." He patted his legs. "When they insisted, I got agitated. I got a little physical, in fact. I was adamant that they weren't going to touch me, and all I wanted was to see my family—in hindsight, very suspicious behavior for someone who supposedly got thrown from a vehicle. Eventually, I made it in to see you. And I found out about your mother.

"I lost it, Justin. I just. . . . To think that all the time I'd spent in the Oikoumene, searching for a way home, praying that I could one day get back to my wife and son. And after all the hellish things *I* managed to survive, I find out my wife was killed in a car accident. Stolen from me, just like that. I saved an entire world from the demons. Yet I couldn't save your mother from one drunk fool. I wasn't even there for her at the end. Wasn't there for you when *you* needed me. The first time I went into your hospital room, you were sleeping, and for some reason, I couldn't even bring myself to wake you up. I felt like I had failed you so badly, so irreversibly, that I—I couldn't even face you."

"Dad. . . ."

"By that point," said Benjamin, pressing on, "my legs had started to go numb. Until then, I hadn't realized that they would stop working. How was I going to explain that? My mind, too, was starting to do some strange things. I wanted to speak to Amphidemus. I thought maybe he could help me make sense of things. So I took a quick trip back to the Oikoumene. At least, it was supposed to be a quick trip. Instead, I arrived in a world overrun by demons again.

"I couldn't believe it. Everything I'd accomplished had been undone. Eventually, I learned that several hundred years had passed during the brief time I'd returned to Earth. Plenty long enough for the demons to regroup and launch a new assault on the Oikoumene. Amphidemus found me. He and his people saw my sudden return as a miracle. And they expected me to rise to the occasion. Again."

Justin watched his father carefully, noting the warring expressions on his face.

"I felt like. . . ." Benjamin trailed off, staring at the gray ground at his feet. Then he set his jaw and added, in an altogether different tone of voice, "After everything I had done and been through—what had it all been for? In the span of a single night on Earth, I lost my home, fought a war, won, returned home, lost my wife, then went back and found out that my war had been for nothing. So many people had died, and for what? Had any of my sacrifices been worth it? I feel like that was the moment when I broke."

"Broke?" said Justin.

Benjamin kept going as if he hadn't heard him. "I learned that Amphidemus had begun training a group of spirit-warriors in the application of a daemyn technique that allowed them to live unnaturally long lifespans, like him. The process involved tapping into something called the Kharon." Benjamin spread his arms, gesturing toward their surroundings. "This place. Amphidemus called his new followers the Brethren. Cyaxares was one of them."

Benjamin looked up, staring intensely at Justin. Behind his glasses, to Justin's surprise, there were tears in his eyes.

"I have to apologize to you," he said. "I don't expect you to forgive me. I don't even *want* you to forgive me because I don't deserve it."

"Apologize for what?" asked Justin.

"I should have gone straight back to you. You were lying in a hospital bed. Plus, you'd just lost your mom. You needed me. But I was so messed up in the head—" Benjamin punctuated this thought by rapping his knuckles against his skull so hard that Justin heard the impact, "—that it was easier for me to fight another war than to live in a world where your mother was gone."

Justin wanted to say something to make his father feel better but found that he could think of nothing.

"Amphidemus, his Brethren, and I took up the fight against the demons again," said Benjamin. "But this time, things would be different—I swore that they would be. Last time, I had been trying to drive the demons out. This time, I would eliminate them. Last time, I'd been a warrior. This time, I would be a general. A leader.

"We fought our way, once again, across the Oikoumene, waging war against the demons as we went, shining a light through the darkness. And, once again, we placed white-winged banners in the cities we liberated. I had to commune with daemyn to keep strength in my legs— still none the wiser to what daemyn actually was. The war went more quickly this time, and we were on the brink of total victory when I made a critical error in judgment. It was another trap, and I walked right into it. You told me that a man named Avagad tried to get you to walk through a strange doorway the first time you met him, right?"

"Yeah," said Justin, and realized that his mouth was dry as paper. "It looked like a sort of windowpane. I almost went through it."

"Thank God you didn't."

At least a full minute of silence passed before Benjamin was able to speak again.

"It was a portal to another world. I stepped through it and arrived in the demonic realm. A world of blackness and fire. A hell all its own. There, a giant being—a creature the size of a mountain—reached down, grabbed my body between house-sized fingers, and picked me up as if I were an ant."

"The Nameless One?" breathed Justin.

Benjamin nodded.

CHAPTER 38

"Cyaxares told me about him," said Justin. "Or *it*. Or whatever the god-king of the demons is. She told me the Nameless One was thought to have been no more than a part of the Ancients' mythology. But she also said she had reason to suspect that it may have been real."

Benjamin was staring off into the distance now. Without looking at Justin, he said flatly, "And who do you think gave her that idea?"

Justin shivered at the haunted expression on his father's face.

"I can't remember much of what happened after that," said Benjamin. "Most of it is a blur in my mind. When the Nameless One took me in his grasp, he did something to me. It was a bit like the transforming touch of a cythraul that turned my legs, only on a *deeper* level, somehow. Mind-deep. Maybe soul-deep. After it was over, the Nameless One sent me back to the Oikoumene. I woke up, alone, and soon discovered that I could no longer use aurym. I had been cut off from it."

"Cut off? From aurym?" said Justin. "Is that even possible?"

"Look at your arm," said Benjamin. "If a cythraul can change a person's body and make a part of them dependent on daemyn, what more can the *father* of the cythraul do? I could no longer call on aurym. Which meant I couldn't even use a keystone. I could never go home again. So, with aurym gone, I called on daemyn instead. Daemyn was easy to use. Sometimes, you don't even need a stone. You just invite it in, and it works. Almost as if you're doing nothing at all. Almost as if it's acting for you."

Justin's mind flashed back to his fight with Lisaac. He remembered what it had felt like to put his own sword to his neck and to be unable to remove it. It had been as if a pair of invisible hands had been wrapped around his. He remembered the voice in his head telling him to do it as those hands increased the pressure, attempting to drive the blade along its path.

The voice of daemyn. The voice of the Nameless One.

"What followed was a period of about two years, which I only partially remember," said Benjamin. "I began to lose control of myself. Looking back, it's almost like being drunk—a few vivid moments floating in a sea of semi-consciousness and blackouts. I returned to my people, and I set myself up as ruler of all those territories that we'd liberated in the war. But I didn't stop there. There were rulers who did not agree with my methods. I made them see things my way. I expanded. My cities became nations, which became an empire. I enforced my will over my people. I made them do as I wished and even made them speak as I spoke. I built monuments of peace, monuments commemorating the war, and monuments to myself."

Benjamin paused to flash a grin at Justin. "Doesn't sound much like me, does it?"

"Hell no," said Justin.

"Exactly. Because I wasn't myself. Or, at least, I wasn't in control anymore. Cyaxares told you I became a tyrant and was corrupted by power, didn't she?"

Justin nodded weakly.

"She is more correct than she knows. It was like I was trapped in my body, a spectator more than a participant, watching my own actions. As soon as I started using daemyn, it took over and started using me. And before long, it *was* me. I was the Nameless One's puppet. I watched myself destroy anyone who questioned my authority. I had occasional moments of clarity, but they were brief.

"Amphidemus tried to help me. So did Cyaxares. But it didn't work. I was too far gone. A shadow of myself. And so, in secret, Amphidemus, Cyaxares, and the rest of the Brethren assembled a military force and launched a surprise attack on my capital city. They fought their way to my fortress and defeated me. I—or daemyn working through me—killed some of the Brethren in the process. Fortunately, Cyaxares managed to bring me to my senses long enough for me to realize what was happening. I begged them to kill me while they had the chance, but Amphidemus, a true friend even to the end, showed me mercy. Instead of executing me, they would banish me from the Oikoumene. The Brethren would use all their aurym combined to power a single keystone to its second form—a Key of the Ancients—and send me home. Cut off from aurym, I would never be able to return to the Oikoumene.

"I didn't know if this process would sever the Nameless One's hold on me, but I agreed to let them try. First, however, I penned a letter that I left in the care of Amphidemus, hoping to warn other 'fallen angels' of the true nature of daemyn."

"Cyaxares had your letter," said Justin. "She gave it to me."

"Cyaxares." A meaningful smile crossed Benjamin's face. "Another true friend. . . . It took all of the Brethren to accomplish it, but with their full aurym strength combined, they did it. They channeled their combined aurym, and the next thing I remember, I was home, holding a dull-looking little stone—the keystone they had used. To my relief, I realized I was free from the hold of the Nameless One. But I was still cut off from aurym. Try as I might, I couldn't make the stone glow as I once had.

"Again, I discovered that only a couple of hours had passed on Earth. I now knew what would happen to my legs, so I acquired a secondhand wheelchair and decided to just lie by omission. I allowed you and others to assume that my legs had been injured in the crash. Sorry about that."

As Benjamin said this, he reached into his pocket and pulled out a small stone. Justin recognized it. It was a gauge stone. A Key of the Ancients.

"There was no going back this time," he said, rubbing his thumb over the stone. "No running away. I decided that I would try to be the best dad I could for you with what I had left. Just as I predicted, my legs quickly lost all function."

Justin's gaze snapped to his father's legs, which were now easily supporting his full weight.

"But if daemyn can control you," he said, "why did you bring us here? If there's enough daemyn here to power your legs, then—"

"I admit, it was a bit of a gamble," said Benjamin without looking at him. "There's *some* daemyn here, but I don't think it's enough for the Nameless One to control me. It was the only way I could talk to you, which is what you needed. And I vowed to be the best dad I could be for you. It's worth the risk."

Nervously, Justin moistened his lips. He wasn't so sure he agreed with him.

"You asked me if *I* sent you to the Oikoumene," said Benjamin. "I did not. But I think it may be my fault that you were taken there."

"What do you mean?" said Justin.

"I was *supposed* to save the Oikoumene from the demons," said Benjamin. "Instead, I just ... *replaced* them. I failed. I wasn't strong enough. So aurym called on my son to finish the job that his father couldn't."

"You mean," said Justin, "you think it was the will of aurym itself that sent us to the Oikoumene?"

"I know it was," said Benjamin. "Daemyn has a will of its own. Aurym does, too. Amphidemus theorized that aurym and daemyn were eternal, opposing forces. But I don't think that's quite right. Aurym is eternal, but daemyn is a corruption—an extension of the Nameless One's own spirit, permeating across the worlds. Every time someone uses daemyn, a part of them, whether they are aware of it or not, is submitting to his will. Including the Brethren, when they use daemyn to prolong their lifespans." He sighed heavily and pointed to his legs. "And you and me, right now."

Justin's gaze drifted to his left arm. It was currently covered from view by the sleeve of the hooded sweatshirt he'd grabbed from his room, but beneath, he knew what it looked like. He squeezed his hand into a fist and felt the tug of his natural flesh against the blackened, bone-like armored material.

Powered by daemyn. Powered by the Nameless One himself.

CHAPTER 39

"You see that too, right?" said Gunnar. "I'm not hallucinating?"

"It's just like yours," said Adonica. "Except that yours is in burnt little pieces at the bottom of the Cervice River."

"Thanks, I almost forgot," said Gunnar.

Hook agreed; the ship below was almost identical to the *Gryphon II*, the vessel that Gunnar had stolen from the demons on the beaches of Gaius.

Beneath a rising sun, high on a wooded coastal hilltop overlooking the ocean strait that separated southeast Athacea from southern Darsida, Hook, Gunnar, and Adonica watched the lone demon ship as it rode the southerly current along the coast.

They couldn't have spotted us, thought Hook. *Not from this distance.*

And yet the ship appeared to be bearing straight toward their position.

Like Gunnar's *Gryphon II*, this one was a double-masted ship made of odd-looking black wood and black sails. As he watched it, Hook found himself wondering where these vessels came from. Did demons *build* ships? And if so, where? From what grim forest had the trees for this black vessel been felled? And from what hellish shores had this boat set sail? Or perhaps the vessels were built by humans who—willingly or otherwise—called these demons their masters. Hook wasn't sure which answer he liked least. On the one hand, it was disturbing to think of humans laboring beneath the whips of demon masters. But, on the other hand, he had always thought of demons as being beneath humans in terms of intelligence, and the idea that demons were clever enough to be capable shipwrights was an unsettling notion. It was easier to think of them simply as monsters.

For days, Hook, Gunnar, and Adonica had been picking their way south, avoiding open country whenever possible, riding mostly at night to avoid being seen. The weather had been kind to them thus far. It had only snowed lightly. Not enough to cause them to leave any obvious tracks as they traveled. They'd ridden past abandoned towns and villages, some that showed signs of besiegement and others from which the population seemed to have evacuated without a struggle. They had encountered no other human beings during their days-long journey by steedback. A few times, they'd spotted a few roaming herds of coblyns at a distance, and yesterday, Gunnar had thought he'd sensed the daemyn presence of a cythraul coming toward them before changing course and gradually moving off in another direction. Thus far, Hook hadn't needed to draw his sword, nor nock an arrow to his bow.

And now, within sight of their destination—a demon ship was coming straight toward them.

Hook shifted his gaze away from the ship to the ruins down along the water, about a mile from their current position. Zechariah had described their destination as a tomb, but to Hook, it looked more like a small castle or a fortress, albeit a run-down and partially sunken one. It was built of stacked stone fashioned into a semicircular shape like an overturned bowl. Hook had once been told that some of Athacea's seemingly picturesque hills were actually old barrows containing the bones of dead Ancients. It occurred to him that if the ruins he was looking at now were covered in grass, they would have formed a shape similar to those mounds.

Inside this set of ruins, according to Zechariah, were the remains of an Ellenean king. And buried with him, supposedly, a collection of aurstones. Gunnar, Hook, and Adonica had only to dig them up. The problem was that the crumbling seaside ruins were set atop a lip of land that had been eaten away by the sea, and the ruins were half-sunken in the ocean.

"What do you think it's doing here?" said Adonica, drawing Hook's attention back on the demon ship coming toward them. Hook replied with a noncommittal shrug.

Over the course of their journey, Hook had taken some time to tutor Gunnar and Adonica on his signs, sometimes writing in the dirt and performing the accompanying sign. They were getting better at understanding him, if not always his precise meaning. Still, there were times when a shrug or a nod did the trick just as well.

Gunnar set the end of his spyglass to his good eye to study the ship. "Maybe it's just, you know, a coincidence. Nothing to do with us. Just passing by on its way to join some other battle elsewhere."

"The more I travel with you," said Adonica, "the more I think you've got the worst luck of any man I've ever met."

"You don't know the half of it," said Gunnar.

Hook thought a coincidence was possible. But the ship was sailing south. So if it *was* on its way to a battle, it was yet another sobering reminder that the League's war was just one of the demons' multiple war fronts. He'd heard plenty of talk about the various civilizations that had fallen to the demons. There were also rumors of other human alliances, like the League, in other parts of the Oikoumene—kingdoms, empires, and republics that had banded together out of necessity to fight for their people's survival. He wondered if the League could somehow connect with these other groups and put up a unified front. Unfortunately, there were vast distances between them, and most roads were no longer safe to travel.

"Guess all we can do is wait here, stay low, and hope it passes us by," said Gunnar. He hazarded a glance over his shoulder, toward the place where their steeds were hidden in the trees. He made a face, then fiddled uncomfortably with his eyepatch as if it pained him. He had been doing that a lot since departing from Cervice.

"You'd think the old man would've mentioned that this place was half underwater," said Adonica, voice brimming with annoyance.

"He may not have known," signed Hook. *"Perhaps sea levels have risen since ancient times."*

When it became clear that Adonica hadn't followed his signs, Hook pantomimed an ocean wave, then slowly brought his hand up to indicate rising water. Adonica nodded her head in apparent understanding.

"Either way, it complicates things," she said. "Whole interior's probably flooded. We might not even be able to get inside."

"That depends," muttered Gunnar.

"On what?" said Adonica.

"On whether we're looking at high tide or low tide."

Zechariah had told them that the grave goods they were looking for would not be in the main area of the tomb itself. The king's servants, he claimed, would have been buried in the upper and outer portions of the tomb, ritualistically standing guard for their king in death. At the center of the tomb would be a sarcophagus, but it would not contain the king; this was a decoy. Instead, Zechariah claimed that there would be a recess in one of the tomb's inner walls marked with the Ancients' royal insignia. Gunnar, Hook, and Adonica would have to find a way to break through that wall to gain access to a tunnel leading to an antechamber below. There, they would find the true resting place of the king. And upon his head, a crown with sixteen aurstones set within it.

An underground antechamber. In a flooded tomb.

Hook rubbed at his jaw. He thought they were currently at or at least near high tide, but he couldn't be sure. If it was high tide, maybe they could gain access when the waters receded. But if he was wrong and *this* was low tide, then high tide would almost certainly submerge the tomb entirely.

"What is *that*?" Gunnar breathed.

Hook looked up. Gunnar was looking through his spyglass. But not at the demon ship or the ruins. Instead, his gaze was directed inland. There, Hook saw that a line of shadows with substance had emerged from the forest.

Dark figures were marching across the lowlands, coming toward them.

CHAPTER 40

At the sight of the figures, Hook, Adonica, and Gunnar lowered themselves to the ground behind the rock where they'd been crouched.

"Damn," hissed Adonica through gritted teeth. "They spot us?"

"I don't know," admitted Gunnar. Again, he glanced toward the place where the steeds were tied. Again, he rubbed at his eyepatch. "Best be ready to ride hard and fast if we have to. On steedback, we can outpace coblyns. Cythraul, too, I think."

"What if they have some of those eight-legged demon steed-things?" said Adonica.

"Then you'd better hope they break at least four, or else we're ox fodder," said Gunnar.

Gunnar did not protest when Hook took the spyglass from his hand. Hook raised his head until he could see over the rock, positioned the glass on the marching figures, and rested his brow against the eyepiece.

The dim light of dawn made it difficult to tell what he was seeing. It wasn't a large group. Two dozen, at most. In the past, he'd had the luxury of assuming that any group of individuals, standing upright and walking on two legs, was human. But these days, such conclusions could not be taken for granted. Upright and two legs did not always mean human. He couldn't yet discern any telling details from here, but they did not seem to have any steeds, pack animals, wagons, or other items indicative of culture, which was another warning sign.

Hook squinted. They weren't big enough to be cythraul. But, then again, they seemed too big for coblyns.

Maybe humans after all, he wondered. *It's possible they don't see the demon ship from there. Maybe we should do something to warn them—*

But the thought was wrenched from Hook's mind. For at that moment, the individual at the front of the procession emerged from the shadows along the edge of the forest, into the full light of dawn.

"General Bard?" said Adonica, apparently noting the change in his body language at the sight of the thing.

Hook blinked hard, trying to clear his eye, but the image stayed the same. He thought at first that he was looking at a male human draped all in black, causing his silhouette to appear shadowed even in the morning light. But as Hook watched, he realized the man was naked from head to foot. He lumbered as he moved, as if he were injured, and a shadow seemed to travel with him, blackening his whole being.

More alarming still were the proportions of this man's body. His legs appeared too narrow—more like those of a stork or an insect than of a man. The same was true of his arms, which had the muscle mass of a desiccated corpse. It almost looked as if his limbs had no flesh or connective tissues to speak of. As the figure drew nearer and new details were made visible, Hook saw that his body was as black as charred wood and appeared to be constructed of interlocking plates, like scales instead of skin. He walked with his head hung low, making it difficult to make out any facial features, but his head appeared to be a black, fleshless skull.

Hook shifted his spyglass. The same was true of the individual behind the man walking at the lead of the procession. And of the one behind that. A line of two dozen figures, human in form yet demon in appearance.

Finally, the individual at the front of the procession raised his head, providing Hook's first glimpse of its face. The sight made his stomach turn. It was as if all the living tissue of the man's face had been peeled away to reveal a blackened, deformed skull beneath. Its exposed mouth was lined with off-white teeth that looked quite human but without any lips or cheeks to keep them covered. There was no nose, just an oddly shaped recess. On either side, bare black cheekbones jutted out below empty eye sockets—deep, wide pits glowing with a fiery red light emanating from somewhere deep within the skull.

A hand gently grabbed the spyglass, and Hook barely had the presence of mind to let go so that Gunnar, who had grown tired of waiting for a report, could take a look for himself.

Hook watched Gunnar take in the sight. The brow over the admiral's eyepatch cocked in appraisal. "Those have got to be some of the ugliest sons of mothers I've ever seen," he said, then handed the spyglass to Adonica.

"By the seas . . ." Adonica whispered when she spotted them.

Down at the shoreline, the demon ship had lowered its sails and was dropping anchor, still about a hundred yards or more from the beach. Even without the aid of a spyglass, Hook could see rope ladders being thrown over the side to hang out into the churning sea.

The ship wasn't coming for us, thought Hook. *It's coming to meet them.*

"Never occurred to me that there might be other types of demons we hadn't yet encountered," said Gunnar. "I wonder if those ones have any nasty surprises—"

"No," breathed Adonica, still watching the approach of the marching figures through the spyglass. "Gunnar, that's no demon. Look again." And Adonica forced the spyglass back into the admiral's hands.

As Gunnar raised it to his good eye, Adonica turned to look hard at Hook.

"The arms," she said. "Do they remind you of anyone you know?"

All at once, the color drained from Gunnar's face. For Hook, it took an additional second or two before the implication hit home.

Demonic limbs as narrow as bones. Interlocking, armor-like plating. Like Justin's left arm. The one that had been turned by the touch of a cythraul.

Hook had been right after all. They were humans.

Or had been, anyway.

CHAPTER 41

Leah's footfalls crunched in the freshly fallen snow. More than a foot of it had fallen overnight, and twice she'd had to get up in the night to remove some of the snow weighing down her tent. But the clouds had since moved on, and the morning had broken cold and clear with an azure sky above. The spruces and pines surrounding her were so heavy-laden with fresh snowfall that it created a wall of almost solid white, further insulating this secluded high-altitude valley from the outside world.

Leah's breath showed in a puff of vapor as she looked up at the rock wall before her. To one side, a series of vertical cracks ran down the facade, webbing outward near the bottom to form patterns with the appearance of river deltas.

Or upward-pointing arrows, thought Leah, *with the fletching at the bottom.*

She turned to face a formation on the other side. Two bulbous hunks of rock protruded from the side of the cliff. When one squinted, it was easy to imagine them as the rounded, curled horns of a ram's head. And between these two distinctive formations was a narrow canyon.

It was not difficult to see how this place had gone unnoticed for so long. The path through the rock appeared to have partially collapsed on one side—not only from overhead but underfoot as well, resulting in a ceiling that was partially caved in and a portion of the floor broken open in a deep fissure. The cave-in had choked the canyon at the top, turning it into something more like a tunnel. A hole in the wall.

It was only wide enough for two people to walk through side-by-side, and the path within ran alongside a crack in the mountain that fell away to unknowable depths. One wrong step would mean a fall down into the chasm, swallowed by the sunless pit to plummet for who knew how long.

Leah turned and looked over her shoulder. Sif, the youngest elder of the Cru nation, was by her side, clothed in the warm brown and black furs of his people. His curly black beard drew a stark contrast to his hairless head, kept ritualistically shaven, as was the practice for all adult Cru men.

"This is the place the head elder asked me to lead you to," said Sif in a quiet, rich tone of voice. "Whether it is what you seek, I will not dare venture to guess."

He glanced at the five other Cru warriors assembled behind him: three men and two women. The males all had beards and shaven heads like Sif, while the females kept their hair in braids so long that they wore them wrapped several times around their necks like scarves. All five carried short recurve bows and longswords. The men were called Tel, Ral, and Wit; the women were called Vox and Enn. But Leah reminded herself that the names by which *she* knew these people were not their true names but, rather, the shortened Waelik versions. In the Cru tongue, the head elder, Thid, had a name as long as a medium-length sentence. The same was true of Sif. He was a younger man with fewer honorifics earned to extend his name, but it was still several times as long as that of the average Nolian. Even the term "Cru" was a shortened version. Their true name, A'cru'u'ol, meant "the trapped people," a reference to having lost their way back to their true ancestral Home under the Shifting Mountains long ago.

On Leah's other side were Banus and Anaxander, two of the surviving members of the High Nolian Guard. They'd been among the soldiers still protecting Cervice under Captain Cimon Endrus when Leah had returned to the city, and they now served as her personal bodyguards. As was the tradition in the High Guard, they were outfitted with spears and kite-shaped shields. They also carried single-edged shortswords designed for slashing. Both men wore their hair short-cropped, but Banus, the older of the two, had a neatly trimmed white goatee and a clean upper lip, while Anaxander kept his chestnut brown facial hair in a style not unlike that of Leah's late father—mutton chops and a long, curled mustache.

Next to Banus and Anaxander was Marcus Worth, dressed in the distinctive bronze cuirass and greaves of the Enden military. Like most of Enden descent, his hair was a rich reddish-brown, and he wore his facial hair in a thin chinstrap. At his waist was a shortsword, and strapped to his back was one of the circular shields that the Endens used to form their notoriously impenetrable phalanx formations.

Next to Marcus was Lycon Belesys, who, like most Mythaeans, opted to wear little armor other than a leather shirt with a series of metal plates riveted across the torso. His brown beard was as thick as wild country brambles, and strapped to his back was a choice of weapon unique to this man: a massive, long, curved blade as black as ebony. He was rumored to have pried it from the hand of a cythraul on the beaches of Gaius. Most men could have hardly lifted such a weapon. Its beastly former owner had wielded it one-handed. Lycon used it as a two-hander.

And, lingering behind them all, arms crossed, was the silent Rorrdvuuk woman with the scar across her head. Megara. Other than the gauntlet on her arm, her only weapon was a long belt knife made of volcanic rock. She didn't seem keen to be here, and Leah was still unsure about Zechariah's suggestion to bring her along.

Sif had proven to be a masterful navigator and woodsman. Based on Thid's instructions and the ancient map provided by Zechariah, he'd led them into the Shifting Mountains. They'd departed from the path at a designated spot and into the thickly wooded wilderness. Banus and Anaxander had had to hack through a nearly impenetrable wall of shrubbery. This morning, after weathering a night of heavy snowfall, they'd finally ambled down a steep ravine and pushed through the snow-laden branches of a thick stand of pine and spruce, to arrive here.

The morning was so young and the snowfall so fresh that it had not yet been disturbed by ground animals or birds. The topmost layer sparkled in the new sun as Leah stared into the dark, narrow tunnel ahead. According to Zechariah, somewhere beyond was a secret back door to an ancient underground city. Where the front door was, even Zechariah did not know.

"Shall we scout ahead, My Queen?" offered Anaxander.

Leah shook her head. "No," she said. "I'll go in first."

"But, My Queen," said Anaxander, "it may be—"

"It could be unstable," Marcus Worth finished for him, eyeing the partially caved-in ceiling and the yawning chasm in the floor. "Any slight disturbance may prove deadly."

Sif spoke up. "This collapse isn't recent. The rock above has supported many winters' worth of icepack and snowfall. Not likely to be shifted by our passage. I cannot, however, speak for the ground beneath."

Leah considered. The path was wide enough that if she hugged the wall, she could keep a few steps away from the chasm. But there was no telling what the state of the path was like beyond her current line of sight.

"Begging your pardon, My Lady," said Lycon. "But we must consider other dangers. Just because a city has been lost to time does not mean it is abandoned."

Out of the corner of her eye, Leah noticed several of the Cru warriors shifting uncomfortably. She made a mental note to choose her words wisely when referring to the Home of their lore, lest an offhanded comment be taken in a negative light.

"Marcus, Lycon, Megara," said Leah. "Stay here and keep watch." Her hand drifted to the satchel slung from her shoulder, resting for a moment on the familiar shape of the Nolian crown tucked within. Then she let out a steaming breath and drew the long, slender saber from the sheath at her belt. "The rest of you, stay close and watch my back, please."

CHAPTER 42

Every scratch and scrape of cloth, every breath, every sharp ping when her sword kissed a stone, sounded as if it were a hair's breadth from Leah's ears here within this little crack in the cliff-side. So loud, and yet so fleeting, the sounds quickly swallowed up in these cramped confines, like the opposite of an echo.

For the first few steps, there was only a low, uneven crag of ceiling above her—a massive chunk of leaning rock that had fallen down into the canyon untold ages before. One side was a rock wall. On the other, a gaping chasm. The opening was only a step away from the current placement of her footing.

Leah ran her free hand along the stable wall of the tunnel as she moved, keeping well away from the chasm on the other side. It was wide enough to easily swallow up a full-grown man, and no light penetrated down through it. She checked behind her and found Banus at her back, followed by Anaxander, both with their machete-like shortswords drawn and held low. Behind them was Sif, but she could see no one else from here. She was surprised to note that the snowy mountain valley behind her was already out of sight around a rocky corner.

There was no snow on the floor of the tunnel, but as Leah proceeded deeper, the ground became slick with ice underfoot, accumulated from moisture dripping down through the fragments of the caved-in ceiling. The shadows grew oppressive, and she had nearly resolved to pull out her gauge stone and instruct the soldiers to light their lanterns when she noticed a shimmer of light reflected on the icy ground and the wall. It was coming from somewhere ahead of her—

A disturbance from behind Leah jolted her to attention. She wheeled in time to see Anaxander fall sidelong toward the chasm, his foot having slipped out from beneath him on the ice. He let go of his sword and reached desperately for the wall.

Sif's arm shot out of the darkness. His hand grabbed hold of the kite shield on the man's back, holding Anaxander suspended over the depth. The man's sword rode the ice a few inches, slipped slowly over the precipice, and dropped into the fissure.

Banus turned and grabbed Anaxander from the other side. Together, he and Sif hauled Anaxander in and helped him regain his footing. He stood still for a moment, staring at the hole that had nearly claimed him, then turned his pale, blank face to Sif. If he thanked him, Leah didn't hear it. He may have been incapable of speech at the moment. Either way, Sif offered him a kind nod in return.

Leah let out the breath she'd been holding, waited for her heartbeat to return to a more normal rate, and then continued forward.

Though she could not see the sky above, the path before her opened wider as she went. She rounded a corner and was relieved to find that the crack in the ground came to a close. The path was now open, flat ground from side to side. And the light she'd noticed coming from ahead, she now realized, was daylight.

Soon, a dusting of snow lay on the canyon floor once again. Sunlight peeked in from overhead.

Presently, an echo of a crack-*clang* sounded from behind Leah. She glanced over her shoulder, fearing that someone else had slipped. But the noise was only an echo and sounded very distant. It took her a moment to recall Anaxander's sword, falling over the edge. How much time had passed since it had fallen? Half a minute? A full minute? Her mind harkened back to her mathematical lessons as a girl—*the distance traveled by a falling object equals one-half the time*—but then she decided she didn't want to know the answer.

Turning the next corner, Leah blinked in surprise. The canyon abruptly ended. She stepped forward and found herself outside again, in a secluded glade. High, stony ridges surrounded her on all sides. The glade could not have been more than fifty yards in diameter, allowing enough room for only a few small evergreens. The snow was not quite as deep as it had been on the other side of the canyon, and it did not sparkle here; with such high walls on all sides, she imagined that this place received probably only a couple of hours of direct sunlight a day.

But it was not the high stone ridges that held her attention. Rather, her eyes were set on the wide-open cave mouth on the opposite end of the glade. The cave had a rather uniform shape and appeared to lead deep into the mountains.

The cave was not dark. Rather, emanating from somewhere deep within, seemingly just out of sight, was an emerald green glow, illuminating the interior of the cave as brightly as a fire in a hearth.

"My Lady!" came a loud voice from behind, startling her.

She turned. The rest of her entourage had emerged from the canyon and were similarly transfixed on the glowing green cave ahead of her. And, to her surprise, so was Marcus Worth, whom she had asked to stay behind. A stern look dominated his face.

"Captain?" said Leah. "Is something—?"

"Megara heard something coming from the mountain path. Steeds' hooves, she thinks," said Marcus. "My Lady, someone has followed us here."

CHAPTER 43

Hook looked on as Gunnar scanned the coastal plains with his spyglass. The former humans down below them—or half-humans or half-demons or whatever they were—marched one after another, moving single-mindedly toward the demon ship anchored along the beach. Black and thin and deformed. Like animated, flame-charred skeletons.

"Any cythraul?" asked Adonica, crouched behind the rock.

Hook knew what she was really asking. Were these people prisoners? Captives being forced to march to the ship? Or were they moving of their own free will? So far as Hook could see, there was no sign of any such masters.

"Don't know," said Gunnar. "They're all human-sized, as far as I can tell."

Hook peeked around the rock. The marching creatures had disappeared briefly behind a small copse of trees, then reappeared on the other side, still making their way toward the ship. They walked with purpose, heads bowed, never deviating from their course.

Gunnar turned his spyglass toward the demon ship anchored on the shoreline. "Ah, hell," he said. "Found one."

Hook directed his attention toward the ship. Even with his naked eye, it was easy to see the nine-foot-tall, broad-shouldered frame of a cythraul standing on the deck.

The first cythraul Hook had ever encountered had boarded Gunnar's first ship, the original *Gryphon*, while they'd been sailing through the Drekwood. The monstrosity had been heavy enough to make the entire vessel rock with a single step. This larger demon ship was sturdier and better able to support the beast's weight. Even so, Hook could see a slight tilt to the ship's berth as the cythraul moved. He could see no distinguishing features from here, but the High Demon's posture was clear enough. It stood with arms crossed proudly, watching with satisfaction as the procession marched toward the ship. Like a king surveying his assets.

Converts, concluded Hook. *Turned by the power of the cythraul's touch. Transformed like Justin's arm, but wholly. Robbed of their free will. Robbed of their very humanity, perhaps.*

"Get down!" snapped Gunnar.

Hook did as he was told. Adonica, already crouched behind the boulder, dropped further still.

Gunnar glanced sheepishly from Hook to Adonica. "It looked at me."

"Blast!" said Adonica. "It saw you?"

"*Looked* at me, I said," said Gunnar. "Or toward me. Who the hell knows how well the damn things can see? Maybe it just happened to be glancing this direction."

Hook wasn't sure about their vision, either. Come to think of it, he wasn't sure how their eyesight worked, if it could be called eyesight at all. Cythraul had no eyes to speak of, just empty sockets in their skulls like deep pits that blazed red as if from an unseen source—like an underground fire in a cave, burning somewhere just out of sight. Perhaps what passed for vision in them was something more like extrasensory perception, the way aurym-sensitive individuals could sometimes sense the spirit. Hook did not even pretend to understand such things. But if they could see aurym—the life force of people and living things—then perhaps distance did not hinder their vision.

Making a snap decision, Hook snatched the spyglass out of Gunnar's hand. He offered no explanation for his actions as he crawled out around the inland side of the rock, ducked low, and raced down the hill.

"What in blazes is he—?" Hook heard Gunnar hiss from behind.

"*Hook!*" whispered Adonica.

He moved quickly down the hill, careful to remain behind cover. He hadn't taken the spyglass to use it but to prevent Gunnar from using it. It was easy to forget, sometimes, that Gunnar wasn't a soldier. He had, no doubt, been trained in tactics and military theory, but he still came from nobility. A life of privilege. Perhaps he had never been taught that it wasn't wise to look through a spyglass from a single location for too long at a time. It was possible that its lens had reflected the morning sun, momentarily catching the cythraul's eye—so to speak.

If the cythraul *had* seen them, they needed to return to the steeds and start riding. To put as much distance between them and the ship as possible. But with their current position compromised, it wasn't worth the risk of peeking out to see what was going on. Hook needed to check the enemy's reaction but from a less compromised vantage point. And fast.

When he was a good way downhill from Gunnar and Adonica, Hook paused behind another large rock. He looked back along the hilltop and was relieved that he couldn't see Gunnar or Adonica from here. Slowly, he moved his head horizontally to peek around the rock to look toward the sea.

The cythraul was still standing in the same position and its arms were still crossed, but its head was now slightly upturned, like a great wolf sniffing the air for a scent. From here, Hook could not see the demonic creatures that had been marching across the lowlands. They had disappeared from view entirely. Had the cythraul sent them back? Were they marching through the trees again—?

Suddenly, dark hands emerged from the sea, grabbing the unfurled rope ladders hanging from the sides of the demon ship. Up out of the churning waters, their naked skeletal bodies climbed. Whether the creatures had swum to the ladders or simply walked out across the bottom of the sea, Hook didn't know, but he did know that a dip in that water, on a wind-chilled winter morning like this, would have been a death sentence for any normal man or woman. These things, however, moved as if they did not feel the cold.

One by one, they climbed up and over the side of the ship to stand on the deck before the cythraul. It continued to sniff the air, its head facing the outcropping where Gunnar had been watching it.

When the last of the human-shaped creatures had boarded the ship, the ladders were pulled up. Who the sailors on this vessel were— whether they were humans, coblyns, or something else—Hook couldn't tell from here. Only after the ladders were up did the cythraul finally turn away from the direction of the hilltop. It waved a massive hand. A few seconds later, the anchor was raised, and the ship began to move.

PART V

STARLESS

CHAPTER 44

Leah waited, hardly able to believe what she'd been told. But sure enough, after a few minutes, Megara emerged from the canyon, leading the way into the glade. Behind her came two Cru men supporting a wicker litter between them. And on that litter, wrapped in furs and seated in the same cross-legged position in which Leah had last seen him, was Elder Thid.

Sif and his Cru soldiers brightened at the sight of their head elder, and all hurried to greet him as he was borne into the glade. Lycon Belesys followed, having escorted them from behind. Beside Leah, Marcus Worth could only shake his head in wonder. Megara, meanwhile, distanced herself from the rest and leaned against a rock wall with arms folded and one foot propped against the stone.

Leah gave the Cru a few moments to converse in their own language before she stepped forward. Thid said something that caused the litter-bearers and Sif's warriors to laugh aloud. Then Sif turned to face Leah.

"Elder Thid knew that any suggestion that he join you on this journey would have been discouraged," he explained. "So, out of respect, he waited a full five minutes before departing from the city to follow us."

Leah tried to hide her grin but failed. "Did you know about this, Sif?"

"I did not, Elder Leah," he said, his dark eyes sparkling. "But I am glad for it." One of the litter-bearers said something in the A'cru'u'ol tongue, and Sif translated, "They brought Thid most of the way in an oxen-pulled wagon. They thank us for our effective trailblazing. Carrying Head Elder through the wilderness would have proven challenging, had the underbrush not been so thoroughly cleared ahead of them."

"And I can see that the time it took us to clear the way was sufficient for you to catch up with us," said Leah, smiling at the litter-bearers.

Thid made a gesture with his hand, and the litter-bearers lowered him carefully to the ground. His only open eye, clouded gray, looked up. But it was not looking at Leah. It seemed to be looking past her, toward the green-glowing cave opening at the other side of the glade.

Thid opened his mouth and whispered, "Cy'mor'ri'ka."

A murmur went up among the Cru. Then Thid turned to face Leah.

"That is the proper name," said Thid, "for our Home beneath the mountains."

"*Cymorrika,*" said Leah.

Somehow the word sounded familiar. As if she had heard it in a history lesson or in a fairytale as a child—perhaps named in a story told by one of the traveling bards during festivals in the capital city.

"Welcome home, Elder," she said. "I respectfully insist that you be the first of us to enter. The first of your people to return Home."

Thid nodded, but the tiny movement carried such levity that Leah got the impression he would have bowed with his face to the ground, had his body still been flexible enough to do so.

Sif helped the litter-bearers carry Thid the rest of the way across the glade. But when they were near the cave's entrance, Thid held up a gnarled hand. The Cru stopped.

"Let me try," murmured Thid, "to enter on my own feet."

Leah glanced at Sif questioningly. But Sif did not look at her. He only waited obediently for the head elder's instruction, a look of wonder on his face.

"Will you assist me, Elder Leah?" asked Thid in an airy voice.

"It would be my honor," said Leah.

Thid turned in the direction of Sif. "Please, my son," he said. "Wrap my beard that I may walk."

"Yes, father," choked Sif, and it seemed to Leah that he was suddenly biting back tears.

Son? Father? thought Leah, wondering if she had heard correctly.

Until that moment, she had been unaware of their relationship; neither of these two men had ever indicated as much.

Sif gently repositioned Thid's long beard, draped and folded in his lap, and wrapped it over and around his shoulders like a shawl. When it was done, Thid reached out blindly with one trembling hand, which Leah grasped. His skin was cold. So very, very cold. To venture out in weather like this was dangerous for an ailing man, let alone one who may well have been over a century old.

With a subtle push, Leah called on aurym, channeling it through the healer's ring on her finger and into Thid's body. His skin seemed to warm slightly, and his frail hand squeezed hers in silent gratitude. Aurym-healing was not magic; it could only speed healing, not create it. It could not undo what was already done, nor divert natural processes from their inevitable course. But it could strengthen, and sometimes it could give people a little more time.

With Sif and Ral supporting him from behind and Leah guiding him by the hand from in front, the ancient man unfolded from his seated stance.

"Lead the way, My Queen," said Thid. "We will enter our new Home together."

"This way, Elder," said Leah quietly, but inside, her mind raced.

Our new Home?

Did that mean he had decided? That he would give his blessing and allow the civilians of Cervice to take shelter here?

Sif supported Thid beneath one shoulder, and Ral held him beneath the other. The old man took a step. Then he took another.

As they crossed the threshold into the cave, there was no sound except for the shuffling of Thid's unsteady steps. All around them, a green glow painted the walls, emanating from somewhere ahead, just out of sight. For a few dozen yards, the way continued like this. The ceiling extended higher above them—or was it that they were moving down while the ceiling stayed in place? Leah could not tell.

Soon the way grew wide enough and tall enough that a Raeqlu war elephant could have passed through with ease. Rounding a slight corner, Leah was surprised to find the righthand wall, previously a craggy, uneven stone surface, had transformed into a curvature so perfectly smooth and geometric in shape that it was almost certainly manmade.

The green glow grew brighter as they proceeded, and the curvature extended above their heads like an archway. One of the walls at their sides suddenly ended, replaced by a waist-high banister with polished stone handrails.

Leah moved forward to the edge of the railing. Gently, she guided Thid's hand to rest upon it. His bent, gnarled fingers curled tightly over the banister.

Carefully, Leah leaned to look over the stone railing, and the breath left her lungs. Below her, a long, empty shaft dropped straight down into the earth—down so far that it dizzied her. Indeed, she could not think of any time in her life when she had looked so far *straight down*. The towering minarets of Cervice's palace could have fit inside, stacked end to end multiple times over. The cylindrical shaft was so deep, in fact, that she found herself wondering if its bottom went deeper than the very roots of the mountains. Distance hindered her view of the details far below, but the lighting did not; there was no lack of that. For partway down the shaft, the walls were lit by a brilliant, jade-green light. Leah had seen this sort of light before, at work in a cavern during her first trip through the Shifting Mountains. Cat's eye, or a'thri'ik, was as dull as any ordinary river stone in the presence of sunlight, but in sunlight's absence, it put forth a brilliant glow.

The place where Leah and Thid stood, she now realized, was a balcony marking the beginning of a path that wound its way downward, like the coils of a spring along the inner walls of the shaft. The a'thri'ik stone in the walls followed alongside the path, taking the forms of flowing, intricate patterns and runes in some places, and artistic designs in others. It was clear that they had been set in the walls to provide light to this place while also serving as a form of artwork. Even from here, she could see, at the bottom-center of the shaft far below, a mass of green light—a solid block of a'thri'ik, as big as a cathedral.

Remembering that Thid didn't have the benefit of her acute eyesight, Leah turned to him and said, "It's. . . . I can't even describe it." Gently, she squeezed Thid's shoulder. "We've found it, Elder."

Thid ran his free hand lovingly over the stone banister. His jaw quivered, and he said, "Home."

CHAPTER 45

"I guess my biggest question," said Benjamin, after a long silence, "is why you would come home."

Justin made a face, caught off guard by the suddenness—and the bluntness—of his father's words.

"This time, I mean," clarified Benjamin. "You returned to Earth once and decided to go back. So why did you leave the Oikoumene this time?"

Justin cleared his throat. "Well, I've been shown and told a lot of things. By Zechariah. By Ahlund. By Cyaxares. . . . And by Avagad. I don't know what, or how much of it, to believe anymore. So I came back to learn the truth from the only person who knows the whole truth, and the only person I can really trust."

"And you have it now, for better or worse," said Benjamin. "So, what are you going to do with it?"

Justin only sighed.

Benjamin turned his back and took a few steps toward the entrance of his rock shelter. Then he paused. "I'm going to say what needs to be said, as long as you won't judge me for it," said Benjamin.

Justin waited.

Benjamin turned back around to face him. "You don't have to go back. Ever."

Justin blinked in surprise.

"Let's look at this thing objectively," said Benjamin. "If you go back, maybe you help your friends—Leah, Gunnar, and the rest—to win their war. Maybe you defeat the demons. Maybe you achieve *everything* you've set out to accomplish. But now that you have what you came here for, the full story, you know that winning the war doesn't really mean you've won. You'll only have delayed the inevitable. Time will pass, and the demons will come back again, just as they did both times *I* beat them. The same scenario will repeat itself. Your work will be undone, and all your sacrifices, like mine, will have been for nothing. Maybe that's the true reality of all sacrifices in the long run, but most men don't live long enough to see it happen. I have. And I don't want you to have to go through that. Or to die in a fight that you could have just walked away from."

"Walked away from?" said Justin. "As in, leave the Oikoumene and everyone in it? Forget about them and pretend none of this ever happened?"

"Pretty much," said Benjamin.

Justin hoped the disappointment didn't show on his face. The course of action his father was suggesting sounded an awful lot like giving up. Like a coward's way out.

"Don't forget," said Benjamin, "you haven't seen what I've seen. We're not talking about a fight to be won or lost. We're talking about a cycle that will repeat itself, with or without you—and with or without your sacrifices. It's just the reality of the Oikoumene. And by inserting yourself in it, all you're doing is endangering your own life."

"And maybe saving the lives of my friends," protested Justin.

"Maybe." Benjamin shrugged. "We just need to be realistic here, Justin. If you go back, you'll be on an island somewhere in the Raedittean, probably with the demons not far behind you. A gauge stone can allow you to travel between worlds, but no one has the power to fly over oceans or hop across continents. You'll be on the run. You don't know where any of your friends are, and you have no way of getting there even if you did. You may never be able to find them. But the Nameless One *will* find you."

Benjamin let the thought sink in for a moment before adding, "*If* you go back."

Again, Justin turned away. His hands were balled into fists. At that moment, he hated his father for putting an idea like that in his head. But he hated himself even more for considering it.

Justin let out a long, slow breath, closing his eyes. "You're right."

"Huh?" said Benjamin, as if he were unsure he'd heard Justin correctly.

"You're right that I can't win the war forever," said Justin. He turned back to face his father. "But maybe *we* could."

CHAPTER 46

Benjamin stared at Justin. Slowly, deliberately, he pushed his glasses up the bridge of his nose and said, "Why would you say that?"

"We were able to come here, together, using one gauge stone under my power, alone," said Justin. "Dad, that means we could both go to the Oikoumene. If one 'fallen angel' can drive back the demons from the Oikoumene, imagine what two could do. We could work together."

"The Nameless One cut me off from aurym, remember?" said Benjamin.

"But maybe there's a way to undo it. Zechariah will know a way, I bet. By working together, we could beat the demons, *permanently* this time! Win the war and not just the battle—!"

"No," said Benjamin. "Out of the question, and I wish you hadn't brought it up."

Justin squinted at his father, surprised. "What do you—?"

"You actually want me to *return* to the Oikoumene?" Benjamin snapped. "Where daemyn's hold on me was at its strongest? So strong that I couldn't even control myself? You want me to become a *slave* again?"

Justin was taken aback. "Dad, no, of course not. You're stronger now. You wouldn't do that sort of thing again."

"You don't know that."

"I'd be there to help you. You and I could—"

"*Please!*" Benjamin shouted.

The air distorted around Benjamin like heat shimmering over a highway. Justin blinked, confused to find himself rocking on his heels, several steps further from his father than he had been a moment before. Benjamin hadn't moved, Justin was sure of it. No, it was *he* who had moved, though he hardly remembered it happening. It felt as if an invisible hand had shoved him. And that voice. His father's voice hadn't sounded like his own. Instead, it sounded as if it had been multiplied into a legion of voices speaking as one, raised to many times normal volume. Now Benjamin stood with shoulders heaving, staring at the ground.

After a few moments and what seemed like a great effort, Benjamin let out a long breath and whispered, "I know you want to help your friends. So did I. But of all the friends I made in that place, *all* of them died. Every. Last. One of them. Some went the way your friend Ahlund did. For others, it was even worse. Most were my fault, and some. . . . Some died by my own hand. Cut off from aurym, I had no defense against the darkness, and I did things that I would never do because it wasn't me doing them. Imagine what happened to Ahlund happening again, except this time, it's *you* doing it. You're trapped inside your body, powerless to stop yourself, unable to even close your eyes to block out the sight of what you're doing to your friends." He looked up at Justin. "And you want me to go back there?"

"It'll be different," said Justin. "You'll have me to help you this time."

Justin expected such loving determination to be met with pride. Or a smile, at the very least. Instead, his father's face was blank.

"Don't you think I could help you, Dad?" Justin asked, almost pleadingly.

"No," said Benjamin.

Justin felt as if a cold needle had pierced his chest. It was the kind of wound only a very dear loved one can give, one that is deep and permanent and, even if someday forgiven, can never be taken back, nor forgotten. His father's utter lack of faith in him was more heartbreaking than Justin could have anticipated.

Benjamin's stern expression broke, as if he suddenly realized what he'd just said. "I didn't mean. . . . It's not because I doubt what you're capable of, Justin. It's because I know what *I'm* capable of. You don't— I can't go back there, and that's all there is to it. And I'm telling you, you don't have to either. We can go back to Earth together. I know it seems impossible to fathom now, but all you need to do is walk upstairs to your bedroom, lie down, close your eyes, and go to sleep. By the time you wake up in the morning, hundreds of years will have passed in the Oikoumene. Just like that, it'll all be over."

"Just like that, huh?" mocked Justin, anger flaring in him. "For me, maybe, but not for them, Dad. You're trying to make me abandon them."

"If I were trying to *make* you do anything," said Benjamin, "I wouldn't have gone through all this trouble to give you the choice."

"Forgive me for not being *grateful* for being given a choice in the matter. What am I supposed to say? You're trying to make me sacrifice my own friends—!"

"I'm *trying* to save my son!" Benjamin yelled.

Justin froze, startled by the outburst. There was nothing unnatural about his father's voice this time. Still, it was so unlike his father to shout like this that the result was no less surprising.

Silence hung in the air for several long seconds. Finally, Benjamin stepped toward Justin with teeth clenched and tears welling in his eyes.

"I'm trying," said Benjamin, his voice unsteady, "to save the only thing I have left in this world. A person whom I desperately love and would do anything for. My son. I would sacrifice anything for that."

Justin looked hard at his father. "Even a world?" he asked.

A tear broke from behind the chipped left lens of Benjamin's eyeglasses, but he set his jaw and stood straight. "In a heartbeat."

CHAPTER 47

Moments passed. It could have been an hour or maybe just a handful of heartbeats; it was hard to tell in the Kharon, a place where time had only a tenuous hold.

Neither said a word. At some point, Benjamin turned and walked away. He took a seat on the gray log outside his makeshift rock shelter, and there, he sat alone, his back to Justin, saying nothing.

He didn't ask me, Justin realized, staring at his father's back from a distance. *He didn't actually ask me not to go back. Not really.*

He doesn't think I can do it. But if he really didn't believe in me, he could have lied to get his way. Could have tricked me into waiting around long enough for time to have passed in the Oikoumene. Or he could have forced me not to go back. He had my gauge stone in his hand, after all. He could have thrown it out the front door or tossed it down the drain or something. But he didn't. Why didn't he?

Finally, Justin spoke.

"Do you remember that time we helped Grandpa Holmes clean up the church?" he said.

Benjamin turned and looked back at him, making a strange face. "Yeah." He smiled a little, then shook his head in surprise. "Can't believe *you* remember that, though. You couldn't have been much older than three or four, though I guess that's plenty old enough to remember, now that I think about it." His expression changed, as if a thought had suddenly occurred to him. "How much of that *do* you remember?"

"I remember an old lady crying," said Justin. "Not really crying, though. More like just dabbing the edges of her eyes with a handful of tissues. Like, trying not to cry.

"I remember that the whole place smelled like how the bowling alley used to smell back when people were allowed to smoke there, but with a little bit of a bonfire smell, too. I remember Grandpa gathering up Bible pages from the floor, and a lot of them were scorched, and the carpet had black streaks in it. I remember asking Mom where you were, and she said, 'Outside.' And when I went and looked out through one of the broken windows—the stained glass one of Jesus on the Mount—I saw you helping some other people lift up one of the headstones that had been overturned."

Benjamin swallowed hard, his face wracked with guilt. "I guess we maybe shouldn't have taken you."

"You said that at the time," Justin cut in. "You said that exact thing to Mom. I heard you whisper it to her as soon as we got there. She said, 'Maybe. But there was no way you could have known it was going to be this bad.' You asked if she thought you should take me home. But she said that since we were already there, we should help.

"There were some broken glass bottles on the altar and on the organ. I remember how they'd rolled out a whole thing of paper towels down the center aisle and lit the end, probably thinking it would burn up all the Bible pages they'd ripped out and catch the whole place on fire. It only burned a little bit of the paper, though, and some of the carpet."

"Jeez," Benjamin said again. "You were too young to have had to see that, Justin."

"It's not like it traumatized me or something," said Justin, almost laughing. "To me, it was pretty uncomplicated. All I remember thinking at the time was that 'bad guys' did this, and they would go to jail for it, simple as that." He paused. "The one detail that I remember most, though, is Mom helping the church ladies clean the writing off the back wall. I couldn't read yet, but I remember that the words were written in bright, *bright* red. To this day, I wonder what they were written in—just red paint, probably—but I remember, even then, thinking that it looked like blood. And you know how everything always seems bigger when you're a kid? Well, those words seem huge in my memory. Impossibly huge. Way bigger than anything that could fit on the wall of a tiny, backwoods church. I never would have known what the words said, except that I overheard one of the church ladies talking to the pastor. That's how I learned what the words said."

Justin hesitated for a moment. "Do you remember what the words said, Dad?"

Benjamin only nodded.

Justin nodded back. But he didn't say the words. He wondered if they were emblazoned in his father's mind, too, as they had been in his mind for all those years: those impossibly huge words, spelled out in sloppy, streaked letters that looked like smeared blood: BURN THE SHEEP.

Benjamin squeezed his eyes shut and shook his head in regret. "I had no idea you remembered so much of that. We never should have taken you there that day, but we didn't know. All we were told was that the place had been vandalized, so we offered to help clean up. We brought you along without really thinking about it. If I'd known the extent of what they'd done, I wouldn't have—"

"No," said Justin. "Actually, I think it was good for me to see that, in a way."

It had been so long ago. And while it was true that the events hadn't traumatized him, he couldn't deny that his memories of that day were quite stark. He remembered hearing the church ladies offering guesses at who had done it—"those teenagers who broke into the Whites' place last summer?" "No, it would take grown men to flip a headstone, don't you think?" But to Justin, the answer had been simple. It was just bad guys. Bad guys like in a movie or a cartoon. The mustache-twirling kind. He'd known it had been "bad guys" with the sort of certainty that was only possible through the black-and-white morality of a four-year-old. And he also remembered that when someone had mentioned the issue of the culprits' identities to his mother, she had surprised him by replying that it didn't matter who they were. Then his father had joined the conversation. He had agreed, adding that not only did it not matter *who* they were, but it didn't even matter *why* they had done it.

In those days, his dad had seemed impossibly big—way bigger than the words on any wall. Almost superhuman in Justin's four-year-old eyes. Bigger than the strongest man in the world. To this day, he remembered the look on his dad's face as he'd looked down at him.

"All that matters," Dad had said, placing a huge hand on his son's little shoulder, "is what we can do to help right now."

"Do you think the bad guys will come back?" Justin had asked his parents later, during the drive home.

"I don't think so," Mom had said.

But Dad, who normally agreed with Mom on everything—especially in front of Justin—had uncharacteristically tilted his head, showing a hint of doubt. "Well, they might," he had said. "And what do you think we should do if they do come back?"

In his booster seat in the back of the car, Justin hadn't even needed to think about it. He had replied, "Help again, right?"

Dad had nodded and said, "Right answer."

In the present, Justin looked at his father, seated on the log before him, head hanging and shoulders tense. No longer did he seem like the strongest, biggest man in the world. Justin was bigger than he was, for a start. In a way, that cold needle to the chest—that terrible wound dealt by his father's lack of faith in him—had driven away any last vestiges of the old illusion. It was as if he was seeing his father for the first time. Seeing him not as Dad, but as a person. As a man. And what was a man, really, but a grown-up boy? Same as Justin. Benjamin was so scared of losing someone he loved that he was acting selfish, willing to put people he didn't even know in terrible danger, and to turn a blind eye to the consequences.

"You know I have to go back, Dad," said Justin.

Benjamin didn't seem caught off guard by this. His melancholy expression, if it changed at all, only deepened, almost as if he felt sick to his stomach.

"You're sure?" Benjamin prodded after a few moments.

There was a brief moment when Justin felt compelled to explain himself. To defend his decision. But then he decided not to.

"Yeah," he said.

Seemingly out of nowhere, a wide grin split Benjamin's face. "Eh, I knew you would," he said, as if the whole thing had been a foregone conclusion. "Gotta learn the hard way every time, like your dad."

Relief washed over Justin at seeing a bit of the old father he knew shining through. He couldn't help but smile.

"Well," said Benjamin, standing up from the log, "in that case, there's something I should probably show you. Let's go for a little walk. I rarely get the chance these days."

CHAPTER 48

"Sorry, girls," said Adonica, "but we can't leave you out in the open where you could be spotted."

Hook watched the countryside behind them as Adonica led the three steeds in through the doorway of the ruins. The animals tossed their heads in discomfort at the darkness of the interior but followed Adonica's lead obediently. They were already panting and huffing, having been pushed to travel at a steady gallop all the way from the hillside and across the lowlands. Now, all Hook, Gunnar, and Adonica could do was hope the demons didn't come ashore and start searching for their tracks. If they did, it would not be difficult to track them here.

There was only one doorway to these ruins so far as they had been able to see, and it was on the land-side. Even here, however, the tunnel leading inward was flooded several inches deep with cold seawater.

"What do you guys think?" asked Gunnar. "Camp here and observe the change in water level with the tide? Or should we head on in quick-smart?"

"Might as well scout ahead as far as we can," signed Hook.

Adonica found an iron bar sticking out of the wall—perhaps a sconce for a torch at some time long ago but now rusted beyond recognition—and tied a length of rope to it, which she fed through the steeds' reins and tied fast.

Adonica's steed, a dapple gray named Ash, snorted and swung her trunk at Adonica in annoyance. Adonica caught the slap before it could land and flashed the steed a smile. She gently lowered its trunk, scolding the creature with a tsk-tsk sound. After Adonica walked away, Hook crossed to Ash and placed a comforting hand atop her head. She was quivering, clearly unnerved by being pushed so hard across the lowlands only to arrive in this dark and forbidding place. Hook scratched the velvety spot between Ash's eyes with the pad of his thumb, and she leaned into it. Seeing the attention Ash was getting, Hook's steed—a fine, big black mare named Stormbringer who'd been with him since Hartla—turned and looked at Hook as if demanding to know just what the hell he thought he was doing. With his other hand, he scratched her between the eyes, too. No sooner had he done so than Gunnar's steed, a fine chestnut with a flaxen tail called Thirsty, tried to push her way between the other two. Gunnar wasn't used to riding steeds and didn't always pay her the attention she was due. Thirsty reached for Hook with her prehensile trunk and grasped his forearm for comfort, like a child gripping a parent's hand. Hook patted Thirsty reassuringly, and the creature let out a sigh of relief through the end of her trunk.

Hook thought it a shame that steeds so often went unappreciated. They were fine animals—as intelligent as dogs at least, and just as loyal, playful, and keen to develop strong bonds with individual humans. Hook and Stormbringer had been through a lot together. She had been gifted to him from Hartla's stables, where the stableboys had warned him that she required a firm hand. Hook, however, had found the opposite to be true. All she'd needed was attention, patience, and a bit of play now and again.

Hook went back to the corridor entrance to peek back the way they'd come. His view of the hillside from here was not entirely clear, but there didn't appear to be anyone following them. Not yet, at least.

"Damn, this water is freezing," said Adonica. She had stooped to test it with her hand. "If it gets high enough to go over our boots, we're liable to catch our death of cold. Can't even build a fire with demons about or we'll be seen."

"In this weather, we'll have no choice but to build one eventually," said Gunnar. "But hopefully we can hold off until we're sure that ship is gone."

A gust of wind came whipping in from outside, producing a noise like the long, low hoot of an owl as it blew down the tunnel. It made ripples in the standing water at Hook's feet.

"Keelhaul this weather!" said Adonica, rubbing at her arms to fight the wind slicing through her.

"Keelhaul everything," Gunnar grumbled. He adjusted his eyepatch, blinking as if it pained him. "Never should've left the damn Brig. Sure, a cythraul might've blown it to bits someday, but at least I'd have died happy and unaware, passed out dead-drunk, nuzzled in the unfaithful arms of a fisherman's wife or two."

"You seem even more deluded than usual lately," said Adonica. "I can't tell if you're trying to impress us or if it's just how you comfort yourself when everything goes to dog shite."

"I wouldn't think too much into it, Miss Lor," Gunnar replied without missing a beat. "I say things just to say them and don't even remember half of what I say, let alone why."

Hook reached into his satchel and fumbled about until he found what he was looking for. He whistled between his teeth to get Gunnar's attention, then handed it to him: a small stone.

Gunnar looked at it. "Is this a gauge?"

Hook nodded. *I asked the old man if we could borrow it.*

"Good, we can leave our lanterns behind," said Adonica.

"As long as I can remember how to use one of these things," said Gunnar. "By the seas, I haven't used one since I was a kid. Brings back memories. Not very good ones either, if truth be told."

Gunnar turned toward the darkness of the corridor leading deeper into the ruins, where the sloshing of the seawater against unseen walls and who-knew-what else could be heard echoing toward them.

"Well," he said, raising the gauge stone in one hand and drawing his cutlass from its sheath with another, "last one in is dimetrodile gall."

CHAPTER 49

At first, nothing happened.

The pause was long enough that Hook worried that Gunnar couldn't power the gauge. During their journey beneath the Shifting Mountains, Zechariah had used this stone to illuminate their surroundings with a cool blue glow to light the way, rendering torches unnecessary. He'd assumed Gunnar would be able to do the same.

Finally, a light appeared in Gunnar's hand. It started as a dim glow no brighter than a firefly on a summer's eve. Then it got gradually brighter. To Hook's surprise, it was not blue like it had been in the old man's hand. Instead, it was a rich yellow color—a bit like the outer rind of a kind of hanging fruit Hook had once seen on an island in the Raedittean.

The reminder summoned unwelcome memories. That had been just after he'd escaped from slavery—the first time. He'd never learned what those fruits were called, but they'd been soft and easy to eat, even without a tongue.

Hook forced himself to breathe evenly as Gunnar raised the stone to illuminate the path before them. The dark tunnel extended forward as far as the stone's light could reach. There were doorway-sized recesses set in the walls, and Hook wondered if they were adjoining hallways, alcoves, or something else. One thing was certain. The waterline was at a distinctly different angle than the rows of stacked stones in the walls. It was clear that the tunnel extended forward at a downward angle. And ahead, the gap between the water level and the ceiling was noticeably narrower. It was just as Hook had feared. Not only were these tunnels flooded, but they extended downward. The water was going to get deeper. Possibly a great deal deeper.

Hook suppressed a shiver that had nothing to do with the cold.

Water, he thought bitterly. *No matter where I go, I somehow end up thrown back in the drink.*

As the three of them strode forward, Hook felt a subtle, rhythmic push and pull of the water lapping against his ankles. The inward-outward flow of the ocean's waves. The sea, breathing. He wondered if his suspicions were correct—that so many generations had passed since the construction of this place that the level of the sea had changed during that time. Or perhaps eons of waves had simply eaten away at the shoreline, causing the ocean to encroach on a previously landlocked location. Whatever the case, its inward-outward movement against his feet confirmed that these waters were an extension of the ocean and didn't originate from a separate source. And that meant the level would rise and fall with the tide.

"You said you hadn't used one of those since you were a kid," said Adonica, her voice echoing through the tunnel. "I always wondered, how do you spirit-user types come about the learning of your skills, anyway?"

"What do you mean?" said Gunnar.

"Just never understood that part of it," said Adonica. "The only aurym I'd ever seen until recently was the healing skill. Like Lycon uses. The talent is passed down in the blood, they say. If someone's mother or father was a healer, they go off for training. Some of them learn how to use the talent, but others never do. But that's healing—how in the bleeding hell did you learn you could grow flowers without water or soil?"

Hook had wondered the same thing. He didn't possess a great deal of understanding about aurym. Like Adonica, Hook had only ever met a few aurym-users, most of whom had been healers like Leah, prior to meeting Zechariah, Gunnar, and Justin.

And Jocasta, he reminded himself.

Or so she'd said, anyway. He'd never gotten the chance to see it.

Hook's hand drifted up to stroke the fabric of the strip of cloth tied over his lifeslave's brand.

"I learned the same way, really," Gunnar answered. "The old Mythaean High King had aurym talent—the ability to turn a lump of stone into a gold ingot, some say, though I don't know if that's really true. Some but not all of Mythaean noble blood carry aurym talent in them. Offspring of the Nimbus line, in particular, are predisposed toward *y'du'ra*."

"Toward what?" said Adonica.

"It's the name of the stone that holds the plant-growing talent," said Gunnar. "Also called godsbreath. It's mined in the north of Darsida. I learned its use from my uncle." He hesitated a moment, then added, "My father didn't have the talent. My uncle used a gauge stone to determine whether Yordar or I possessed aurym potential when we were boys. I managed to make the stone light. Yordar did not. It was the first time I saw Yordar get angry. Truly angry, I mean. I *thought* I'd seen him get angry before, but it turned out, I hadn't seen anything."

Hook suppressed a grimace as the water got high enough to pour in over the tops of his boots, quickly filling them with frigid seawater. His toes were already partially numb. He made a mental note to pay close attention to that. They would all have to monitor their body temperatures carefully. A fire's ability to warm a freezing body was only as effective as that body's ability to build a fire in the first place. If their hands went numb, or if one of them lost consciousness before they could make it back to the entrance, it could mark the beginning of a slow, quiet death. Perhaps for all of them.

"I didn't develop my true talent until after I left the Thalassocracy," said Gunnar. "If I'd done so earlier, I probably would have been relegated to city gardener like I am back in Cervice—to grow a harvest's worth of wheat and grain in an afternoon and keep it up every day. Or to make us rich with an endless supply of sugarcane for trade. If only

Yordar could have seen the more creative uses I've developed!" Gunnar laughed a little at this but came up short, shifting his gauge to light a portion of the wall. "Hey, look here. Tide must be going out."

Hook moved forward to take a look and concluded the same. About half an inch above the current waterline, the wall was damp. The level appeared to be dropping slightly.

"With any luck, we'll be able to follow the tide as it goes down, and get in and out without our arses getting wet," said Adonica.

"I've spent the better half of my life on the water," said Gunnar, "but I've had nothing but negative associations with it of late. Let's hope this isn't another one."

Hook rolled his eyes. The gall of Mythaean royalty to complain about negative associations with *water*.

Gunnar had never owned slaves; Hook had to constantly remind himself of that. But the man was still a product of a life of privilege—a noble son born of an empire built on the backs of enslaved people like Hook and Megara, sentenced to row and row until they died in the bowels of ships like the *Manticore* and the *Lion of the Sky.*

The *Lion of the Sky* was the name of the ship that Megara said she'd been enslaved on. But something about that name struck Hook as wrong. It was not uncommon for Mythaean ships to be named after beasts, real and imagined alike, but most were single-word names. The *Dragon*, the *Wyrm*, the *Serpent*, the *Manticore*, the *Gryphon*—

Hook froze in mid-step.

The gryphon. A mythological creature with the body of a lion, and the head, front legs, and wings of an eagle.

A lion of the sky.

Hook's dark eyes narrowed on the back of Gunnar's head. Quietly, he continued into the tomb, following him.

CHAPTER 50

As Adonica had predicted, the tide continued to recede as they went deeper into the ruins. Still, they were waist-deep in it now, and Hook was having a hard time feeling his feet.

Everything about this place unnerved him. The tight confines. The water itself. Even the sound of the constant, irregular sloshing got under one's skin. Back at the entrance, it had sounded like water under a bridge. But now that they were deep in the ruins, the water made sounds that were somehow both muffled and unnaturally loud all at once. It sounded like they were inside the mouth of a giant who was rinsing his teeth. And while the theory of following the tide's recession made sense, Hook wasn't at all convinced by Adonica's assertion that they would have plenty of time to return to the entrance when it came back in. In waist-high water, the fastest pace that one could hope to achieve was that of a slow walk. In water any higher than that, speed was further reduced. And if they had to *swim* through freezing-cold water, fatigue would set in fast.

The yellow light of Gunnar's gauge stone showed that the waterline along the wall, which had previously been a damp band down at their feet, now made up almost the entire wall. The only dry stones were those along the very top of the wall: a thin strip just below the ceiling. Which meant that this tunnel would flood almost completely when the tide came back in, leaving only a few inches between the water and the ceiling.

Hook's mind flashed with an image of himself frantically treading water to stay afloat. Just enough clearance to keep his nose and mouth above the surface. Lips grazing the roof of the tunnel as he tried to suck in gulps of damp air, spoonfuls of seawater coming in with each breath—

Hook stopped walking. He steadied himself against the wall, trying to ignore the trembling of his own hand. He took a deep breath. A breath of thick, stagnant, wet air.

In an instant, he was back. Inches between the rising water and the roof above him. Men wailing for their mothers. Bodies all around him, some flapping their arms desperately, others already lifeless below the surface, anchored down by the same sets of chains that held Hook to his seat, pulling him steadily down as the water came steadily up. Knowing he had only a few seconds to suck in what would be his last breath. Wondering what drowning would feel like.

A moment too late, Hook realized that his breathing had gotten too loud and too fast. It had drawn Adonica's attention.

She turned and cocked an eyebrow at him. "What's your problem?" she asked.

He raised one hand and signed slowly and deliberately so that she would understand, *"I do not like water."*

"Can't you swim?" she asked.

Instead of replying, Hook turned and stared at the back of Gunnar's head again. The admiral wore a bandana to tie back his long, curly black hair. But it wasn't a bandana. It was the flag from the original *Gryphon*, which he had carried with him ever since it had sunk on the Greenspring River.

Lion of the Sky.

Hook turned back to Adonica and repeated the same signs. *"I do not like water."*

Adonica took an exaggerated look around. "You came to the wrong place, pal."

He closed his eyes to block her out, doing his best to steady his breathing. His body was already working overtime to keep itself warm in these conditions. He didn't need the additional stress of reliving past horrors.

"I won't say anything to the admiral if you turn tail," said Adonica. "If it makes you feel any better, I'm sure the tide won't come gushing in here all at once. And, at any rate, we're more likely to freeze to death than to drown."

Hook signed, *"Thanks."*

"I think we're coming up on the main chamber!" came Gunnar's voice, calling back down the tunnel.

Hook breathed a sigh of relief. It wouldn't be much longer now. At least, he hoped not.

Adonica turned to him. "Now or never, mate," she said. "You coming?"

Hook walked past her and proceeded on down the tunnel.

The tide, the cold, and the prospect of making it back out of this place—he forced all of it to the back of his mind and locked it there. Analyzing a situation could save your life, but overanalyzing one could distract you and compromise your awareness. Sometimes, it was just best not to think so much.

"Oh, yeah!" confirmed Gunnar from up ahead, visible only as a silhouette cast by the yellow light of his gauge stone. "There's definitely a larger chamber here. Maybe the burial area the old man told us about. Just have to find the—"

All at once, Gunnar's light shifted wildly. There was a dull *plop* sound—the distinctive sound of a stone hitting the water—and all light went out, plunging the tunnel into blackness.

"Um," Gunnar said from somewhere up ahead. "Oops."

CHAPTER 51

The only consistent thing about the a'thri'ik patterns on the walls was their intricacy. The designs ranged from geometric patterns to the runes of forgotten languages to landscapes featuring animals the likes of which Leah had never seen before.

The wall presently to Leah's left was a glowing panorama of mythological creatures doing battle: anthropomorphic deities rode enormous lizards, charging at club-wielding cyclopes who sat astride massive, long-necked indricoths.

Leah ran her finger along one of the lines of cat's eye stone used to create the images. It was the outline of a large foot—the bottom of an image depicting a cyclops pulling a tree out of the ground. The creature stood at least fifteen feet tall—three times as tall as Leah. Its single, glowing green eye seemed to be looking straight down at her. She would have to remember to take a few samples of cat's eye stone from somewhere in these caves before she departed. Prior to seeing Justin use this type of stone—with deadly effectiveness—she hadn't even been aware that a'thri'ik was an aurstone. Maybe someone else among them would be able to use it, if not as effectively.

Leah had sent Anaxander and Banus down this twisting path to scout the lower levels. But over an hour had passed since then, and Anaxander and Banus still had not returned. Thinking back to the giant scorpion-spiders that had assailed their group the last time she'd been beneath these mountains, she wondered if it had been a deadly mistake to send them ahead.

Right is right, rang her father's words in her head. *If you can remember that, you have all you need to lead.*

A fine saying, in theory, thought Leah. *But when it comes to commanding soldiers and armies, it's a bit more complicated than that, Father.*

Marcus and Lycon flanked Leah as they walked, while the Cru soldiers—Sif, Ral, Vox, Tel, Enn, and Wit—led the way. Bringing up the rear was the silent, hulking form of Megara.

Leah glanced back at the Rorrdvuuk woman. She returned the glance with a blank expression. In the green glow from the walls, the interlocking triangles and circles of the tattoos on her face looked darker than usual. And the long, angry scar across her forehead stood out all the more.

"This place is more extensive than I ever would have imagined," said Lycon. "To call it an underground city is perhaps not an exaggeration."

"So close to Nolia's borders," said Marcus Worth, "yet undiscovered, unknown all this time."

"The Cru knew of it," said Leah. "They just did not know the way."

At the front of the procession, neither Sif nor any of the other Cru warriors offered any comment. Leah wondered how they felt about the idea of potentially opening up their ancestral home to outsiders. Was it up to the head elder to make the decision uniformly? Or would the point be deliberated among the rest of the council? And how much did they know about the true origins of the map and Zechariah's involvement in its discovery?

Thid will not be their head elder forever, thought Leah. *Perhaps not even very much longer. The sentiments of their council may shift once he is gone.*

"Perhaps it is too much to hope for," said Lycon in a whisper, apparently hoping that the Cru could not hear him, "but there are civilians in Castydociana who are also at great risk. Perhaps the refugees of Hartla and other Mythaean city-states could find sanctuary here."

"Perhaps," was all Leah said.

Megara stopped walking.

As the others continued forward, Leah turned to face Megara, realizing that the tall, broad-shouldered woman had her hands clutched into fists. Her eyes blazed.

Leah caught Megara's gaze and attempted to communicate a questioning look. But rather than respond, Megara scowled and turned away.

Leah turned to continue forward, then stopped again. After a moment's hesitation, she turned and walked back to Megara.

"My Queen?" asked Sif from the front.

"Keep going, please," said Leah. "All of you, please. I'll catch up." To her relief, she did not have to give the command a second time.

Megara still had her back turned, her fists hovering to either side of her. Cautiously, Leah stepped in front of her.

"Something wrong?" Leah signed.

With some effort, Megara unclenched her fists. *"No,"* she signed back. A lie.

Leah gave her a few seconds, then signed back, *"I trust that if something is wrong, you will let me know."*

Leah had begun to turn away when Megara suddenly grabbed her by the shoulder and forcibly turned her around to face her—so fast and hard that Leah might have been thrown to the floor if not for Megara's tight grip on her, holding her fast.

Leah looked up in alarm at the huge warrior, trying not to wince at the force of her grip on her shoulder.

For a moment, Megara only stared down at her, grim-faced and wild-eyed. Her grip on Leah's shoulder loosened, though she still did not let go. Slowly, she bent her great frame down until her face was inches from Leah's. Then Megara raised one finger and pointed to the place where her slave's brand, a raised, whitish-pink band of scar tissue, ran in a perfectly horizontal path across her forehead. From this close, Leah could see that the brand had been burned overtop of the tattoos on her forehead. She noted the way the otherwise perfect, blue-inked lines were distorted on the edges of the scar tissue.

Megara pointed silently at the scar for a moment. Then she pointed ahead. At Lycon.

"There's no need to worry about that," Leah whispered, though she wondered if she ought instead to cry out for help. "You are one of us now. Part of the Athacean League. Anyone who would dare say otherwise would have to answer to—"

Megara's grip on her shoulder retightened, and this time, Leah could not help wincing. A moment too late, Leah realized her mistake.

Megara tapped her finger hard against her scar. *"You condone this?"* she signed.

"No, I—" Leah began to say, but she was cut off by a grunt from Megara's throat—a warning to say no more.

"I can see to my own safety," signed Megara. *"What about the safety of others? Those who yet labor in the bellies of Mythaean ships, with festering lash wounds?"*

Leah's nostrils flared. "Neither I nor my people have ever engaged in such practices," she said in a whisper. "And I certainly don't condone them."

"Perhaps you do not hold the whip," signed Megara. *"Perhaps you did not lock the chains. Perhaps you do not wield the knife to cut out our tongues. But if you are allied with the men and women who do, and benefit from the bloodstained riches it brings them, then your guilt is no less."*

"Some of the Mythaean city-states in the League hold slaves, but Lycon is from Hartla!" Leah protested under her breath. "They do not practice slavery!"

"Others in your League do," signed Megara. Slowly, she pointed to her own forehead again, forcing Leah to focus on the scar. Then she signed phonetically: *"Nimbus."*

For a moment, Leah couldn't breathe. "What. . . ?" she said.

Megara only tapped her scar again.

Leah swallowed hard. She opened her mouth to say something, but Megara's face suddenly changed. She raised a single finger to her lips, and her eyes went distant. Then Leah heard something too.

Leah turned toward the rest of the group, now well ahead of them on the path. "Halt," she commanded.

The group stopped walking. For a moment, the sound of their footfalls against the stone walkway echoed on, up and down the empty shaft. Then everything faded away to be replaced by silence.

Or almost silence.

An echo floated up from the bottom of the shaft, still very far below their current location. It was a voice.

"My *Queen*—!" it said, and then was cut off with a pained cry.

Leah pushed back her cloak and drew the saber from the sheath at her belt. To proceed with caution would have been the wisest choice, but Anaxander and Banus were in trouble down there.

"Follow me!" she commanded, and she took off running.

"We do not know what's down there," said Sif calmly.

"Wait!" said Marcus, reaching for Leah as she bolted past him.

"My Lady!" objected Lycon.

But Leah slipped past them all, sprinting ahead of them. Soon, she realized she was not running alone. Sif was sprinting alongside her. And there, running on her other side, was Megara. The others hurried after, trying to keep up.

CHAPTER 52

With her saber drawn and at the ready, Leah raced down the coiling decline of the path leading deeper into the underground city of Cymorrika. Sif and Megara were at her sides, and the clamor of footfalls from behind told her that the others were following her lead.

Passing beneath an a'thri'ik pattern in the wall—an outline of the constellation Yaress and its connecting point with the Wolf's Paw—it shamed her to realize that she hadn't even known Anaxander or Banus by name until a few days prior. Both were Nolians, both members of the High Guard, both tasked with dying for her if duty called for it. Yet she barely knew them. There were so many people to keep track of. So many people relying on her. Above all else, she longed to protect and save them all. Yet she had sent these two men so far ahead, alone, that she had more than enough time to ponder her failure as she raced to their aid.

Leah redirected her course slightly to glance over the stone banister. She was getting close to the bottom now—nearer to the source of the pained cry a few moments before. From higher up, she'd been able to see a formation of a'thri'ik in the center of the floor below. Now that she was closer, she could see a defined symmetry to the sides of the formation, and although she could not yet discern its exact shape, it was clearly not a natural deposit but an elaborate sculpture carved of pure a'thri'ik.

And nearby, previously hidden by the lip of the spiraling walkway, two human bodies lay on the rocky cavern floor.

No, thought Leah. *Please, no.*

She pumped her arms harder as she ran, passing beneath more patterns in the wall—detailed depictions of ranks of soldiers arrayed in full sets of glowing, green armor. She did not have time to study the imagery closely, but she could not help but take note of the enemy they marched against: a giant creature with a frighteningly familiar skull-shaped head and empty sockets for eyes. The monster had a massive hand raised. A shape like a comet seemed to be pouring out of its palm, into the ranks of soldiers.

Moments later, the walkway finally reached ground level, and Leah skidded to a halt, momentarily disoriented by the sight that met her. The shaft through which they had descended stretched straight up for what seemed like a thousand feet.

The chamber was a convergence of several great, high-ceilinged halls—eight enormous tunnels extending like the spokes of a wheel, away from the central chamber. Down each of these tunnels, more deposits of a'thri'ik could be seen glowing brightly, and to Leah's astonishment, she realized that she could see for at least a mile in each direction. This place had been described as a city. She had expected something more like an underground fortress. But *city* was the only proper word to describe this place. One that stretched for miles in multiple directions, making it several times larger than Cervice or Hartla.

In the center of the chamber was an enormous sculpture carved out of solid, semi-transparent a'thri'ik—a twenty-foot-tall cyclops seated on a massive throne. Elephant-like tusks protruded from between the cyclops's lips and hung curled and jutting outward, and atop the monstrous creature's head was a crown. The single, great eye appeared to be looking straight down at her. At the base of the throne, a pair of similarly green, similarly glowing human-sized statues stood flanking the cyclops at either foot as if standing guard.

But Leah didn't have time to marvel at any of this at the moment. For ahead of her, lying side-by-side on the ground, were the bodies of Banus and Anaxander. The pools of blood spreading outward from their bodies were large enough to have combined into one.

Leah started forward only to be seized from behind by a strong grip. She wheeled to find Lycon holding her wrist in his big hand, gentle yet unyielding. She glared at him, prepared to rebuke him for restraining her. He was an aurym-healer, too, was he not? Did he not understand—?

"Apologies, My Queen," he whispered. "But we don't know what did this. Please. May I have your blessing to search the floor for traps before you proceed?"

Leah stifled her objections and replied with a quick nod.

Lycon let go. Cautiously, he approached Banus and Anaxander, moving slowly and testing the ground as he went.

Leah shot a look over her shoulder. Marcus Worth was close behind her, his circular shield raised and his sword drawn. Sif had his bow nocked with an arrow. The other Cru also had weapons drawn but were gazing in wonder at the monumental architecture that surrounded them.

Behind them all, Megara had her volcanic-rock knife drawn and was studying one of the two statues flanking the feet of the cyclops statue. The human-shaped figure appeared to be an armored soldier. In one hand was a large shield in the shape of a crescent moon. The other hand supported a tall, cleaver-headed polearm in a vertical position. The weapon was called a voulge. Leah had once seen a man called Lisaac use one. The armor consisted of plates that covered nearly every inch of their bodies. Even the helmet showed hardly a gap, with a narrow horizontal slit along the eye line and an even smaller slit at the mouth. Leah found herself wondering if such soldiers had really existed or if, like the carving of the cyclops, they were based on mythology and legends.

As Leah watched, Megara leaned closer. She seemed particularly interested in the cleaver-like blade of the glowing statue-guard's voulge. Although it glowed like the rest of the a'thri'ik, it did not appear to be made of the same stuff as the rest of the sculpture. The cyclops was semi-transparent like cloudy glass—you could see straight through its large, lone eye for a distorted view of the hall behind it. The same was true of the throne on which it sat. But the voulge held by the statue-guard looked more like Justin's sword—deposits of glowing a'thri'ik forged into some other type of metal. The shields and armor, too, had a similar look to them.

In the silence of the cavern, Leah heard a single drip. Megara suddenly looked down. It was then that Leah noticed the spots of blood at the statue's foot.

Leah opened her mouth to yell just as the statue swung its crescent-moon shield, slamming it into Megara.

CHAPTER 53

Darkness. Darkness the likes of which Hook had never known.

Deep within the ruins, cut off from all daylight, and now without the assistance of Gunnar's gauge stone to light their way, there was no difference between having one's eyes open or closed. It had been only a few seconds. He knew that Adonica was nearby and that Gunnar was not far ahead. But in the blackness, with the lapping of the water drowning out all other sounds, it was not difficult to imagine that they were gone, and he was alone in the flooded crypt.

"Well, Admiral Erix Nimbus," said Adonica, "we're waiting."

Gunnar grunted. "I'm trying," he said. "Can't find the damn thing."

Hook began digging through his pack and immediately cursed himself. He had left his lantern hanging from his saddlebag, stupidly assuming he wouldn't need it since Gunnar could light the way.

That's what you get for relying too heavily on a single individual, he thought. *And for not being prepared.*

"You can't light it up from a distance?" asked Adonica.

"And how would one do that?" demanded Gunnar.

"I've seen you use your plant-growing powers from a distance," said Adonica. "Do the same thing with the light-stone."

"It doesn't work that way," said Gunnar. "Some stones require direct physical contact to. . . ." He made an exasperated noise. "Why am I explaining this right now? Get your ass up here and help me find it. Hook, you still back there?"

Hook resorted to replying via a grunt-like sound in his throat. He rarely did that. He didn't like the way it sounded.

"All right," replied Gunnar. "Just follow my voice. The thing's gotta be right here in front of me."

Hook pushed forward through the waist-deep, frigid water. He kept one hand on the wall as he moved.

He paused, his heart pounding in his chest. Maybe it was just his imagination, but the back and forth lapping of the water seemed to have swelled suddenly. He was almost certain that it was deeper than it had been a moment ago.

It was getting harder to keep those bad thoughts locked away in the back of his mind. Once again, he found himself wondering how long it would take to get back out of this crypt, moving at the slow pace afforded by wading through deep water. Enough time to find somewhere with a little breathing room?

Probably.

Maybe.

"Whoa, there," Gunnar suddenly said from ahead. "Nice to see you, too."

"Shut up. Where did you drop it?" asked Adonica.

"Right in front of me here," said Gunnar. "I think. . . . I think I may have kicked it. Could be wrong. Can't really feel my feet anymore."

A few seconds later, Hook could sense that he was near the others. The sloshing sounds of their movements seemed to be directly in front of him, but when he heard Adonica curse in annoyance, he realized he was still several yards away. He followed the wall forward until his searching hand touched the back of Adonica's shirt. She stifled a cry of surprise, then said, "There you are. Somewhere around here is where his royal highness got slippery fingers."

Hook let go of the wall with his hand and moved out into the center of the hall, to Adonica's opposite side, and began tentatively feeling around with the toes of his boots for objects on the ground.

There was a thud from the other side of the hallway, and Gunnar cursed under his breath. Hook gathered that he had just bumped into the wall.

"Of all the stupid . . ." hissed Gunnar. "We can't search for this thing forever. If we don't find it soon, I'll try to light a torch. I've got a bottle of pitch in my bag, but the little bit of kindling I brought has got to be sopping wet by now. We may have to turn back to find some dry fuel."

As Gunnar was finishing that thought, Hook stopped moving. He thought he felt something on the floor at his feet, so he bent over and reached beneath the water. He slid his hand across the slimy stone floor, but there was nothing.

He pulled his hand back up out of the water. He'd been doing his best to keep as much of himself dry as possible, to keep his body temperature up. Now, his good arm was damp with cold seawater all the way to his underarms. He could already feel the cold sapping his strength, making him sleepy, making it difficult to think straight.

"If we go back out," said Adonica, "we'll have to wait for the tide to come back in, then recede *again*. That'll take hours."

"You think I don't know that?" said Gunnar. "It'll give us a chance to watch the waters and time their rise and fall. We'll have a better idea of how much time we have, and we can time our reentry."

The toe of Hook's boot bumped up against something hard and solid. He reached his arm forward but realized he wasn't close to the wall. He reached down into the water, groping for the obstruction.

Hook's fingers found a long object so thick that his hand barely fit around it. It seemed to be lying on the floor of the tunnel. It felt slightly slimy to the touch, much like the stone of the tunnel's floor, but the texture was different. A fallen piece of rubble, perhaps. It was long and cylindrical in shape, like a large tree root that seemed to be stuck fast to the floor.

He tightened his grip slightly to try to lift the thing, and it began moving—slipping through his hand like a rope being pulled out of his grasp. A very large, slime-covered rope. The movement startled Hook so badly that he jerked his hand away—

Hook felt the rope-like object wrap around his arm like a great coil. In an instant, the pressure was so great that it nearly snapped his arm at the elbow, causing him to cry out involuntarily in pain and alarm. His mouth was still open as the snakelike appendage jerked him downward, pulling him under the water. He felt his head slam against the floor of the tunnel, and everything faded away.

PART VI

ECHOES

IN THE DARK

CHAPTER 54

The entire body of the statue-guard pulsed as its shield connected with Megara, striking her like a club. A bright flash of aurym energy—like an extension of the shield—carried her up and back, lifting her from the floor. Flailing and flipping, she sailed backward in the wake of the blast.

Even before Megara's limp body had hit the ground, Leah saw the statue on the other side of the cyclops's graven throne shift in place, leveling its voulge into a lance position. The blade lit up like a sunburst, and a blast of green aurym energy shot out at Sif's Cru warriors, wide enough to hit three of them at once. Tel and Wit were thrown back by the blast, the edges of their furs bursting aflame. But Enn, caught in the center of the blast, was not so fortunate. Leah could only watch in horror. The Cru woman's lower body continued to stand for a second, her knees locked in place. Then it fell forward, smoking from the waist, above which nothing remained.

"To arms!" Leah shouted, but the others were already moving.

Megara's body landed and rolled across the floor. Marcus rushed to place himself between Leah and the source of the aurym blasts, his circular bronze shield raised, and Lycon ducked for cover while Sif and the Cru warriors scrambled to react to the blast that had just cut through their midst.

The statue-guard that had batted Megara aside quickly turned to face Marcus. It leveled its crescent moon-shaped shield, and a bright burst of green aurym energy shot forth from it like liquid fire. Marcus ducked behind his shield, holding it high in front of himself and Leah. He let out a sound that was part war cry, part shout of alarm as flames leaped along the edges of his shield. The blast sent him sliding back a step, bumping into Leah, but he kept his shield raised high and steady. Almost casually, the statue-guard with the leveled voulge turned its weapon on the Cru warriors still recovering from the first shot. They were defenseless, completely out in the open. The cleaver blade pulsed with energy again—

A twang of a bowstring was heard over the war cries, followed by a meaty thud. The aurym energy pulsing in the voulge's blade faded, and the guard wobbled on its feet, the feathered butt of an arrow suddenly protruding from the narrow eye-slit of its helmet.

The statue-guard dropped its weapon to the floor with a clang and raised its hands desperately for its face. Red blood rolled from the neckline below the helmet, painting the front of its glowing green breastplate. Sif was already nocking another arrow to his bow with cold calculation.

Blood, thought Leah. *That's a good sign.*

The blast of aurym from the first statue-guard's shield was still pounding in a steady stream of liquid green flame, dousing Marcus's shield, forcing him further and further back.

"My Lady!" groaned Marcus through gritted teeth. "My shield won't hold much longer!"

Ducked behind the shield with him, Leah realized that its interior was starting to glow red; it was increasing in temperature like an ingot in a smithy's furnace. Marcus cried out in pain as smoke rose from his gloved hands.

"Ral! Vox!" shouted Lycon. He snatched Banus's kite shield from the ground and tossed it like a skipping-stone, then kicked Anaxander's shield to send it skidding across the floor, too. "Protect the Queen!"

Vox caught the shield thrown her way, and Ral gathered the other one up off the ground in mid-run. Both of them dashed toward Leah and Marcus's position. Sif let fly with another arrow at the wounded statue-guard. But by this time, the guard turned to the side. The arrow struck a glancing blow to the shoulder-plate of his armor without leaving a scratch.

Marcus's shield was starting to fold in on itself like a flower's petals closing for the evening when Vox and Ral reached Leah's side. Leah dove sidelong, abandoning the cover of Marcus's failing shield in favor of Banus and Anaxander's shields, now held in new hands. From her new vantage point, she could see Tel and Wit charging at the statue-guard pouring aurym from its shield against Marcus's shield. With its shield still raised in one hand, the statue-guard raised the voulge in the other hand and promptly rattled off a series of quick shots. They were not as powerful as the one that had ripped Enn in two. They were, however, strong enough to knock Tel and Wit to the ground again.

Lycon, meanwhile, had his massive black demon sword in hand and was trying to reach the statue-guard with the arrow in its head, but it saw his approach. Despite the blood pouring down its front, it retrieved its voulge from the floor and fired a superpowered shot at him. The attack missed but forced Lycon back. Sif shot at it again. The arrow hit the side of its helmet. It bounced off ineffectually, but the statue-guard's head jiggled with the blunt force of the impact. Now turning away from Lycon, it focused its full attention on Sif and fired a full-powered blast directly at him.

"*Sif!*" screamed Leah.

Sif jumped almost in time.

CHAPTER 55

"Can't you talk?"

Hook looked up, searching for the source of the whisper. It was difficult to see anything in the dark of night, deep within the ship. The single lantern, hanging from a hook at the center of the ceiling, provided barely any light.

In shadows tilted by the steady churn of the sea, Hook found Haystack seated beside him, his bald head cradled in his blond-haired forearms, rested against the oar. The man was snoring. On the other side, Curly was propped against the wall, also fast asleep.

"Hey."

The voice was coming from across the aisle. Hook turned toward the source.

He could only see her silhouette in the darkness, but he knew by the tilt of her head that she was looking at him. The woman who had taken Toad's place at the oars. Row-master Cadmus had taken to calling her Fawn.

Fawn had been serving aboard the *Manticore* for two months now— long enough that her striking silver hair had grown out and she now kept it tied back. Where she had managed to find something to tie it back with, Hook did not know, but he suspected she had torn a strip from her shirt.

Though Hook could not see her face, he knew that those blue eyes of hers were looking in his direction. In all the time Fawn had been here, she hadn't said a single word to him or anyone else. She'd been silent so long that although she didn't have the brand scar of a lifeslave, Hook had begun to wonder if her tongue had been removed by the Mythae-ans, like his.

"Can't you sign?" Fawn asked in the dark, lower than a whisper.

It had been a long time since Hook had heard a woman's voice, and it took him a few moments to shake his head, not understanding her meaning.

"Can't anyone on this ship sign?" she said.

Hook shrugged.

The woman's chains jingled as she extended her hands, moving them into the narrow shaft of light that shone down in the aisle separating them.

Fawn made a purposeful gesture with her hand. "That means *yes.*" She followed it with another gesture. "And that means *no.*"

Hook stared at her hands, so much like his. Work-worn, scarred, and calloused. And yet so unlike his.

"Yes and no," she said, repeating the gestures.

Hook shifted his hands into the aisle as far as he could. The chains prevented him from getting any closer than a foot from where her hands were positioned in the light. Clumsily, he mimicked her move-ments.

"Yes," he signed. *"No."*

And for the first time in years, he had a voice.

"I'm Jocasta," she said. As she spoke, she accompanied the words with gestures that Hook took to stand for words or letters or sounds. "I could teach you to sign your name." She made two quick signs, say-ing, "Dark-eyes."

Hook wished he could see her face in the dark, but all he could see was her shadowed silhouette and her hands. He considered for a moment, then signed, *"No."*

Jocasta was silent for a moment, then said, "No?"

Hook balled his right hand into a fist and raised a single finger to form the shape of a fishhook. With his other hand, he pointed to it, tracing its outline with deliberate movements.

"A hook?" said Jocasta from the darkness.

"Yes," he signed.

"Hook. Is that your name?"

"Yes," he signed.

"Hook," said Jocasta.

CHAPTER 56

Hook's eyes shot open. He was underwater.

No way to tell how long he'd been out—not too long, evidently, as he still had breath left in his lungs. All was blackness. The sound of rushing water bubbled against his eardrums. By either luck or some bodily instinct, he hadn't attempted to breathe in, even in his unconscious state.

A snakelike appendage still held him by the arm with crushing force. He flailed against it, but it only tightened and continued pulling him along, dragging him across the stone floor of the underground tomb. The rush of water in his ears, the feeling of being pulled end over end, dragged along the bottom—deeper into the crypt, he presumed—was so disorienting that he soon couldn't tell up from down, let alone forward from back.

Just don't open your mouth, he told himself. *Keep your mouth closed, no matter how bad it hurts.*

With his free hand, Hook tried to draw his falchion from its scabbard, but it was pinned in place by the same appendage that gripped his arm. Fumbling at his belt, he managed to draw his knife. His movements felt unbearably slow, restricted by the water's resistance as he hauled back, preparing to strike.

Hook's hand collided with the wall. The knife was knocked from his hand.

Hook felt air escaping through his nostrils and mouth, forced out by the turbulence of being pulled along. His lungs were burning, a sensation compounded by the frigid temperature of the water. He grabbed at the tentacle-like thing, kicked desperately against it, and tried again for his sword, but he still couldn't draw it.

He'd narrowly escaped from drowning once before, and ever since, it had been his greatest fear to die like this. Now that it was happening, he thought there was something almost poetic about it. Perhaps, having eluded this fate once, he'd been steadily marching toward it ever since. A lifeslave living out his sentence, destined to die at sea, whether above or beneath it.

Keep your mouth closed, he told himself, trying to banish any thoughts about things like destiny and poetic justice and other drivel. *Make yourself pass out if you have to, just don't breathe in water. It isn't hopeless. Even after you're out, Gunnar or Adonica could free you somehow. Or the thing might let go. Just keep your mouth closed as long as you can. That's all you can do.*

All he could see was blackness. All he could hear was the gurgling of passing water. And all he could feel was a burning in his chest, a freezing everywhere else, and the crushing pressure on his arm.

Bright flashes formed at the center of his vision. Everything within him cried for him to open his mouth—to try to take a breath in the illogical, impossible hope that somehow air would flood his aching lungs rather than seawater.

Keep your mouth shut, he thought, reaching for his sword one more time. *Keep your mouth—*

Before Hook's fingers could find the hilt of his sword, a second snakelike thing—arm or tentacle, he didn't know which—curled around his other side like an old friend embracing him for a hug. It felt almost gentle as it looped under his armpit, dragging him toward some unknown source. He'd been dragged too far; nobody was going to make it in time to free him. And this thing wasn't going to let go.

Ah, the hell with it, Hook thought.

Hook opened his mouth. He leaned down and clamped his teeth on the arm that held him. The slime that coated its surface was as thick and syrupy as mucus. The small stump of a tongue he'd been left with, far at the back of his mouth, tasted the tang of salt water and a sickly sour, viscous slime. But the next thing he tasted was a mouthful of blood as he flexed his jaw muscles as tight as they would go and bit a chunk out of the thing that held him.

Hook felt it move. But rather than loosening its grip, it further tightened until it felt as if his shoulder would be pulled from its socket. The flashes in Hook's vision grew brighter. He spat the snotty meat from his mouth. Water was going down his throat, but he focused singularly on finding the same bite mark. He did not adjust the placement of his bite, only its depth.

CHAPTER 57

Yes, it had been Hook's greatest fear to die like this. He very nearly had, once. That time, it had been chains holding him beneath the water as the ship sank around him, pulling him down with it. This time, it was a slime-covered tentacle. He hadn't given up then. He wasn't about to now, either.

His second bite found tissue much more tender and much easier to get through. He ripped through it with vigor and tasted blood—so much blood that it warmed the chill water around his face and stung his eyes.

With a spasm, the tentacle-like thing straightened. There was a noise from somewhere in the water ahead that sounded like a muffled scream, and suddenly, Hook's arm was free. He felt the flat surface of the tunnel floor beneath his feet. He put both legs down, then kicked with all his might to propel himself upward.

Hook's head broke the surface of the water. He was on the verge of unconsciousness but still had the presence of mind to cough out as much seawater as he could *before* gasping for air. Blood and seawater went in with it despite the effort, and he coughed wetly, all the while, drawing his sword and frantically turning to try to find the thing before it could grab him and pull him under again.

Wherever he was, the water was up to chest height here. And to his surprise, he realized that he could see. He was no longer in a tunnel but in a large, open chamber. Portions of the walls and the surface of the water were bathed in yellow light, while the corners and the adjoining hallways were dark. The water extended wall to wall, except for a rectangular stone platform in the center of the room, high enough that its top was a few inches above the waterline.

"Hook!" screamed Adonica.

"Hang on, Hook!" came Gunnar's voice.

Hook was still gasping, coughing, and sputtering out blood and seawater as Gunnar and Adonica came rushing his direction. Gunnar had his cutlass drawn in one hand and held his glowing yellow gauge aloft in the other. Adonica, too, had her cutlass raised and at the ready.

Hook looked around but saw nothing else. The only signs that anything else had been there were the unnaturally strong waves rushing back and forth through the chamber—and the fluids coating his facial hair.

"You gonna make it?" asked Adonica, wading through the water to reach his side.

Hook's throat had a dry, metallic taste to it as he coughed hard again, but he managed a nod.

"What was it?" asked Gunnar, pushing his gauge stone brighter and squinting into the darkness that surrounded them.

Hook shook his head to indicate that he didn't know, peering cautiously out into the adjoining tunnels. He was grateful that Gunnar had managed to relocate the gauge.

"Well, whatever it was, at least we know it's here now," said Adonica. "If it tries again, it'll have to deal with all three of us."

"Sod that," said Gunnar. "After a dunk like that, Hook's liable to freeze."

"We're *all* liable to freeze if we don't get what we came for and get out of here," said Adonica. "I vote we get this over with."

"You don't get to *vote*," said Gunnar. "This is a military operation, not a town hall election, and what I say goes."

"Funny how you pick and choose when you want to be the man in charge," Adonica snapped back.

Gunnar's jaw muscles twitched. "He needs to warm up. All of us do."

"Slogging all the way back out won't change—"

Hook raised a hand, interrupting Adonica mid-sentence. But instead of signing his thoughts, he touched his head to make sure the strip of cloth that covered his lifeslave's brand was still there. He froze for a moment when his hand found only the band of scar tissue that ringed his forehead. He lowered his hand and found that the strip of cloth had slipped off his head. Fortunately, the knot hadn't come undone, and it was hanging around his neck. He breathed a sigh of relief as he caressed the fabric between his fingers. Gunnar and Adonica watched him wordlessly.

Hook gritted his bloodstained teeth to prevent them from chattering, then raised his sword to point at the rectangular stone platform rising from the water in the center of the room. Without explaining himself, he waded through the water to the platform and started to climb up onto it. Adonica followed.

"Hey!" said Gunnar. "Admiral talking here. We're going back."

Hook shot a look over his shoulder at Gunnar. He thumbed his chest and signed, *"General."*

Gunnar raised his hands in defense.

CHAPTER 58

The floor where Sif was standing erupted with an explosion of green energy. He made no sound as his body went spinning through the air and slammed down onto the stone floor.

"Stay on me!" Leah shouted to the two Cru shield-bearers protecting her.

Leah took off sprinting toward Sif, leaving Vox and Ral with no choice but to run along with her, their newly procured shields raised.

The wounded statue-guard had focused all its attention on Sif to unleash that last attack, which meant Lycon Belesys finally had his chance. With a roaring war cry, Lycon charged with his demon sword raised high over his head. The statue-guard tried to turn in time to defend, but it was too late. The demon blade came down on the back of his armor.

The bleeding statue-guard dropped to one knee from the strength of Lycon's blow. But Lycon, too, was nearly knocked off his feet by the recoil. The surprise was evident in his body language. His demon blade had bounced off the guard's armor like a mallet against a drum. The armor held true. The statue-guard quickly recovered and swung an armored fist in an arc, batting the sword from Lycon's hand.

Leah slid to a halt beside Sif's body, quickly calling on aurym and letting it flow through the healer's stone in her ring. His eyes were open, and his chest rose and fell with rapid, heaving breaths. He was alive, but the entire left side of his body was a single, solid burn. His lower left leg had been burned bone-deep.

Before Leah could place a hand on him to start healing the burns, Sif grabbed her by the wrist. Fighting agony, he stared at her with bulging eyes and said, "Their helmets—your saber is thin!"

Leah looked down at her sword, his meaning dawning on her.

A flash. A sound like roaring wind.

Suddenly, the cavern lit up as bright as the sun. It was the first light Leah had seen in this underground city that was not green, and it appeared blindingly white-yellow in the corner of her eyes, causing her to raise her hand to shield her eyes out of reflex.

Leah turned, hand still raised to protect her vision, and saw a beam of sunlight slicing through the chamber. It struck the shield of the statue-guard who'd been assailing Marcus. Instantly, the shield was torn from its hands. On the opposite side of the beam of light, Megara stood with her hand raised. The bracer on her forearm glowed with pure sunlight so bright that Leah couldn't even look at it.

Marcus was finally able to lower his red-hot, melting shield. He fell to his knees with a curse, hands trailing smoke. Tel and Wit also lay on the ground, wounded. And on the other side of the chamber, Lycon was now unarmed and at a disadvantage. The bleeding statue-guard swung its voulge wildly at him. He managed to jump out of the way, and the voulge's glowing green blade bit into the side of the cyclops's throne and stuck there. As Lycon retrieved his demon blade from the floor, the statue-guard pulled a shortsword from its belt and advanced on him. If it was bothered by the arrow protruding from its face, it gave no indication.

Leah gave Sif one last look. "Stay with him!" she commanded Vox and Ral.

Without waiting to see if they would obey, Leah ran at the statue-guard attacking Lycon. It swung its sword at Lycon, feeding a blast of aurym energy into the blade—like the voulge, it had also been forged of a'thri'ik. There was a crackle like green lightning at the point of impact, and Lycon's demon sword went flying out of his hands and across the room. The statue-guard simultaneously raised a foot and sent a kick straight into Lycon's chest, knocking him to the ground.

On the other side of the chamber, Megara fired repeated blasts of sun power at the enemy that had struck her with its shield. Each time one of her shots connected, it threw the statue-guard off-balance. But the armor held, and the statue-guard was still standing. Presently, it planted its feet and began marching toward her, wading through Megara's blasts as if they were nothing more than high water.

As the statue-guard on the other side of the chamber raised its sword to bring it down on the defenseless Lycon, Leah leaped at its hulking back.

CHAPTER 59

Leah wrapped her arms around the statue-guard and clung to the thing's back like a climber on a cliff face. As quickly as she could, she pulled herself up to hang from its shoulders.

The statue-guard faltered. Leah heard a voice inside the helmet growl in annoyed surprise—a very human voice, Leah thought, albeit distorted by a gargle of blood.

Suddenly, the armor beneath her pulsed with power. The temperature of the surface she clung to was instantly as hot as the volcanic rock of the Orlia Flats beneath a blazing sun. Leah gritted her teeth against the searing pain, feeling it burn her flesh at every point where her skin was exposed, resisting the urge to dive off the thing's back.

The statue-guard jerked crazily from side to side, trying to throw her off its shoulders, but she held on. Smoke stung her sinuses, and flames jumped from her cloak and shirt. She brought her saber forward, in front of the statue-guard's helmet, but an armored fist closed around her wrist. The fingers glowed bright green, and Leah screamed despite her resolve. It felt as if her wrist was being held over open flames.

Lycon slammed into the statue-guard, trying to take it down in a grapple—enough force to cause the statue-guard to momentarily loosen its grip on Leah's wrist. She took her chance. Through the agony, she shifted her saber until its tip rested on the edge of the narrow gap in the statue-guard's helmet. The statue-guard suddenly realized her plan, and in desperation, it threw Lycon to the ground and swung its sword up and back at Leah. Its aim was true.

The impact felt strange. Burning pain was already overriding so much of Leah's perceptions that what registered first was only a blunt impact against the side of her head. A bright flash erupted before her vision.

Stunned by the blow, she nearly dropped her saber but managed to hold on. She wondered for a split-second if she'd been hit with the hilt of the weapon rather than its blade. Then she heard a wet sound as the blade pulled away from her head for another strike, and she felt an odd flapping sensation and a cold breeze. She was struggling not to black out when she realized what she was feeling—a loosened section of her scalp.

Willing herself not to succumb to the encroaching blackness, Leah tightened her grip on her saber's hilt, and, as neatly as threading a needle, she slipped the point in through the narrow eye slit of the helmet. Her roar was a combination of pain and rage as she pulled the blade into the helmet with all her strength. When she felt the saber's momentum impeded by an obstacle within, she threw all her weight backward. Something gave beneath the tip of the blade. She heard a sound like the crack of an egg, and the white-hot grip on her wrist suddenly went slack.

The statue-guard's shoulders seized once, then drooped. Leah could only ride the body as it fell forward to the ground. As soon as it landed, she leaped to her feet. Although she knew she was injured, she seemed somehow removed from the sensation of it—nerves dulled by adrenaline, perhaps. Lycon, lying on the ground, was looking up at her in amazement. But also, she noted, he seemed to be staring at her with no small degree of horror. The place where she'd been struck. How bad was it? How badly was she—?

A loud noise from the other side of the chamber jolted Leah back to the present. The fight wasn't over.

The first statue-guard was raising its voulge, attempting to fire at Megara, when Marcus's spear came flying across the chamber and struck the guard in the wrist, knocking its voulge sidelong at the critical moment. The resulting beam of green energy doused the overhanging ceiling of the cavern in liquid fire instead of Megara. In its wake, a large, glowing stalactite was blown free and plummeted to the floor, where it exploded into thousands of stony, crystalline shards.

Marcus ran forward, drawing his shortsword and charging at the statue-guard. Smoke was still rising from his gloves. "Come on and finish the job, if you can!" he roared.

Vox was still using a shield to cover Sif as Leah had ordered, but Ral now charged alongside Marcus. The two of them would die before they even got close.

"Megara!" Leah shouted. "The eyes!"

Megara's eyebrows went up in understanding. She adjusted her aim, then unleashed another beam of sunlight.

Megara's sunlight hit the face of the statue-guard with full force. Most of the energy was deflected to the side, dispersed by the armor. But a portion made it in, pouring in through the eye slot. The statue-guard's head jolted backward like a sunflower in a stiff breeze. Then the green glow faded from its armor, and the figure fell backward and hit the floor with a clatter of metal plates.

"My Lady," said Lycon from behind her. "Queen Anavion, you're. . . !"

Leah turned to face him. He was still staring at her in horror.

She felt a stinging sensation in her wrist and looked down to realize that blood was running into the burn left by the statue-guard.

She blinked in surprise. Blood. Her entire arm was coated in it. But it wasn't coming from her arm. It was running down her body in steady rivulets, dripping to the cavern floor, creating an alarmingly wide puddle. Where was it all coming from?

Leah raised her hand toward her head. She'd almost forgotten she'd been struck by the sword.

The cavern suddenly seemed to tilt sideways. She took a step to try to steady it, but the world refused to cooperate. It turned the wrong way and seemed to fall away beneath her feet. She heard multiple voices shouting, sounding very far away, as her vision closed inward and her body crumpled.

CHAPTER 60

Justin was amazed at his father's stamina. What had started as a walk had quickly evolved into a run, and despite all the time Benjamin had spent confined to his chair, he was still able to keep a grueling pace.

For a time, they jogged through sparse, gray woods. They took several turns, following along a barely visible path through the trees. The features of this place were so monotonous and singular that Justin felt like he was passing the same place over and over again with the backdrop repeating itself around him on a loop—like the background of an old cartoon. He was huffing and puffing by the time the scenery changed. The trees came to an unnaturally abrupt end, and Benjamin skidded to a stop at the edge of what appeared to be a vast desert studded with rock formations rising out of the gray sand.

Justin bent over, propping his hands on his knees for support as he gasped. The rock formations before him were spires that rose out of the badlands in irregular, lumpy towers like totem poles.

"Hoodoos," said Benjamin, and Justin noted that he was barely breathing hard.

"Huh?" said Justin between sharp intakes of breath.

"The rock formations," said Benjamin, pointing. "They're called hoodoos. Formed by erosion when deposits of hard rock are surrounded by softer sediments. The soft rock is worn away, leaving the tougher rock behind."

"Erosion," said Justin. He thought about that for a moment. "How does erosion happen in a place that has no passage of time?"

"Exactly," agreed Benjamin.

He lowered himself to a squat and looked out at the formations as if casually admiring the scenery. His shoulders rose and fell with deep, steady, controlled breaths.

"This place is full of contradictions," he said. "How can certain bodily processes stop—the effects of aging or the need for sleep, both of which have to do with the life cycle of cells in the body, as well as the circulation of cerebrospinal fluid—while others, such as the circulatory system—breathing heavily after a run to oxygenate your blood, for example—are still hard at work?"

"I don't know."

"Me neither," said Benjamin. "I brought you here to show you something else. Something on the other side of this desert."

"On the other side?" said Justin. "Will it take long to get there?"

"Does that matter?"

Justin shook his head. "You sound like Zechariah. Or Cyaxares, come to think of it."

Benjamin grinned a little. "Cyaxares," he said, staring out at the desert. "I've tried not to think about her."

Justin cocked an eyebrow and was about to ask why when his father continued.

"Justin," he said, "there's something I have wanted to ask you. You said several times that you have been able to 'call to' your sword in times of need, and it came to you each time. Is that accurate?"

"I did it a couple of times," said Justin. "The last time I tried, though, it didn't work. Avagad had taken it. When I tried to call it to me, he said he could feel it trying to come to me. Even after Ahlund blasted Avagad with the fire, I still couldn't get the sword to come to me. By then, there was no time. I had to leave without it. . . . What sort of aurym power is that? Where did it come from?"

"That's what I was going to ask you," said Benjamin. "Using aurym requires the use of aurstones. Did you use an aurstone to do it?"

"None that I'm aware of," said Justin.

"Then there's only one explanation. It must be a daemyn ability."

"Daemyn?" Justin furrowed his brow.

"Daemyn isn't like aurym," said Benjamin. "It wants to be used—and wants to use its host. It doesn't require stones. It can be selective about who it uses, but if one calls to it, it may let itself in. Once that happens, an individual can call on daemyn and channel its power without the aid of any stones. That is what I was able to do, in the end. It's not really the individual using daemyn. In reality, it's daemyn that is using the individual."

"It never really felt like using any sort of power," said Justin. "It just felt like asking for help, and the help came. The first time it happened, it helped me kill three cythraul and get away. Why would daemyn help me do that?"

"Because in addition to being powerful, it also has a will of its own. And it is a master manipulator," said Benjamin. "What about with the tiger? The time when you 'told' it to leave."

"Same deal," said Justin. "Something told me to just close my eyes and drop my sword, so I did. After that, I was able to see aurym everywhere if I focused."

Benjamin hesitated, then turned away slightly. Justin stepped forward until he could see his father's face again. He appeared troubled.

"Dad?" said Justin.

"Justin," said Benjamin, "I've never heard of anyone using the abilities you're describing—with a stone or otherwise."

"But they're not abilities," said Justin. "I couldn't even use aurym. Zechariah tried to teach me, but I couldn't even make a gauge light up."

"You couldn't?" said Benjamin.

"No," said Justin. "Could you, on your first try?"

"Yeah," said Benjamin. "Amphidemus said he had never seen anyone create such a light."

"Well, I never got it to work. Not even a flicker. It was only when. . . ."

Justin trailed off, leaving the rest unspoken.

It was only when I was at the end of all hope, he thought, *with my own blade pressed against my neck, fighting the invisible hands of daemyn, that aurym came.*

"I had failed," Justin continued quietly. "I was completely powerless. When I realized I couldn't win, I asked for help. And help came."

Benjamin was watching him closely now. He had already heard this part of the story, but he still looked as if he were hearing it for the first time. But after a few silent moments, he seemed to decide to drop the subject for now. He stood up and turned his attention back out over the rock formations. "We'll have to proceed cautiously from here," he said.

"Why?" said Justin.

"I don't think we're in any danger," said Benjamin, "but I'm not entirely sure. Come on."

CHAPTER 61

Only by walking among the hoodoo formations did Justin get a true appreciation for their size. From a distance, he had mistaken them for structures the size of people, but he'd soon realized that the smallest ones were the size of two-story buildings, and the larger ones were like lighthouses. They were so thick and numerous that he could see no farther than a few hundred feet in any given direction. It was like being in a house of mirrors—no matter which way he turned, everything looked the same. Before long, he would have been hard-pressed to say which way they'd come from.

Finally, Benjamin stopped in his tracks and pointed upward.

Justin looked up. A tingle ran down his spine, and his fingers felt as if they had gone numb.

"Is that. . . ?" he said, but his question faded away before he could finish.

"You tell me," said Benjamin.

Directly above him was the largest of all the hoodoo spires he had seen so far. It stood nearly twice as high as the next runner-up—more like a small skyscraper than a lighthouse. At the top, a roof extended upward to a pointed spire. Windows were set in the stone. Above the spire, colorless clouds rolled slowly across a gray sky.

"That's it," Justin whispered. "That's the place where he first spoke to me. It's Avagad's tower."

Benjamin scoffed. "*My* tower, more like it."

Justin shot a look at him. "What?"

"Your description sounded familiar," said Benjamin. "I found this place the first time I came to the Kharon. I used it as a sort of base of operations for a while. A place where I could get away from it all, from time to time. But after a while, I started to get nervous. Paranoid that someone would come here and find it. So I cleared out my things and found a less conspicuous place to stay. I guess this Avagad person found it and decided to use it for a similar purpose." He glanced at Justin. "Want to take a look inside?"

Instead of answering, Justin grabbed Benjamin by the shirtsleeve and pulled him behind the nearest rock formation. "Dad, we've got to get out of here! For all we know, he could be up there right now!"

"That is unlikely, bordering on impossible."

"How do you know?" demanded Justin.

"Remember," said Benjamin, "time does not pass while we are in the Kharon. I don't think it stops, exactly, but somehow, we are separated from its flow while we're here."

"But what if Avagad was *already* here when we arrived?" said Justin.

"How?" said Benjamin. "If the flow of time ceases when one is in the Kharon, then for anyone else to be here at the same time as we are, they would have to enter at the very same second we entered. Right?"

Justin made a face as he attempted to follow this logic. "Okay, but what about the time difference between the worlds? A second on Earth means—what? Hours in the Oikoumene? It's still possible."

"I'll give you that," said Benjamin, "which is why I said *bordering* on impossible. In any case, I have never, in all my time in the Kharon, encountered another human being here. Ever."

Justin snuck a peek around the rock pillar to look up at the tower, but his caution was rendered pointless when Benjamin sauntered casually out in the open, in full view of the tower's windows.

"If your friend Avagad uses this tower the same way I used it," said Benjamin, "as a sort of hidden base of operations, then who knows what he might keep up there?"

Justin's mind raced with the implications. A secret hideout. A place that Avagad probably assumed no one would or could ever find, let alone enter. What might be up there?

"Worth taking a peek, don't you think?" said Benjamin, and he started walking toward the rock tower. After a moment's hesitation, Justin followed.

He kept his eyes trained on the glassless windows, expecting Avagad's silhouette to appear in one of them at any moment. A wooden ladder extended up the side of the rock, ending at a door built into the upper portion of the formation.

"Wasn't much up there the first time I found this place," said Benjamin. "Some uncomfortable furniture. Some books I couldn't read. I filled it with my own stuff over time and used it as a private study for a while. I moved most of my stuff out after I started using the rock shelter."

Justin continued to stare up at the windows.

It's so close, he thought. *So close to Dad's cave.*

If his father had found the tower and the cave, wasn't it possible that Avagad had found them both, too? Maybe he'd even been inside Benjamin's hideout. Avagad's words echoed in Justin's head: *My boy, I knew who you were from the very beginning. Not many alive today know the name Benjamin Holmes, but in my position, I am privy to a great deal of otherwise unobtainable knowledge.*

"Justin?" said Benjamin. "You all right?"

"Yeah," said Justin. "Fine. But Dad, I . . . . I think you should stay here."

Benjamin had moved forward and already had one of his hands on the bottom rung of the ladder. He cocked an eyebrow at Justin, and for a moment, Justin thought he was going to argue with him. Instead, he slowly removed his hand from the ladder.

"This is your fight, so I'll trust your judgment," said Benjamin. He took a step back. "Shout if you need anything."

"I will," said Justin, and he grabbed the ladder and started climbing.

CHAPTER 62

Stripping down to one's underclothes seemed like a counterintuitive solution for fighting the cold. But soaked to the bone as Gunnar, Adonica, and Hook were, it was their only option. They sat huddled together around a meager fire built upon the raised, tabletop-like platform in the center of the flooded chamber. As luck would have it, Gunnar had managed to keep his satchel above the water level, and although there wasn't any proper kindling, the fabric of the bag itself and some of its less essential contents were dry enough to burn. After soaking a coil of rope in pitch and striking a spark with a flint and steel, they'd managed to get a small fire going. It wouldn't last long. Hopefully long enough to prevent their body temperatures from dropping too low. Maybe long enough to dry out their clothes.

The water level was going down around them, and Hook now felt only moderately miserable. Thanks to this fire, his head-to-toe dip in the freezing water wasn't going to be the death of him.

As a distraction from thoughts of tentacles slithering through the shadowy waters around him, Hook took a piece of salted, cured meat from his pack and began to tear it into thin strips. He then placed the strips on the bare stone in front of him and used the butt of his knife to pummel and grind it until it bore the consistency of a lumpy paste.

Hook sensed Gunnar opening his mouth to make a comment. He looked up at him, and the admiral wilted beneath Hook's dark-eyed glare. Gunnar cleared his throat and said nothing, and Hook placed the meat-paste in his mouth and slid his teeth back and forth over it, sucking on the juices. Even eating was a challenge, thanks to what the Mythaeans had done to him. But he had to keep his strength up.

Adonica cursed under her breath, shaking her head. "This thing we're after better be here, and it better be worth it." When no one offered any thoughts on the matter, she turned to Gunnar and said, "Can't you grow us some firewood?"

"I am temporarily unable to do so," said Gunnar. "Zechariah *borrowed* my stone to keep the people fed, just in case I never returned. Knowing my bad luck, it was probably a smart move."

"Haven't you survived two shipwrecks?" said Adonica. "I'd say your luck is pretty good."

Gunnar gave them both a sour look, then slowly raised three fingers into the air.

"*Three*?" said Adonica. "By the seas, fortune has its hands full with keeping you alive."

"The first time wasn't fortune," muttered Gunnar, staring into the flames. "It was my royal flagship. A vessel handed down to me from my father, the former Admiral of Eppex, upon his passing. The *Siren* was a mighty vessel and an heirloom of House Nimbus for generations."

Gunnar idly prodded at the edge of the fire. "Many of my friends went down with the *Siren* when she sank during the siege of Skyre. Somehow, Yordar and I made it to shore. There, we rallied our forces and broke through the city's defenses. It seemed like a lost cause, and it would have been, if not for some clever arrangements made by Yordar beforehand. He'd made the right promises to the right people, and Skyre's own city guard betrayed their benefactors and rallied in support of our assault, assured that they would be well rewarded once Yordar and I took power.

"I have been through several battles since, but I've never seen as much blood as I did that day staining those gray-bricked streets. After a lot of fighting and a lot of death, we made it to the palace with its distinctive design, built with a waterfall pouring straight from between two high towers with a ceremonial promontory extending to the side, where the count would give his addresses to the city. In those high towers, Nimbus, Count of Skyre, had taken refuge, so we climbed the towers to launch our final assault."

The Count of Skyre was a Nimbus?" signed Hook.

"My uncle," said Gunnar. "The same one who taught me to use a gauge stone. Yordar and I fought side by side through the palace, cutting down any who attempted to defend our uncle. Inside the second hall, Yordar took a blade to the leg that slowed him down, and from there, I took the lead. Finally, I faced my uncle. He had retreated all the way to the promontory that overlooked the waterfall. The place where he had made his royal decrees had become his last refuge. I ordered my soldiers to stand down, and I stepped forward to face him. He, like me, was gifted with the power of the godsbreath stone, and I was well aware that some trickery might be at hand. All the same, I stepped out onto the promontory, alone, to do battle with the man who killed my father."

Adonica looked up sharply at this. Gunnar paused. He seemed to have trouble continuing.

Slaveholders who kill their own siblings for power, thought Hook. *And you, Hook Bard, call them your allies.*

Almost unconsciously, he caressed the headband in his hand, drying in the warmth of the fire.

Not for much longer, he reminded himself.

"My uncle did not draw his blade," continued Gunnar. "Instead of giving me the battle I longed for, he looked at me and asked, 'Why have you done this?' For a moment, I didn't know what to say. Just imagine—*me* speechless. But, even though his words confused me, I didn't hesitate in my mission. I told him plainly that no tricks would save him.

That I was there to avenge my father. My uncle's expression did not change. He said, 'I can see the determination in your eyes. I see that you will do what you have come here to do, or you will die trying. So much like your father. I can only pray you live long enough to realize your folly.' Then my uncle turned, and he jumped.

"I rushed forward, trying to catch a glimpse of his descent. I saw his body flail, turn, and disappear into the mists rising from the rocks below. Instead of wondering about his words or actions, I was just furious at the coward for robbing me of my chance to put a blade through his heart. I stared into those rising mists and churning waters for several long moments. When I turned around, Yordar was standing behind me.

"The wound to Yordar's leg had slowed him down; I didn't see his blade coming in time to dodge it, but I was able to pull back enough to turn a killing strike into a glancing blow. He would have cut my throat or maybe beheaded me. Instead, he did this." Gunnar lifted a finger, pointing to the long scar that ran down his face, behind his eyepatch.

"Next thing I knew, I was falling. I spun once, enough to see my brother looking down at me as I followed the same course I'd forced my uncle to take moments before. Then I saw nothing but mist. I hit the water, and it was goodnight."

Gunnar stopped here. It was clear to Hook that he was lost in thought now and had no intention of continuing the story.

"Guess it's no wonder you wanted to find Yordar so badly," Adonica muttered. "*He* was the one who killed your father, I assume. Set the whole thing up, didn't he?"

Gunnar scratched at his eyepatch. "Yeah," was all he said.

After a few moments, he stood up, holding his yellow gauge-stone aloft like a lantern and gazing out into the dark, quiet chamber.

"I'll keep watch," he said. "No reason the two of you shouldn't get some shut-eye while you can. Might help you warm up a bit."

Hook didn't argue. He repositioned himself on the stone platform. He didn't know if he would be able to sleep in a place like this, but he'd been through enough long and sleepless missions to know not to turn down the chance of rest when it was offered.

Gunnar untied the bandana he wore. His long black locks fell free without anything to hold them in place.

He looked at the bandana for a moment. Not a bandana at all, in fact, but the flag of the original *Gryphon*, retrieved from its wreck when it went down in the Drekwood. Without a word, Gunnar dropped it into the fire. It blackened at the edges. Then a hole opened up in the middle, and it began to burn from the center outward.

Hook took one last look at the burning flag of the *Gryphon*, then allowed his head to droop and closed his eyes.

CHAPTER 63

Leah heard someone talking near her. Saying something about stopping the bleeding. She tried to move, only to be held down by unseen hands. Sometime later—no way to tell how long—she woke up with a headache that rivaled the worst pain of her life. With no little effort, she opened her eyes and was met by a wall of green light. When she tried to move, it felt like a rod of iron was being repositioned inside her skull, and she cried out involuntarily. She couldn't help but think that her voice sounded pathetic, like a scared little child, before her vision faded to black again.

When she next came to, the pain was still there but less severe. She opened her eyes and realized that the wall of bright green was the broad side of the cyclops sculpture in the center of the underground chamber. She lay on the ground with blankets, coats, and cloaks around her and a pack beneath her head to keep her in an upright position.

Leah turned and found Lycon on one knee beside her, watching her closely. She opened her mouth to speak, found her throat too dry, and gagged on her words. Lycon put the nozzle of a waterskin to her lips, and she took it as gratefully and eagerly as a blind kitten.

Lycon said nothing as she drank, only looked hard at her. When she'd had enough, Leah took a breath and asked, "How bad?"

The big man let out a sigh of relief so great that Leah could tell he'd been sampling their rations of goat cheese and dried beef. "The fact that you are speaking to me, My Lady," he said, "means it is not nearly as bad as I feared."

Leah nodded. She, perhaps more than anyone, understood his concerns. When it came to head injuries, there were things that went on deep below the surface where no healer's aurym could touch. If things went wrong in there, there was nothing anyone could do about it. Sometimes people were never the same again. She'd seen it happen.

"I feel all right other than the pain, and I remember taking the hit," said Leah, answering the questions she knew Lycon would ask—questions she would have been asking in his place, at a time like this. She wanted to reach up to touch the injury—the point where she'd felt the hot sword peel back her scalp—but she resisted the urge and instead asked, "The others?"

Lycon frowned. "There was no hope for Banus or Anaxander," he said. "Or Enn. And we lost Wit to his injuries."

Leah took the news like a kick to the stomach. "What about Sif?" she asked.

"Everyone else, I was able to heal." Lycon gestured over his shoulder, and Leah repositioned herself to see past him. Sif was kneeling reverently beside two blanketed bodies. Leah assumed that beneath the blankets lay Wit and what remained of Enn.

"He may never walk the same again," said Lycon, "but he made it."

"And Megara and Marcus?" asked Leah, looking around. "They took injuries as well, didn't they?"

"Dog bites compared to what you got," Lycon said.

He blinked rapidly, then shook his head as if trying to clear the fog. Leah knew from experience how draining the aurym-healing process could be. Multiple healings in short succession caused great fatigue in body and mind alike.

Thank the spirit we had another healer with us, thought Leah. Aloud, she said, "Thank you for keeping me alive, Major."

Lycon's tangled beard shifted upward in a grin. "Just returning the favor." His grin faltered as his gaze fell on Leah's forehead and the right side of her face. "I. . . . I did the best I could."

Finally, Leah raised her hand to examine the wound.

She decided not to show any visible reaction, no matter what she felt beneath her fingertips. She had been on the other side of this exchange too many times in her life, and she knew how excruciating it was for a healer to watch the patient come to terms with the scars left by her work.

The wound was wide and long, and it began at her hairline. The outer layer was healed with a scar as wide as a butter knife. Touching it, she could feel the sensitive, raw tissue beneath the surface; the new scar tissue would act as a living bandage while she healed. Given the location of the wound, and the extent of the sensitive flesh beneath the scar, she realized that the sword had peeled a good three or four inches of her scalp back.

No wonder there was so much blood, she thought.

If Lycon hadn't been present, no amount of field dressings would have been able to reverse such damage. She ran her fingers over the scar, following the angle of the blade. It was a straight line running down from her hairline, across her forehead. It passed alarmingly close to her right eye and was still quite wide at the point where it ran over the hinge of her jaw, before ending at—

Leah's fingers froze in midair as they arrived at her right ear.

She reminded herself of her vow not to visibly react. Lycon was watching. So she did her best not to let her expression change as she probed at her ear. The bottom half—the lobe and some of the cartilage—was gone.

"I tried to reattach it," said Lycon. "But the aurym power of the hot blade. . . . It burned as it cut. In a few places, I had to excise burned flesh to grow new skin. I'm afraid I failed to get the severed portion to take. I'm terribly sorry, My Lady."

Leah set her jaw. She touched her halved ear once more, then traced the wide scar back up her face to the hairline again, trying to imagine what it must look like but unable to conjure an image.

"I'm sure I couldn't have done any better," said Leah.

"I'm terribly sorry," Lycon said again, hanging his head.

Leah wasn't sure if he'd forgotten that he'd already said it or was re-iterating his apology. She found herself wondering: What would she want someone to say to her if she was the one doing the apologizing? If their roles were reversed, how would she hope Lycon would react?

Leah squinted at him. "Say again?" she said, and made a show of cupping her hand to her injured ear.

Lycon opened his mouth and was about to repeat himself when he noticed Leah's twisted grin.

"Are you. . . ? Oh, for the love of—!" he growled. "That is not funny."

Leah shrugged, then blinked hard against the pain in her head as she sat up straighter against the side of the cyclops's throne. "Do not apologize to me again," she said. "I won't have anybody apologizing for saving my life—what sort of precedent would that set?"

"Yes, My Lady," said Lycon. "I just wish I could have helped the others."

Leah's heart sank. "So do I," she said.

Looking around, Leah realized that she wasn't far from where one of the statue-guards had been standing when they'd first entered the chamber. Other than Lycon, the only other person she saw was Sif, still kneeling quietly over the bodies of Enn and Wit. Not far away, one of the green-armored statue-guards lay on the floor—the one Leah had killed. On the other side of the chamber was the second one, and a short distance from that, she could see the bodies of Banus and Anaxander. An ear was the least of her losses today. She had failed miserably in her leadership here, and good people were dead because of that.

"Where are the others?" she asked.

"Scouting the city," said Lycon.

Leah frowned. "Carefully, I hope."

"I know we ought to have waited for you, but there was no telling—"

"I understand," she said. "I only meant that I hope they don't find any more of those. . . . What were they?"

"Beneath the armor, just ordinary men," said Lycon. "And old men, at that."

"What did they look like?" Leah asked quietly, and when her gaze wandered to the still-praying form of Sif, Lycon seemed to guess her meaning.

"Not Cru," he said.

Leah nodded. If these attackers had been Cru or even relatives of the Cru, it surely would have complicated things. But now, her greater concern was that there might be many more of them throughout this city.

"No attempt at diplomacy," she muttered. "They killed Banus and Anaxander and attacked us outright."

"Their armor and weapons are remarkable," said Lycon. "I've never seen pieces of such craftsmanship, much less with cat's eye stone forged into them."

Leah thought back to Justin, deep beneath these mountains, holding a two-hander sword whose blade shimmered with veins of cat's eye forged into the metal. He had found it by accident when he'd stumbled upon a skeletal corpse in the caves. She remembered wondering who that individual had been, but she hadn't given the matter another thought since. She glanced again toward the heavily armored corpses, their shields, helmets, and plate armor, all glowing brightly even in death.

Two men. Just *two men* had been enough to kill Banus, Anaxander, Enn, and Wit, and to injure Marcus, Sif, Ral—and her.

I wish Justin were here, she thought. *To help us. . . . To help me.*

Part of her had thought it a great mistake to send Gunnar, Hook, and Adonica off on a treasure hunt for an ancient relic at a time like this. But Zechariah was right; they needed more aurym-wielders among them. If even one spirit warrior was discovered among their ranks by retrieving those aurstones, it might all be worth it.

Her eyes wandered up to the lone eye of the giant cyclops on the a'thri'ik throne towering over her. She considered its stature, then turned to study the twenty-foot-high ceilings of the adjoining tunnels. She thought back to the great walls and the massive gates leading through the fortifications along the base of the mountains—

"My Queen," said a voice from across the chamber.

Marcus, Megara, Ral, Vox, and Tel were returning via one of the massive adjoining tunnels. And they had someone else with them.

CHAPTER 64

The old man walked in front, his hands bound with a length of rope. He had an odd look about him: a clean-shaven face and long, white hair tied in a loose ponytail. He was barefoot and dressed in plain clothes, but behind him, Megara, Ral, Vox, and Tel had their arms full of glowing green pieces of armor. Between them, they carried a helmet, a crescent moon-shaped shield, greaves, a breastplate, pauldrons, a mail skirt, and other pieces that Leah didn't recognize. And propped on Megara's shoulder was a long, cleaver-bladed voulge, just like the two guards had wielded.

When Leah started to stand, Lycon helped her up instead of trying to hold her back. An onslaught of pain dizzied her and nearly sent her back to the ground, but she managed to gain her feet with Lycon's aid.

"I didn't think we'd find you standing, My Queen," announced Marcus as the group crossed the room. "It lightens my heart!" As an afterthought, he nudged his prisoner with the tip of his spear to force him forward.

"Major Belesys saw to it that I would stand for at least one more day," said Leah. "Though I may have lost my looks long before my time."

Despite everything, this prompted a chuckle from the warriors assembled.

"We found this one in a makeshift camp," said Marcus, shoving the prisoner while also keeping a tight hand on his shoulder. "He was wearing the same armor as the others, but he surrendered to us without a fight. Hasn't said a word."

Leah shot a look at the cat's eye armor and weaponry carried by Megara and the others, wondering what sort of proximity a person gifted with the power needed to be from one of those stones in order to use it. Some aurstones required direct physical contact. Others did not. But the prisoner seemed to have no intention of moving. Instead, he was staring at the corpse of the armored guard whom Leah had killed by driving her blade through the eye slit of his helmet. Leah noted that there were tears in the old man's eyes. He turned to look at the other guard, dead on the floor on the other side of the chamber, and he sniffed. The tears then broke from his eyes and rolled down his cheeks, and he bowed his head.

"You found no one else?" asked Leah.

"Not yet," said Marcus. "But this place goes on for miles. It'll take some time to clear it."

Leah stepped forward, approaching the prisoner. Marcus tightened his grip, and she saw the old man flinch in pain. His eyes were still downcast, and his weeping was growing more audible. The sound of his tears dripping against the cavern floor reminded Leah of the dripping sound she'd heard—the blood of her countrymen falling from the first guard's weapon—just before Megara had been attacked. A bit of dried blood clung to Megara's short-shorn orange hair, but she looked none the worse for wear.

The sound of footsteps brought Leah's attention to her side, and she turned to find Sif approaching, limping quite noticeably. Without a word, he took up a protective position beside Leah.

Leah turned back to the prisoner. "Can you understand me?" she asked.

The old man made no indication that he had heard her. Marcus gave the old man a push that seemed to surprise him. He looked around as if confused.

"Can you understand me?" Leah said again.

"Apologies," said the old man. "I am hard of hearing."

Leah wasn't the only one taken aback by this response. Megara cocked an eyebrow, and Marcus looked astonished.

"Can you understand me?" Leah repeated more loudly.

The old man nodded.

"Are there more of you down here?" she asked.

This time, the old man did not respond even though he had clearly heard the question. Sif started to step forward, but Leah raised a hand to his chest, silently ordering him to stay back.

"We meant no harm when we entered this place," said Leah, loudly and clearly. "These men attacked us without provocation and killed four of our people. They almost killed me. We did what we had to do to defend ourselves."

The cavern swayed before Leah's eyes. Even something as simple as raising her voice was almost too much exertion all at once. The dizziness made her stumble, and she might have fallen forward straight into the prisoner had Lycon not grabbed her by the shoulders from behind to steady her.

Whether it was due to her words or because she had nearly fallen over, the old man finally looked up at Leah. He was not clean-shaven; she had been mistaken about that, she now realized. Rather, his wrinkled face was as hairless as that of a boy, without so much as a bit of stubble on it. His eyes were a deep orange-brown, and the green glow of the cavern was reflected in his tears.

The sorrow on the old man's face changed to something else as he looked at Leah. No—not at Leah, she realized. But at the brutal new scar carved across her face and forehead, ending at her half-missing ear. She wasn't used to being gawked at or seeing this look of revulsion on someone's face. Her father, King Darius, had worn his dueling scar—his smite—as a badge of honor. Maybe she could do the same. Still, the gut reactions of others were going to take some getting used to.

"There were only the three of us here," the old man said. "There is no one else. There has been no one else for many years."

Marcus, Sif, and Lycon exchanged dubious glances.

"This is your home, then?" asked Leah.

"It was never meant to be. But yes." There was an odd time signature to his speech, as if he couldn't get further than a few words before needing to take a breath, and his words were heavily accented to Leah's ears. "We should have left long ago."

Leah waited, but the old man offered no other explanation.

"I will ask you one more time," said Leah, placing a hand on her saber's hilt and stepping forward. "Speak true. Are there any more of you down here?"

"Only three," insisted the old man. "Now just one, it would seem."

CHAPTER 65

In the dark of night, somewhere far out on the Raedittean Sea, the *Manticore* swayed with the waves. And below its decks, Jocasta's hands shone in the light of the hanging lantern, teaching Hook how to form words and sentences. She had conducted her lessons every night for the past several weeks. Hook's technique was poor, but his vocabulary was expanding.

Hook extended his hands as far as his chains would allow so that he could practice his signs in the dim light of the aisle. The chains kept their hands about one foot apart at all times. The bolt that held Hook's chains to the floor was loose, but it was a false hope. It had been loose since the first day he'd been brought aboard the *Manticore*. He sometimes wiggled it back and forth at night and picked at the surrounding wood with his toenails, hoping that someday it might come all the way free. But those bolts were long. Despite all those years and all that wiggling back and forth, it had gotten no looser. It would probably still be loose and still doing its job long after Hook was dead. But still, he pulled at it, wishing his hands could reach hers.

"Where did you learn signs?" he asked, doing his best to replicate what he'd been taught.

"When I was a girl, I lived in a fishing village with my mama, papa, and sisters," she whispered, moving her hands to sign along with her voice. "We sometimes traded with a local monastery. For some reason, they didn't speak, but they used a system of hand signs to communicate."

Beside Hook, Haystack snorted in his sleep and shifted his hairy arms against the oar. After a few moments, he resumed his steady breathing.

"The last ship I was on," Jocasta continued, "the lifeslaves used the same signs to communicate with their hands when the row-master wasn't looking."

There was a long pause, and Jocasta lowered her hands. The shadows prevented a clear view of her face at night, but judging by the tilt of her head, Hook thought she was looking at the floor. To a certain extent, it was his inability to fill silences like these that made him eager to learn more.

"When they brought me to this ship," Jocasta whispered, this time forgetting to sign as she spoke, "I had hoped to find one of my sisters."

She placed her hands in her lap.

"Misplaced hope, of course," she breathed. "The only kind of hope there is."

For a moment, Hook only stared at the floor too. He reached out in the darkness, extending his hand toward her, silently trying to offer comfort. He had never done anything like this before, and he knew exactly how far his chains extended—knew it was a pointless gesture. But a gesture, perhaps, was what she needed.

Jocasta's head turned toward him in the dark. At first, she made no sign of reacting. Then her hand extended too, as far as her chains would allow.

In the shaft of light from the swinging lantern, their hands hovered suspended in the air, a foot away, reaching for one another across the gulf of the aisle. The bolt holding Hook's chains to the floor wiggled.

CHAPTER 66

Hook's eyes snapped open to an underground world bathed in yellow light. Beside him, Adonica sat with her arm over her knees and her forehead resting in the crook of her elbow—a classic sleeping position for soldiers in the field, which was not so different from the way Haystack had always slept on his oar.

Hook stared at his hand. His fingers trembled. He closed them into a fist, then placed it to his head, driving his knuckles into his temple.

Why can't the memories just leave me alone? he wondered. *Must I constantly be reminded of what I've lost?*

He let out a breath to steady his nerves.

He and Adonica were still in the same position on the raised platform where they'd taken refuge from the water, but Gunnar was missing. Judging by the angle of yellow light emanating from his gauge-stone, he was close by. And if the light was still glowing, it meant he was alive, at least. Good enough.

The fire they'd made of their supplies had nearly burned out, and Hook found himself cold but, mercifully, almost dry. He checked the clothes he'd lain out before the flames. Not only dry but almost warm. He stood and began putting them on.

"Morning," said Gunnar.

The admiral approached at ground level, below the raised platform. The water level in the tomb had dropped substantially, so that he now stood in only about a foot and a half of water. He had his gauge up like a lantern and seemed to be studying the side of the platform on which Hook and Adonica slept.

Gunnar glanced up at Hook with his lone eye. "Guess what you've been sleeping on," he said.

Hook cocked an eyebrow, then carefully lowered himself over the edge of the table-like stone platform. He shot a glance up each adjoining hallway, gazing into the distance as far as the limited vision of Gunnar's glowing stone would allow. Still no sign of tentacles or arms or whatever had grabbed him.

Hook left his boots off. He wasn't eager to get back into the frigid water again, but it had to happen sooner or later, and he preferred to keep his boots dry if possible. He turned alongside Gunnar to study the stone platform. The many runes etched into its side were unreadable to him, but the meaning was clear enough. He knew a coffin when he saw one.

"*The king?*" signed Hook.

"Looks that way," said Gunnar.

Adonica stirred atop the platform. After stretching her neck back and forth a few times, she stood, braced her lower back with both hands, and thrust her hips forward. The resulting pops that resounded from her spine were followed by a scratching of her rear end.

"Do rest a little longer if you like, my fair lady," said Gunnar.

Adonica replied by instructing him to do something creative though thoroughly impossible to himself. After dressing, she hopped down to join them.

"Symbol of the eye," she said with a yawn. "Behind the coffin. Right?"

"That's what Zechariah said," said Gunnar.

The three of them turned to the wall behind the raised sarcophagus. Now that the waters had receded, Hook could see that the back wall was lined with symbols and runes. Most were easily recognizable. Animals, fish, trees, the sun, the moons. Some of the figures were as small as a person's fist, while others were nearly life-sized. Dead-center in the wall, directly behind the sarcophagus, was a carving of a stag's head with a rack of antlers larger than any Hook had ever seen in reality.

The three of them split up to study the wall. But as much as Hook tried to focus on the task at hand, he again found himself fighting memories. He'd always wondered about Jocasta's striking silver hair. He hadn't known it back then, but silver hair was a defining characteristic of the Castydocian people, who populated the far-northern shores of Athacea as well as some of the westernmost islands in the Raedittean Archipelago. Their hair was a brilliant silver from birth and turned white with age.

Over time, Jocasta had told Hook the whole story of how she'd come to be a slave. The fishing village where she and her family lived had been raided. At the time, she'd assumed the attackers were pirates. She would eventually learn that they were privateers under the employ of Arillion.

Arillion. A Mythaean city-state. One of the founding members of the League, in fact.

State-sanctioned piracy was not a policy that the Mythaeans endorsed officially or publicly, but, like slave labor, plundering vulnerable communities and raiding unlucky ships were keystones of their economy.

The Arillion privateers had ransacked the village, capturing anyone young or strong enough to fetch a fair price in the Thalassocracy's slave trade. Jocasta and all six of her sisters had been taken and sold as slaves to other Mythaean colonies. She'd ended up in Lyphix. Where her sisters had gone, she did not know. Her father and mother had had everything stolen from them.

Presently, Hook came up short at a spot on the wall, the carven image making his blood run cold. It depicted a young deer, in mid-leap, being struck by a loosed arrow. He raised his hand and ran a finger across the length of the arrow, then over the expressionless face of the fawn.

"Think I found it," Gunnar's voice echoed through the tomb.

Hook removed his hand from the image as if scalded, then crossed the room to stand at Gunnar's side.

"It's not exactly what I was expecting," admitted Gunnar. "But it fits the bill, wouldn't you agree?"

He had stopped before a carving in the wall of a larger-than-life face about the size of a wagon wheel. But it was not a human face. A pair of curled, elephant-like tusks protruded outward from the jaw, and rather than two eyes, it had a single large one in the center of its face.

"A cyclops," said Adonica. "No offense intended, Admiral."

Gunnar, in vocabulary no less creative than Adonica had used earlier, instructed her to do something no less impossible.

"I guess we just—" began Adonica.

Before she could finish her thought, Hook whipped his knife from his belt and stabbed the blade straight through the center of the cyclops's eye. The brute force with which he thrust it sent his entire hand into the wall. A layer of thin, clay-like pieces fell inward—into a hollow pit behind where the eye had been.

CHAPTER 67

Without waiting for the others to help, Hook struck at the edges of the hole with his knife, breaking free chunks of the thin clay that had been used to seal the entrance. When a larger section refused to give, he and Gunnar grabbed hold and pulled while Adonica kicked at the base. When they were done, the face of the cyclops was gone, and a narrow tunnel was revealed in its place. It was only about two feet in diameter, and it led straight into the wall—and down.

Gunnar ducked down and shone his light into the tunnel. The interior appeared dry, but, looking at the water level in the main chamber, Hook realized that it wouldn't stay that way. The entrance was far below the high water line. Now that they had unsealed this tunnel, it would be flooded with seawater when the tide came back in.

"Torch-bearer should always lead the way," said Adonica.

Gunnar slung his satchel over his shoulder and climbed in, crawling on his hands and knees. Gradually, the light from his gauge stone faded until it was only a dim beam shining from the hole. The tomb around Hook and Adonica was doused into almost total darkness as a result, and suddenly, every smack and slurp of the gently sloshing seawater against the sarcophagus and the tomb walls sounded like a probing tentacle.

"Lor, are you behind me?" Gunnar called back from the tunnel.

"No," Adonica replied frankly.

"What? Why not?" he demanded.

"What do you need me for?" she demanded right back.

Gunnar hesitated. "Hook?" he called.

Hook made a series of semi-visible signs to Adonica, who relayed the message down the tunnel to Gunnar: "Do you see anything yet?"

"Looks like it opens up ahead," he called back, grunting a bit as he repositioned himself within the tight confines of the tunnel. "Can't tell yet if it's a room or just a slightly bigger tunnel."

Hook looked down at his feet. Maybe it was only his imagination, but the water level seemed to be rising already. He envisioned himself within that same tunnel, squeezing his shoulders into a section he thought he would fit through, only to find himself stuck fast—unable to proceed forward, nor able to back out—struggling to kick himself free as the tide rushed in and filled the trench like slop in a barnyard trough. Salt water rising higher and higher until only his lips and eyes were above the murky depths. Gulping one final breath before—

Hook steadied himself against the wall and closed his eyes. He could almost feel the drag of the chains that had anchored him to his rower's bench, pulling him down with the rest of the ship as it sank. He could hear the screams. The cries for help from his fellow oarsmen.

"I can't swim!" some of them kept screaming. And Hook kept thinking, *Neither can I.*

The water was up to his chest.

Then it was over his shoulders, and some of the shouts became gurgles.

Then it was up to his chin.

At least Jocasta isn't here for this, he thought.

She had been gone by then. Thanks to him—

"Hook," whispered Adonica.

Hook jerked in surprise and turned to face Adonica, taken aback at how uncharacteristically soft her voice sounded. Almost caring. With Gunnar's light almost gone, he couldn't really see her face in the darkness. Just her silhouette. And her hands, reaching out to touch his shoulder as if to steady him. Her hands—

Get a hold of yourself, damn it.

"You still with us, General?" Adonica asked.

Hook tightened his jaw. *"Watch out for things in the water,"* he signed.

Hook didn't wait for a reply. He took off his sword belt and handed it to her. Then he ducked low, climbed into the hole in the wall, and began to crawl.

PART VII

THE

PINNACLE

CHAPTER 68

Something about the climb felt odd. By the time Justin pulled himself up over the last rung and onto the suspended stone platform of the entryway, he realized what it was. There was no wind. The air was still—as still as if he were standing in a closet. Before him, a door led into Avagad's tower.

Justin licked his dry lips, tightened his grip on Ahlund's broken sword, and glanced down. Far below, Benjamin was looking up at him. He grabbed the doorknob and found it to be unlocked.

Pushing the door open, Justin found a stone stairwell on the inside, leading still higher up into the interior of the tower. A haunting sense of deja vu arose in Justin as he entered and began to ascend the stairs. He had trod these steps before. Or, at least, part of him had, in the dreamlike experience that had led him to meet the man with the crown for the first time. Now, here he was again—this time, not merely his consciousness but his full physical self. And despite his father's assertion that Avagad couldn't be here, Justin found himself less than convinced. How could he be sure that the rules of this place applied to someone like Avagad?

At the top of the stairs, Justin opened another door, and any speculation that this might not be the same place evaporated in an instant.

The small tower room was exactly as he remembered it, except that back then, the sky had been blue outside the windows. Now, it was gray. There was a globe on a stand on the floor. A desk. A finely upholstered chair. The only noteworthy difference was that the last time Justin had been here, there had been a swirling pane of light on the other side of the room: the portal Avagad had tried to coerce Justin into walking through. By all appearances, it looked as if the occupant had only stepped out for a moment. A candle was even burning on the desk. The sight made Justin want to leave before whoever had lit it came back.

Time doesn't exist in the Kharon, Justin reminded himself. *Maybe candles don't burn down. Maybe here it would burn for a hundred years.*

Justin walked through the room in a daze. He wasn't sure if Avagad had survived Ahlund's blast of flame during the escape from Esthean, but the man's cunning couldn't be overstated. Deception was his mother tongue, after all. Perhaps such a man would lay a trap within his base of operations.

Justin suppressed a chill. Daemyn was thick in this place. He could feel it coursing so strongly through his arm that it felt like he was wearing a blood pressure cuff. He crossed the room to the globe, thinking back to his first time in this room. "So. Here is where you are," Avagad had said, spinning this globe and pointing to a spot on it.

Justin turned the great sphere on its stand. Most of it was water, but, spinning it a quarter-turn, he found a series of landforms in the southern hemisphere.

The Oikoumene, thought Justin.

The continents were labeled in a language he could not read, but he recognized the small continent of Athacea by its shape, recalled from maps he had seen in Gunnar's cabin aboard the *Gryphon II*. Justin was astounded to realize how tiny it was, relative to the rest of the Oikoumene—just a few square inches on the surface of the globe. Most of the Oikoumene was in the far south, but a series of islands north and northeast of Athacea—the place Justin knew as the Raedittean Archipelago, the territory of the Mythaeans—extended far enough north that they approached the tropics. Turning the globe, Justin realized that there were other landmasses outside of the Oikoumene. One, on the opposite side of the globe, was itself as large as all the continents of the Oikoumene put together. He had never heard anyone mention anything beyond the Oikoumene.

On a table nearby was a stack of paper maps. They were annotated with ink—large circles and Xs. The one on the top was a map of the Athacean coast and the islands of the Raedittean Archipelago, with hand-drawn fleets of ships on the waters and sweeping arrows drawn to indicate their movements.

Avagad's war maps, thought Justin.

His hand hovered over the stack. For a few seconds, he was unable to convince himself to touch them. But finally, he did. He flipped through them slowly, careful not to do anything that might reveal that they had been tampered with. He saw maps of Athacea and the central continent of the Oikoumene—Darsida, he remembered Ahlund calling it. He also found maps of Erum, the largest continent of the Oikoumene, which lay in its east.

Justin paused. One map, above all others, seemed to have been of particular interest to Avagad. It depicted the eastern coast of Erum, and it, like the others, had been annotated in ink. The most heavily marked portion was a strip of land between a bay on the coast and a small inland sea. Around this area were what appeared to be notes that marked the positions of fleets and armies. In the center was a circular dab of dark reddish-brown, but the texture and color were unlike that of ink.

Blood, Justin realized.

At the bottom of the pile, Justin found a map that gave him pause. He picked it up, returned to the globe, and began to turn it, searching for an area that matched up with the landmass depicted on this map. But there was none. Most curious of all, this map had the same mark: a dark reddish-brown dab of blood. There were no other such marks on any of the maps; these did not appear to be drops that had found their way on the parchment by mistake.

I could take the maps, thought Justin. *They might be helpful. But if he returned and found them gone, he would know to alter his plans.*

Justin looked around the room and noticed a stack of blank sheets of parchment on the table. Beside the still-burning candle were an ink well and quill.

He couldn't take the maps. But maybe he could still take the information.

CHAPTER 69

Justin started with the unknown map. The one that didn't seem to match any landmass on the globe. He made a crude sketch of its shape, and although he could not read the language that had been used to label these maps, he did his best to copy the letters. Hopefully, when he returned to the Oikoumene, someone would be able to read them.

When he had finished copying the first map, Justin did the same with the others, copying down all the symbols Avagad had drawn. There were ten in all, and he endeavored at first to diligently copy them all. But as he went on, he realized that the ink in the well would get lower the more work he did. Hopefully Avagad—if he was still alive and if he returned here—wouldn't notice a disturbance as small as a few missing sheets of parchment or a lower level in his ink well. But Justin didn't want to take any chances. He settled for copying five of the maps that seemed most important and did his best to commit the details of some of the others to memory.

Justin rolled up the copies he had made and stacked the originals in the same order in which he had found them. He searched the desk and its drawers. Then he checked the bookcase on the far wall.

Most of the books were in tatters, and all of them had titles that Justin could not read. But on the top shelf, situated beside a small wooden box, was one that he recognized. It was the book that Avagad had once used to try to tempt him. Avagad had called it *The Book of Unfinished Dreams*. And it contained the handwritten account of an ethoul from Earth.

Dad's words, Justin now knew.

Justin reached up and pulled the book from its place beside the wooden box. He noted burn marks on the binding and remembered how Avagad had held it over an aurym-flame in his hand, threatening to destroy the book if Justin didn't do as he said. Justin started to open it.

But instead, he found his gaze unexpectedly locked on the wooden box that the book had been sitting beside. Something about it, too, was oddly familiar. Where had he seen it before?

Justin put the book back and took the box from its place on the top of the shelf. The instant he touched it, it came to him.

Esthean, he realized. *The box Cyaxares gave me.*

The box had contained a faded, ancient-looking high school yearbook photo—of himself. She'd given it to him to prove that she had known his father. That Benjamin really had been a fallen angel in the Oikoumene long before Justin's time.

This looked like the same box.

But what's it doing here? thought Justin, suppressing a chill.

Slowly, he opened it.

His yearbook photo was not inside. Instead, it contained only a small, folded piece of fabric. And unlike the box Cyaxares had given to Justin that day, the underside of this box's lid had a series of symbols carved into it, forming two words.

Justin unfolded the fabric inside. It was torn and frayed at the edges, and he could see nothing remarkable about it. He carefully refolded it and placed it back in the box, returning his attention to the engraving beneath the lid and thinking back to Cyaxares's description of Avagad.

According to Cyaxares, many years after his father's time, a young man had joined the Brethren and quickly rose up the ranks to become one of the most powerful among them. Eventually, that young man betrayed them all to the Nameless One, leading to the breaking of the Brethren.

This wasn't the same box that Cyaxares had given to Justin, but it was practically identical. Had this box come from her, too? And if so, why did Avagad have it? A single piece of cloth lay folded inside the box almost lovingly. Like a keepsake.

A light thud tore Justin from his thoughts. It sounded like it had come from outside.

Justin approached one of the windows. He looked down to see Benjamin preparing to throw another rock. When he saw Justin in the window, he made a questioning gesture, asking if everything was all right. Justin replied with a thumbs-up.

Justin placed the wooden box back on the top of the bookshelf. *I can always come back and look at the books later*, he thought, gathering up his copies of Avagad's maps. *Maybe Dad can read these maps.*

He took one last look at the wooden box, then exited through the door.

CHAPTER 70

Spikes of impure a'thri'ik hung from the ceilings and rose out of the floors—stalactites and stalagmites formed not by the hands of the Ancients but by natural processes. The presence of such formations made Leah wonder about the age of this place. Every corner of Cymorrika begged thorough investigation. But more important than her curiosity at the moment was determining if the underground city was safe for her people. And, short of investigating every possible hiding place in this labyrinth, the answer to that question appeared to lie in their old prisoner.

Leah had permitted the strange old man to spend a few private moments with his dead comrades. She had also allowed his hands to be unbound. Sif guarded him closely, an arrow constantly nocked to his bowstring to ensure that the old man did not get too close to the a'thri'ik armor, shields, or weaponry. So far, he had done nothing but sit quietly next to the bodies, praying silently over them much as Sif had done for Enn and Wit, moments prior.

Leah and the others watched from a distance. As always, Marcus was at her side. Lycon sat examining the blade of his great demon sword, and Ral, Vox, and Tel were at the ready, prepared to come to Sif's aid at a moment's notice. Megara, meanwhile, busied herself with examining the exotic-looking pieces of a'thri'ik armor.

"I don't think we should trust him," said Marcus.

"Neither do I," said Tel. "There could be more of these trespassers." There was special disdain in his pronunciation of *trespassers*.

"If there are," said Lycon matter-of-factly, "we need more soldiers."

Leah frowned. That would mean sending a messenger back to Cervice to request aid. And it would further delay—and possibly complicate—the message she *wanted* to be able to send: "Come one and all to a place where you will be safe."

"The others attacked right away," said Vox, running a thumb thoughtfully over her long braid. "But this one surrendered. Perhaps he is of a different mind."

"This one would have killed Enn and Wit, no different than the others," said Tel. "He surrendered because he was alone and did not hear us coming. These trespassers spilled Cru blood. In our Home." His gaze shifted meaningfully toward Leah. "I want to know what they were doing here. And then I want him dead."

Slowly, Lycon stepped in front of Leah and cleared his throat.

"Something on your mind, Major?" said Leah.

Lycon hesitated, just staring at the black blade in his hands. Leah looked at it, too. She did not know what sort of metal the demon blade had been forged from, but it was an object of the blackest black. And unlike the Rorrdvuuk people's blades of sharpened volcanic rock, Lycon's sword had no luster—even beneath the bright glow of the a'thri'ik in this chamber, there was no reflection from its surface. Rather, it seemed to absorb any light that came near it. Finally, Lycon spoke.

"I claimed this weapon from a slain cythraul on the beaches of Gaius. The beast wielded it with one hand. I wield it with two. And in the battles I have fought since then, I have used it against demons and humans alike. I have cut creatures in half in a single swing. I suspect that with this blade, if I so wished, I could fell a tree more quickly than a woodsman with an axe. I have even seen it cleave steel armor in twain and pass through the man inside as if he were wearing no protection at all. And in all the time I have wielded it, it has never required sharpening. Its blade has never dulled. There is, I think, a foul power in this thing. I both love it and hate it for that. But today, I brought it down upon my enemy with as much force as I could muster. My life depended on that swing, and I did not doubt that my strike would split the enemy's armor, as it has done in the past, and slay my foe."

Lycon reached into a pocket of his jerkin to retrieve something and held out his closed hand to Leah.

Leah held out her palm, and Lycon dropped into it a small piece of metal. It was triangular in shape, about as long as a sewing needle, and as black as the blackest night, with no trace of luster.

Lycon presented his demon sword and gently ran his thumb along the middle portion of the demon blade. His thumbnail nicked an imperfection in the black metal—a jagged notch in the blade.

"That a'thri'ik armor not only turned my strike," said Lycon, "but the impact damaged my demon blade for the first time." He gestured toward the armored corpse on the floor. "I checked his armor and found not a scratch to mark my strike. As for the other warrior, after you instructed Lady Megara to direct her attack to his armor's weak point, he was quickly killed. But his armor bears no signs of any lasting damage, despite her many attacks."

Leah turned the shard of demon metal over between her fingers. To her surprise, the tiny fragment was as heavy as a merchant's weights. She wondered if she would even have been able to lift the weapon that the broad-shouldered, barrel-chested Lycon Belesys wielded as deftly as a longsword.

"My point is twofold," said Lycon. "First, if there is any chance that other warriors like these might be found in this place, then we can't handle this alone. Even if we bring more soldiers here to aid us, we'll risk losing many lives in the attempt."

Leah handed him back the broken piece of his sword. "And point number two?"

"If a'thri'ik-forged metal is strong enough to do *this* to a demon blade," said Lycon, "then full suits of a'thri'ik armor, worn by the right individuals, could turn the tide of almost any battle."

Leah thought back to the image of Justin fighting with his a'thri'ik sword. How its glowing blade had cut through the cythraul.

Before Leah could consider the matter further, Megara suddenly stepped toward Lycon, a look of open challenge on her dour face. Lycon blinked in surprise at the display. Megara watched him icily for a moment before turning to face Leah.

"There is no need for more soldiers to secure this place," signed Megara.

CHAPTER 71

Leah waited for Megara to elaborate. After a few tense moments, she finally did.

"The men who attacked us," signed Megara. *"You speak of them as if they were guards. They were not."*

Leah furrowed her brow at the assertion, then grimaced as the scar tissue on her forehead pulled against itself. She kept forgetting about her injury.

"Guards do not allow intruders to enter and then attack," signed Megara. *"Guards raise the alarm to call everyone else to come to the defense."*

"You're right," Leah realized aloud. "If there were others here, why wouldn't the guards raise the alarm?"

"Perhaps because their only reinforcements were an old man with bad ears." Megara finished this sentiment by flashing a brief grin that showed a missing canine tooth in the side of her smile.

Leah returned the smile. For a moment, the rest of the group could only wait, as none of the others were versed in the language of signs. As if as an aside, Megara gestured to Leah's face, then to her own lifeslave scar, and signed, *"You'll get used to it."*

Leah tried to smile, but Megara's slave brand was an unwelcome reminder of the conversation they'd had prior to the battle. It was a subject she didn't feel equipped to tackle in her current state of mind.

But you'll have to deal with it, she thought. *And sooner rather than later.*

"I think I'll have a word with our prisoner," said Leah. When Marcus and Lycon attempted to follow her, she added, "Alone, please."

Leah approached Sif and put a gentle hand on the man's shoulder. He took the hint and backed away but kept his bow in hand and an arrow between his fingers.

The prisoner looked up, surprised at Leah's approach. His eyes were red-rimmed and bloodshot, and he quickly wiped at them with the edges of his tattered shirt. He remained kneeling.

"I'm sorry about what happened to your friends," said Leah.

The old man shook his head. "Not friends. My younger brothers."

Leah's gaze shifted toward the helmets of the two dead guards. One was stained with blood and had an arrow jutting from the eye slit. The other had black ash along the edges of the eye slit where Megara's aurym attack had found its way in. Despite the losses on her side, Leah pitied the old man. She knew what it was to lose brothers to violent deaths.

"There are no more of us here," said the old man. "You have my oath."

Leah kneeled down beside him and sensed Sif edge a bit closer behind her.

"If that is true, then what are you doing here?" she asked.

The old man sighed. "My name is Itzacoatl. Many years ago, my four brothers and I departed from the Ecbatan Empire and journeyed west, following a map said to lead to an underground city made of theynrald. Five of us set out to find this lost city and uncover its secrets. We prepared for our journey by studying the region we would be traveling to. Learning its language. We set out with an entourage and faced many perils to get here.

"We lost our entourage along the way. Only we five remained. And after searching deep in the mountains, we finally found this place. Our map led us to its rear entrance. What we found was a marvel greater than we had dared to hope. We could not risk this place being found. Three of us stayed behind. The other two ventured out to find wagons to help transport our riches back with us." He paused. "Neither ever returned. The three of us have been here ever since, guarding this place against outsiders."

A sudden realization dawned on Leah. "Itza . . ." she said. "I'm sorry, what was it?"

"*Itz-a-co-atl,*" he said slowly.

"Itzacoatl," said Leah. "I think I may know what happened to your brothers. Or to one of them, anyway."

She proceeded to relate the story of her passage through the Shifting Mountains and how Justin had stumbled upon a skeleton carrying a satchel with a few coins, a silver flask, and a claymore sword with a'thri'ik forged in the blade. By the time she finished, Itzacoatl's eyes were brimming with tears.

"Your guess is right, I think. That matches the description of my youngest brother. And although I suspected as much, it still pains me to learn the truth."

"But he looked," said Leah, choosing her words carefully, "as if he had been there for a very long time."

"As have we remaining three," said Itzacoatl. "A similar fate likely befell my other brother, too. All this time, we have been waiting for them to return, and it's possible that neither of them ever made it out of these mountains. . . . We guarded our find too zealously, I think. Had the five of us returned home together, instead of fearing to leave this place behind, our dreams may have been realized."

For a few moments, Itzacoatl was silent. Then he looked hard at her.

"I'm sorry," he said. "Had I been here when you arrived, I may have been able to reason with my brothers. Then they *and* your people would still be alive." His gaze wandered to her scar and her partially missing ear. "They did that, too, didn't they?"

Leah didn't answer.

She said nothing for a while, trying to see this situation from every angle. If this man truly had been here all these years, then he didn't know the state of the wider world—the demon invasions, or the fact that his homeland, the once-great Ecbatan Empire, was rumored to have been the first to fall.

"I also regret what happened here," said Leah. "Much like you, it was a dream for my people that brought me to this place. I am about to lead an army to war. I have made peace with the fact that my soldiers and I may never return, but I need a place where our civilians will be safe. There are many moving parts. But perhaps, if you and I can find it in our hearts to put this bloodshed behind us, we can help each other."

"If it is a sanctuary you seek, you will find none better than this," said Itzacoatl. "It is well hidden and easily defended. There is fresh water. Food sources, too, if you know what to look for."

"And there are no others here who would do us harm?" Leah asked yet again.

"It is safe here," said Itzacoatl.

"There's one thing I don't understand," said Leah. "What was it that you found here that was so important? What riches were you guarding?"

"Not riches," said Itzacoatl. He gestured toward his two dead brothers on the ground, then back toward Marcus, Megara, and the others, where his own armor was piled on the ground. "The armory of the Ancients."

CHAPTER 72

"It's all right," Gunnar called back down the tunnel. "Solid ground here. Room enough to stand, even. And dry, too, thank the seas, though that won't last."

Hook hurried his crawl.

The passageway was more like an animal's burrow than a tunnel. The floor was uneven and craggy, and although he'd had the good sense to cover the palms of his hands with his sleeves, he could already feel himself bleeding from a few small cuts on his bare feet. Despite the cuts, he still didn't regret his decision to keep his boots dry. Nothing was worse than cold, wet boots.

After a few more pushes forward, Hook reached the end of the tunnel. There, Gunnar extended a hand and helped him out of the opening and onto a level stone floor.

There was, indeed, room to stand, though just barely. Hook's inner compass told him that they had crawled not only downward but further seaward. But if that was the case, this room had been exceptionally well sealed off from its surroundings. In stark contrast to the rest of the tomb, it was quite dry here. And far from the salty damp air of the hall outside, the atmosphere in here had an almost earthy richness to it.

How old is the air I'm breathing? wondered Hook.

Sealed since the times of the Ancients. He had never heard it rightly said just how many years had passed since those lost ages.

Gunnar raised his gauge to cast a brighter light on the room. Ahead of them, just as Zechariah had said there would be, were two miniature versions of the sarcophagus in the main hall of the tomb, said to contain the grave goods of the unnamed Ellenean king for whom these ruins had been constructed as a resting place.

"Damned if the old man wasn't right," Gunnar said. "He's always right, isn't he?"

"Yet we still never believe him," signed Hook.

"I think his delivery needs some work." Gunnar studied the floor for traps before stepping toward the first of the stone sarcophagi. "Help me with this thing, will ya?"

Careful to travel in Gunnar's footsteps, Hook moved to assist. The stone boxes weren't nearly as intricate as the grand one in the main chamber but were covered in the same kinds of runes. As Hook positioned himself on the opposite side of the sarcophagus and touched the lid, he couldn't help but think of the warnings of his Islander mother. Tampering with the dead who had been lain to rest was an invitation for the worst kind of luck.

Gunnar, on the other hand, seemed to harbor no such reservations. He slapped at the top of the box with his hand, clearing a layer of dust away, and grabbed the edge of the lid. But instead of lifting, Gunnar shot Hook a one-eyed glance and said, "Bet you're wondering how I survived."

Hook cocked an eyebrow at him.

"After Yordar attacked me and I went over the falls," said Gunnar.

Hook didn't reply. It took a special kind of ego for Gunnar to assume that Hook would be thinking about *him* at a time like this, when he was about to raid a tomb untouched for untold years, in a cavern poised to be flooded with seawater at any moment.

"Yordar's blade didn't kill me, and neither did the fall," said Gunnar. "Didn't kill my uncle, either. He'd been jumping from that waterfall for laughs ever since he'd been a boy, after all. Turned out, it was his escape plan."

To Hook's annoyance, Gunnar now leaned on the sarcophagus lid with one elbow, examining his fingernails as he related the tale.

"The crafty devil had his ship, the *Gryphon*, tucked away in a cove hidden behind the falls," he said. "He dove into the water, swam to his ship, and was prepping it to set sail when his dimwit of a nephew came crashing down into the same waters behind him—with half as many eyes in his head as his mother gave him, to boot."

Hook glared, then tapped one finger meaningfully against the lid of the coffin.

"Right, right," said Gunnar. He looked at the yellow-glowing gauge stone in his hand unsurely, then placed it between his teeth, where it continued to glow with his flow of aurym power. Then he grabbed hold of the lid.

"On three," Gunnar mumbled through the stone held between his teeth. "One, two, *three*."

Hook braced himself and gave a heave. With a series of grunts of effort—between which Gunnar peppered various oaths and curses, badly enunciated due to the obstruction between his teeth—the two of them managed to slide the stone lid to the side and let it topple to the floor with a loud thud.

The air hanging in the room had smelled of rich earth before, but the heady aroma that rose from inside the box was something quite different. It was not a terrible smell, but it was pungent and unlike anything Hook had smelled before. Perhaps this was the scent of an atmosphere that no longer existed in all the world.

And to Hook's surprise, a green glow—equally as strong, if not stronger than the light from Gunnar's gauge stone—was emanating from within the sarcophagus.

CHAPTER 73

Gunnar spat his gauge stone into his hand to shine its light into the green-glowing sarcophagus.

"A bullseye on the first shot," announced Gunnar.

Within the confines of the casket were two items set upon a bed of soft fabric as if lain there with great care. One was the source of the green light: a long, golden lance with a blade that appeared to have been carved from a single, solid chunk of cat's eye—or a'thri'ik, as Zechariah had called it during their journey through the Shifting Mountains.

The other item was the object of their search. Zechariah had described it as a crown, but to Hook, it would have been more fittingly described as a helmet. The base appeared to be made of pure gold but with two elaborate structures jutting from either side: a pair of antlers that measured almost a foot wide.

Hook thought that the golden antlers atop the crown looked remarkably similar to those of the stag carved into the wall in the chamber outside. Each of the helmet's antlers came to eight points, making for a total of sixteen. And set atop each was a cut stone, mounted in the gold like a gem in a ring.

Some of the stones looked precious as rubies; others were as dull as gravel. But Hook knew better. They were all aurstones. Sixteen of them.

"Wonder if it's my size," said Gunnar, reaching for the crown.

Hook quickly raised a hand to stop him. *A trap?* he signed.

Gunnar shrugged. "I don't see as we have much choice but to find out the hard way."

Gunnar hesitated for only a moment, then reached in to gingerly pick up the crown. It appeared to be lighter than he'd anticipated, and he heaved a sigh of relief when he pulled it clear of the stone box without incident. To Gunnar's credit, he didn't try it on but simply placed it in the satchel slung over his shoulder, then gestured at the gold lance with the cat's eye tip.

"That'll make a handy torch," he said.

Hook looked at him.

Gunnar shrugged again. "It ain't doing anybody any good in here. And you're already a grave-robber."

Hook hesitated, but Gunnar was right. He could see no reason not to take it.

"Hurry up!" Adonica's voice suddenly echoed through the tunnel. "It's as dark as a coblyn's armpit out here, but I can feel the tide coming in fast."

Hook snatched the lance from the box and started for the tunnel, but Gunnar didn't follow. Instead, he was busy hurrying to the other stone box.

"Just enough time," he said. He slipped his yellow gauge stone into his pocket, and the room remained lit by the green glow of the lance's blade. "Help me with the other coffin."

Hook raised his hands to sign in protest, but Gunnar shook his head.

"Ah-ah-ah! Listen. The less you argue with me, the quicker we can crack this sucker open and get out of here. And if you weren't too good to take that lance, then you aren't too good to see what else is here that might be useful. Once you're a grave-robber, the size of the haul doesn't make you more or less of one—let's be smart about this."

Hook growled in annoyance, then propped the lance against the wall and hurried to help him.

"Anyway, like I was saying before," groaned Gunnar beneath the weight of the stone lid, "My uncle did me the kindness of dragging me out of the water. While I was unconscious, on the brink of death, and leaking from the place where my favorite peeper used to be, my uncle singlehandedly sailed the *Gryphon* away from Skyre, right under the noses of Yordar's forces—my forces, too, technically. Heave-*ho*!"

The stone lid hit the floor. Inside were several long, narrow objects. They looked like brass bedposts lying in heaps of dust and cracked pieces of fabric.

Gunnar grabbed one of the bedpost-like objects and lifted it up. A few clinging pieces of fabric that were still intact crumbled to dust. He held the object out like a weapon at first, vertically, until Hook reached out and turned it sideways for him.

Hook gestured to the dusty, fabric-like remains strewn throughout the coffin. *"Scrolls,"* he signed.

"Huh?" said Gunnar, unfamiliar with the sign.

"Paper roll books," signed Hook. *"Decayed with time."*

Gunnar made a disinterested face and tossed the scroll-holder irreverently over his shoulder. It produced a sharp clang as it landed in the corner.

"Well, it was worth a shot," said Gunnar. Nevertheless, he continued to fish through the decayed fabrics in the box for a moment, evidently hoping to find something worthwhile at the bottom. "To cut a long story short, my uncle had *not,* as it turned out, betrayed and killed my father. As you may have already guessed, it was Yordar. Part of the reason he accused my uncle was to trick me into helping him launch an assault on Skyre. Fool that I was, I fell for it. I was too conservative for his lofty ambitions, so, two fish with one hook—he got rid of me that day, too. At least, that was his plan."

"You coming or what?" Adonica shouted down the tunnel.

"Coming!" Gunnar shouted back.

The word had hardly left his mouth when a sound met Hook's ears. It sounded like wine being poured from a decanter. He looked toward the tunnel and saw that a trickle of water was flowing from the opening, creating a quickly spreading puddle across the floor of the room.

But the sound of the water was soon drowned out by an altogether different noise—a guttural roar loud enough to shake rubble loose from the ceiling of the chamber.

"Get out here!" came Adonica's shout from outside.

Hook grabbed his lance and sprinted for the tunnel.

CHAPTER 74

Leah stared at the architecture around and above her. The tunnel through which they now traveled was as astonishingly tall and wide as the rest and seemed to go on for miles.

The strange old man named Itzacoatl had led them through huge rooms and halls. He'd taken them to what he claimed had once been a massive library, its walls lined with shelves sitting empty, piles of dust and tatters of parchment scraps strewn across the floor. There were rooms that appeared to have been grand dining halls, with massive stone tables built into the floors. And he'd shown them a great smithy with ancient anvils that seemed almost illogically large. Leah wondered, had they been for some sort of ritualistic or symbolic purpose, as opposed to serving a practical function?

Occasionally, Leah noticed holes in the ceiling that she surmised were vents leading above ground to allow for the circulation of airflow. The old man claimed he was leading them to the treasures that he and his brothers had devoted their lives to guarding: an ancient armory. And thus far, Itzacoatl had proven true to his word. They had encountered no one else in these depths, and he had made no attempt to escape from them. Still, this did nothing to put Sif's nerves at ease. The Cru elder walked with a noticeable limp from the aurym blast that had nearly killed him, sustained in the battle against Itzacoatl's brothers. Sif kept an arrow nocked to his bow as he walked behind the old man. The other Cru warriors, and Megara, also remained vigilant. As for Lycon and Marcus, they, like her, were more focused on the wonders of the ancient city.

Leah had lost track of how many rooms they had visited so far. All of it was lit by deposits of a'thri'ik. Once upon a time, in a cavern deep beneath the Thucymoroi, she had gazed upon thick deposits of glowing a'thri'ik and promised herself that if she ever got the chance, she would return to see the beautiful sight again. In a way, she had fulfilled that promise. But she had never imagined that it would be like this.

Leah's gaze wandered to Megara. The Rorrdvuuk woman was neither watching Itzacoatl nor admiring the view. Once again, her eyes were boring into the back of Lycon's head. Apparently sensing Leah's attention, Megara shifted her focus toward her. For a few moments, they walked in pace, regarding each other silently. Then Megara touched one finger to the scar on her head and, with the other hand, discretely flashed Leah the sign that meant, *Slaveholder*.

Leah felt her own brow furrow. Once again, she thought back to Megara's claim.

But Gunnar told us he never owned slaves, thought Leah. *Is it possible that he lied to us?*

Of course it was possible. The man's past was checkered with various deceits and indiscretions.

But there was also a much larger problem. It was a fire that had been kindled long before, warming a pot that Leah now realized she had been a fool to have let come to a boil.

Whether or not Gunnar Erix Nimbus had partaken in that morally repugnant practice of slavery, the fact remained that Leah had—albeit unintentionally—become allies with nations and city-states that used slave labor to power their economies. And their ships. Most Mythaean slaves were convicted criminals serving sentences of hard labor or prisoners of war, which was bad enough. But she had also been told that some city-states raided islander communities and hauled away their young men and women in chains.

Thus far, Leah had managed to distance herself from the fact that some of her allies engaged in this practice; there had been so much going on that she had managed not to think about it.

But that would not last. There would be a reckoning.

"You entered through the mountain-side stairway," Itzacoatl explained as he walked, "but there is another entrance. A tunnel that leads to a cave system. That is the way through which my brothers and I discovered this place after long years of searching."

"*Years* of searching?" said Lycon.

Itzacoatl did not seem to hear him. He pointed down an adjoining hallway. "Down that way is a staircase that leads deeper underground to a labyrinthine system of caverns, which are connected to an exit on the northern side of the mountains."

Suddenly, Tel raised a hand in warning, causing all assembled to stop short. Itzacoatl kept walking for a few more steps, none the wiser, and only stopped when Sif reached out and grabbed him hard by the shoulder.

Sif whispered a question to Tel in the A'cru'u'ol language.

"Something ahead," Tel replied in the Waelik tongue. His eyes were trained on a doorway ahead. "Shapes. Figures. Possibly more armored soldiers."

Lycon drew his massive demon blade. Marcus, who had replaced his ruined Enden shield with one of the glowing green a'thri'ik shields, leveled it and stepped in front of Leah.

Leah drew her saber. "How many?"

"Many more than two," said Tel, his gaze never leaving the doorway. "It is possible that they have seen us."

Without asking, Megara stepped forward, her arm raised, a spark of sunlight dancing on the stone set within her bracer. Judging by her body language, she saw them now, too.

Megara turned to look back at Leah. Leah nodded for her to proceed.

"There is no need to—" began Itzacoatl, but he went silent when Sif's grip tightened on his shoulder.

Leah and the others remained in place as Tel, Marcus, and Megara inched forward as quietly as the echoes of the cavernous tunnel allowed.

Realizing that she was holding her breath, Leah forced herself to breathe slowly in and out, trying to steady her racing heartbeat. At full strength, they had barely survived against two of these warriors. If there were more. . . .

Leah grimaced in pain. Perhaps it was only her imagination, but the wound across her head—from her hairline down to her missing earlobe—seemed to ache.

Finally, they reached the large doorway. But to Leah's surprise, Marcus's body language relaxed, and Megara lowered her bracer. For a terrifying second, Leah feared that they were surrendering without her permission, perhaps upon seeing the insurmountable odds that awaited them. But then Marcus looked back at her and waved his hand in an informal gesture for her to come forward.

"You see?" said Itzacoatl. "Nothing to fear."

But Sif did not remove his hand from the old man's shoulder.

After a few steps forward, Leah saw what Tel had initially spotted: the same armor that had been worn by Itzacoatl's brothers while they had been posing as statues in the main hall. Through the doorway ahead, she saw green-glowing breastplates, shoulder guards, and helmets—complete sets of a'thri'ik armor lined up in a row of a dozen or more. From here, it looked like ranks of soldiers standing at attention.

But as Leah continued forward to join the others and her line of sight changed, her perspective shifted. The helmets were not set on the shoulders of the breastplates and shoulder guards. Rather, the breastplates and shoulder guards hung suspended from iron hooks mounted in the wall, and the helmets rested in small alcoves above them. As for the greaves and leg plates, they either lay fallen on the floor or leaned against the wall. The wooden stands that had once supported them must have rotted away with the passing of the ages.

As Leah drew closer, she saw that the row of armor was one of many. The room extended for several hundred yards, and the entire wall was lined with sets of a'thri'ik armor. Megara and Marcus stepped in, and Leah followed.

Leah heard gasps from Marcus and the others. The opposite wall of the room was lined not with armor but with swords, spears, axes, claymores like Justin's sword, shields like the one in Marcus's hand, and voulges like the ones Itzacoatl's brothers had been wielding. There were hundreds of sets of armor and perhaps twice as many weapons, all shining with the brilliant green glow of cat's eye. Some of them had a'thri'ik forged into the metal, while other pieces seemed to have been carved out of solid blocks of the stuff.

But when Leah noticed the armor at the far end of the hall, she stopped in her tracks, unable to take another step.

"The treasures of the underground city," announced Itzacoatl from behind.

Leah turned. Itzacoatl stood in the doorway, a pained look on his face. Finally, Sif let go of him, and the old man rotated his shoulder and rubbed at it gingerly.

"The Armory of the Ancients," he said. "Arms and armor from before the fall of the Elleneans, preserved here for eons. Untouched. Forgotten to the rest of the world."

Leah, suddenly thinking back to the carving at the entrance to the city—a depiction of an army of glowing, armored soldiers advancing on a cythraul—could only nod her head dumbly.

She turned her attention back to the armor at the far end of the hall. It was another row of arms and armor, similarly arranged, but these ones were different. At first, she had mistaken them for more of the statues of solid a'thri'ik that decorated and lit this city. But now she saw them for what they were: swords as long as barn beams. Polearms the size of small trees. Breastplates as large as castle doors. Shields that would have dwarfed the throne of Nolia itself.

And helmets. Helmets as wide as rain barrels. With large, singular, oddly centered eyepieces.

CHAPTER 75

Justin stepped down to the bottom rung of the ladder, then hopped the last bit of the way to the bottom, sending up a small puff of gray dust as he landed. His father stood not far from his position, hands in his pockets, standing as casually as if he were waiting for a ride.

"So?" said Benjamin.

Wordlessly, Justin handed over the rolls of parchment on which he had laboriously copied Avagad's maps.

Benjamin leafed through them, pausing to study each one. "Hmm. If he's sending ships this way . . ." he said, tracing a finger over a set of arrows drawn on a map of the central region of the Oikoumene. "I see. Sending ships south around Lower Darsida to invade from the *opposite* coast is a classic tactic for invading the central continent. It's an unexpected route—unless you know your history, of course. That tells us he's already got the western coast of Erum secured. It's the only way to pull off that maneuver and keep the element of surprise intact."

"I tried to copy down a few of the notes he had written on the maps," said Justin, "but I can't read the language, so I'm not sure how well I copied the letters. I was hoping maybe you could read them."

"Well," said Benjamin, pausing to look at the next map. It was Justin's copy of the one that had been marked with the red blotch. "This looks like the Bay of Anemoi in the far east of Erum. In my time, there was an old city there, but I don't recognize the name he's used to label it on his map. This word here means 'The Pit.'"

There was something about the way his father said the word that caused Justin to suppress a shudder.

"And this one," said Benjamin. He had found the map of the unknown landmass, the one that had featured the second red blot. "This is labeled as 'Mu.' That's the name of the demon world. Supposedly, anyway. I've certainly never seen a map of it before." Flipping through the other maps, he nodded in satisfaction. "These could be valuable. Maybe your friend Zechariah could put this knowledge to good use. If you feel you can still trust him, that is. There wasn't anything about *him* up there, I take it? No sign he had been there?"

"I didn't see anything," said Justin. "But then again, I can't read the language, so if there was something—"

"You sure you don't want me to go up?" said Benjamin.

Justin gave his father a sideways glance, surprised by the suggestion.

"*Any* bit of information we can find could make all the difference." Benjamin gestured to the maps. "I mean, don't get me wrong, this is a good start. But when else are you going to have an opportunity like this?"

Justin hesitated. "The daemyn up there is strong."

The disappointment was obvious on Benjamin's face. "You don't think I could handle it."

"No, I didn't. . . ." Justin stopped himself, then continued carefully, "*You* said earlier that daemyn could enslave you again."

"Right," said Benjamin. He closed his eyes hard and shook his head, as if suddenly remembering something. "Right. Of course."

"Besides," said Justin, "maps are useful, but it's like you said. The real fighting ultimately falls on me."

"Or us," said Benjamin. "If we do it together."

Justin opened his mouth to speak but, for a moment, wasn't sure what to say. Finally, he managed, "But when I asked you before, you said you couldn't go back there."

"I was nervous about the idea before," said Benjamin. "But seeing you here, looking at these maps and talking everything over, gets me thinking maybe we really could do it together."

Benjamin smiled at Justin. A warm, excited smile. The sort of smile Justin remembered from birthdays and Christmas mornings and basketball games.

And yet, somehow, it was not like that smile at all. It was like a bad imitation. A computer-generated recreation of the real thing. Sure, it looked good, but there was something wrong about it, on a fundamental level, that was at once obvious and yet difficult to define. And behind it was. . . .

Darkness.

Justin took the papers gingerly from his father's hands. "Let's talk about this later," he said, trying to sound casual. "Right now, I'd just like to get away from this tower, if that's all right with you."

Benjamin nodded, still smiling. "Yeah. Probably a good idea."

Justin tried to hide his sigh of relief. He started to turn away from the tower when, out of the corner of his eye, he saw his father moving in the opposite direction.

When Justin spun back around, Benjamin already had both hands on the lower rungs of the ladder, preparing to make the climb.

"Dad," Justin said loudly.

"Hmm?" Benjamin said, tossing a glance over his shoulder at him.

Justin stared at him. "What are you doing?"

"Going up in the tower, like we agreed."

"No," said Justin. "That isn't what we agreed on."

Benjamin made a face. "Yes, it is. We just said—"

"Dad. No, we didn't."

"Justin," said Benjamin with a dismissive shake of his head, "you're going to have to learn that you can't control everything in life. There's caution and then there's cowardice. Sometimes, you just have to grow a pair."

Justin took a cautious step forward. "Dad, I don't think you're thinking clearly right now."

Benjamin exhaled a single sharp, bitter laugh. "You and your mother. So alike sometimes. In all the wrong ways."

"What are you—?"

Before Justin could finish the thought, Benjamin wheeled on him. He let go of the rungs of the ladder and ripped the maps out of Justin's stunned hands.

For a moment, Benjamin said nothing. He only stared at Justin. It was a dad stare. *The* dad stare. An expression that at once bespoke disapproval, disappointment, and command—the sort of look that, from a young age, had always been able to stop Justin in his tracks.

But this version of the dad stare made Justin's skin crawl. There was something in it that had never been there before. Anger bordering on rage.

Benjamin tightened his grip on the sheets of parchment, partially crumpling them under his fingers. He lifted them to hold them out in front of Justin's face.

"You think a few badly copied scribbles will be enough to save you when you get back there?" he demanded. He shook the papers in Justin's face, then began to violently flip through them. In an exasperated, almost sarcastic voice, Benjamin read from them, one by one.

"'Mu.' 'The Pit.' 'Beloved Son.'" In frustration, he shook the wad of papers as if strangling an invisible foe. "For all your searching, this is all you turned up. It's not enough, Justin!"

"Beloved. . . ?" breathed Justin.

Justin's gaze came to rest on the topmost paper in Benjamin's hand. It was the piece of parchment on which he had copied the unknown inscription on the inside of that small wooden box.

Benjamin tossed the papers to the ground and turned. In two quick strides, he reached the ladder. "If you don't *trust me* enough to let me come back with you, at least let me do this."

Justin, momentarily stunned by his father's words, hesitated a moment too long. By the time he'd regained his wits, Benjamin already had his hand on the bottom rung of the ladder.

"Dad!" said Justin, reaching out for his father's arm. "Wait, please—"

As soon as Justin touched his father, there was a loud pop—as if he were standing too close to a firecracker.

Justin felt his body jolt, and his vision blurred. Suddenly, all he saw was gray—a blurry gray sky. He was airborne. He didn't remember leaving the ground, but he was moving, through the air, with unbelievable, shocking pain reverberating through his head, drawing a searing line from one ear straight through to the other.

A long moment passed, and his blurred vision tumbled over itself. He saw gray ground again, and Avagad's tower, which should have been close, now seemed far away. It spun like the hand of a clock as his vision rotated in midair. Then his body connected with one of the rock structures. His neck snapped back like that of a shaken baby doll. He felt a crack as the back of his skull hit the stone. And all light went out.

CHAPTER 76

Gunnar was first back into the tunnel, using his gauge stone to light the way, his speed hindered a bit by the grave goods he carried.

Hook was right behind him, his way now lit by the glow of the pilfered a'thri'ik lance he gripped in his hand. If nothing else, it was comforting to know that if Gunnar dropped his stone again, they would not be entirely in the dark.

Ahead, there was another rumbling roar, and Hook heard Adonica cry out. He tried to hurry, but the tight confines of the tunnel made it difficult. The water coming through the tunnel was more than a trickle now; Hook felt like he was crawling on his belly through a shallow stream.

Gunnar disappeared ahead of Hook, and a few moments later, Hook pushed himself through the broken tomb wall—through the broken eye of the cyclops carving—and back into the central chamber. The chilly water was up to his waist now.

Ahead, Adonica crouched behind the stone sarcophagus with her sword drawn. Hook's eyes narrowed on a pair of tentacle-like appendages groping around the edge of the sarcophagus, reaching toward her. She was batting at them with her sword to keep them at bay.

"The hell—?" said Gunnar, coming up short at the sight.

Hook pushed past him and jumped up on top of the sarcophagus, lit by the light of the glowing green lance in his hand. No sooner had he mounted the sarcophagus than a tentacle-like appendage shot out of the water and wrapped around his ankle.

But this time, he was ready.

Grasping the lance with two hands, Hook stabbed downward with all his might. He felt the blade bite into the tough meat of the tentacle, and it quickly let go and retracted. The other tentacles seemed to react to the blow as well. The water ahead of Hook began to bubble and churn. He held tightly to the lance, keeping it primed in a downward position, like a fisherman's gaff, prepared to strike again.

In the green glow of the lance's tip, a large, lizard-like head emerged from the water. Bony nodules ran down the back of its head in parallel ridges. Two overlapping sets of eyelids opened—one set splitting open from top to bottom, the other set sliding apart from side to side—to reveal a pair of blackened, globular eyes.

As the head continued to rise from the water, Hook expected to see something like a snake's mouth. Instead, its lower jaw was more like that of a crocodile, with an underbite of off-white fangs and an odd cleft in the center.

The head didn't rest atop the water. It continued to rise, mounted on a long, muscular neck. It rose until it was high out of the water, several feet above Hook's head, so high that the bony ridges atop its skull nearly scraped the ceiling of the crypt. A pair of nostrils opened, and it breathed out in a huff, spraying salt water.

The creature opened its mouth, and to Hook's surprise, its lower jaw split in two along the cleft. Instead of opening downward like a door hinge, the lower jaw separated down the middle in opposite directions, forming two halves that hinged both downward and outward. A leathery flap of skin stretched between the two portions of the lower jaw, creating an opening larger than the monster's own head. Hook found himself wondering how close he had been earlier to being pulled into this three-hinged jaw, when he noticed the water churning and bubbling again, from both sides of the creature's extended neck.

Another lizard-like head poked up out of the water to its left. Then another to the right. Then another to the left. And another to the right. One of the heads had a scar across its face that had whitened one of the eyes. Another seemed to have a problem with one of the two portions of its lower jaw—one side hung open lopsidedly. But all of them were the same size, and all of them had the same sets of under-biting fangs.

As the five heads rose up, Hook got a glimpse of a set of shoulders. A single set of shoulders, from which sprouted five necks.

Ten tentacle-like arms, each as thick as Hook's thigh—one dripping blood from the place where his lance had cut through it—rose out of the water to hang in midair, curling and uncurling like steeds' trunks. Ten eyes glared down at Hook. And five three-sided jaws opened. In unison, all five heads boomed out a gut-shaking roar so loud that the sound slammed against Hook's chest like an invisible fist. Rubble fell from the ceiling, and Hook tightened his grip on the lance, glaring back.

CHAPTER 77

Each of the creature's five heads was two to three feet long. The shared body, partially submerged in the water of the flooded tomb, was larger than a Raeqlu war elephant.

Hook set his jaw, staring the creature—or creatures—down. He couldn't tell how many arms or tentacles it had, but ten were currently visible, suspended before him like curled vipers primed to strike. All he knew for sure was that the one that had pulled him under had been surprisingly strong. All his strength hadn't been enough to loosen its grip on him. He did not doubt that if two of them grabbed him at once, he would be torn apart like dough.

The only light sources in the chamber were the gauge stone in Gunnar's hand, behind Hook and at the base of the sarcophagus, and the glowing green tip of the lance in Hook's hands. The movements of the creature's tentacles threw wild serpentine shadows on the ceiling and adjoining walls. All eleven good eyes, plus the injured, whitened one, stared back at Hook as the heads inched forward. A deep exhale was issued from all five sets of nostrils at once, simultaneously producing ten misty jets of salt water.

Breathing in unison, Hook noted, backing up slightly on the top of the stone sarcophagus as the creature advanced. *A single set of lungs, then. Maybe a single heart, too?*

A valuable piece of information. After all, knowing whether the thing coming toward him was one creature with five heads or five creatures melded together could make all the difference.

The long, parallel shadows of the creature's necks cast on the ceiling reminded Hook of the shadows that a jailor's lantern cast when it passed prison bars. It was a sight so familiar to him that, for a split-second, he found it almost comforting.

One of the necks broke from the rest, leaning in closer to Hook than the others. Its two-sided jaw split open down the middle, separating at the central hinge, revealing a forked tongue as wide as a man's hand. Then the jaws snapped shut again. The other heads, however, did not open or close their jaws. It reared back as if to strike, and Hook braced himself, preparing to drive the lance into the webbed, leathery corner of the mouth—a spot that, he surmised, might at least loosen the jaws that were inevitably about to clamp down on him.

But before the central head could strike, one of the other heads turned its attention away from Hook. It moved to the side to peek around the sarcophagus, apparently noticing Gunnar or Adonica behind it. The interested head then loosed a growl from deep in its throat, and the other four heads all turned their attention in its direction.

Communicating with one another, thought Hook. *Not seeing in unison. Or thinking together. Separate minds, then. Good to know.*

One of the five heads lowered itself. The neck seemed to extend longer than it ought to have been able, then disappeared into the inky water like a snake. If Hook had been capable of speech at that moment, he would have shouted a warning to Gunnar and Adonica. But he wasn't. And he couldn't risk letting go of his grip on his weapon to flash a sign in their direction.

All at once, the central head let loose a roar, and a tentacle flew out of the water and swiped at Hook. He turned toward it, prepared to defend with his lance—

Almost too late, he realized his mistake. The tentacle was coming at him from the left when a loud splash erupted from his right. He turned to see the fifth head shooting out of the water at the edge of the sarcophagus, its double-jointed mouth so wide that it could have swallowed a creature at least twice Hook's size. He had just enough time to swing his lance around, tip-first, at the oncoming head.

The impact was so jarring that the lance was nearly knocked from Hook's grasp. But his aim was true; the blade bit into the meaty web of flesh at the side of the creature's jaw, slicing through it. Still, the head was simply too big. It kept coming. Its bite bore down, and Hook felt multiple dog-like teeth puncture his arm.

Clenching his teeth against the pain, Hook raked the lance sideways, forcing a wider gash in the leathery webbing of the jaw, and the head retracted with a scream.

Hook let go of the lance with his off hand and drew his shortsword from the sheath at his belt. He brought it down like a hammer, aiming the tip at the back of the head where, if this monster's anatomy was consistent with most biological creatures, the spinal cord connected with the brain stem—

A thick slab of meat struck Hook in the back with full force. The tentacle knocked him to his stomach on the stone surface of the sarcophagus lid. He managed to hold on to the lance, but his sword was knocked out of his other hand.

Hook rolled onto his back, trying to escape, but a tentacle lassoed his ankles in a bone-crushing embrace. As the head that Hook had struck reeled back, part of its lower jaw now hanging grotesquely to the side, the tentacle's iron grip pulled Hook across the platform, toward the edge. There, two heads—one of which was missing an eye—waited for him, their hinged jaws wide.

CHAPTER 78

Hook felt blood seeping from the place where the teeth had punctured his arm. He struggled against the tentacle holding him by the ankles, but he could only watch as he was pulled closer and closer to the two reptilian mouths.

Adonica came in fast. Impossibly fast—so fast that Hook wasn't sure what he was seeing at first. She darted past him like a falcon in mid-dive. And something was moving beneath her. At first, he thought she had somehow managed to mount one of the creature's necks and was riding it. But upon closer inspection, he realized she was straddling a large vine—more like a tree trunk, really.

Adonica leaped off her unorthodox steed. Propelled forward by the momentum of the rapidly growing vine, she flew through the air, leading with her sword. With a war cry, she swung it in a two-handed chop at one of the two heads that awaited Hook at the edge of the sarcophagus.

So thick were the necks of this creature that Hook expected Adonica's sword to become lodged partway through. Instead, the blade sliced cleanly through muscle, tissue, and bone alike. Blood sprayed across Hook's front as the huge reptilian head dropped from its neck. At the same instant, at least three tentacles hovering over the water around it fell limp.

Adonica's war cry took on an almost comical cadence as she continued along her trajectory, now out of control. Her body pinwheeled through the air and hit the water behind the monster with a *kerplunk*. Two heads and multiple tentacles plunged in after her.

The second head in front of Hook—the one with a single eye—was momentarily distracted by seeing the head of its conjoined fellow roll across the stone. By the time it regained its focus and prepared to bite down on Hook, the vine that had transported Adonica had made a loop around its neck. It pulled fast like a noose and wrenched the one-eyed head away from Hook.

Hook threw a confused glance behind him. Gunnar stood in the waist-deep water. Atop his head was the plundered crown of the Ellenean king, which looked oddly exotic yet somehow appropriate on the one-eyed admiral. At the pinnacle of one of the horns on the Ellenean crown, one of the sixteen aurstones produced a dull glow.

As Hook watched, Gunnar swung his cutlass this way and that, fending off attacks from groping tentacles, even as he twisted his free hand in the air, guiding the movements of the vine that had looped around the second head.

At Gunnar's command, a thick branch, grown to a sharpened point, shot forth from the water and punched through the creature's upper body. It turned one of its other heads to inspect the wound.

"To the depths with you, ya motherless cur!" growled Gunnar, hacking off the tip of a tentacle, which caused the head before Hook to cry out in pain.

Hook regained a strong grip on his lance and brought it down in a raking, sideways slash at the tentacle holding him and chopped through it just below its grip on his ankles. One of the creature's heads screamed in response, but not the others.

Certain appendages belong to certain heads. Hook kicked his legs free of the spasming severed arm. *That's worth knowing.*

The head with the bad eye, currently held in place by the vine, was right in front of him. It wrenched violently back and forth, trying to free itself, roaring in frustration. Two tentacle-like arms rose from the water and grabbed at the vine to try to pull it away. Quickly, Hook jammed the glowing green blade of his lance into the creature's remaining good eye.

The monster opened its mouth and roared in fury and agony so loudly that Hook flinched involuntarily, ears immediately ringing. Before he could push the blade further into the creature's head, it ripped itself free of Gunnar's vines. The head pulled back with blood seeping from its eye, the lance still embedded in it.

The wicked strength of the recoiling neck jerked the weapon out of Hook's hands, but it also fell free of the eye. It clattered to the stone in front of him, just short of dropping over the edge of the sarcophagus. At the same instant, Adonica's head finally broke the surface of the water. She heaved in a desperate breath. Her hair had come undone and was plastered to her face by the chill seawater. In the contrast of the yellow and green aurym light, Hook saw that a tentacle was wrapped beneath Adonica's armpits, tight across her chest. Judging by the look on her face, it was doing its best to squeeze the life out of her.

Hook snatched the lance from the floor, but before he could move any further, another tentacle grabbed him by the ankle, pulling him away from Adonica. Behind her, a reptilian head rose from the water and opened its mouth.

Adonica was blue in the face. Her fingers tried to pry at the tentacle that held her, but it was too strong. She watched Hook with bulging, desperate, horrified eyes as the tentacle began to pull her back down again.

On impulse, Hook tossed his lance toward Adonica. He tried his best to spin it so that the shaft would be within her reach. As the tentacle pulled her down, she extended her arm to catch it. But Hook's aim had been off. The butt end of the lance bounced off of her outstretched fingertips, turned like the hand of a clock in the air, and sank into the water behind her.

Hook hoped the look in his eyes was enough to communicate his regret as Adonica took one final look at him before the tentacle pulled her under. A reptilian head went down after, mouth wide open.

Hook felt an intense pressure on his leg, followed by sharp, blinding pain. He looked down. The head whose mouth he had wounded now had its triple-hinged jaw clamped around his lower leg.

Twin rows of teeth sank into Hook's flesh.

CHAPTER 79

The injured half of the monster's lower jaw hung to the side, but the upper jaw and the other, uninjured lower half were still strong enough to push teeth straight through Hook's leather greaves, creating a series of puncture wounds in his calf muscle and the bony part of his shin. Before Hook could react, more tentacles shot out of the water and grabbed him from behind—one around his shoulders, another beneath his chin, squeezing his neck. The eyes of the creature biting him rolled back in its head in a state of reverie. Only the whites of the eyes were showing as the jaw loosened slightly, adjusted its grip on Hook's leg, and bit down twice as hard.

Hook cried out as rows of dog-like teeth punched through new places in his leg. Part of his mind registered that the creature was no longer biting him—it was chewing on him, pulling the flesh off the bone.

The tentacle around his neck tightened, and the one around his shoulders and chest started to pull him back, toward the edge of the platform to the water. He looked around frantically for something, anything, to grab on to. Or something to use as a weapon, even if only to delay the inevitable. But he'd thrown the lance to Adonica. His shortsword lay at the other end of the sarcophagus, beyond his reach, beside the disembodied head that still lay where it had fallen. And his belt knife had been lost in his previous encounter with this thing.

Hook heard Gunnar cry out. He managed to shift his head enough to see the admiral dangling in midair. A muscular tentacle had wrapped itself around his waist and held him suspended above the water, upside down. The head coming after him was contained; Gunnar had somehow managed to ensnare it with a cluster of vines that had wound themselves around its jaws like a flowering muzzle. But a second head now shot from the water and snapped at Gunnar, its attack barely thwarted by a log-sized vine cracking it across the head. In retaliation, the tentacle holding Gunnar swung him like a mallet and bashed him off the wall. The admiral's arms immediately went limp, the spiked helmet fell from his head, and the yellow glow of his gauge stone went out.

Hook tried to move his chin, hoping to bite the tentacle, as he had done before, but he couldn't reach it. Its grip was so tight that his windpipe was pinched shut. He felt the teeth adjust their position again, gnawing at his leg, and this time, the grip on his neck was so strong he couldn't even cry out.

The green lance beneath the water still provided a dim glow to the surroundings, but now, solid blackness encroached at the edges of Hook's vision. His world looked as if it was retreating from him down a long corridor.

At the center of Hook's narrowing vision, Adonica suddenly shot out of the water. She didn't bother taking a breath, opting instead to use the precious little air left in her lungs to let loose a banshee-like war cry. A severed tentacle hung from her shoulders, illuminated by the green light emanating from the tip of the lance in her hands. She put her full weight behind the lance as she drove it into the bulk of the monster, just below the necks, between the shoulders.

Multiple heads cried out as one. Hook felt the jaws gripping his leg give a slight shudder, but they did not let go. Adonica withdrew the lance and stabbed again. And again. And again. The green light of the glowing blade repeatedly winked out, intermittently plunging the room into darkness and then flashing back again as it penetrated, retracted, and re-penetrated the creature's hide.

Finally, the jaws around Hook's leg loosened. All four remaining heads—including the one rearing back from Hook's leg, with his blood dripping from its teeth—let out screeches of agony. The tentacles around Hook's neck and torso slackened.

After sucking in a breath, Hook had the presence of mind to scramble on all fours for his sword. He saw, across the room, the tentacle holding Gunnar aloft release its grip, and his body plummeted to the water with a splash.

Hook grabbed his sword from beside the severed lizard-like head and wheeled toward the bulk of the creature. But Adonica stood alone. The heads and necks were gone. Some of the tentacles lingered behind for a few moments longer, but soon they, too, were gone, leaving only churning water as the creature retreated down one of the adjoining hallways.

A final, forlorn screech resounded, echoing through the tomb, but after a few seconds, all that was heard was the slopping of water as it lapped against stone—and the sounds of three humans breathing heavily.

Three, thought Hook, recalling Gunnar's limp body falling into the water. He turned to find the admiral standing in the water, leaning against the corner of the sarcophagus for support and shaking his head dazedly. The antlered crown he'd previously been wearing was nowhere to be seen.

"Think we scared it off?" said Gunnar.

Adonica frowned. "I was hoping to do a little more than scare it. Tell me you didn't lose the artifact."

Gunnar raised his other hand. In it, he held the antlered crown.

Adonica nodded, then turned toward Hook. "Hey, loudmouth. Your aim needs work." She punctuated the thought by throwing the lance back at him.

Hook caught it with an outstretched hand. He grinned, trying to ignore the pain in his leg and the blood pooling in his boot.

Adonica gestured to the crown in Gunnar's hand. "So now that you've got your power back, how about you grow us a lily-pad boat or something and sail us out of here?"

"By the seas, do you ever shut your. . . ?" said Gunnar, but he trailed off, noticing the blood on the floor surrounding Hook's leg.

"Hook," he said, now speaking in a very different tone of voice. "You all right?"

Hook replied by planting the butt-end of the lance against the ground and leaning heavily on it, using it as a makeshift cane to support his weight. He didn't know the extent of the damage, but it had bled a lot already and was still bleeding.

Hook raised his free hand and signed, *"We got what we came for. Let's go."*

CHAPTER 80

Leah sat cross-legged on the floor of the Armory of the Ancients. In her lap was a shortsword with a slender, leaf-shaped blade and a stout hilt with a broad circular guard to protect the wielder's hands instead of a more traditional crossguard.

With a finger, she traced the swirling veins of a'thri'ik forged into the blade and was reminded of Justin's two-hander cat's eye claymore. This shortsword had been forged in the same manner. She thought back to the way he had wielded it—and the deadly efficiency with which he had used it against the demons. And here was an entire chamber filled with weapons and armor made of the same stuff.

Across the room, Megara and Marcus were rifling through the arms and armor, taking time to examine each piece. Sif and Ral had gone to the surface to fetch Thid, now that Leah was reasonably certain that the city presented no immediate danger. She, meanwhile, sat quietly in thought with Itzacoatl. Lycon, Vox, and Tel stayed close to the old man. None of them were content yet to let their guard down.

"This is the treasure you and your brothers came for?" asked Leah.

Itzacoatl nodded. "Our bloodline is strong in aurym," he said in his slow, halting manner of speech. "In Erum, aurym warriors are called warlocks and are feared for their power. Equipped with these weapons and outfitted with this armor, our family could have become the most powerful house in all of Ecbata. But our dreams of power, it seems, were not destined to come to fruition."

Again, Leah traced her finger over the sword's blade. Even after the untold centuries, or perhaps even millennia, hidden far beneath the earth, the cutting edge was keen enough to have given a man's face a close, comfortable shave.

Zechariah had once told her that spirit warriors who could call on aurym through a'thri'ik were rare. But if one *could* use its powers—like Justin and Itzacoatl and his brothers—then these surely were treasures worth protecting with one's life.

Leah watched Megara pluck a weapon from a metal hook in the wall. It was a glowing green trident, long as she was tall. The central prong of its fork was like a great, long needle, while the outer two were half as long and tipped with wicked barbs like a fisherman's hook.

"This could change everything, My Queen," Lycon said in a whisper, low enough that Itzacoatl, whose ears were not so good, did not seem to hear him. "We came in search of a sanctuary, but we have found a boon. The way the a'thri'ik armor turned my demon blade, and the way Sir Justin used his blade against the demons. . . . There is enough here to outfit a legion. Perhaps ordinary humans could even stand against cythraul."

Leah scanned the room. How many suits of armor were here? Several hundred, maybe. "Cymorrika rightfully belongs to the Cru people," she reminded Lycon—and herself. "If Elder Thid allows our people to stay here, only then can this place be considered our sanctuary."

Tel, standing off to the side, offered no comment. Instead, he turned and wandered off toward the other side of the room.

Leah watched as Tel stopped before the mysteriously massive sets of armor—so impossibly big that it would have taken a squad of men just to lift one of the breastplates. Just looking at it inspired a thrill of fear in Leah. Those massive weapons. Those oversized helmets. Were they meant as symbolic? Had the Ancients forged them in a ritualistic fashion? Or as works of art?

Or had these weapons and armor truly seen use? And by whom?

She chewed her lip and suppressed a shiver. This place felt haunted—haunted by the ghosts of creatures that every ounce of logic told her were only fairytales and myths.

"There we are!" Marcus suddenly announced. "Took a bit of searching, but I believe I have found a suitable fit."

He gathered up the several pieces of armor he had collected into a small pile beside him. It must have been quite light, for he was able to carry the full set in the cradle of an overturned shield as effortlessly as if they were light garments. At first, Leah assumed that he had collected the set of armor for himself. But then he came to her side and set the plunder down at her knees.

"Nearly a full set," he said, scratching at his chinstrap of orange facial hair. "I'm afraid I couldn't find a—"

There was a soft sound from behind him—the kind of mouse-like squeak produced by a controlled intake of breath through pursed lips—and Marcus turned toward Megara. He only barely got his hands up in time to catch the glowing green helmet that she flung at him. Marcus examined it, then playfully spun it on his hand before setting it down atop the rest of the pile of armor.

"Something in your size, My Queen," he said. He gestured grandly toward the wall of weapons. "And despite what Megara might have you believe, *she* doesn't get first pick of the plunder. It's only fitting that our Queen—"

"Thank you, Captain," Leah cut in. "But this is not plunder. None of this belongs to us. This city—and everything in it—is the property of the Cru people."

Marcus cleared his throat. "Of course, My Lady."

"Well spoken," came a loud voice from the doorway.

Leah turned to see Sif standing in the entryway to the room. Ever since they'd first entered the underground city, the smile usually present on his face had been missing. But it was finally back.

"Any news from above?" asked Marcus.

"Elder Thid," said Sif, "speaking on behalf of the full council of A'cru'u'ol elders, has decided to open the doors of Cymorrika, our ancestral Home, to the people of the League. A portion of the resources here will be kept here to defend this city. The rest will be used in the war against the demons."

Leah stood, trying and failing to suppress a relieved smile. "I thank the Cru people for their generosity." She grabbed the glowing green helmet from the pile at her feet, testing its weight in her hand. "Marcus. Lycon. Megara. Pick out some armor and some weapons. We ride for Cervice to bring our people Home."

PART VIII

ENIGMATIC

OCEAN

CHAPTER 81

A world of black on black. A silhouette of a towering figure. A sword with a blade of flowing, molten magma dripping with flames—

As Justin opened his eyes, the image gave way to the view of a gray sky above him, interspersed with darker gray clouds.

His lips parted in confusion as he tried to remember where he was. There was a pain in his head that throbbed and pulsed. It felt as if a great armored hand was squeezing him from the front of his skull all the way to the base of his brain stem. He shut his eyes tight against the pain—

The towering figure with the fiery sword was waiting for him behind his eyelids. But it had moved closer. A shadowed face beneath a set of curved horns was coming toward him. A fanged mouth opened with a roar so deep that it shook Justin's bowels. A wall of heat struck him, so hot that it felt as if the flesh would melt from his cheekbones.

Justin forced his eyes open again, gasping for air. He was beneath the gray sky again.

Justin raised his hand and touched his cheek. He winced in pain as he brushed against raw skin. His fingertips came away coated in a watery discharge—the sort of fluid one might find inside a blister.

The pain had been real. The illusion, if it could be called that, had burned him.

He continued staring at the gray sky, forcing his eyes to remain open for as long as he could stand it, afraid to close them again. Afraid to even blink. Finally, he could hold his eyes open no longer. He blinked.

Nothing was waiting for him behind his closed eyes. Just darkness.

Gradually, it all came back to him. Climbing down from Avagad's tower. His father trying to climb up himself. He had reached for Benjamin to try to stop him. And then. . . .

Dad, thought Justin. *Oh, Dad, no.*

Gritting his teeth against the pain in his head, Justin turned. But instead of Avagad's tower and the hoodoo rock formations that surrounded it, Justin saw gray trees and undergrowth. Before him was the mass of branches that marked the entrance to his father's makeshift shelter. From somewhere within came sounds of rattling and shuffling, interrupted by an occasional crash.

Dad, Justin thought again. *What did you do?*

Justin took a slow breath, trying to steady his nerves, realizing he must have been knocked out by. . . . By whatever his father had done to him. But what happened after that? Had Benjamin climbed the tower? Had he called on daemyn?

Was he himself?

Justin called on aurym—so difficult to feel here in this strange place—and tried to draw courage from its flow. His hand drifted to the hilt of Ahlund's sword, tucked into the belt at his side. He drew a firm grip.

What am I doing? he thought. *I can't hurt my own dad. But what if he's not himself? To save him, I might* have *to hurt him. Dad, please be okay. Please don't make me. . . .*

But he couldn't make himself think any further than that.

Still lying on the ground, eyes still closed, he flexed his fingers around the handle. He fed a sliver of power into the sword. When he opened his eyes, the blade was glowing red, as if fresh from the smith's furnace.

C H A P T E R   8 2

Justin did his best to remain silent as he transitioned to a crouch. He steadied himself and realized that his right ear was ringing badly. Actually, it was more like a sustained whine—as if a mosquito were buzzing around inside it. The burn on his face felt terribly raw and sensitive. The feeling of air touching a deep place that air was not supposed to touch inspired waves of pain across his face.

Another rustle came from within the cave before him, followed by his father's voice saying, "Got to be here somewhere, damn it!"

Cautiously, Justin took a step toward the camouflaged entrance to the cave. He walked the way Kallorn had taught him to walk during his training in the jungles outside Esthean: knees bent, using the balls of his feet to step up, but always stepping down with a flat foot to keep his weight as widely distributed as possible.

After a few more steps, he reached the entrance to the rock shelter. He bent slightly to peer through the branches and shrubbery that hid the entrance.

Inside, Benjamin stood with his back to the entrance. As Justin watched, his father frantically threw aside a pile of books to dig through an assortment of items in a corner of the cave. He made a frustrated noise in his throat, turned on his heel, and quickly crossed to the other side of the chamber. There he opened a small wooden chest, only to growl in annoyance and shove it roughly aside.

Justin's gaze wandered down to Ahlund's glowing sword in his hand. The man inside that cave was his father. The man who had told him bedtime stories and slept on the floor beside his bed when he had nightmares. The man who'd lifted him up so he could put his basketball into the hoop when he'd been too small to reach.

And now, Justin was sneaking up on him from behind, holding a sword in his hand.

Justin looked down, suddenly sickened by the sight of the glowing sword in his hand. He retracted his aurym from it. It went dark as he tossed it to the ground beside him.

At the sound of the sword hitting the ground, Benjamin spun to face him. His glasses sat precariously on the tip of his nose, slick with sweat. He hurriedly pushed them up into position to get a better look.

"Justin!" he said.

Benjamin rushed toward him, but Justin took an involuntary step back, which made Benjamin come up short. The sight of Justin recoiling from him seemed to jog his memory. A look crossed his face that was part regret, part disbelief. Instantly, there were tears in his eyes. His fingers trembled as he raised his hands up as if in surrender, looking nauseous.

"I—" he said, choking on the word. His lip quivered. The tears broke from the corners of his eyes. "Justin. I am so sorry."

Justin stared at his father. He felt tears threatening at the corners of his eyes, too, but he resolved not to let them go. He balled his hands into fists, clenched his jaw, and said nothing.

"As long as I live," Benjamin said, "I will never forgive myself for what just happened."

Justin said nothing, and a moment of heavy silence passed.

"It wasn't me," said Benjamin. "Something did it through me—you touched me, and I heard a loud noise, and I turned, and—"

Benjamin drew in a shuddering breath, so worked up that it looked as if he might pass out.

"I would never do anything to hurt you," he whispered. "You know that. It. . . . *That* wasn't me, I swear."

I believe you, Dad, thought Justin. *And that's what scares me.*

But he decided not to say it.

Benjamin looked back at the interior of his rock shelter, at the items scattered across the ground. "I was looking for a healer's stone," he said. "I know I've got one around here somewhere, but I can't seem to find it, not that I was ever very good at using it. And I can't even call on aurym, so I'm not sure what I'd have done even if I had managed to find it. But you're all right. Thank God you're all right."

"Did you go up?" asked Justin.

Benjamin's brow furrowed in confusion.

"Into the tower," said Justin.

"What? No!" gasped Benjamin. He closed his eyes tightly, causing more tears to spill out. "No, of course not. When I turned and saw you lying there and realized what I'd done, I brought you straight back here. For a few minutes, I thought I'd lost you."

"Was it some sort of daemyn power that struck me?" said Justin.

"I think so," said Benjamin.

He shook his head. Then, all at once, as if weak from prolonged exertion, he plopped down on the ground. He hung his head and crossed his arms over his knees.

"Either the daemyn here is stronger than I realized," he muttered, "or I'm a lot weaker than I thought."

"Is that how it used to happen?" said Justin. "Back when you were in the Oikoumene?"

Benjamin nodded without looking up. "It was me doing it," he said. "But I had no control over it. And as time went on, my body did things and my mouth said things that weren't coming from me. I was still there, deep down. Like a spectator trapped inside of myself. A captive audience, watching as daemyn took over." He closed his eyes in defeat as he whispered, "Amphidemus and Cyaxares should never have allowed me to live. As long as I'm alive, and as long as daemyn exists, I'm a danger to everyone. Even my own son."

Justin's breath caught in his throat at the mention of Cyaxares. In the moments prior to the incident at the tower, Benjamin had been reading aloud from the papers Justin had brought down from the tower.

Mu.

The Pit.

Beloved Son.

Several memories came flooding into Justin's mind at once.

"Cyaxares. Another true friend," Benjamin had said, a meaningful smile on his face.

And later: "Cyaxares. I've tried not to think about her."

"After all these years," Cyaxares had said, looking deeply into Justin's eyes the first time she'd met him. "It really is you. You really are Benjamin's son."

Beloved Son—words etched on the inside of a wooden box in Avagad's tower. A box identical to the one in which Cyaxares had kept Justin's school photo, given to her by Benjamin during his time in the Oikoumene.

"Are you sure you're okay?" Benjamin asked.

Justin realized that Benjamin was squinting at him.

"That mark on your face," said Benjamin. "It wasn't there before."

Justin raised his hand to his cheek to touch the edge of the burn.

The image of the giant creature with the flaming sword.

The feeling of intense heat eating away at his flesh.

"I don't think we should stay in this place anymore," said Justin. "I think it's time we go home."

A look of hope flashed across Benjamin's face. Hope that, to Justin's regret, it was his responsibility to dash.

"It's time for you to go home," Justin clarified. "And time for me to go back."

CHAPTER 83

Crack. Crack. Crack. Crack.

Again and again, Adonica struck the flint against her dagger, attempting to produce a spark strong enough to light the small pile of fallen limbs, dry grass, and twigs they had gathered from outside the entrance to the ruins. Her hands shook violently from the cold as she worked.

It was night—closer to morning than to dusk, judging by the constellations, though Hook had never been a very accomplished stargazer. Not an ideal time to light a fire, the light of which would probably be visible from several hundred yards away on a clear night like this. But they had no choice. Their clothes were sopping wet yet again, and the longer they were exposed to below-freezing temperatures, the less likely it became that their bodies would regain enough warmth to sleep and travel the next day. Although there was no snow on the ground, the winter winds cutting through them as they traveled across the open country would be more than enough to be the death of them.

That is, thought Hook, *if I even live long enough to die from that.*

Stormbringer, Ash, and Thirsty had been grateful to see the humans and seemed to be watching Adonica's attempts to light the fire just as eagerly as Hook and Gunnar. They stood close together for warmth and kept their trunks curled tight, and Hook had positioned himself strategically behind the steeds, so their bodies partially blocked the breeze. He sat with his back propped against the cave wall, his trousers stripped off to expose the dozens of puncture wounds that lined his lower leg. It was not a pretty sight.

Hook's calf muscle was not its usual shape; rather than the rounded bulge of a healthy muscle, it looked more like a half-filled wineskin. In several places, the beast's chewing had widened the punctures to ragged tears, and blood continued to leak lazily from every one of them. Even with Gunnar and Adonica's help, it was all Hook had been able to do just to get back here using his new lance as a crutch. The pain was only getting worse, and he was feeling weaker by the hour.

"Regrettably," said Gunnar, kneeling beside him, "I ain't all that well-versed on the medicinal herbs." The antlered Ellenean crown was on his head yet again, and he fished a handful of seeds from the pouch at his side. "I spend more time on the weaponized and recreational varieties, but I've picked up a few things along the way."

With a flourish of Gunnar's fingers, the seeds in his hands burst to life, growing to full size right there in his palm. Quickly, he tossed the herbs into a travel-sized stone mortar and began to crush and grind them with a pestle, producing a rich, heady aroma.

"Can't promise a miraculous recovery," he said. "But I'll do my best."

Crack-crack-crack went Adonica's flint. "I couldn't have gotten paired up with the one who can shoot fire," she mumbled, stammering a bit as her jaw quivered with the cold. "Had to get the gardener."

"Remind me what you bring to the table?" said Gunnar.

"Poise and s—sophistication," Adonica said, then, logic notwithstanding, loudly slandered the mother of the flint in her hand.

Gunnar grew another handful of plants—these ones small flowers with indigo petals—then stripped the petals and mashed them into the mixture.

"Don't expect to run any races anytime soon," said Gunnar as he added some water from his canteen into the mortar, "but this stuff should stave off infection until we can get you to a real healer. Unless old ten-eyes utilizes some brand of poison or toxin in his bite. In which case, damned if I know what to do."

Hook considered signing to tell Gunnar that his bedside manner needed some work, but he didn't have the energy.

After some further mixing, Gunnar tilted the mortar and began applying the syrupy concoction to Hook's leg.

Hook tried to keep the noises to a minimum as Gunnar pushed the ointment into the deep holes in his leg. After a few moments, the work was done, and the liquid began to harden, forming a sort of paste.

Gunnar reached into his satchel and pulled out two objects: a sewing needle and a spool of thread.

"This will only work for some of them," said Gunnar, slipping the thread through the eye of the needle. "A few others will need a hot brand, once Adonica gets us a fire going." He tied the thread and bit off the loose end. "Are you the type to hold a grudge?"

Hook gave no reply.

"Great," said Gunnar, taking hold of Hook's leg. "Well, here goes nothing."

Hook rested his head against the wall of the tunnel and closed his eyes. He felt Gunnar tightly pinch the opposite edges of a tear in his thigh, then felt the needle pierce through.

Crack-crack-crack went Adonica's flint against the steel, falling in a steady rhythm.

And suddenly, Hook was back.

Back aboard the *Manticore*, watching helplessly as, with slow, steady repetition—almost as perfectly timed as the pacer's mallet-beats on his drum—the whip came down on Jocasta's bare back.

Crack. Crack. Crack.

CHAPTER 84

Crack. Crack. Crack.

Hook, seated across the aisle from Jocasta, clenched his teeth so hard that he tasted blood. Jocasta, just beyond his reach, sat with her head down, flinching each time the whip struck. Somehow, she had managed not to cry out, even as the skin of her back was split open in long, gaping lacerations, over and over again. Her unusual silver hair had grown out long in the months she'd been aboard the *Manticore* and was tied back by that strip of cloth.

As another blow landed, Hook shot a glare at Haystack, his benchmate, fellow oarsman, and fellow slave. Haystack looked away in shame. It had been he who, in his misguided zeal to please their captors, had revealed to Row-master Cadmus that Jocasta was teaching hand signs to the lifeslaves.

And now, she was paying the price. The pain of the lashings from the coral-studded leather was supplemented by the indignity of having been stripped of her upper garments, leaving her bare to the waist, exposed for all to see, with nothing to soften the blows of the whip.

In the aisle, not far from where Hook sat, Cadmus raised the whip again and brought it down on Jocasta's back.

Crack.

Cadmus was only a foot away from Hook. He paused to shoot a satisfied glance at Hook, whom he called Dark-eyes, then raised the whip and brought it down.

Crack.

He raised the whip and brought it down again.

Crack.

And again.

Crack.

Crack.

Crack.

With each strike, Hook found himself convinced that this one *had* to be the final one. In his rage, he had forgotten to keep count, but never had he seen so many lashes delivered in a single beating to a single slave. If Cadmus kept it up, he was going to kill her. And it suddenly occurred to Hook that perhaps that was his intention.

Maybe they weren't watching a punishment. Maybe they were witnessing an execution.

Crack.

Crack.

Crack.

With each successive strike, Jocasta's shoulders twitched a little less, and she slumped a little more. And with each twitch of her shoulders, Hook pulled harder against the chains that kept his wrists and ankles bolted to the floor—wrenching and twisting back and forth against the loose bolt that he had been wrenching and twisting at every single day since he'd been brought aboard this ship and placed in this spot, years before.

Crack.

Crack.

Crack.

Hook pulled. The shackles bit into the skin of his wrists. He felt the blood trickle down his forearms, felt the bolt in the floor wobble, but no more or less than it had wobbled on the first day he'd been put here. Two years ago, by his rough estimate. Maybe they all wobbled like this. Maybe they were supposed to.

Crack.

Finally, Cadmus lowered his whip and rolled it into a coil. Jocasta sat slouched forward, arms draped over the shaft of the oar for support, breathing heavily. Her back oozed red from muscle-deep slices.

Casually, Cadmus adjusted his belt. He scanned the assemblage of rowers. None dared look back at him.

None except the dark eyes of Hook Bard.

"Our newest team member has violated one of the principles set down by sacred Mythaean law," said Cadmus, making it a point to look straight into Hook's eyes as he spoke. His tone was conversational, as if he were sitting down to dinner with an old friend. "I don't make these rules, but it is my duty to enforce them. I want you all to know that I will do what I must, though I do not enjoy it. This little Fawn uses her hands to speak, I am told."

Cadmus reached into a satchel hanging by a strap around his shoulders and withdrew a small chunk of wood, a pair of tongs, and a paring knife.

"Lucky for her, then," he said, "for she will not miss her tongue."

"No—" whispered Jocasta. It was the only sound she had made, all this time.

CHAPTER 85

Cadmus grabbed Jocasta by the hair, yanked her head back, and shoved his hand into her mouth. He positioned the chunk of wood this way and that until her jaw was wedged open. She threw her head wildly against him. Her arms flailed. But the scourging had left her weak.

Hook pulled.

And the loose bolt holding his chains broke.

The single length of chain—fed through the shackles on his wrists and ankles—fell away like a fisherman's line unspooling from its reel as Hook shot to his feet.

Hook's freed hands grabbed Cadmus by the neck. His fingers closed around the row-master's windpipe with an iron grip.

In his shock, Cadmus dropped the tongs, but, to his credit, he managed to keep hold of the paring knife. He swung it sidelong, stabbing

Hook solidly in the shoulder, and the tiny blade stuck there. Hook barely felt it.

Hook looked deep into Cadmus's eyes. He was a big man. But he wasn't that big.

Hook picked him up by the throat, lifting him until his boots dangled inches off the ground. Cadmus beat against Hook's hand to try to free himself, but fingers that had spent years grasping an oar were not so easy to pry open. Hook squeezed harder, and Cadmus's face contorted, turning blue.

"Dark-eyes, don't you—!" Cadmus choked out from beneath Hook's grip.

Even now, the severity of the situation didn't seem to have yet dawned on Cadmus. He glared at Hook as if scolding an out-of-line child. Hook could not tell if it was a brilliantly disciplined bluff or if this man had spent so long entrenched in authority that he was incapable of contemplating what was happening—so out of touch with his own vulnerability.

At the front of the aisle, Pacer Hil had already cried out in alarm, and several marines were rushing down the stairs from the deck above. Hook knew he had precious little time to make his mark.

Hook let go with one hand and pulled the knife out of his muscular shoulder. The thin blade had broken in half, but it would do.

He raised it to Cadmus's forehead. Only now did the row-master's expression change. His disapproval turned to terror.

"No, please—!" said Cadmus.

Please, thought Hook. *He's saying please. To me.*

The audacity was stunning.

Cadmus squealed and flailed as Hook inserted the blade beneath the skin of his forehead, wedged it upwards, and dragged it along, sideways. Like peeling an apple, he flayed a long strip of skin from Cadmus's forehead, from one temple to the other, roughly equivalent in size and shape to the burn scar of a lifeslave's brand, while Cadmus wailed and cried tears like a child.

The marines converged on them from both sides. They tackled Hook, wrested the knife from his grip, and rained fists upon him. Others grabbed Cadmus to pull him to safety, shouting for a healer.

By now, even Captain Gelon had made it below-decks. "What is going—?" he demanded. When he saw Cadmus's red-streaked face, he gasped. "By the seas!"

Even as the marine's blows struck him again and again, Hook kept his dark eyes trained on Captain Gelon, who had turned to look at the unchained lifeslave in horror. Never had he so longed to be able to speak again, so that he might properly convey his message: *You, Captain, are next.*

"P—put him in chains! Now!" ordered Gelon. "Our row-master needs medical attention—all hands, prepare to row!"

But as the marines hauled Hook to his feet and dragged him down the aisle, the rowers sat motionless. Their hands were in their laps.

"All *hands*, I said!" shouted Gelon. "That's an order!"

And still, no one moved.

Just before they dragged him up the stairs that led to the deck, Hook managed to turn his head far enough around to see Jocasta. Her blue eyes were watching him. She was still breathing deeply from the whipping. But despite the agony she must have been feeling, she was smiling a crooked smile at him.

Crack.

"Got it!" Adonica said.

Hook blinked in surprise, snapping back to the present as Adonica dropped the flint and dagger and cupped her hands around the pile of sticks and grass where the spark had finally taken.

Adonica pursed her lips into a careful circle and blew gently. Smoke rose from between her trembling fingers. Gunnar, halfway through stitching one of the segments of torn flesh in Hook's leg, rushed to her side. He grabbed a few small pieces of bark and bits of twigs to feed the tiny ember, but Adonica slapped his hand away to prevent him from interfering. Dutifully, she tended to the precious flame, and, in a few moments, it had multiplied—hopping from one branch to the next.

"Grow us some kindling," Adonica demanded.

"You know, I hate to pull rank here—" Gunnar started to reply.

"Will you shut up and do as I say?" Adonica snapped, turning toward him with a clenched fist raised.

Gunnar retreated quietly from the fire and occupied himself by growing a series of woody vines. Hook, meanwhile, took advantage of the reprieve from medical treatment to rest his head against the stone wall, close his eyes, and fall asleep, thinking about Jocasta's blue eyes.

CHAPTER 86

"How much more of that cured beef have we got?"

Hook searched through his pack, coming out with three thin sticks of the stuff, wrapped in paper. Not even enough for a meal for one, in his opinion, let alone to split three ways. But it was all they had.

Days of hard traveling lay between them and Castydociana, where they were to meet up with Leah and the others—provided, that was, that all had gone according to plan on her end. Any other sources of food between here and there would either be grown by Gunnar or hunted or scavenged along the way.

"Here," said Adonica, reaching into her own satchel. "Might not be bad roasted."

She sat several long cuts of raw meat down beside the fire.

"Is that what I think it is?" said Gunnar.

Wordlessly, Adonica offered him a piece.

"Tentacle?" asked Gunnar.

"Wasn't keen to try tentacle," she said. "It's jowl."

"Jowl?"

"It's the best bit of bacon from a hog." She shrugged. "Thought the same might be true of a sea monster."

Gunnar looked at the morsel suspiciously for a moment, then flicked his finger. A small vine shot up from seemingly out of nowhere, skewered the piece of meat right out of Adonica's hand, and then curled to bring it down to hang over the flames.

When Adonica offered a piece to Hook, he shook his head. He hadn't enjoyed his first bite of the beast. He would need to be a bit closer to starvation before he resorted to forcing down another.

Hook sat, staring into the fire, his mind wandering back through the years. He'd expected to be killed on the spot for attacking Cadmus. But, evidently, Captain Gelon had had a greater sense of propriety than that. He'd opted to follow protocol—to take Hook to the nearest Mythaean port and turn him over to the local magistrate for his crime.

Upon their arrival at the port, a delirious Row-master Cadmus had been carried off the *Manticore* and taken to the healers. It was not until Hook had been brought up on deck, wrists chained behind his back and ankles chained as well, that he'd recognized where he was. Ephixes—the very city where he had been branded and assigned to the *Manticore*.

It started here, Hook remembered thinking, as they'd hauled him off for judgment. *Appropriate that it would end here as well.*

The magistrate had ordered an obligatory whipping to start with, followed by swift sentencing. It was to be as Hook had guessed: the most public of executions, at dawn the following day.

Hook remembered the way the magistrate had eyed him after announcing the sentence. Waiting for a reaction. Perhaps thinking Hook would try to beg for amnesty. Instead, he had stared at the magistrate in satisfaction, knowing he had done the one thing that scared these people. He had made one of them bleed.

Following the hearing, Hook had been thrown into a cell. His sentence was to be carried out so soon that there had been no need for the healers to tend to the lashes on his back—or the small hole in his shoulder where Cadmus had stabbed him with his paring knife.

It had felt nice to be on firm, solid ground, even if it was the floor of a jail cell. He hadn't realized how accustomed he'd become to the world constantly rising and sinking beneath him with the ups and downs of the sea.

He wouldn't have long, he knew. The execution was to be at daybreak, and it would be a grand and grotesque spectacle—naturally, in full view of the slaves aboard Hook's old ship, to demonstrate what happened to those who tried to fight back. He remembered a friend from his childhood who claimed to have seen a slave's execution. The methods employed in his friend's story had been quite creative; apparently, prolonging the victim's life, and therefore his suffering, was just as important, if not more important, than the end result.

As Adonica tore through a piece of jowl meat, Hook closed his eyes and remembered the feel of the cold stone beneath him as he'd sat in the corner of his cell, clenching his teeth against the sharp pain of the open lash wounds on his back, wincing with each steady throb of Cadmus's stab wound in his shoulder, carefully watching the two guards nearby playing cards at the table by the door.

The rest of the cells, so far as he'd been able to tell, had been empty. He'd waited until he was certain the guards were sufficiently absorbed in their game before reaching up to his shoulder and digging his fingers into the hole in his skin. It'd been a challenge to stay silent as his fingers probed inside the wound, but if there was one thing Hook Bard had plenty of practice at, it was being silent.

Finding the broken tip of Cadmus's paring knife hadn't been difficult. Pulling it out had been the hard part.

It was fortunate that Cadmus had opted to use such a small knife. Much bigger, and the blade wouldn't have fit into the keyhole of the shackles on Hook's wrist and ankles. He'd made quick work of those; he'd encountered more challenging locks on street merchant's lockboxes as a youth. The cell door took a bit longer, but he had plenty of time. The guards' lanterns lit their card game and not much else.

Hook waited until one of the guards stepped out, leaving the other one alone at the table. There was no sense in sneaking. The better chance was to rush him—hit him hard before the man knew what was happening. Injured as Hook was, he knew that getting the jump on a healthy soldier would be easier said than done. But it was his only shot.

The guard had barely had time to draw his sword before Hook had been on him. Hook had clamped a hand over his mouth and relieved him of his sword, laying it carefully atop the cards on the table. He couldn't afford for there to be any blood. He needed the man's uniform.

When the second guard had returned, Hook had been waiting for him behind the door, dressed in the attire of the first guard. He'd made short work of him.

When Hook took his leave, the first guard was sitting in the corner of the locked cell, dressed in rags like a slave, and chained like a prisoner. The second guard sat propped in a chair at the table, his arm positioned beneath his head as if he'd fallen asleep at his post. Hook slipped the second guard's helmet on to cover the scar of his slave's brand. The scene he was leaving behind wouldn't fool anyone for longer than a few seconds, but a few seconds was sometimes all you had.

Hook had marched out in the guard's attire, estimating that it couldn't have been past midnight yet. The intelligent course of action would have been to head for the stables, pick himself out a steed, and put as much distance between himself and Ephixes as possible before anyone noticed he was gone. But he had a responsibility. He had done the one thing that scared these people. He had made one of his masters bleed.

One wasn't nearly enough.

Hook had stuffed one of the second guard's socks into the hole in his shoulder, knowing that the threat of infection wouldn't matter much if he didn't make it out of here; he had to avoid bleeding out and staining the uniform. As for the wounds to his back, there wasn't much he could do about it. He walked straight-backed and with a measured step, knowing that a confident stride would be the key to maintaining his disguise in the shadows of torchlight.

He remembered this place well. He followed his mental map to the dungeon chambers beneath the jailhouse, opting to venture deeper into the enemy's domain than to flee from it. After all, he'd made an oath, and a promise was a promise.

CHAPTER 87

Hook walked every corridor with a confident stride in his step, proceeding as if he belonged there. He entered every doorway as if he had full authority to enter it. So when he finally pushed open the door to the room he'd been searching for—a room that was never far from his thoughts—it was with the professional, matter-of-fact demeanor of an officer.

It was exactly as he remembered it, though perhaps a bit smaller than it loomed in his memory. A furnace in the corner. A large bucket of water to the side. Tools on the wall. A chair in the center of the room with shackles on its armrests.

Hook's entrance was so casual that the two men in the room looked up at him not with alarm but mild curiosity. The bigger of the two was in the process of hanging up his apron, and his apprentice was sweeping the floor. A bit late at night for a message from the magistrate, they were probably thinking.

Hook almost found himself feeling grateful. In a way, all the wretched lots he'd been cast in life were worth it, just for this small bit of luck today.

"Help you?" asked the big man.

Hook closed the door behind him and threw the bar across it. He cast a glance at the coals in the stove. They were burning low, but they would do.

He removed his helmet. Realization flashed across both men's faces as Hook advanced across the room. The apprentice tripped over his broom as he tried to scramble away. The big man grabbed an iron rod off the wall and held it out in front of him like a duelist's saber. At that moment, perhaps more than any other moment that had preceded it, Hook longed to have his tongue back, just so he could say, "I told you I would be back."

A gentle prodding woke Hook. He looked up from the ground and found Stormbringer standing over him. The steed was nudging him with its trunk.

Hook blinked in surprise. He hadn't even realized he'd drifted off, but he'd evidently been sleeping for several hours; the first light of day was creeping in through the entrance to the ruins.

"You were making noises in your sleep," said Gunnar from the other side of the fire. He gestured to Stormbringer. "Poor thing seemed upset by it."

Hook reached up and nuzzled the steed reassuringly. Stormbringer huffed in relief.

Gunnar sat before the fire with the antlered helmet in his lap. A few freshly grown logs now burned in the fire while new ones lay at the edge of the coals, drying in the heat. Beside him, Adonica sat with her back to the fire. She had removed her clothes to allow them to dry, and one of the steeds' saddle blankets was draped over her shoulders for warmth. She glanced over her shoulder at Hook, and for a split-second, her yellow hair almost looked silver in the firelight.

And her eyes.

Hook swallowed hard. There were times when she reminded him so much of Jocasta that it hurt.

"Nightmares again?" Adonica asked.

Hook's jaw clenched. He raised his hands, hesitated for a second, then signed, *"I should have let those men live."*

Adonica's brow furrowed. She exchanged a glance with Gunnar.

"The night I escaped from slavery," signed Hook, *"I killed some people. Two of them deserved it. The others, I do not know."*

Neither Gunnar nor Adonica was very familiar with Hook's signs, but his lessons had apparently paid off, as they seemed to be following his meaning.

Hook looked hard at Gunnar. *"Did you own slaves?"*

"I told you, I never did," Gunnar replied evenly.

"I know what you told me," signed Hook. *"But did you?"*

Gunnar stared at him with his lone eye. Slowly, he raised his hand and gave the sign that meant *"No."*

Hook stared at the man until he felt satisfied.

"I escaped from slavery," signed Hook. *"Twice."*

"Twice?" Adonica signed back.

Hook nodded. *"The first time, I broke the chains that held me and cut a brand into my ship's row-master. I was arrested for my crime. I escaped from my cell, killed my guards . . . and found the two men who had cut my tongue out and branded me. In return for what they had done to me and countless others, I cut out their tongues and branded them. Then I killed them.*

"I returned to my ship. A small detachment of guards was posted there. I killed them all. And I killed the captain of the vessel, Gelon. Then I took the ship for myself and freed the slaves from their chains. We rowed out to sea, for once at our own command, and sailed away. Finally, we were free."

Hook paused. He left the next part of his story unsigned: *Finally, I could touch the hands of my beloved. The hands that had given me a voice again.*

"Time passed," signed Hook, *"and we joined forces with another vessel. Together, we took to raiding Mythaean ships."*

"Raiding?" said Adonica. "You mean piracy."

Hook glowered at her. *"You truly have no idea what your own people are like, do you?"*

Adonica's only response was a look of confusion.

"The Mythaeans were the pirates," signed Hook. *"We raided ships to free the slaves they had captured. Each time we took a ship and freed the slaves from Mythaean galleys, we added to our numbers."*

And each time, thought Hook, *Jocasta did not lose hope that we would someday find her sisters.*

"We grew into a small fleet. My escape, and my ruthlessness in our raids, became legendary among the crew, and I became a sort of leader to these people. My. . . ." Hook paused. *"My most trusted friend, she soon tired of this life. She was an aurym-user. A healer. Like Leah and Lycon. She wanted to help in a different way. One day, she came to me and said she wanted no more of this life. No more revenge."*

Hook paused. He stared into the fire as he signed, no longer caring if Gunnar or Adonica were paying attention to his story.

"She, as much as anyone, deserved to hate the Mythaeans. But she said that she believed mercy was stronger than revenge. That forgiveness was stronger than hate. I did not believe that. She said she would have left this life behind long before, if not for me. She asked me if I cared for her enough to leave this life behind and follow her. Before I could give her an answer, our vessels spotted a Mythaean trireme alone in calm waters, at the Bay of Rysh near Lyphix. A perfect target."

"Oh, no," said Gunnar.

Hook looked up at him.

"I. . . ." said Gunnar. He hung his head. "I think I know what happens next."

"I could have left it alone," signed Hook. *"Could have used the moment to prove to Jocasta that I cared more for her than for revenge. Instead, at my orders, we gave chase. Straight into a trap.*

"The undefended ship was bait, meant to lure us into the bay, where we were quickly boxed in by Mythaean ships hidden among the inlets.

"They swarmed us. A few of our ships got away. Not mine. They boarded us. They took us down one by one."

Hook paused. He remembered the feel of Jocasta's hand in his as they ran, attempting to flee the *Manticore*. Remembered the sound of a loud twang, followed by Jocasta's sharp, surprised intake of breath. Remembered looking down to see the barbed arrowhead protruding from the front of his beloved's chest. Remembered turning to see Cadmus standing on the deck of the *Manticore*, lowering his crossbow with a satisfied smile on his face.

He'd tried to catch her, but his fingers had only grazed Jocasta's silver hair as she fell, snagging on the strip of cloth she'd always used to keep it in place. He remembered watching as it pulled free of her hair, and she tumbled overboard, trailing blood, looking up at him in shock before she splashed down into the waters below.

Hands had grabbed him, then. Too many hands to fight off. And they'd dragged him to *him*. Cadmus had looked down, eyes staring at Hook from beneath a nasty, raised scar that ran across the length of his forehead like a lifeslave's brand.

"Couldn't save your pretty Fawn this time, eh Dark-eyes?" Cadmus had said.

Presently, seated beside the fire with Gunnar and Adonica, Hook reached up and rubbed his fingers over the strip of cloth tied around his forehead.

CHAPTER 88

"Most of us were killed," Hook signed. *"The rest became slaves once again. Cadmus, the former row-master of the Manticore, became its new captain. I was wanted for public execution for my crimes. But first, he sat me in the same seat where I had labored for all those years. And I rowed again. To fill in all the newly emptied rowers' seats on the Manticore, Cadmus stopped at an island village along the way and captured a few of the young locals."*

"What?" Adonica suddenly spat. "What fleet did this Cadmus sail for? That's barbaric! What city-state sanctioned enslaving islanders who had done no wrong?"

Hook shot a look at her, then at Gunnar. Signing proper names wasn't easy, especially to people who weren't already familiar with the signing system. So instead, he grabbed a burnt stick from the fire and leaned over to write the name on the stone of the tunnel floor.

For a few moments, Gunnar and Adonica both stared at the name, dumbstruck.

"Winhold!" Adonica finally gasped. "An ally of Hartla?"

"And one of the founding members of the League," said Gunnar. "One of the fleets that came to assist us after the Battle of Gaius, no less."

But Hook ignored Gunnar for now. He stared Adonica in the eye. By now, he'd spent enough time with Mythaean soldiers to have learned what little understanding most of them had of their own cultural legacy. Many of them seemed completely unaware of the barbarism that made their way of life possible.

"Your people's power was built on the backs of slaves," signed Hook. *"Some of those slaves are criminals who are sentenced to life at the oars. Like I was. But others, like my beloved, are victims of state-sanctioned piracy and worse. Every day, people are being captured. Enslaved. And eventually murdered."*

Hook paused to write another name on the floor. Then he gestured at Gunnar.

"*Megara*?" Gunnar read aloud.

"You mean that Rorrdvuuk woman?" said Adonica.

Hook nodded. *"She was an enslaved rower on the Gryphon."*

This, too, took some writing on the floor before he managed to get the meaning across. When he did, Adonica's eyes went wide.

"I thought you never used slaves," she said, shooting an accusatory glance at Gunnar.

"I didn't," he retorted, hands clenched into fists. "But the *Gryphon* wasn't always my ship. It belonged to my uncle—"

"But wasn't the *Gryphon* a sailing ship?" said Adonica.

"There were seats for oarsmen below deck as well," said Gunnar, "but I didn't think. . . ." He shook his head.

"Megara recognized the name Nimbus," signed Hook. *"You are lucky that before we left Cervice, she did not do to you what I did to my former captors."*

Gunnar ran a hand over his forehead, visibly shaken.

Hook adjusted his position on the floor and winced as a terrible pain shot up from his leg. This time, he was unable to hide his discomfort from Gunnar and Adonica. Gunnar had done his best to treat and bandage the wounds from the monster's bites, but Hook knew that without some real, proper treatment, a wound like this could kill him. And perhaps sooner rather than later.

"It took us a two-day ride to get here," Adonica said meaningfully, turning to face Gunnar. "We're gonna have to move faster than that on the return to Cervice, or he may not make it."

Gently, Hook grabbed Stormbringer's trunk for support. The intelligent animal understood what he was doing and kept his trunk steady as Hook pulled himself to his feet. Gunnar and Adonica both moved to assist, but Hook waved them off. When he'd gained his footing, he signed, *It is almost morning. No use talking the day away. Let us leave now. I will make it.*

Gunnar and Adonica both nodded, then began gathering up their things. Hook, feeling the blood trickle down his leg, chewed on the inside of his cheek, trying to mask the pain.

I will make it, he thought.

It was always good to tell yourself things like that, whether they were true or not. After all, if it wasn't true, being wrong would be the least of his worries.

CHAPTER 89

In the light of early evening, in the hidden grove tucked into the cleft in the mountains, Leah's a'thri'ik armor had lost all of its glow. Beside her, Marcus, Lycon, and Megara were similarly adorned in their own procured sets of cat's eye armor.

Leah had never seen anything like this armor before, and it had taken some time—and some instruction from Itzacoatl—to put it all on. There were a'thri'ik breastplates and plackarts to cover the chest and torso, pauldrons that went over the shoulders, and vambraces that slipped on like metal-plated shirtsleeves. There were plates that closed around the thigh on hinges and attached by straps and buckles, and smaller versions that went around the shins and calves, partially covering their boots. There were gloves over their hands and circular plates of armor that attached around the neck and throat. And there were helmets with visors on hinges that, due to some magic or expertise of engineering, moved as if well-greased despite their unknowable age.

Magic perhaps was a simplistic way of thinking about such things, but Zechariah had once described the walls that protected these mountains as having been built with the "magic" of the Ancients as mortar. Perhaps some such magic or lost craft had gone into the forging of these pieces of armor and weaponry, too, which had survived millennia underground without rusting or even losing their keen edges.

Down in Cymorrika, these suits of armor had been an impressive sight. With the full suits donned and the helmets on, Leah and her soldiers had taken on the appearance of glowing green apparitions in the blackness of the mountain underworld, looking a great deal like the two powerful warriors who had attacked them—Itzacoatl's brothers. They did indeed look more like unbreakable carven statues than humans. The armor left hardly a gap exposed. It was a chore to put it all on, but it was not nearly as heavy or awkward as Leah had feared. Presently, she stood with the visor of her exotic helmet raised, allowing her to see unhindered. When the visor was lowered, it left only a narrow slit to see through.

Or to run a saber through, thought Leah.

Over it all, Leah wore her blood-red cloak, an emblem of Nolian nobility. The crown was still packed away in a satchel at her side.

Thid and his bodyguards had entered the city. The plan had been for Leah, Marcus, Lycon, and Megara to depart immediately. But a report from a member of Thid's entourage had altered their plans. Travelers had been seen coming up the mountain paths far below. At such a distance, the scout hadn't been able to identify them, and after a few minutes, the travelers had moved beyond sight. It was possible that they were humans. It was equally possible, however, that what the scout had seen had been demons.

Tracking us into the mountains, thought Leah.

If that was the case, the location of the hidden city might have been compromised, meaning everything they'd gone through had been for naught. Time would tell if that was the case. If they were coming up the same paths, following them here, then they would eventually appear below.

"Almost three hundred full sets," Marcus said to no one in particular. He rapped his armored fist against his breastplate. "And even more weapons."

"We'll leave some of them here for the soldiers who will serve as guards for the city," said Leah. "As for the rest, with Thid's blessing, we'll take them with us. To Castydociana."

Megara made a series of signs with her hands. She did not wear the gauntlets or gloves of the Ancients' armor; Leah suspected that this was not only to ensure that her signs were clear, but also because the gauntlet she already wore, with her sun-stone set into it, was a greater boon than any amount of reinforced protection.

"You truly mean to go set sail?" she asked. *"To take your army across the ocean and invade your enemy's territory?"*

"I do," Leah signed, then said aloud, "and I hope that your people will join us."

Megara considered this for a moment, as if she was unsure if she should answer. Finally, she signed, *"As do I."*

A rustling in the trees ahead drew Leah's attention forward. A moment later, a hemlock bough bent back, and the Cru scout, a young woman, came through, her chest rising and falling from her run.

"It is the people," she said.

Leah's brow furrowed, wondering if there was a language barrier hindering her understanding of the young woman's meaning.

"The people," Marcus spoke up. "As in *our* people?"

The scout nodded.

"The people of Cervice?" said Leah.

"Yes," the scout said. "The citizens. Women, children, elderly—nonfighters. I can see Nolians, Endens, Lundens, Cru, Raeqlu, and others. If I were to guess, there are enough to account for most of the civilians of Cervice. Only a few soldiers among them."

Leah's nostrils flared. "Zechariah," she fumed. "He was to wait for my orders before proceeding with the plan. Without fail, he does as he pleases with no regard for. . . !" She trailed off, biting her tongue to prevent herself from saying something she might come to regret later.

"Begging your pardon," said Lycon. "But do you think he *could* do that, My Queen?"

Leah turned to face him.

Lycon stroked his bushy beard with an a'thri'ik armored hand. "Olorus would never disobey your orders, would he?"

Leah hesitated. That was true.

"The League forces are loyal not to Zechariah, but to you, Olorus, and the others who journeyed with us from Hartla," Lycon continued. "And I cannot imagine a scenario where even old Zechariah, for all his political wiles, could convince Olorus to disregard your orders."

"The same is doubly true for Endenholm, I assure you," said Marcus, puffing out his chest. "I left my orders. My officers would not have disobeyed without great cause."

"You're right," Leah said, the realization dawning on her. "That can only mean something went wrong."

Megara touched Leah's arm to get her attention. She signed a question, which Leah quickly translated to the scout: "You didn't mention Rorrdvuuk. Did you see any Rorrdvuuk among the people?"

The scout shook her head. "None, Elder Leah."

Leah turned back to face Megara, but the big woman's face was even more impassive than usual.

CHAPTER 90

When the first waves of the mass of humanity came marching up the mountain path, rounding a corner for a heavily wooded area, Leah was there waiting for them.

Snow had begun to fall from gray, mid-morning clouds hanging overhead, forming a layer of moisture on her armor. Her royal cape flew behind her like a flag in the mountain breeze. And on her head, she wore the crown of Nolia. If something catastrophic truly had occurred in Cervice, then now more than ever, she needed to be a symbol for these people. It was the least she could do to serve that purpose for them, and be waiting for them as their weary bodies labored up the mountain path.

From what she could see, the young scout's initial observations had been correct. There were some soldiers here, but most of these people were citizens from the city. The very people Leah had been hoping to return to Cervice and lead here personally.

General Olorus Antony led the procession. Every time Leah saw him, it seemed there was more gray in his beard. He approached Leah and the others with a haggard look on his face—an expression that turned to curiosity at the sight of their new suits of armor they all wore, then to concern when he noticed the scar across Leah's head and the missing portion of her ear.

"Trouble?" was all Leah said.

Olorus, to his credit, did not hesitate nor falter in his delivery. "A demon army," he said. "The biggest we've seen to date, marching toward Cervice from the southwest. We learned of it two days ago, My Lady. Based on our scouts' reports, they probably arrived at the city gates either last night or early this morning."

Leah's heart suddenly felt out of place in her chest. She struggled to remain stoic as she thought of warriors manning the walls of Cervice, bracing the gates against a demon onslaught, dying by the scores or the hundreds, to give these civilians a chance to flee.

"Why is our army not here, Olorus?" she whispered when she could wait no longer. "Please tell me they did not—"

"They are safe," Olorus cut in. "So far as I know, at any rate, no one has been harmed. When the fate of the city became clear, Zechariah and I—along with the officers of the League, Raeqlund, the Holy Army, and the rest—decided that our only course of action was to evacuate the city. It pained me to do such a thing, but the alternative would have meant our assured destruction. Cervice is emptied, My Lady."

The breath Leah had been holding came out in a great, shuddering sigh.

Thank the spirit, she thought.

"There was nowhere else for these people to go," said Olorus, "so Zechariah provided us with a map that led to the location of the hidden city. We had no choice but to proceed on faith that the sanctuary you came to find was a reality. And faith that we would be allowed access."

"Your faith was not misplaced," Sif spoke up. "Cymorrika is open to the people of Cervice."

Olorus beamed. For a moment, his old self shone through. He turned to face the quiet crowd assembling on the mountain path behind him—who, Leah now realized, had been waiting for a verdict. Olorus raised one hand for all to see, then closed his hand into a triumphant fist. A cheer erupted from the crowd. Leah smiled, then raised her hand and mimicked Olorus's gesture, causing the cheer to grow in volume.

"And the army?" Lycon was asking Olorus when Leah turned her attention back to the matter at hand.

"Zechariah is leading them to Castydociana to connect with the rest of the League forces," said Olorus. "I believe he intends for you to meet him there via the route north of the mountains, if that is your chosen course of action. There, he hopes you will be able to convince Wulder Von Morix to commit to the plan to set sail and invade Erum."

"But the demon army," said Marcus. "When they find Cervice empty, they'll surely follow you into the mountains—"

"It's been taken care of," said Olorus. "We shut the gate. Permanently."

Leah nodded in satisfaction. The Walls of the Ancients. The great fortifications, leftovers from the same civilization that had built Cymorrika, were hundreds of feet tall and ran the entire length of the mountains. Zechariah had once described them as having been constructed with the "magic" of the ancients as mortar. When those gates were shut, it was said, nothing could get through—not even aurym or daemyn.

Leah did not know how true the claims were, but those walls were the only defenses she had ever seen effectively thwart a cythraul's advances. On her first trip into these mountains, Ahlund had destroyed the winch holding up one of the Ancients' great gates. Only the dropping of that gate had allowed Justin, Leah, and Zechariah to escape. If Olorus had done something similar, then perhaps these people still had a chance after all.

But as these thoughts were running through Leah's mind, Megara stepped forward to address Olorus. *"And what of my people?"* she signed.

Olorus's countenance fell. "There was . . . an incident."

CHAPTER 91

As Lycon, Sif, and Marcus began the arduous process of leading the civilians to the secluded glen that marked the entrance to Cymorrika, Leah did her best to remain in full view of her people—while also holding a private council with Olorus and Megara.

"The Rorrdvuuk," said Olorus, "are no longer with us."

Leah avoided looking at Megara to try to gauge her reaction. At least, for the moment.

"Zechariah and I spoke to your king, Folgruuth, prior to the evacuation," said Olorus. "We encouraged him to do as we had done. To send his civilians into the mountains and his warriors to Castydociana. But he insisted on sending all of the Rorrdvuuk into the mountains with us. To help protect the civilians on their journey, he claimed. A few are still with us. Maybe twenty-five or so. No more. The rest are gone, along with most of the several hundred Darvellians we had taken in, and almost a hundred other Athaceans."

Leah touched Olorus's arm. "What happened, Olorus?"

He looked hard at her. "Asher."

"Who?" signed Megara.

"The former prime minister of Nolia," said Olorus. "A masterful manipulator and a traitor to the crown. There was a brief struggle. Not much blood was shed, thankfully. No fatalities. I didn't think it was worth it to go after them. Not under the circumstances. If I was mistaken, I apologize."

For a moment, Leah didn't understand what Olorus was trying to tell her. Then it all clicked into place, and two massive blunders now stood plainly exposed before her.

In her willingness to help the Rorrdvuuk people, she had placed a great deal of trust in Folgruuth, Megara, and their people, without a full understanding of where they truly stood. She had believed—had *wanted* to believe—that Folgruuth would follow her lead for the good of his people.

But Asher. The man had a tongue silver enough to have connived his way to the highest civilian post in the Nolian government, only to betray the crown. A group of people as displaced and desperate as the Rorrdvuuk—driven from their homelands, seeking refuge in Nolia, only to be asked to march even farther, beneath the banner of a military alliance they had no reason to trust. . . . She didn't know how Asher had managed to gain an audience with Folgruuth, but a few delicately planted ideas and properly timed suggestions were all Asher would have needed to influence the king of the Rorrdvuuk into opting for a seemingly more beneficial alliance.

"They set him free," said Leah. "Didn't they?"

Olorus nodded. "We were transporting him and the Darvellian assassin as prisoners. Folgruuth and his Rorrdvuuk warriors ambushed the guards in the night and set Asher and the assassin free."

"So the Rorrdvuuk have left us," said Leah. "Taking Asher with them. But you say we lost Athaceans, as well? And Darvellians?"

"At least a hundred Athaceans," said Olorus. "And the several hundred Darvellians we took in out of mercy. Almost all of them pledged allegiance to Asher and then departed with him and the Rorrdvuuk." Olorus dropped his voice to a whisper. "And there were some Nolians, too, Leah."

Leah shook her head, trying to hide the pain this brought her.

It was discouraging that the Darvellians to whom she'd shown mercy would betray her. But the idea that Athaceans and even Nolians—people who *knew* of Asher's treachery—had opted to follow him and his liberators anyway, struck her a hard blow.

How could they? she wanted to say. *After everything that's happened, how could they?*

"Initially, we tried to stop them," said Olorus. "But we have precious few soldiers with us. Chasing after them seemed like folly—"

"I agree with you," Leah reassured him. "You were right to let them go. But where could they be going?"

"I'm not sure," said Olorus. "Our last reports said that the city of Isabelle was still standing in Darvelle. It's possible he means to take them there. Asher clearly saw no future for himself in Nolia or the League."

"So he created a new one," said Leah.

The snake, she thought, and not for the first time.

Leah glanced at Megara. The big woman stood rigid and stone-faced.

"As I said, not all of the Rorrdvuuk left under Folgruuth's command," said Olorus. "A few, to their credit, saw the wisdom in staying with us. . . . I hate to pour more troubles on you, My Queen, but there is one more thing. It's the map. We cannot locate it."

"The map," said Leah. "The map that shows the way here?"

"Yes, Leah," said Olorus. Then he added in a whisper, "It is possible that the deserters have it."

Leah closed her eyes, only now feeling the full impact of her failure. Asher had the map that led to her people's only sanctuary. A man who would not hesitate to use such knowledge to his advantage, whatever the cost to others. If the demons or any who followed them somehow got a hold of that map. . . .

Father, thought Leah, eyes still closed. *I thought I was doing the right thing. I thought I was being merciful. Helping those in need. Acting in accordance with our moral code and our nation's laws. And here is where my faith has led me. Should I have turned the Darvellians and the Rorrdvuuk away, to protect my own? Should I have had Asher killed when I had the chance?*

When no answer came, Leah turned away from Olorus and Megara. She stepped into the shade of a copse of evergreens for a moment, alone with her thoughts.

If I had, she thought, answering the question for herself, *none of this would have happened. A real leader would have anticipated something like this. Or been wise enough to avoid a situation where it could have occurred.*

There were so many moving parts. She'd been trying to do whatever was necessary to maintain her political alliances and stay strong. She had no other choice, did she?

She continued a few more steps into the trees. When she felt quite certain that she was out of sight of the rest of the people, she closed her eyes, removed the Nolian crown from her head, and rested her forehead against the trunk of a tree.

"You're not even meant to be here," she whispered to herself. "You were never supposed to lead anybody. Your brothers were supposed to be the leaders. You weren't trained the way they were. You were supposed to be a healer, maybe a professor at the Academy someday. If you can't even handle *this*, how do you expect to lead an army halfway across the world?"

Leah shut her eyes and leaned more heavily against the tree trunk, gritting her teeth.

"I can't do this," she heard herself mumble through her clenched throat. "Father. Mother. I'm just not strong enough. . . ."

CHAPTER 92

Hook didn't even remember falling from his steed. One moment, he was riding. The next, his body was hitting the ground, bouncing, and rolling through weeds hard with frost.

"Hook's down!" called Gunnar from somewhere ahead.

"I've got him!" Adonica replied. "Keep going and flag it down! It's flying the League's flag—they have to listen to you, right?"

"That's right!" Gunnar shouted, then gave a cry for his steed to hurry its pace.

Hook heard all this from the cold ground, his bleary eyes staring into the sky. He felt Stormbringer's prehensile trunk probing gently at his hand, and he stroked the trunk to calm the worried creature.

His leg was getting worse. The pain was hot, throbbing, and relentless. Infection had set in, as they all had known it would. If something wasn't done soon, he wouldn't last much longer. In some cases, the amputation of an infected limb could save an injured soldier from death. Hook suspected, if it came to that, Adonica would have to be the one to make the hack. He doubted Gunnar had the stomach for it.

"Come on," said Adonica, appearing suddenly over his head. She crouched and grabbed him beneath the armpits.

She uttered a curse as she hauled him to his feet. Hook managed to get an arm around her shoulders for support and leaned heavily against her, his vision swimming.

"Think you can climb back into the saddle?" she asked.

Hook managed a nod.

"They've got to be able to see us by now," she said. "With any luck, you'll get to lie down real soon."

She clicked her tongue, and Stormbringer drew close. It took the combined efforts of two humans and one very patient steed, but Hook made it back into the saddle. He felt himself swaying back and forth. In response, Adonica forced his hands around the steed's neck and wrapped his wrists with a length of rope to prevent him from falling off again. Then she climbed into her own saddle, grabbed Stormbringer by the reins to lead him, and resumed riding toward the beach.

Their plan had been to travel north along the same route that had led them south to the ruins. However, a near-encounter with a roving heard of coblyns shortly after daybreak the first morning had forced them to veer eastward and follow the coast for a while. It had been while skirting the coastline that they had seen the ship. Not a demon ship, as they'd first feared, but a vessel flying the flag of the Athacean League.

A friendly ship. Not only did that mean allies and a chance at procuring much-needed supplies, but there was a chance that an aurym-healer would be aboard. And that chance, Hook was now quite sure, was his only hope of survival.

Hook looked up as they rode, trying to see the ship, but he found it difficult to focus his eyes. He saw the green-brown ground beneath him and gray-blue water somewhere ahead, but he had only a vague idea of where he was in relation to the coast, or where he was going.

"He's got it!" Adonica cried out. "Gunnar got their attention—the bastard managed to do something right! They're coming this way!"

Hook offered no reply. He kept his eye on the water ahead. Then he saw only black. When his vision returned, the water seemed much closer than it had a few seconds before, and he realized that it must have been longer than a few seconds; he must have blacked out for a moment.

It happened again. And this time, when his vision returned, he knew that several minutes must have passed because he could hear ocean waves. He was off the steed and being carried by several sets of hands.

Suddenly, he was in a small dinghy. Adonica and Gunnar were beside him, and some men he didn't recognize were rowing them out over the water. Hook tried to sign to them, to tell them not to leave Storm-bringer, Ash, and Thirsty behind, but when he tried to raise his hand, he blacked out again.

A jolt of pain brought him awake suddenly and with full, ruthless awareness. He was indoors somewhere, and he'd been lowered onto a bed, jarring his leg badly enough to make him cry out in agony. Someone began unwrapping the rudimentary bandages that bound the bite wound, and all at once, the pain became too much.

"Jocasta," he tried to say, forgetting for a moment about the tongue that hadn't been in his mouth since he'd been a youth. He had always wished he could say her name. It left his lips as a pitiful mumble.

CHAPTER 93

The woman drew a tighter grip on Leah's hand and bore down hard, clenching her teeth to stifle a scream.

"No need for that," Leah said. "Shout if you have to. If you do, make it loud enough for the whole city to hear."

The Cru woman, an adolescent younger than Leah, took a deep breath. Her shortened name was Kiin, and she had done well. Enduring the ride all the way from Cervice and up along the difficult mountain path while swollen with child would have been difficult enough, but she had done it while in the midst of labor pains that had begun while they were still within Cervice's city walls.

The past few days had been an arduous affair for the woman, but she'd made the journey along with the rest of them. Made it all the way up the steepest portion of the path, in fact, and through the tiny, partially collapsed canyon. She'd made it all the way into the entrance of the hidden city of Cymorrika.

And now, here on the causeway of the Ancients leading below the earth, her time had come.

Hours had passed since Leah had spoken to Olorus on the mountain path. The procession from Nolia now traveled the wide, spiral road straight down into the underground city. This mass of humanity migrating underground together was an impressive sight. Most of them walked. Those who could not walk rode on steeds or were carried on litters as Thid had been. As for Kiin, she had made it over halfway to the bottom before her true quickening had begun.

A bed of thrown-together garments and fabrics served as a bed for Kiin, but she held herself up in a position more akin to a squat. The green glow of a'thri'ik emanating from the intricate designs on the walls reflected off her sweat-coated face. She kept her eyes closed, gripping Leah's hand on one side and her husband's hand on the other. Meanwhile, several Cru women were at work, helping the birthing process along in a few capacities with which Leah was familiar, as well as a few that she had never witnessed before. She had been trained in these things at the Cervice Academy and had learned that traditional ways were often observed for a reason. To Leah's surprise, Olorus's elderly mother was helping, too. She had become quite close with some of the Cru women during their time at Cervice.

Leah could see the tightening of Kiin's abdominal muscles as the next contraction came.

"Now," Leah instructed.

Kiin bore down. The shout that came through her gritted teeth reminded Leah of the roar of a warrior on the field of battle. There was a bulge.

"You're making progress," said Leah, caressing Kiin's knuckles with her thumb. "The next one may be it."

Kiin nodded, though she did not open her eyes.

Moments passed. Her abdominal muscles grew tight again.

"Now," Leah said.

Kiin bore down again.

All at once, there was a massive release, and Kiin's face went slack. She slumped to the ground in relief and might have fallen hard had Leah and her husband not been supporting her.

Immediately, one of the women took hold of the child, turning it this way and that, examining it. They cooed with encouragement, but their faces were stern and unreadable. Leah held her breath. The child made no noise. Kiin looked at her husband. Her husband looked back at her.

Leah let go of Kiin's hand and rushed to check the child.

A shrill wail rang out, and the stern faces of the women examining the child broke into joy. Kiin and her husband heaved gasps of relief.

Leah watched as the women brought the child to Kiin's breast. Tears plowed trails down Kiin's sweat-soaked face.

"A girl," said Leah, squeezing Kiin's shoulder. "A beautiful girl."

Around them, a crowd of onlookers, previously maintaining a proper distance out of respect, pressed in and clambered for a look at the child.

Kiin looked up at Leah and spoke in the Cru tongue.

"She says," one of the midwives said in fluent Waelik, "that A'cru'u'ol do not name their children until the end of their first year. But she already knows what she will name the child." The midwife recited several syllables that Leah had trouble following, then followed it up with an explanation: "A simplified form would be Eka. The full name means, 'one born at home.'"

Leah smiled. The significance of this child's name would be lost to no one.

"Elder Leah," said someone from behind.

Leah turned to find Sif standing behind her. He glowed as bright as a green sunrise in his full suit of a'thri'ik armor and was keeping his distance from the scene of the birth, though he had a look of joy on his face. Leah suspected he had been there for some time.

"Might I have a word with you when you have a moment?" he asked.

Leah gave Kiin one more squeeze of the shoulder, then turned to the midwife who had spoken to her. "Seek me out if anything appears irregular with the mother or the child," she said. "I will do whatever I can."

"Yes, Elder Leah," said the midwife.

Leah went to Sif, who led her away from the bulk of the procession. Walking to the edge of the causeway, Leah saw that the procession stretched all the way to the bottom floor far below; the first of the civilians had made it and were dispersing down the massive adjoining hallways, all beneath the single-eyed gaze of the great cyclops statue.

"With Itzacoatl's help, Olorus is seeing the people to suitable living quarters," said Sif, "and a Raeqlu man named Alcaeus is using his powers with the growing stone to create a garden that should be suitably irrigated by the spring. Our council of elders is overseeing everything. As for the herds—the bison, oxen, goats, and steeds—they can be kept in the mountain valleys, and milk and meat can be transported up to the city entrance as needed. By all appearances, our people shall want for nothing here. Save sunlight, perhaps. But this is an acceptable substitute." He grinned at the glowing designs in the walls. "I will rest easier knowing that they are safe here."

Leah looked at him. "They?"

Sif nodded.

"I'd assumed that you would remain here with your people."

"Many of us will remain here," said Sif. "But not me. My father and the other elders will be here to lead them. Some of our warriors will help guard this place, including Ral. But Tel, Vox, and I, along with any others who are able-bodied enough to fight, will join you in your march to the east, Elder Leah."

"Are you certain?" Leah asked. "To leave your Home so soon after finding it. . . . If it were me, I don't know if I could bring myself to leave this place behind."

Sif's grin widened, and he gestured to Leah's forehead—at her new scar. "I have seen firsthand your willingness to place yourself in harm's way for the sake of your people. Your willingness to sacrifice yourself, even for the least of us." He looked over the edge of the banister at the people filing into the hallways far below. "Maybe I will never return to see this place again. Either way, my path is the same as yours."

Sif's gaze drifted back to the path to rest on Kiin and Eka.

"Those of us who can, must risk great sacrifice," he said, "so that new life can have a fighting chance."

A figure stepped up behind Sif, overshadowing him, and Leah looked up at the towering frame of Megara. The lifeslave's brand on her forehead stood out in the green glow from the cat's eye walls as well as her armor.

Sif hazarded a glance over his shoulder but did not turn to face Megara. Instead, he continued to address Leah.

"I shall go and see if Olorus needs any help getting our people settled," said Sif. "After that, I'll start preparing the soldiers to depart."

"After a night's rest, first," said Leah. "We need some time to get set up here, and I will not leave until I'm certain our people have everything they need. Spend time with your families. Hold them tightly."

Sif flashed a smile of gratitude, then departed.

And Megara stepped forward to take his place, grim-faced.

CHAPTER 94

The two of them stood alone together at the edge of the causeway—one at barely over five feet in height, the other at several inches over six feet.

Megara's grim face did not change. Normally, Leah would have attempted to fill such silence with a comment or a question to encourage a response. But this time, she said nothing. She waited quietly as people passed by on the causeway behind them, chatting and marveling at the sights.

Leah knew that Megara had been speaking with the twenty-five Rorrdvuuk—the only members of her people who had rejected Folgruuth's betrayal and chosen instead to accompany the people of Cervice in their journey to Cymorrika.

I wonder what state Cervice is in at this very moment, thought Leah. *Being torn to bits by the demons, perhaps. Burning. . . .*

She bit the inside of her lip and tried not to think about it.

Finally, after what felt like several minutes, Megara raised her hands and signed, *"Some of my people have asked if they might stay here in the city. Eleven of them. Would you grant them this request?"*

"Yes," signed Leah.

Megara nodded. *"The rest will leave with me."*

Leah bowed her head slightly. *"I understand,"* she signed. *"May I ask where you plan to go?"*

"To war, of course," signed Megara. *"If you will still have us."*

Leah hesitated.

"If the rift between our people cannot be mended—" signed Megara.

But Leah shook her head and raised her hands, interrupting her. "I would welcome you at my side. I would call you a general among our people. I hesitate only because I know that a very difficult task lies ahead of us. So difficult that I find myself wondering if it would be unjust for me to ask you to join me in it."

"My warriors and I do not fear death," signed Megara.

"It's not the war I am worried about," said Leah. "Not yet, anyway. The task I refer to is of a more . . . *political* nature."

Megara cocked an eyebrow at her. *"Is it a challenge greater than going to war?"*

"In a way," said Leah.

Leah stared down the path leading into the city, thinking about all that had transpired among her people.

She'd had some time to think about everything that had happened. In her zeal to uphold what she believed was the individual's right to a fair trial, she had kept Asher imprisoned until a time when a fair trial could be had. It was a gesture intended to show the people that her country's civil standards would be maintained even in dire circumstances.

Others might have seen an outright execution as the swift justice of a strong leader. But executing *anyone* without a trial would have set a dangerous precedent. It would have implied that the crown wielded unchecked power, and further, that Leah would not hesitate to use it. Some might have considered her decisive and just for such a course of action, but others would have considered it the actions of a tyrant. But now that Asher had escaped, she knew she would be painted a weak bleeding heart.

Not only that, but he'd taken the map with him. The location of the city of Cymorrika, hidden for untold centuries or millennia, would remain hidden no longer. If he or anyone else got it into their head to use the secret of its location as a bargaining chip against Avagad and the demons, the consequences would be disastrous. All because she had tried to please too many sides.

No longer.

Leah's gaze wandered to Megara's lifeslave brand. Only half aware of what she was doing, Leah raised one hand and touched the scar on her own head, running a finger across it. She thought of Hook's scar. She thought of the innumerable scars on the heads of so many others like him and Megara. And she thought of the fencing scar her father had had—a smite, he'd called it. A badge of honor.

Honor.

"Right is right," her father had once told her. "If you can remember that, you have all you need to lead."

Leah turned to face Megara. Carefully, she lowered her hands so that no one else might see her signs, though there were precious few around who would have been able to read them anyway.

"I am going to ask you not to repeat what I am about to tell you," said Leah. *"Not yet, anyway."*

Megara was visibly caught off guard by the request but nodded nonetheless.

"You were right," signed Leah. She paused to point meaningfully at the slave's brand on Megara's head. *"Allying myself with the kind of people who would do* that *is as good as holding the whip myself."*

Megara furrowed her brow.

"Tomorrow morning," signed Leah, *"we will leave this city. We will journey to Castydociana to rejoin the army that departed from Cervice. There, we will be reunited with the rest of the League, including slave-holding Mythaeans. As planned, I will ask for ships to transport us eastward to Erum. I will then announce that under my command, all slaves under the yoke of the Mythaeans are to be freed."*

Megara blinked in surprise, then grinned widely—wide enough to reveal the gap left by the missing canine tooth on the side of her mouth.

"And if they refuse?" Megara signed.

Leah breathed a bitter laugh and ran her tongue over her teeth. Beneath her breath, she whispered, "Then woe to them."

CHAPTER 95

"We can have more than this life, Hook," said Jocasta. "I know you want to keep fighting, but there's no future in it, and you know that. I don't want to see any more blood spilled. Not ours or the Mythaeans'. You may be free, but as long as you keep chasing this obsession for revenge, you're still living for *them*. Someday, you'll have to live for yourself. When you do, you'll realize that mercy is a stronger healer than revenge. And forgiveness will always win over hate."

Hook opened his eyes, the words still echoing through his mind.

He shook his head in confusion. He was in a small, windowless room lit by a low-burning candle, but the all-too-familiar feel of the world swaying around him told him everything he needed to know about his environment; he was at sea. And the fact that he wasn't dead was proof that an aurym-healer had been aboard this ship after all.

Tentatively, he moved his leg. There was pain. But it wasn't as bad as he might have expected.

An aurym-healer's gift was truly an amazing thing, to be able to heal wounds and fight infection so effectively as to reel a man back from the gaping maw of death.

I've never been that close before, thought Hook.

He pushed the covers off and sat up in bed. He didn't know how long he'd been out, but it hadn't felt like long, and his sleep had been dreamless. Of all the times to not have nightmares.

Wearing only his underclothes, he swung his bare legs over the side of the bed and examined his injury. They had bathed the wound well—not even any dried blood left. There were only scars and indentations in his leg where the monster's teeth had gone the deepest. It looked years old, not hours. Or had it been days?

The door to Hook's cabin opened slowly, and Adonica backed in, holding a pitcher of water. She turned and jumped a bit at the sight of him sitting upright on the edge of the bed, just a couple of feet away.

"So you're up," she said.

Hook's brow furrowed. There was something about Adonica's choice of words and her tone of voice that gave him pause. This woman, so quick to jest, even in the midst of life-and-death combat, was as close to disturbed as Hook had ever seen her.

"What is it?" he signed.

"Hook," said Adonica. She swallowed hard. "The ship.... We couldn't have known. We're not going to stand for it—I know that. But I wanted to warn you, before you go out there—"

But Hook was already on his feet.

"Wait, Hook!" she said, grabbing his arm.

Hook ripped his arm out of her grasp and pushed through the door so hard that it cracked against the wall outside. He took a single step, then froze in place.

He'd never seen it from this side before, and what struck him most was how small they all looked from here. Small and weak.

Many *were* small and weak, of course. They sat hunched over their oars, every vertebra of their bony spines looking sickeningly pronounced in the dim lanternlight. At the moment, there was no pacer to pound the drum. But the row-master was there—a thick-armed woman outfitted much the same as Cadmus always had been, with a coiled, coral-studded whip hanging from her belt. Hook imagined that the slaves assembled here would normally be doing their best to keep their eyes downcast in the presence of their row-master—to do anything to avoid drawing attention to themselves. But Hook had drawn everyone's attention his way when he'd thrown the door open.

All eyes—all those sunken, haunted eyes—were on him. And above so many of those eyes were foreheads striped with long, horizontal scars like grisly halos.

Hook took in the many seats filled with slaves. Then his eyes wandered to where the row-master was standing. On the bench directly beside her, the aisle seat was unoccupied. Empty. Hook knew from experience what that meant.

Hook felt Adonica's hand touch his bare shoulder. Whether she was trying to comfort him or restrain him, he wasn't sure. Either way, he ignored it.

He walked forward, moving purposefully toward the row-master. She watched him coming. She appeared confident at first. But, as he drew nearer, one of her hands drifted toward the knife at her belt.

Hook stopped before the row-master and looked down at her. He could feel the many eyes of the galley slaves on him, and a murmur began to go up from the hundred-some rowers. Hook, bare-chested and still only in his underclothes, knew that by now, many of them could see the layers of old whip scars on his back—scars so much like their own.

The row-master stared up at Hook for a moment, matching his silence. Finally, Hook turned toward the empty seat and sat down.

The row-master cautiously backpedaled down the aisle, putting a bit of distance between her and Hook. She moved up the aisle, toward the door where Hook had emerged. A casual observer might have thought Hook was staring daggers at the row-master. In fact, he was looking over the row-master's shoulder, at Adonica.

A League ship, Hook thought.

Hook reached forward, placed his hands on the oar, and waited. If this was how things were to be, he would take his place beside his true allies.

The row-master, still cautiously eyeing Hook from the aisle, suddenly buckled and went down on one knee, kicked in the leg from behind. Adonica's hand slipped forward, tore the knife from the row-master's belt, brought it up, and rested the tip below the row-master's armpit.

"Move, and I stick you like the swine you are," Adonica hissed into the row-master's ear.

Before anything else could happen, a whistle cut through the tension. It was the un-melodious, idle, up-and-down sort of whistle of a man taking great pleasure in his work.

As the whistle grew louder and footfalls could be heard approaching above-deck, neither the slaves nor Adonica nor the row-master dared to breathe or say a word. Hook half-expected a sailor with a mop to come wandering down from above, none the wiser to the situation taking place. Instead, an overhead hatch suddenly opened, allowing evening light to spill down into the guts of the ship, and Gunnar Erix Nimbus stuck his head down through the hatch, still whistling cheerfully through his teeth.

With his head sticking upside-down through the hatch, Gunnar's one-eyed gaze came to rest on Hook seated on the rower's bench. "Ah, good morning!" he said. "Glad to see you're finally up."

Gunnar then turned his attention to Adonica and seemed neither surprised nor unhappy to see her holding the ship's row-master at knife-point.

"Dar-*liiing*," he said in a doting, singsong sort of voice. "Correct me if I'm *wrong*, but I thought we had agreed to wait for the sig-*naaal*."

"Yeah, well, I got tired of waiting," muttered Adonica. She prodded the row-master with the knife and whispered, "Keys. Now."

Looking around at the stunned, disbelieving slaves, Hook found himself grinning. But then he noticed the look on the row-master's face and knew that freedom would not be so easily bought for these people.

"*Mutiny!*" the row-master screamed. "*Traitors!* To arms—!"

Adonica cracked the woman in the back of the head with the handle of her knife, and her eyes rolled back in her head.

No sooner had the unconscious woman dropped to the floor than Hook heard the shouts of alarm and the sounds of boots stomping across the deck up above.

"Stupid pig!" Adonica hissed, grabbing the keyring from the row-master's belt.

Gunnar made a frustrated sound in his throat. "See? *See*? This is why you *wait* for the *sig-nal*."

With an acrobatic somersault, Gunnar dropped to the floor below, then quickly slipped on the Ancient Ellenean helmet that was already in his hand. As Adonica began unlocking the chains that held the slaves to their seats, Gunnar drew his cutlass and tossed it to Hook, who snatched it out of the air.

"Well, you heard the woman," said Gunnar. "Let's have ourselves a mutiny."

PART IX

THE RETURN
TO FOREVER

CHAPTER 96

"You know, there's no rush. Literally."

Benjamin gestured toward the gray wasteland surrounding them.

"I mean," he added, "can you think of anywhere else where time stands still?"

"I know," said Justin. "But I'm not sure any amount of time would get me more prepared than I already am."

Benjamin slipped his hands into his pockets and looked away.

"For what it's worth," Benjamin said after a few moments, "I'm sorry again. Don't forgive me for it. I certainly will never forgive myself."

Justin looked sternly at his father. Benjamin looked back at him, and for an instant, his father seemed almost like a boy.

"I forgive you," said Justin.

Benjamin lowered his head.

Beloved son, thought Justin.

He couldn't shake the words he had found carved on the box in Avagad's tower. Or the implication they carried.

"Dad?" said Justin.

Benjamin looked up.

"Do you think . . ." said Justin before trailing off. He cleared his throat, trying to work up the courage to ask the question that was on his heart. Instead, he decided to ask something else. "Is there a possibility that what happened to you could happen to somebody else?"

"You mean being taken over by the Nameless One," said Benjamin— it was not a question.

Justin nodded.

"Absolutely," said Benjamin. "And you *cannot* be too careful, Justin. That's why I wish you wouldn't go. I went through hell. I couldn't bear the thought of the same thing happening to my son."

Beloved son.

Justin swallowed hard, his mouth suddenly dry.

Benjamin gestured to Ahlund's broken sword, tucked in Justin's belt. "You still haven't shown me what you can do with that thing."

Justin pulled out the half-sword, giving its broken blade a close inspection. He'd gotten it to light up before by feeding a small amount of aurym into it, but even he wasn't sure to what extent he could use it.

Justin called on aurym, feeding it through the sword. Instantly, Ahlund's blade came alive, red as coals. He aimed it into the sky, then allowed his power to flow in earnest.

It was not like Ahlund's fire had been—red and orange flames spurting forth from the blade like a jet of napalm. Instead, the blade turned blue, and a churning beam of a white, plasma-like substance shot out of the blade in a blinding column.

Instantly, Justin cut off the flow of power, crying out involuntarily. The sword hit the ground and faded back to its normal color as Justin reeled back, cradling his hand. The radiant heat of the blast had singed his knuckles and wrist. High above, the column of white bored a hole through the gray clouds, which parted and swirled around it like smoke.

As Justin shook his hand, Benjamin made a face that seemed to say, "not bad." Then he wandered into his makeshift shelter.

"There are a couple of things I've got here that you might as well take with you," said Benjamin, tossing odds and ends out of the way.

Justin followed Benjamin into the rock shelter just as he moved aside a whole stack of books. The stack toppled as he put it down, but he paid it no mind.

"Ah, here it is," said Benjamin. He reached into the corner and pulled out a circular shield with a wooden back and a bronze, hammered face. "Can't leave home without one of these," he said, handing it to Justin.

Justin was surprised by how heavy it was. He accepted it, holding it up by way of a set of leather straps and wooden handholds at the back.

"Now all you need is my old cuirass and greaves—if I can find them—and you'll be ready to go," said Benjamin. "Should fit nicely under that cloak of yours. And boots. Oh, and another sword, of course. An unbroken one."

"Are you kidding?" said Justin, struggling just to hold up the shield. "I won't be able to move."

"A soldier's panoply is what separates him from the rabble," said Benjamin.

"A soldier's *what*?" said Justin.

"Panoply," said Benjamin. "Your gear. Armor and weapons. You'll just have to get used to the weight. Uncomfortable's better than dead. If you've been running around without proper gear all this time, then you've been lucky so far. That'll only last you so long. Believe me."

CHAPTER 97

Piece by piece, Benjamin gathered up his old armor. And with no small degree of regret, Justin changed out of his Earth clothing and into his father's otherworldly garb. Tennis shoes were traded for his father's boots, and his hoodie and jeans were switched with a linen tunic that wouldn't draw much attention in the Oikoumene.

The cuirass was a plate of hammered bronze—or perhaps it was some other sort of otherworldly metal with which Justin was unfamiliar—that tightened at the sides by way of straps and buckles, and the greaves were curved tubes that slid on like a pair of metal socks to protect his shins. The circular shield hung from his shoulder by one of its straps. At his hip was a sword belt with a sheath holding a long sword that his father had called a hand-and-a-half sword, able to be wielded with one hand or with two, depending on the situation.

For Ahlund's broken sword, Benjamin had found Justin a baldric, a sort of belt worn slung over the shoulder. The baldric supported a short sheath that was meant for a dagger, into which Ahlund's broken sword luckily fit. As Justin had anticipated, he felt as if he were carrying an extra hundred pounds, but maybe his father was right. He'd been lucky so far, running around fighting demons, without any proper gear.

Benjamin scooped Justin's cloak from the ground and draped it over him.

"There," said Benjamin. "That's more like it. Now, there's just one more thing. . . . One more thing."

Then Benjamin sighed and looked away. For a moment, Justin thought he was having second thoughts about allowing him to leave. But then he noticed that his father's shoulders were tense, almost locked in place.

"Dad?" said Justin, placing the shield on the ground beside him. "What is it?"

"Daemyn must have a tighter hold on me than I realized," Benjamin muttered. "Why else would I be having such a hard time giving you this last thing?"

Justin watched his father closely. "What is it?" he asked.

"It's an aurstone," said Benjamin. "I don't actually have it here with me. I always keep my keystone with me, even though I can't use it any-more." He raised his hand and lifted a chain worn around his neck, revealing a locket on the end. "But the aurstone I mean to give you. . . . After everything that happened, I felt no need to keep it close anymore. Which is why I left it where I did. It was my strongest weapon, Justin. My most reliable source of power. Until I made my mistake and was cut off from aurym."

"What does it do?" asked Justin.

Benjamin shook his head. "I'm not going to tell you."

Justin frowned. "Why not?"

"Because aurstones are fickle things," said Benjamin. "Certain stones can only be used by certain people. And vice versa. And sometimes, even when two people can use the same type of stone, the effects can vary. It may not work for you at all. Or it may not do the same thing for you that it did for me. If I told you about what it *could* do, only for you to have it fail. . . . I think it would frustrate you. If it's not to be, then it's best not to dwell on it. But if it is to be, you'll figure it out without my help. But it's almost like. . . . It's like I want you to have it, but there's a part of me that couldn't bear to see you take it."

"Where is it?" asked Justin.

Benjamin hesitated.

"Dad."

"Your mother's coat pocket."

Justin opened his mouth, but he didn't know what to say.

"When we get back to the house," said Benjamin, "I'll leave the room. Then you can go and get it. Don't let me see you take it, okay?"

"Are you sure you won't come back with me?" said Justin.

Benjamin stared at him. "Back to the Oikoumene? You're *still* asking me that? Even after what I did to you?"

Justin stared right back at him. "You slipped up. It happens. Dad, you can do it. I believe in you."

"Then you're the only one," said Benjamin.

Silence hung in the air for several long moments.

"I hope you know how much I love you," said Benjamin. "How proud I am. And how proud your mother is."

It did not go unnoticed by Justin that his father had used the present tense.

"You know, there really are times when I think she can see me," said Justin. "Not in a sunshine-and-rainbows 'looking down on me' sort of way. I mean, really, actually *see* me."

Benjamin looked hard at his son.

"I don't know," said Justin with a shrug. "I know she's dead. But maybe, just like how *we* can go to different worlds like this one and the Oikoumene, maybe part of *her* is in another world right now. Maybe she can see us from time to time. And maybe we'll get to see her again someday—the way some people say, or maybe in some other way we don't know about."

A grin suddenly tugged at Benjamin's lips. "I'm sure you're right," he said.

"Yeah," said Justin. "But either way, if I never see you again—"

"Nope. Cut it out," Benjamin said. "If you start with that sort of talk, I'll never be able to let you go."

But Justin pressed on. "You'll need some sort of story about what happened to me. If the police are already investigating you because of the car accident like you think they are, it will look even worse if I go missing. You've got to have an explanation. Right?"

Benjamin shook his head. He wasn't disagreeing with Justin, but this was clearly not a conversation that he wanted to be having.

"Do you have any paper here?" asked Justin. "A pen?"

Benjamin let out a sigh, then rummaged through a corner of the rock shelter and found, of all things, a yellow legal pad and a mechanical pencil.

"What are you going to do?" Benjamin asked, handing Justin the pad and pencil. "Write a letter saying you ran away to join the circus?"

"Something like that," said Justin.

He sat down on the ground, cross-legged, and began to write.

CHAPTER 98

To reach Castydociana, the capital city of the small republic of Castydocia, Leah and her small force of soldiers had to pass through several miles of the outlying countryside—dairy farms and vineyards stretched across the coastal plains, with cozy-looking whitewashed brick structures and sawn-log roofs. She was grateful to see no sign of damage from demon attacks as they traveled, and by the time their force was on approach to the city walls, they had picked up an escort of silver-haired Castydocian soldiers.

Three days had passed since Leah's force of one hundred and fifty had set out from Cymorrika. Itzacoatl had told her that there was another entrance to the underground city, and the old man had been willing not only to guide her and her people through the caves to it, but had even acquiesced to her plan to have him lead an entourage of civilians back, from Castydociana to Cymorrika.

All one hundred and fifty of Leah's soldiers wore a full set of a'thri'ik armor as they traveled. Some carried additional armor with them, along with as many of the weapons as they could manage. If their theories proved correct, this a'thri'ik armor would prove resistant to demon weapons—and perhaps daemyn power.

Leah hadn't wanted to rob Cymorrika's vulnerable population of steeds or oxen, so they had brought only a few steeds. The rest traveled on foot. Marching in their identical sets of exotic armor—many with helmets covering their heads—these mismatched soldiers looked to Leah, for the first time, like a somewhat uniform group. She had to smile at the wide berth given to them by the Castydocian soldiers escorting them. They were, after all, an intimidating sight.

Familiar faces were waiting to meet them at the open gates of Castydociana. Zechariah stood beside the hefty frame of Wulder Von Morix.

"Hail, Anavion, Queen of Nolia!" Wulder boomed before anyone else had a chance to speak. He lumbered forward to meet her with a horned helm, the symbol of Mythaean nobility, set atop his head. "What a strange turn of events this has been! We sent you to Nolia in hopes of recruiting soldiers. You sent back word that there were no soldiers to be recruited—indeed, that *you* were the one who needed reinforcements—and now, your general, Zechariah, returns to us with greater strength of arms than I ever would have hoped for! All thanks to you!"

Leah nodded to Wulder and gave the traditional Mythaean greeting, "Hail, Morix, Count of Hartla." Then she turned to Zechariah. "And greetings, old friend. Was there any trouble on the road?"

"Greetings to you as well, my child," Zechariah said. "No trouble. We were able to leave Cervice before any demons arrived, and we encountered none on the journey here." He paused, looking hard at the scar across Leah's forehead and her partially missing ear. "It seems you were not as lucky."

"It was a trifling matter," she said.

"It's quite becoming, I think," Wulder said, bending to make a show of examining her. "The crown of a warrior queen! And your forces, garbed in new armor, too!"

"Better equipped for war," Leah said and rapped her knuckles against the a'thri'ik breastplate. Then she gestured to Olorus, Sif, Marcus, Megara, Lycon, Vox, and Tel, similarly outfitted behind her.

A bit farther back stood Itzacoatl. He was the only individual among them not wearing a'thri'ik armor or wielding a sword. She was not ready to trust him to *that* extent.

"Count Morix," said Leah, "I have also brought a guide who can lead some of your civilians to a newfound sanctuary in the mountains."

"Very thoughtful, but I should think that would be unnecessary," said Wulder. "We have fended off every demon attack thus far, from the land and the sea alike, and our walls are strong. I daresay Castydociana is one of the safest places in all the Oikoumene!"

"The walls of Endenholm were strong, too," Marcus suddenly said, speaking up from behind Leah.

Wulder's gaze snapped toward the man, a hint of fire in his eyes. But he directed his rebuttal toward Leah, not to Marcus. "I understand that

My Lady must be *shaken* after having to evacuate Cervice, but I've grown this city into the seat of power for the entire League. I assure you that we are safe here, despite what any doom-saying advisors might have you believe."

"For now," offered Leah, undeterred by the fire in Wulder's eyes.

"Indeed," said Zechariah. "The trouble will be when the same army that our scouts saw approaching Cervice follows our trail here."

Olorus looked up at the city walls as if scrutinizing a wagon for sale. He made a tsk-tsk sound through his teeth and shook his head in disappointment. "Not sure this'll do, I'm afraid."

Wulder looked on the verge of an outburst, but suddenly noticed the murmur that had gone up among the city guards and the Castydocian soldiers who had escorted Leah and the others. Wulder clamped his mouth shut and chewed on his tongue.

"This is hardly the place to discuss such matters," Wulder finally said in a low voice. "Bring your . . . *generals* into the palace with you. The others can rejoin your people in the Old Town quarter."

Wulder started to turn away but came up short. He was staring over Leah's shoulder, where Megara, a lifeslave's brand on her head, stood shoulder to shoulder with one of Hartla's most decorated soldiers, Major Lycon Belesys. Wulder looked as if he might say something to Major Belesys. Instead, he turned without another word and proceeded into the city, assuming without looking back that he was being followed.

Before Leah could proceed into the city, Zechariah touched her by her armored wrist and pulled her close. Silently, she communicated to her generals and confidantes to join her, and Olorus, Lycon, Megara, Sif, and Marcus approached and gathered around. Tel and Vox, still loathe to let Itzacoatl far from their sights, escorted him into the city along with the rest of the one hundred and fifty soldiers.

"What is it?" Leah asked.

Zechariah gave each listener a firm look before he spoke. "Things are far more tenuous here than Wulder wants his people to know," he said in a whisper. "He was all too overjoyed by our arrival—even announced his intent to order *our* army out into a skirmish on the northern border, before we'd even settled in. I managed to distract him from that idea for the time being. Naval battles rage up and down the coast. But he's managed to secure an alliance that has helped him maintain balance."

Zechariah shot a meaningful look at Lycon. "He's joined the League with the remnants of Yordar Erix Nimbus's confederacy."

Lycon's face soured in disbelief. "Yordar's confederacy?" he fumed. "But. . . . But Yordar *invaded* Hartla and kept *us* trapped there after the demon attack! His soldiers killed Hartlan city guards! Why, it was Yordar *himself* who beheaded Drexel—Wulder's own brother!"

Zechariah nodded. "But now that Yordar is dead, too, the incident is water under the bridge, as far as Wulder and his contemporaries are concerned. Mythaean politics at their finest. Some of the soldiers who have been with us since Hartla nearly deserted when they found this out. It took all the diplomacy I had to convince them to stay. I tell you, this place is a boiling kettle, and it's only getting worse."

"Sailing east and leaving this place behind is sounding better and better all the time," said Olorus. "Have you brought *that* up with Wulder yet?"

Zechariah shook his head. "No. But with all our many soldiers here now, intermingling with his forces, he's surely heard rumors. Before we can consider *that* matter, however, there is another complication that needs to be addressed. Now."

"What is it?" asked Leah.

"Come with me," Zechariah said, and pointed at Lycon and Megara. "The two of you should come, too." Then he turned his attention to Olorus, Sif, and Marcus. "I think the three of you should go with Wulder. Tell him that Leah was needed to tend to a wounded soldier and will be on her way shortly. Stall for time, if you can."

"Now see here, just one moment!" objected Olorus.

Zechariah looked at Olorus. They had a history of disagreements—including incidents of near bloodshed between them. In the past, Zechariah might have ignored the soldier's comment, made a belittling remark, or overruled him by opting to go over his head by speaking to Leah instead. But this time, he looked at Olorus as if he were an old friend and said, almost pleadingly, "Trust me, Olorus."

There was a long pause. Olorus looked from the old man to Leah. Then, finally, he nodded.

Olorus led the way as he, Sif, and Marcus departed to follow Wulder. Before he left, Marcus placed a hand on Leah's arm. "Stay safe," he said, looking into her eyes.

Leah looked back at him but said nothing. He smiled at her, then left to follow the others.

When the three of them had faded into the crowd, Zechariah turned to Leah, Lycon, and Megara.

"It's Hook," said Zechariah.

Leah's brow furrowed in concern. "Hook?" she said. "What about him?"

"We may not have much time," said Zechariah. "Follow me."

CHAPTER 99

Zechariah pushed the door shut behind them and threw the bolt. He crossed the room to a small window and pulled back the curtain to peek out, as if checking to see if they had been followed. Judging by the shelves of books and the desks covered with quills and pots of ink, Leah surmised that this was a counting house. No candles or lanterns were lit, and with the curtains drawn, the far edges of the room were doused in shadow.

"It's us," Zechariah said to the empty room.

From behind one of the desks stood Adonica Lor. "Nice armor," she said.

"Private Lor!" said Lycon.

He moved forward as if to embrace her, then seemed to think better of it and extended his hand in a more professional manner. Adonica smiled, took his hand, then pulled him in for a hug.

"It ain't half-bad seeing you either, Major," she said. When Lycon let go of her, she turned to face Leah. "Queen Anavion."

Leah nodded. "Welcome back, Private."

"Actually, it's Captain now," said Adonica. When Lycon looked quizzically at her, she shook her head. "Long story."

"You'd better tell them what you told me," said Zechariah. "And quickly. Wulder will only wait so long before he realizes something's amiss."

As Megara stepped up to stand beside Leah, Lycon shifted his weight and glanced over his shoulder. He was noticeably uncomfortable at the idea of sneaking around behind his count's back. Still, the news of the

League joining with Yordar's confederacy had clearly shaken the man's confidence in Wulder.

"Well, for starters, we didn't return empty-handed," said Adonica. She reached behind the desk and brought forth a crown with several antlers jutting from its apex. In her other hand was a small bag.

Adonica tossed the bag to Leah, who caught it out of the air and peered inside. It was filled with small, finely cut stones.

"I managed to remove the aurstones from the crown easily enough," said Zechariah. "A skilled stonecutter will be able to divide those into at least a dozen stones apiece. If anyone among our forces proves capable of using these stones, we will grow exponentially stronger. Especially if, spirit willing, someone proves capable of using the hydstone."

Leah closed the bag. "But what about Hook? And Gunnar?"

"I *think* they're here," said Adonica. "Somewhere. And that's the problem."

A few moments later, Adonica had told them the whole story.

"A League ship?" said Lycon. "With *slave labor* at the oars?"

"Several member-nations of the League practice slavery," said Zechariah. "And now that Wulder has negotiated an alliance with Yordar's confederacy, there are even more of them."

"So that's how you became captain," Megara signed, smiling at Adonica.

"I thought it was high time for a promotion," Adonica replied. "And Gunnar will probably tell you it was his plan, but *I* was the one who started the mutiny. When it was all over, the ship's marines and sailors were chained in the rowers' seats, and the slaves were running the ship, under my orders. Some of the sailors had heard a rumor that Cervice was being evacuated and its people were being moved to Castydociana, so we set sail in this direction. The marines and sailors weren't too keen to do the manual labor themselves until we explained that they could either row or swim.

"We knew we'd have some explaining to do when we reached our destination. And we figured if Wulder had sanctioned the use of slave labor by the League, then showing up with a bunch of freed slaves wouldn't go over so well. We didn't know how the count was going to react to the whole situation, but Gunnar felt sure he could talk him down. Still, we put ashore south of Castydociana and let the slaves go. We decided that I should go with them. Since the nature of our welcome here was naturally questionable, I took the artifact with me to bring it north by land. Gunnar and Hook, meanwhile, would sail for the city, where we would all reunite."

"But they never arrived?" asked Leah.

"That's what we're trying to find out," said Zechariah.

"The *ship* made it here," said Adonica. "I enlisted the help of an old friend of mine who spotted it at the docks last night."

"So either it arrived without them—" said Lycon.

"Or it arrived *with* them," Adonica said, "which is even worse. Wulder has stayed silent on the matter. But some of our soldiers heard rumors of a ship that had been taken over by its slaves. They say the leaders of the revolt are in the dungeons—awaiting execution."

Leah felt the blood drain from her face.

"The count wouldn't do that," said Lycon. He looked around, exchanging glances with the others. "Would he? Not to Gunnar, surely!"

"If Gunnar and Hook were aboard that ship when it arrived," said Adonica, "it means that Wulder has them."

"And if he has not announced that they are imprisoned," said Zechariah, "it means he does not want anyone to know about it. Which does not bode well for them."

Leah shook her head. "Perhaps he was waiting for my arrival," she said. "So we could discuss all this and come to a quiet, diplomatic agreement."

"Perhaps," agreed Zechariah.

Megara raised a hand to sign, *"Doubtful."*

"Agreed," said Adonica, then turned to face Lycon. "Major, the count wants victory. He sees it as his duty to Hartla and to his people to see that, above all else, we *win*. By whatever means necessary." She paused, sighed, and shook her head. "I don't know about you, Major. But I'm not okay with that anymore. I think Wulder *does* have Gunnar and Hook. And I think if I hadn't gotten off that ship in time—my years of loyal service to Hartla notwithstanding—he'd have my head on the chopping block, same as theirs."

Leah watched the exchange. Her gaze shifted from the blunt conviction on Adonica's face to the bitter disbelief on Lycon's.

"All this does," said Leah, "is confirm the decision I have already made."

Zechariah, Megara, Lycon, and Adonica all turned their attention to Leah. Only Megara understood the meaning of Leah's words. Even Zechariah looked as if he had been taken unaware.

Leah stood from the table. "It's time to fix this."

CHAPTER 100

Iron bars and brick walls.

And this time, no blade to dig out of his shoulder to pick the lock.

Misfortune no longer upset Hook Bard. Rather, it felt like the natural way of things. What was important was that Adonica had made it out and had the artifact with her, and the slaves aboard the *Naiad*, the ship they'd taken over, were free. Even if Hook died here, at least he would go to his grave having done something Jocasta would have been proud of.

"Far be it from me to tell you how to do your jobs," Gunnar said, leaning casually against the bars of their shared cell, "but I still think this is a case of mistaken identity. Just wait until Wulder hears about this—boy, is he gonna laugh!"

The guards didn't take the bait. It was a credit to their discipline and training that they hadn't responded to any of Gunnar's taunts or goading so far.

Gunnar turned away from the bars to face Hook, adding loudly, "But forget about the blunder of locking up Admiral Gunnar Erix Nimbus. Just wait until they find out General Hook Bard was mistaken for a common mutineer."

As Gunnar prattled on, Hook discretely signed, *"Use your plants to get us out of here."*

Adonica may have taken the artifact, but so far as Hook knew, Gunnar still had the small godsbreath stone he'd pried off the antlered crown—hidden away somewhere on his person. Their belongings had been confiscated. The guards had even taken Jocasta's headband, and it had taken everything in Hook's power not to attack them the moment they touched it. It now sat on a table on the far side of the room, along-side Gunnar's cutlass and the a'thri'ik-tipped Ellenean lance Hook had taken from the tomb. Knowing Gunnar, Hook assumed he had some of his seeds hidden away, too. But even if he didn't, there were several patches of moss growing in the corners of this jailhouse. Surely that was enough for Gunnar to work with to do something creative.

Gunnar lowered his hands to keep them out of the line of sight of the guards and signed back, *"I do not want to hurt anybody. I want to talk to Wulder first."* Meanwhile, he said aloud, "Imagine that! From lifeslave to general. Doesn't get more rags-to-riches than that, eh?"

Hook shook his head. In spite of everything, it seemed, Gunnar still wanted to believe that Wulder would do the right thing.

"Regretting your decision yet?" signed Hook.

Gunnar smirked at him and said aloud, "Getting there."

At that moment, the door to the room was pushed open on sagging hinges. Its bottom ground across the stone floor, and in stepped the hefty frame of a round-bellied man. He was clothed in the garb of Mythaean royalty, complete with a feathered Mythaean Admiral's hat on his head.

The guards clicked their heels together to stand at attention. The newcomer kept his head lowered, the hat's brim blocking his face. At first glance, Hook assumed Wulder had finally granted them an audience. But these were the trappings of a Mythaean Admiral; Wulder was a Mythaean Count and usually wore the traditional horned helm that identified him as such.

Then Hook noticed the coiled whip hanging from the man's belt.

The admiral removed his hat, revealing a long, jagged scar running across his forehead. He smiled congenially, and his cool, detached gaze came to rest on Hook.

"Every time I think I'm rid of you, you come crawling back," said Cadmus. His strangely soft-spoken tone of voice was just as Hook remembered it. "Hello, Dark-eyes."

CHAPTER 101

Wordlessly, Cadmus brushed past the guards and approached the bars of the cell, his gaze never leaving Hook.

"Who the hell are you?" Gunnar asked.

Cadmus favored Gunnar with a grin. "Orbus Lox Cadmus, Admiral of Hartla. And you must be the famed Gunnar Erix Nimbus."

"Lox Cadmus?" Gunnar said. "That's no royal house."

"Count Von Morix is more concerned about skill and experience than royal blood," said Cadmus. "After the demon crisis is over, Hartla stands to become a powerful player in the new world and will be in need of strong leadership—"

Cadmus took another step forward, still looking at Gunnar, and Hook took his chance. He closed the distance to the front of the cell in two strides, wholly unconcerned with the impact against the bars. He lunged for Cadmus, throwing both hands through the bars, reaching for his neck.

Hook's left hand brushed the brim of Cadmus's hat, but the admiral managed to step back in time, and Hook bounced his face so hard against the iron bars that his teeth cut the inside of his lip.

The guards rushed forward, swords drawn, but Cadmus raised a hand to stop them. "No need for that, if you please," he said. "This animal *belongs* in a cage. But he won't be staying in this one for long. Mutiny is bad enough. But a repeat offender like this slave deserves special treatment—"

"That's no slave," Gunnar said. "General Hook Bard is one of the highest-ranking officers in the Athacean League. And as officers of the League, we were within our rights to commandeer a League ship."

Cadmus waved a hand, brushing this off. "The Raedittean Alliance respects the Athacean League, but that does not mean that its officers have diplomatic immunity in acts of war."

"Raedittean Alliance?" said Gunnar.

"You've been away from your homeland too long, Admiral," said Cadmus. "Preoccupied with external affairs. The Athacean League has proven weak and ineffectual. Moving forward, the new Raedittean Alliance, led by a council of Mythaean oligarchs, will govern the regions of the archipelago and coastal Athacea. Nations such as Nolia, Raeqlund, and others are eligible to benefit from the Alliance's protection. In exchange, they may become client states of the Raedittean Alliance after the demon crisis has been dealt with."

Gunnar, for once, was speechless.

Cadmus inched a bit closer, staring at Hook. For the first time, Hook got a look at the scar he'd left on Cadmus's head. He had done a good job at replicating the shape and location of a lifeslave's brand, but it lacked the uniformity. It was an angry-looking wound. Raised up and bubbled in places. Like stretched animal fat.

Finally, Cadmus turned away and strode across the room, toward the table where Hook and Gunnar's belongings were laid out.

"An underground city has recently been located in the mountains, I am told," he said. "A suitable seat of power for our new empire. We hope to incorporate as much of the League as possible. But we can't overlook acts of open insurrection. I'm sorry, Admiral Erix Nimbus. Wulder didn't want it to come to this. We won't make a show of it—not in this political climate. Better to do away with traitors quietly. Something humane and dignified for you, Gunnar. We owe you as much for your lifelong devotion to the Mythaean race. For Darkeyes. . . . Well, I have something in mind."

Cadmus paused. He leaned over the table, and Hook's heart seized in his chest.

"I recognize this," Cadmus commented.

With sausage-like fingers, Cadmus plucked the strip of fabric from the table. Jocasta's headband.

Able to control his rage no longer, Hook thrashed against the bars. He shook them with his hands, hoping against all logic that he might tear them from their mounts—as he had once done to a loose bolt holding a length of chain aboard the *Manticore*.

Cadmus tossed a casual glance over his shoulder to observe Hook's thrashings. "Even animals are not without the occasional sentimental streak, it seems."

Idly, Cadmus wiped a bit of sweat from his upper lip with the strip of cloth. Then, without looking back, he stuck Jocasta's headband into his front-left jacket pocket, and left via the same door through which he'd entered. Hook threw himself against the cage door one last time, then slumped to his knees on the floor, his face pressed heavily against the bars.

"All right," Gunnar announced loudly. "Time to try a different approach—two hundred and fifty kreels to the man who unlocks this cell."

The guards ignored him.

"Five hundred," said Gunnar.

The guards still said nothing. Even as he increased his bribe, Gunnar was signing to Hook, trying to ask him if he was all right. But Hook only stared at the door through which Cadmus had disappeared, curling his fingers around the bars of the cell so hard that the iron bit into his palms.

CHAPTER 102

Leah looked down from a third-story balcony of the renowned Castydociana Library, a center of learning nearly as old as the city itself. Above was a rooftop flower garden. And below, the entire central square of the Old Town quarter was an uproar of raised voices—shouted questions, arguments, and debates that seemed in some places to be on the verge of crossing the threshold from civilized to belligerent.

"This will not go unnoticed," Zechariah said below his breath, standing beside Leah.

For the first time in all the time she'd known him, he was wearing something other than the unassuming robes of a clergyman or scholar. He, like Leah and Lycon on her other side, had donned a full set of a'thri'ik armor. The old man was hardly recognizable.

Leah nodded in agreement. "I can't imagine it will be long now."

She toyed nervously with the satchel of aurstones at her belt, distracting herself with the way they clacked against each other. There was no turning back from this plan once it was set in motion—no mending the ties that she was about to sever.

And good riddance, she thought.

In response to a particularly loud shout from below, Lycon stepped forward to the edge of the balcony and raised his hands. "Patience!" he shouted. "The Queen will make her announcement shortly!" He returned to his place beside Leah, whispering to himself, "Come on, Lor. It's up to you now."

Leah turned and glanced back into the room behind her. Itzacoatl, Tel, and Vox nodded to her reassuringly.

For the first time, Leah had allowed Itzacoatl to wield an a'thri'ik weapon—a long two-hander sword he had picked out himself. Lycon, Tel, and Vox hadn't been happy about the idea of trusting him, considering the power his brothers had wielded against them. For Leah, it was more of a gesture than a matter of practicality. She was not quite ready to trust the little old man with a full set of armor like the others, but he had proven trustworthy so far and seemed willing to help. He deserved the ability to defend himself at least, in the midst of what was about to happen.

The late-afternoon sun shone in an orange-pink hue off the white-washed walls of Castydociana's architecture, and as Leah looked out over the crowd, a contingent of Mythaean guards rounded a corner onto the main thoroughfare and rushed toward the scene. Bobbing in the center of their formation was the horned helm of Wulder Von Morix.

Tagging close behind Wulder's entourage were Olorus, Sif, and Marcus. All three looked up at Leah, unspoken questions written across their worried faces. She raised one hand and, trusting that there were few individuals present who would be fluent in the hand signs of slaves, signed to Olorus, *Follow him up. Close the doors behind him.*

Olorus's face hardened, and he nodded. She saw him lean in and whisper a translation to Sif and Marcus.

Upon the count's arrival, the crowd grew all the more impatient. They shouted questions at him, to which he responded with half-answers and continued forward with an air of confidence—confidence that Leah knew he did not feel. He and his soldiers were soon in front of the library. Several of his Mythaean soldiers formed a defensive ring around the door, while others followed him inside.

Leah backed away from the balcony into the third-floor room, where she waited by the closed double-doors. She exchanged looks with each of her allies. No one said a word as they listened to the heavy footfalls of Wulder ascending the stairwell.

Wulder pushed open the double-doors so violently that they bounced against the walls. He paused just inside and stared down at Leah, his shoulders heaving.

"I thought you were following me to the city palace," he huffed, clearly winded from his quick pace through the streets. A half-dozen Mythaean soldiers filed in through the doors, followed by Olorus, Sif, and Marcus. "Instead, you disappear. And now plan to address my people, without my permission?"

"I plan to address *the* people," said Leah.

And before Wulder could stop her, she turned and stepped back out onto the balcony.

CHAPTER 103

Gunnar sat with his back to the wall, head back, staring at the ceiling. One might have thought he was sleeping. Thus far, the moss had spread slowly out from the corner of the jail room across the floor and up the leg of the table where their belongings had been placed. What Gunnar hoped to do, Hook wasn't sure, but Hook was out of ideas. He stood with his hands on the bars, staring at the place where Jocasta's headband had been.

"You believe any of this stuff?" one of the guards asked the other. "About the Nolian princess wanting to sail east?"

"Queen," said the other.

"Huh?"

"She's the queen now, they say. And I don't know, but it'll never happen. Wulder won't allow—"

The man's words were interrupted by a tiny, almost inaudible knock at the door.

The two guards looked at each other questioningly. Both drew their swords and moved toward the door. The first stepped behind it. The second grabbed the handle and cautiously pulled it open.

Hook blinked in surprise. In the doorway, a little girl stood beside an elderly man. The girl couldn't have been much older than five or six years old, and the old man was hunched with age and leaning heavily on a cane.

"Oh!" said the old man. "I think we took a wrong turn, Maera."

"Maera?" whispered Gunnar.

The soldier at the door gestured for the second guard to join him. "Check the hall," he commanded. As the second guard exited the room to do so, the first guard stepped aggressively toward the old man. "How'd you get in here?"

"I'm not, eh . . ." said the old man, recoiling a bit. "Well, I—"

"I was looking for Justin," said the little girl. "Have you heard of Justin? The ethoul?"

"Sorry, kid, but he's not. . . ."

The guard trailed off. He leaned toward the door as if hearing something. When he ducked his head around the corner, there was a bright flash—so bright that even from here, out of direct line of sight, Hook recoiled. The guard staggered back, clutching at his eyes. He raised his sword, prepared to start hacking blindly, when a large hand shot into the doorway and grabbed him by the wrist.

A big woman with pale white skin and geometric tattoos lining her face stepped in. She turned the guard's arm to pin it behind his back and the man cried out, attempting to raise an alarm, but Megara quickly swung an elbow, cracking him across the jaw so hard that he went limp in her grasp.

Gunnar was now standing, and Hook had finally let go of the cell bars. As Megara tossed the unconscious guard to the floor, the old man and the little girl stepped aside to make way for Adonica, who emerged from the hallway dragging the other guard's body by the ankles.

"You did good, kid," Adonica told the little girl as she pulled the key from the guard's belt.

"Thank you," said the little girl, beaming.

"You too, Feliks," Adonica added.

"Acting like a confused old man isn't much of an act, these days," said the little man with a shrug. "But after everything you did for us at Hartla, I'm more than happy to help."

"Will I get to see Lycon?" asked little Maera Evin.

"Maybe," said Adonica. "I hope so."

Adonica crossed the room to the cell and inserted the key to unlock the door.

"A few more minutes and I'd have had us out of here, you know," said Gunnar.

Adonica paused short of turning the key in the lock, shooting him a look. "I could come back when you're ready, if you prefer."

Gunnar made a face, then gestured with his hand to urge Adonica to speed things up.

Hook exited the cell as the door swung open, but Adonica remained standing in his way. He looked down at her in surprise, and she raised a hand and patted him across the cheek—a friendly gesture but nearly hard enough to be considered a slap. "Glad to see you're still alive," she said.

Her hand lingered on his jaw a moment, and she grinned.

"I'm beginning to think Hook's got nine lives," said Gunnar, pushing past the two of them. "Is it even worth asking what the hell is going on?"

"Mythaean politics," answered Adonica.

He grimaced. "I was afraid of that."

Megara dragged the two guards across the room, one in each hand. After tossing them into the corner, she flashed a quick *"Hello,"* to Hook.

"It was Gunnar's uncle, wasn't it?" Hook asked as he crossed the room to retrieve his things from the table. *"It was a different Nimbus who captained the Gryphon when you were a slave."*

Megara nodded.

"Gunnar is different," signed Hook. *"And Adonica. And Lycon."*

Megara considered. *"A few days ago, my people betrayed your people."*

Hook's brow furrowed. *"But not you?"* he asked.

Megara smirked, revealing a gap in her smile where a canine tooth was missing. *"The only thing the members of this group have in common, it seems, is that we are all exceptions to the rule in some way or another."*

"We'd better get moving," said Adonica. "Leah is about to burn some bridges, and we need to be on the right side when it happens."

Gunnar reattached his sword belt and checked his cutlass, and Hook grabbed his a'thri'ik-tipped lance from the table. For a moment, he stared at the place where Jocasta's headband had been, remembering

the way Cadmus had wiped his lip with it. He looked up to find
Adonica watching him. Together, they left the room.

CHAPTER 104

"By now, many of you have likely heard the rumors!" Leah shouted to
the crowd in the streets below.

She waited until the people below quieted down enough that she
could be heard in a normal speaking voice.

"I am here to confirm much of what you have heard," she said.

Leah heard the doors suddenly slam shut in the room behind her,
followed by some scuffling and a series of grunts. She heard Wulder
start to cry out, but his voice was quickly cut off, followed by a thud as
something hit the floor hard. Leah continued gazing serenely out over
the crowd, hoping that the disturbances couldn't be heard from below.

"This League is nothing short of a miracle," Leah called out. Her
words echoed from the building façades as she continued, "And like
many miracles, it was destined, from the very outset, not to last long."

A murmur rose from the crowd, and Leah quickly pressed on before
it could increase in volume and drown her out.

"Prior to the invasion of the demon armies, many of us never would
have called ourselves allies. But we made the logical choice. We put aside
old grievances in the interest of joint survival. In short, necessity
brought us together. Since then, as allies, we have been fighting a war.
A war that we are *losing*. For that reason, we can be allies no longer."

She paused, allowing her gaze to drift from one side of the square to
the other, then back again.

"To win this war," she said, "we must be *one*."

She heard a muffled voice attempt to cry out from the room behind
her, but she resisted the urge to turn around.

"Hartla has fallen," Leah said, allowing her voice to increase a bit in
volume. "Endenholm and Lundholm have fallen. We know that parts
of Darsida have fallen. In the east, the Ecbatan Empire is said to be in
ruins. Even as far south as Otunmer, people have become refugees fleeing demon hordes. And my homeland of Nolia, just a couple days' ride
from your walls, had to be abandoned in the face of a looming invasion.

"When we formed this League, I—like many of us—thought that if we could come together as allies, it would be enough. It is not. We thought that if we supported one another in defending our homelands and pushing back the demons, it would be enough. It is not. We haven't pushed them back. We have only *held* them back, in only a few places, and even there, only just barely." Leah rested her hands against the balcony's railing and leaned forward. "The demons are *legion*. They will *never stop coming*. By building up our defenses, all we can hope to win is the privilege to be destroyed last."

Only now did Leah finally hazard a quick glance over her shoulder. The double doors were shut, and the bar had been thrown across them. Most of the guards who had been with Wulder lay in unmoving heaps on the ground. Others were subdued and being held in place by Olorus, Tel, and Marcus. In one corner, a guard sat with hands raised in surrender. Itzacoatl had his sword pointed at him, the blade glowing bright green with the threat of aurym power.

Wulder's horned helm lay on its side on the floor. At the center of the room, Wulder was on his knees, motionless, arms behind his back, eyes wide and blazing in a mixture of surprise and outrage. The count of Hartla was being restrained by none other than the Hartlan major, Lycon Belesys, who had one armored hand clamped over Wulder's mouth and the other holding a knife with the tip pressed to the count's collarbone. Sif and Vox, meanwhile, had their bows drawn and arrows nocked and pointed at the count's chest.

As Leah watched, Zechariah stepped into view. He reached down, seized Wulder's sword by the hilt with his hook-hand, and deftly pulled it free of its sheath. He admired the weapon for a moment, then winked at Leah and flashed a grandfatherly smile.

Leah turned back to the people in the square below. "The demons' seat of power is in Erum," she announced, louder now than ever. "Half a world away. It is the source of their seemingly endless numbers. So that is where I am going, along with my generals, my trusted advisors, and as many soldiers as will volunteer to follow us.

"It will be no alliance or league that invades the enemy's territory. There will be no nations or governments among us. Only a fighting force. There will be no queens, counts, or royalty—our world no longer has room for such luxuries. Only commanders, generals, admirals, and soldiers on the warpath. Stay here and try your best to live, but I would rather die well! The Army of Light will invade the heart of darkness. To push back the demons? No. To crush their bones beneath our boots."

The majority of the people below seemed unsure—disturbed by her words rather than inflamed. But a small minority cried out with a loud cheer. It made Leah's cheek twitch with a grin.

There are our volunteers, she thought.

"Count Von Morix has graciously pledged as many ships to this cause as we will need," Leah continued, "as well as a good deal of supplies. There is no time to waste, so we shall leave by nightfall."

Leah heard Wulder struggling against Lycon's grip in response. When she glanced over her shoulder, she saw Zechariah casually sticking his hooked hand under Wulder's chin. At this, the count went silent.

Leah almost felt bad for Wulder. But not quite. This was a man who had sided with the remnants of Yordar's confederacy, tolerated if not endorsed slave labor, and had imprisoned Gunnar and Hook for freeing a ship of slaves from their chains.

Hopefully, Megara and Adonica had managed by now to free Gunnar and Hook. Leaving by nightfall was going to be difficult to pull off, but they'd have to leave quickly to escape the repercussions of absconding with part of Wulder's fleet.

"If there are any volunteers, bring any gear you can find and meet us at the docks as soon as possible," Leah called out. "But there are two other matters of business I must also mention. Several days ago, my people discovered a hidden sanctuary. An ancient city below ground in the mountains. Its owners, the Cru people, have generously offered to allow civilians to take refuge there. For anyone who cannot fight, I will be organizing a march to lead you to this sanctuary. Those who wish to go there should gather whatever belongings they can carry and meet at the southwest city gates. And now, one final order of business."

Leah paused, then raised her voice to a shout.

"As an army without a nation, we will consider all peoples to belong to us, and us to belong to them! Whenever and wherever we encounter populations who are oppressed or weakened or enslaved by the demons, we will fight to free them, no matter who they may be."

To Leah's satisfaction, this drew a cheer of support from the crowd. She allowed it, then continued.

"And that goes for populations enslaved by entities other than the demons as well."

Suddenly, even the clearing of a throat was like a thunderclap in the crowded square.

"Today," announced Leah, louder now than before, "I declare all enslaved peoples, Mythaean and otherwise, freed from their bonds forevermore. Any nation found to be in violation of this edict will be considered our enemy. Member-nations guilty of this crime will be ejected from the Athacean League, effective immediately. And *any* human who takes or keeps another human against their will is no better than a demon, and shall fare a fate no better than that of any other rabid beast when they fall beneath the swords of the Army of Light."

There were whispers of shock. There were dubious mutterings. There were vicious objections. And yet, there were also many, many cries of fervent approval.

Leah raised her hands to ask for quiet, then added, "Any able-bodied fighter who wishes not to join our Army of Light, and would rather remain behind, beneath the governance of the League, does so with my blessing. I will also grant a grace period to the members of the League, and to other nations of the Mythaean Thalassocracy, to allow them time to adhere to my declaration. But after the Army of Light has banished the evil of the demons from this world, rest assured that we shall turn our focus to ridding our lands of other evils next. Perhaps we will never return from this warpath. If that is to be the case, then we are all doomed. But if we do return, we will bring with us a reckoning for the enemies of free people everywhere."

This drew an even louder cry of support from portions of the crowd, but Leah did not miss the other groups, whose members were darkening their countenances and leaning in to share secret words.

"I hope you will follow me," Leah said, "Warriors of Light."

CHAPTER 105

Leah left the balcony amid cheers and boos alike. There was no time to muse on the implications of what she had just done. There were many down there—officers of the League, Wulder's people, and others—who would note Wulder's absence and realize that something was amiss. They would be coming soon.

"Is our exit secure?" Leah asked.

"We've extended planks across to the adjoining rooftop," said Vox, adjusting her long braid, "through the flower garden."

"We ought to be able to make it all the way to the docks via the rooftops, if need be," said Lycon.

"That shouldn't be necessary," said Zechariah. "Some volunteers from the Holy Army are waiting for us three blocks from here to serve as an escort, and a half-dozen Raeqlu footmen have the adjoining side streets blocked off to keep our route secure."

"Well played, Elder Leah," said Sif, staring down the length of his arrow at Count Wulder.

"I wouldn't mind a bit more notice next time, if I'm being honest," said Marcus, currently standing over a downed Mythaean guard.

Olorus, who had one arm wrapped around a Mythaean guard's neck to keep him in place, smiled and shook his head in giddy astonishment. "Glorious!" He punctuated the thought by shaking the guard—not aggressively, but more like he was a drinking buddy who was in on a good joke.

Leah could already hear the streets outside erupting into an uproar in reaction to her announcements. It would be chaos out there for a time, as some prepped to join her army sailing eastward and others attempted to make ready to march to Cymorrika. Hopefully, in the midst of such chaos, it would be easy to hide the city's missing count. Leah was opening her mouth to say this when one of Wulder's guards suddenly lunged forward from the corner.

Before anyone else could react, a flash of green light arced across the room. The guard came up short, skidding to a halt in front of a smoking scorch mark. A hole had been burned straight through the stone before his feet.

The man looked up at the source of the warning shot—Itzacoatl, who now had his glowing green sword pointed at the man's head.

"Stand down, young man," said Itzacoatl.

The guard raised his hands over his head and dropped to the floor. The rest of Wulder's guards looked at one another uncertainly.

"Major," Leah said, turning her attention to Lycon. "I would like a quick word with the count of Hartla."

Lycon removed his armored hand from Wulder's mouth, but he did not remove the knife he held against the man's collarbone.

"You have made enemies today, Princess," growled Wulder.

"The right enemies," said Leah. "And it's 'Queen,' if you please."

"Have you any idea, *Queen*, what sort of maneuvering it took to develop the alliances?" Wulder demanded. "You've pulled the bottom out of a house of cards!"

"Then if anything, I did you a favor by doing it early, if it was so delicately constructed," said Leah.

Wulder growled in rage. "You don't understand what you've done! If you had only trusted me enough to come to me with this idea—if you'd just told me that you had something like this in mind—we could have negotiated a solution!"

"*Trust* must work both ways, Count," said Leah, "and you lost mine when you imprisoned Gunnar and Hook."

"How do you think you'll get out of this?" Wulder hissed. "My people will not take kindly to seeing their count like this, a traitor holding a knife to his throat."

Leah sighed in disappointment, noting that Wulder did not deny imprisoning Gunnar or Hook. He couldn't even be bothered to feign confusion at the charge. She looked around at his guards and noted that some seemed to be shaken by this.

A knock came from the other side of the barred door, and Lycon wisely clamped his armored hand back over Wulder's mouth before the big man could cry out. An increase in the light from Itzacoatl's glowing sword was all it took to keep the rest silent.

Leah gestured toward the stairs leading up to the rooftop garden.

As the knocking on the door steadily increased, her people began to move. As silently as possible, their prisoners in tow, they moved toward

the stairs. Leah retrieved Wulder's horned helm from the floor and followed.

CHAPTER 106

They passed several other guards as they made their way through the
torchlit hallways of the jailhouse—all incapacitated. Most had their
wrists bound. Some were gagged. And some sat where they had fallen,
knocked out. Megara and Adonica had been quite thorough.

"Does it really glow green *all the time* there?" asked Maera, skipping
playfully as they passed another unconscious guard.

Megara smiled broadly and nodded at her, then signed.

"She says it's the most beautiful place you'll ever see," translated
Adonica.

Maera responded by sticking her tongue out of the side of her mouth
and making an excited noise.

Adonica turned to Feliks. "Be at the southeast gate by morning. Assuming everything goes to plan, there'll be a whole caravan of people
heading to Cymorrika. You'll all be safe there. Every one of you."

"And you did get the artifact to the old man, right?" asked Gunnar.
"I was nearly eaten alive over that stupid thing, so I hope—"

"Relax," Adonica snapped. "He's got it. And he didn't even seem to
mind that you kept one of the stones for yourself."

"Hey, you can never be too careful," said Gunnar.

The group stopped at a corner, and Megara and Adonica checked the
adjoining hallways before proceeding.

Ahead, Hook could see the light of day. He tapped Adonica on the
shoulder and signed, *What about the people we freed from the ship?*

"Most headed inland as a group," said Adonica. "Said they were
headed for Lonn."

"Perfect place for a new start," said Gunnar. "I ought to know."

"The rest, believe it or not, came north to the city with me," said
Adonica. "Said they want to help fight the demons as free men."

Megara and Hook exchanged silent smiles.

"I'm not sure Wulder will be okay with that," said Gunnar.

"He doesn't get a say in the matter," said Adonica. "I just hope everyone's able to prepare by sundown."

"Sundown?" said Gunnar. "You don't mean we're setting sail *tonight*?"

"It's the only way we could convince the good count to donate some ships," said Adonica. "By which I mean that we are stealing them while he's tied up in a closet somewhere."

At the doorway to the jailhouse, Hook was relieved to find Stormbringer, Thirsty, and Ash tied to hitching posts. The three steeds had boarded the *Naiad* along with them, and Adonica had taken all three with her when she'd disembarked with the crown, south of Castydocia. Stormbringer's eyes lit up, and she stomped her hooves excitedly as soon as Hook appeared. He started toward her, but Adonica suddenly came up short and looked down.

Hook followed her gaze. A length of frayed rope lay on the ground. A few feet away were several drops of blood. And a few feet away from that, more.

"Blast," breathed Adonica. "Somebody got loose. If he raises an alarm, it could complicate things real fast."

Adonica started to follow the trail, but Hook put a hand on her shoulder.

"I will do it," he signed. *"I am the better tracker."*

"We're meeting at the docks," said Adonica, "after I can get Feliks and Maera somewhere safe."

Hook nodded. *"You may need Gunnar to talk your way through. Or Megara's sunlight. I will meet you there."*

Adonica nodded but didn't look as though she liked the idea much. Meanwhile, the others mounted up on the steeds.

Gunnar mounted up, mumbling, "Setting sail *tonight*. A guy can't get a decent night's sleep to save his life."

Adonica climbed atop her steed with Feliks Evin in the saddle behind her.

"Bye!" said Maera as Megara pulled her up into Stormbringer's saddle with her.

Hook patted Stormbringer reassuringly to calm the girl down.

"See you at the docks," said Adonica.

Hook nodded.

She continued watching him with her green eyes for a long moment.

As the three steeds set off at a canter, Hook adjusted his grip on the a'thri'ik-tipped lance and set off, following the blood trail. Somewhere, out over the rooftops, the sun was starting to go down.

CHAPTER 107

"You can't leave us in here!" one of Wulder's guards protested.

"This storehouse has been empty for weeks—nobody will be looking here!" said another.

Wulder, meanwhile, said nothing. He only glared at Leah as he sat on the floor, surrounded by his guards. They were all bound at the feet. Their wrists were tied behind their backs, secured to the building's support beams. One by one, Lycon and Olorus tied gags over their mouths.

Leah looked down at Wulder. "My army, whether it's a few hundred or a few thousand, sets sail tonight," she said. "And tomorrow morning, some of my people will set out from the southeast gates, leading civilians to the city in the mountains. Before setting out, my people will inform the city guards of your location." She paused. "Unless you wish to join us."

Wulder's glare only hardened. Leah had her answer, it seemed. She did not know what sort of action Wulder would take come morning, but she and her newly acquired fleet would be far from here by then.

"So be it," said Leah. "Count Von Morix, I pray you can continue to keep your people safe here. And if I ever return, I pray we can be allies and build a new world together."

Leah gave him a hard, measured look.

"Out of curiosity," she said, "if I *had* come to you with this plan before taking action, would you have joined me?"

Something in Wulder's glare changed, but it did not soften. "Now we'll never know," he said.

They were the last words he spoke before Olorus pulled the gag tight between his teeth and tied it around the back of his head.

Wulder gave Lycon, his former major, a particularly withering look. Then Leah and the others exited the storehouse. Lycon shut the door behind them, turned a key in the lock, and promptly tossed the key up onto the roof.

Zechariah and Marcus, along with several dozen armed volunteers of the Holy Army, had already gone ahead to help facilitate things at the docks. It was now just Leah, Lycon, Itzacoatl, Sif, Tel, and Vox—and almost fifty Raeqlu infantry men and women.

Leah truly did not know how many of the people who had heard her declaration would answer the call to action, but *some* seemed to be, at least. Even from here, Leah could see, down the adjoining side streets, groups of people making their way toward the docks. It was a start.

"Itzacoatl," said Leah, turning to the old man. She raised her voice so that he could adequately hear her. "This is where we part ways. Thank you for escorting the civilians to Cymorrika tomorrow morning. We met on terrible terms, but you have proven to be a stalwart ally."

Itzacoatl offered a sad smile. Then he looked away.

"What is it?" she asked.

He turned back. "Erum is my homeland," he said. "I can be of use." He gestured to the sword in his hand. "You *know* I can be of use. If you were to trust me to don my armor once more, I could help."

"No," said Leah. "I need you to guide the civilians to Cymorrika."

"I can do it," Vox said.

Leah glanced at her in surprise.

"With your permission, of course, Elder," Vox clarified. "I remember the way. And my husband and child are in Cymorrika. There, I could still serve by guarding the city. I would rather join you on the warpath, My Queen, even if it means going to my death." She let out a laugh, gesturing toward Itzacoatl's sword. "But I should think Itz will be of more use!"

Sif and Tel also laughed, and Itzacoatl grinned in response.

Itz, thought Leah. The shortened version of the old man's name sounded almost Cru.

Leah considered for a moment. A guide who knew Erum would be valuable. And the old man's rare talents would be highly useful, so long as she could trust him. After the betrayal of Folgruuth, the Darvellians, and even some Nolians, she worried about misplacing her trust again.

"General Sif?" said Leah.

Sif, who bore resentment toward Itzacoatl more than anyone else, only bowed to Leah—a silent indication that he approved of whatever decision she made in this matter.

"Then I leave the decision with you, Vox," said Leah. "I trust your judgment in this."

CHAPTER 108

When Justin was finished writing, he ripped the page from the top of the yellow legal pad, folded it up, and handed it to his father.

Benjamin started to unfold it, but Justin grabbed his hand to stop him.

"You said you didn't want to see me take the stone from Mom's coat pocket," said Justin. "I'm asking you—please don't let me see you read that. It's there for you only if you need it. I plan to come back home again someday or die trying. And, considering the time difference between Earth and the Oikoumene, I guess it won't take very long before you know, one way or the other. A day or two on Earth has got to be decades there, right?"

"Something like that," said Benjamin.

"So if I'm not back by then," said Justin, "chances are I never will be."

Benjamin's hand tightened on the note, crumpling it a bit. "I hate this sort of talk," he said.

Benjamin lowered himself into his wheelchair. He'd retrieved it from the bottom of the hill where he'd kicked it, and it appeared to be relatively unscathed other than some dings and scratches.

For a moment, both of them were silent again. In the silence, Justin took out his gauge stone.

"When you were born," said Benjamin, "and I first held you, it was like. . . . It was like they had handed me a best friend who I just hadn't known about until that day. Instantly, I would have died for you. You were so little and helpless, but I could see that you were strong, too. For the time being, your strength was trapped within the limitations of a tiny, defenseless little body, but it was there—even from day one, I knew it! So until that strength could come out, it was up to me to be strong for you. That became my most important responsibility. And, you know what? That feeling never goes away."

He hung his head. His fingers curled tightly over the arms of his wheelchair. Tears threatened at the corners of his eyes.

"All I want is to be able to protect you," he said. "So to let you go like this, knowing what's ahead of you, feels like a betrayal of everything that was entrusted to me."

Justin checked that he had everything, then slung his new shield to hang from his back. He leaned down, grabbed his father by the shoulders, pulled him in, and held him.

"You did your job, Dad," said Justin.

Benjamin made a noise against Justin's shoulder, and he leaned heavily against him, allowing his son to hold him up.

Justin patted Benjamin on the back and began to feed his aurym power into the keystone.

CHAPTER 109

Tel wiped the tears from his eyes as he gripped Vox's arm tightly.

"No need for sadness, my friend," said Vox. "I return to our Home. Our Central Mountain. And you take yours with you."

Tel forced a smile. "I look forward to the day when the two shall be one again, my friend," he replied.

"Take care of our people, warrior," said Sif.

"I will, Elder," said Vox. Then she turned to Leah. "Thank you, My Queen." She raised her voice as she added, "And as for you, Itz, *our* Home will be waiting for you when you return."

Moments later, Vox had departed, and Leah found herself watching the corner where she'd turned, thankful for the woman's bravery and service, and quietly praying for all those she would be leading to Cymorrika.

"Leah," said Olorus.

She turned to face him. Even after all this time, it felt odd when he referred to her by her first name. Odd and nice.

"I know," she said. "Time to go."

She looked around at Olorus, Lycon, Sif, Tel, and the Raeqlu soldiers surrounding them. Almost unconsciously, her hand wandered to the satchel of aurstones at her belt, then to the other satchel she had been carrying since leaving Cervice—the one that contained the Nolian crown. In spite of everything, she didn't think she would ever get used to the sight of people waiting for her to tell them what to do, let alone when her decision might lead to their deaths.

Leah said nothing. She simply nodded, then started off down the city streets toward the harbor.

CHAPTER 110

Like a transition between scenes in a movie, the gray expanse of the Kharon gave way to the Holmes family's living room.

The same vinyl record was playing on Benjamin's record player—still blaring the same solo from the same progressive rock track, in fact—as if no time had passed whatsoever. Because, of course, it hadn't.

Justin let go of his father, and Benjamin sat back, rubbing his eyes behind his glasses. The paper Justin had written was still in his hand. Back in the Kharon, he had seemed like an ordinary, vulnerable man. But somehow, being back in his childhood home, Justin saw him as his invincible father once again. Tough but gentle. Knowing but humble. And, as always, grinning as if he knew something Justin didn't.

Benjamin tapped his fingers against the arm of his wheelchair in time with the prog rock. "Well then," he said. "Time's wasting. You already know what I'm going to say, right?"

Justin nodded. "I know. 'Do your best, and don't look back.' I will."

"Love you, kid," said Benjamin.

"I love you too, Dad."

They hugged one last time. Then Benjamin stood from his wheelchair, turned, and walked into the kitchen.

Justin crossed the living room, approaching the front door where his mother's green jacket still hung from the coat hanger. He reached for it.

His hand hovered in mid-air in front of it. The green jacket had hung there, untouched as far as Justin knew, for over a year. He could see her, with this same coat folded in her lap, cheering for him from the stands at one of his playoff games. She'd always been there. Always. That was part of what had made it so hard to have had her taken from him.

He rubbed his fingers together, took a deep breath for courage, and reached into the jacket.

Inside the left front pocket was a stone.

It was larger than his gauge—about the size of a chicken's egg but rough and uneven. It might have easily passed for a piece of limestone from a gravel driveway. But when it came to aurym, looks could be deceiving.

Justin turned to take in his father's wheelchair sitting empty in the middle of the room. Again, the words flashed through his mind: *Beloved son.*

For a moment, he second-guessed his choice to hide the words from his father. But he set his jaw, shook his head, and raised his gauge stone.

He held out his hand and let his aurym power flow into the gauge. It became a swirling torrent of green energy that slowly expanded until it encapsulated him like a chrysalis. The power swirled around him, causing his mother's jacket to flutter. Framed family photos swung from their hooks on the wall.

The last thing he saw was his father's empty wheelchair. The last thing he heard was the scratch of the record player's needle being abruptly and none-too-gently pulled off the spinning record in the next room. Then the Holmes house disappeared.

CHAPTER 111

Hook leaned against a building to peek around a corner. The dribbling blood trail had led him toward one of the city's multiple waterfronts. Small fishing boats could be seen moored ahead, along the edge of a canal that led to the sea. The harbor where Leah had asked her volunteers to assemble was on the other side of the city, but here, residents had their own private docks up and down the city's coastline. Hook could hear the commotion of excited voices a few streets away, but here, it was strangely quiet.

Ahead of his position, the blood trail led beneath a covered archway that connected two buildings. He checked his surroundings, adjusted his grip on his lance, and followed it.

Drops of blood led past a stucco house and into a small garden that was only a patch of loose dirt now that the winter months had set in. He picked the trail up on the other side, heading toward the house's private dock—a few uneven and rickety planks of wood extending out into the water, supported by piles.

Hook felt the entire dock move beneath his weight as he tiptoed out onto it. The man wasn't bleeding badly. Probably no more than a broken nose, which, knowing Adonica, made sense. The trail led down the dock to a boat.

A short gangplank spanned the gap between the dock and the boat. There was blood here, too.

Hook studied the boat. There was a small cabin, big enough that Hook couldn't see inside it from here, especially in the dying light as the sun went down. But he could hear someone milling about in there.

Not a bad idea, actually, he thought. *He's planning to take the canal to the acropolis to raise the alarm.*

But at that moment, Hook noticed a shape on the water.

It was a large ship, at the terminus of the canal's flow to the sea. It was a Mythaean tall ship, and it appeared to be traveling along the coast, probably headed toward the harbor. But there was something about it. Something familiar. Or perhaps just odd.

For one thing, there appeared to be no one on deck. Not a single soul. Oars were extended out the sides and rotating, propelling the vessel along. But Hook had spent years at oars just like those ones. He knew the proper optimal rhythm—lived with the sound of drums beating in his head like an internal metronome. But *this* ship—

The twang of crossbow arms sent memories flooding through Hook even before he felt the bite of the bolt's barbed head penetrate his back.

PART X

THE MEETING

OF THE SPIRITS

CHAPTER 112

The impact alone was staggering. Like getting kicked in the back by a steed.

Hook cried out—a pitiful noise when one didn't have a tongue to form sounds—and fell. His knees hit the planks of the dock. He nearly tumbled over the side into the water below, but tightened his grip on the lance and used it as a support to prevent him from falling. The pain was extraordinary, but he knew he only had seconds before the next bolt was loaded and fired. It had come from behind, and he was out in the open here on the dock. Nowhere to hide except. . . .

Hook rushed forward, over the gangplank and onto the small fishing boat, aware of a wet sensation pouring down him from the front. He rushed into the cabin.

A shortsword came slashing at Hook in an overhand chop like a hatchet coming down on kindling.

Hook sidestepped and watched the blade pass by him. At his best, he would have reacted swiftly and taken the attacker down, but the simple effort of avoiding the attack sent waves of agony and nausea flooding through him, radiating outward from the crossbow bolt sticking through his back, all the way out his front. He stumbled into the wall of the cabin with a groan.

Did it catch my lung? Hook wondered. *Might have missed it. Can't tell.*

Hook's eyes lost focus for a second. He blinked hard and regained his vision just in time to see the sword coming at him again, this time horizontally. No time to dodge it, so he pulled the lance toward his face. The guard's sword hit the haft, stopping inches from Hook's neck. The blade bounced back, which knocked the guard off-balance for a moment, and Hook looked up and realized he'd been right about the broken nose; the Castydocian guard's silver mustache had a trail of red running down from his nostrils, but he seemed otherwise uninjured.

But he's in here, thought Hook. *So who shot me?*

"Slave scum!" the guard hissed, brimming with rage.

I don't want to kill you, Hook would have said, if he'd been able.

This time, the guard tried to stab him through the belly. Hook spun the lance. With the business end, he slapped the incoming sword aside. In the same motion, he brought the blunt side up and rapped it against the guard's already broken nose. So stunned was the guard that he dropped his sword and raised his hand to his smarting nose.

"Slave *scum!*" the man barked, blinking in surprise.

You said that already, thought Hook.

There wasn't much space to work with in the small cabin, but there was enough. Hook stepped forward, leading with the lance. The guard was turned, his side to Hook as he looked for his dropped sword, completely open and defenseless. All too easy.

Hook jabbed the blunt end of the lance straight into the hinge of the guard's jaw. The man didn't so much as twitch in response; instantly, his every muscle went limp, and he collapsed to the floor of the cabin.

Hook collapsed, too. He sat back heavily on his rear end and stifled a scream as the motion bumped the butt end of the crossbow bolt sticking through him. He looked down. The barbed head had passed all the way through him—in through his back, beneath his shoulder blade, and out just below his collarbone.

Figures that I wouldn't be lucky enough for it to hit the shoulder blade, thought Hook. *Not bleeding all that badly, though. Didn't hit any arteries. I have time.*

Probably. But who the hell really knew.

Hook pulled out his belt knife and looked down at the bolt again. A bloody, barbed broadhead. He saw Jocasta standing in front of him, looking down with helpless, doe-like eyes at a bloody, barbed broadhead protruding from *her* chest. He remembered reaching for her just before she toppled over the side of the ship, only managing to rip the strip of cloth from her hair.

Hook blocked out the pain as he grabbed the bolt just behind the head. He used his knife to carve a notch in it to weaken the shaft, then snapped the front end off. Reaching over his back to do the same with the reverse end was a far greater challenge, but he managed it. He could think of no better way to make things worse than to try to pull the thing out. But at least he could shorten it and reduce the risk of it bumping against something and tearing up his insides even worse.

He stayed low. He could hear his own panting and a bubbly sort of snoring coming from the unconscious guard in front of him. Other than that, he couldn't hear anything. But the crossbowman was still out there, waiting for him to stick his head out.

Suddenly, Hook heard a dull crash, followed quickly by a *whoosh*—like a sharp intake of breath. He wasn't sure how, exactly, but he recognized the sound immediately. Some deep-seated, latent memory, perhaps. He turned toward the door of the cabin and confirmed what he already knew. The flames were already growing from where the oil lantern had been tossed onto the deck of the fishing boat.

CHAPTER 113

The screams were what Leah noticed first. Then she saw the unarmed citizens fleeing through the streets, rushing in the opposite direction of the way she was heading—the harbor. She had her new a'thri'ik sword drawn and was running before a word was spoken among her entourage, and they followed without needing to be told.

The closer they got, the louder the screams became. And then she heard—and felt, through the extrasensory perceptions of aurym—the first daemyn blast.

No, thought Leah. *Not here. Not now.*

She glanced over her shoulder. Itzacoatl was lagging behind, but he was still with them. There was an a'thri'ik sword in his hand, but he wasn't armored like the rest of them. The Raeqlu soldiers escorting them were in ordinary steel plates and chainmail. But Leah, Olorus, Sif, Lycon, and Tel all wore full sets of a'thri'ik armor.

"Soldiers, fall back!" Leah ordered. "Protect our rear and our flanks! Olorus, Sif, Lycon, Tel—helmets on, and stay with me!"

Leah pulled her own helmet over her head. Her field of vision became limited but also focused. Focused only ahead. Where smoke could now be seen rising from the harbor.

Zechariah and Marcus were there. Possibly Gunnar, Hook, Adonica, and Megara, too.

Leah pumped her arms and ran, not caring who, if anyone, was following her.

CHAPTER 114

The flames were growing with each passing second.

Hook squeezed his eyes shut against a fresh wave of pain, then opened them to take in the unconscious soldier before him, the flames outside the door, and the blood beneath him—his blood. He sighed in annoyance, then pulled himself to his feet.

He crossed the cabin and grabbed the lid off of a barrel in the corner. Judging by the smell, this was where the captain stored his catch between the open water and bringing it back home. Hook tested the weight of the lid in his hand, then grabbed a nearby coil of rope, hacked off a piece, and wrapped the length around the barrel lid in a triangular pattern. He tied it to the middle of the lance haft. All the while, the flames outside the cabin door grew.

The pain in Hook's back made him dizzy as he grabbed the unconscious Castydocian guard, picked him up, and threw him over his uninjured shoulder. His leg still pained him where the teeth of a sea monster had bitten him to the bone, and the weight of this man was no help. With his other hand, he held the lance up, the barrel lid facing outward to cover his face as a makeshift shield.

Hook thought he might be all right if there was only one of them out there. The reload times on crossbows—loading the bolt and cranking the lever back to pull the arms into place—were sometimes as long as fifteen to twenty seconds. But there was no telling. Maybe there were ten crossbowmen, all lined up in a row and waiting for him. He did a mental countdown, then ran out onto the burning deck.

Hook felt his skin being seared by the flames, but he ran through them as quickly as possible, toward the gangplank to the dock, careful to keep his head lowered behind the barrel lid.

He heard a twang, a sound like a bird flying by at high speed, and a woody thump against the deck at his feet. Whoever they were, they didn't care enough about the unconscious man over Hook's shoulder to hold their fire.

As Hook ran, he considered the implication of the angle of the shot. *Above me. Firing from the roof.*

In a few quick strides, he made it across the gangplank. He wasted no time. As soon as he was on safe ground, he tossed the soldier to the ground and looked up at the roof of the fisherman's stucco house. In the fading twilight, Hook saw a silhouette. A silhouette that was currently pulling a bolt from a quiver on its back. And only one of them.

Hook grimaced again against the pain but heaved a sigh of relief nonetheless.

He took his time. He had fifteen to twenty seconds, after all. All the time in the world.

Hook pulled the knife from his belt and hacked loose the rope he had used to tie the barrel lid to the lance. He could hear the steady click-click-clicking as the crank of the crossbow turned.

He dropped the barrel lid to the ground. Behind him, the flames on the boat sucked and roared, and he heard deck boards cracking. Carefully, he tested the weight of the lance. He bounced it up and down on his palm to find its center of balance.

Click-click-click went the crossbow's crank.

Still not quite there. Too slow.

Hook braced himself for the pain that this was about to cause the wound in his shoulder, then hauled back, took a crow-hop forward, and threw the lance.

The man dropped the crossbow. He tried to leap sidelong. Too late.

The lance caught him. He cried out and spun in a full circle before dropping off the back of the roof. A second later, Hook heard the impact of his body hitting the ground on the other side of the house.

Hook fell to his knees, nearly blacking out from the pain. He sucked in a deep breath and glanced over his shoulder at the fishing boat. The weakened deck had split down the middle, and the two sides, engulfed in flames, were sinking at different angles.

He looked down at the unconscious guard beside him and signed, *"You're welcome."*

Hook drew a tighter grip on his knife, stood, and walked toward the house.

C H A P T E R   1 1 5

Finally, Leah saw them. Shadowed bodies running through the streets. Attacking the people.

But even in the dim light of dusk, she knew they weren't coblyns. They weren't humans, either. Or cythraul.

They were something else.

From somewhere farther ahead came a daemyn blast. Quickly after, a burst of sunlight flashed over the rooftops.

Megara.

Leah's feet faltered. She was closer now, and she could not only see that these things were not coblyns, but they held weapons—something she had never seen a coblyn do. Swords. Axes. Bows and arrows. Many were locked in combat with soldiers from Raeqlund, Endenholm, or Nolia. They stood taller than any coblyn she had ever seen, though far shorter than a cythraul. Instead, they appeared to be about the height of a man.

Presently, she saw an Enden soldier hack a hand off of one of the creatures. The thing did not even seem to notice. It responded by thrusting its longsword into the Enden soldier's throat and driving it down all the way to the hilt. The Enden soldier clutched desperately at the attacker's arm as if trying to hold himself up, but the creature pulled sideways, wrenching his sword free and sending a shadowed spray across the street.

"What, in the name of all that is holy, are these things?" Lycon breathed beside her.

"Forward!" Olorus shouted. He ran past Leah and Lycon, rushing toward the fighting like a man possessed. In one hand, he wielded a new a'thri'ik shield. In the other hand, an a'thri'ik shortsword. "We outnumber them!" he bellowed. "Find your courage! Cut the devils down!" Sif and Tel were already rushing forward, right behind him.

Olorus's cry jolted Leah from her daze. Together, she and Lycon charged.

An outside observer might have found it difficult to tell Leah and her soldiers apart, covered in matching sets of armor, with their faces hidden behind helmets. But Leah knew her allies both by their choices of weaponry and the body language of their unique fighting styles. As for her, the blood-red cloak of Nolia flew behind her as she ran.

They passed by human corpses, coblyn corpses, and several corpses of these monstrous, human-sized creatures, too. She resisted the urge to pause and look at them. She couldn't—whatever they were, if they were attacking her people, they had to die.

A child-sized coblyn launched itself out of the darkness, coming at Olorus from the side. It wrapped its hands around his side and lunged for his chest with its jaws gaping, but its teeth shattered against the armor. Olorus didn't so much as slow his pace; with a roar, he threw the creature down, and a half-second later, Sif stomped down on its head, crushing its skull beneath his heel. Another coblyn jumped at Lycon, and the big man responded with a sidelong swipe of his demon sword that separated the creature's top half from its bottom. Black blood sprayed across the street.

There don't seem to be that many of them, thought Leah. *But where are they coming from?*

Ahead, she spotted a group of human noncombatants huddled against the side of a building. Some Enden soldiers and Holy Army volunteers had created a defensive ring around them and were fending off a herd of the human-sized demon-like things.

Olorus led the way straight to them. He wasted no time on honor in his first attack, driving his a'thri'ik sword through the back of one of the creatures, then swiftly retracting his blade and spinning toward another. But the second one raised a sword of its own, blocking Olorus's attack. It counter-attacked by driving its sword at Olorus's stomach, an attack that Olorus just barely managed to parry. It slashed at him again, and Olorus stumbled over his own feet, thrown off-balance by the surprising effectiveness of the attacks.

They're fast, thought Leah. *And they've had training.*

As the rest of the man-sized demons turned to face Olorus, Sif, Tel, and the other newcomers, Leah suddenly found herself toe-to-toe with one of them. And instead of flying at her in animalistic fury like a coblyn, it squared off against her. Two Mythaean-style hatchets—short-handled weapons typically used in close quarters when boarding enemy vessels at sea—were clutched in its bony hands, and it held them in proper defensive positions as it stared at her.

Sizing me up, she realized. *Looking for weaknesses in my form. Planning its attack.*

Leah stepped to the side, circling, and the creature matched her movements. This thing was unlike any demon she had ever seen before. Though its limbs were narrow like those of a coblyn, it stood a full foot taller than Leah. It was dressed in ragged clothing, but she could see that its body was not made of the same black, leatherish material as a coblyn's hide. It was more like black bone armor like a cythraul—chitinous, bony scales that overlapped one another across its arms and chest.

And the face. Like a cythraul, the face was a fleshless black skull with empty eye sockets that glowed with a deep, red light from somewhere within. Yet, unlike a cythraul, the skull was not oversized, monstrous, or deformed. Rather, it was disturbingly human in shape and appearance.

The creature suddenly flew at her in a spin, leading with one hatchet, with the other leveled to follow up. In her new armor, she found that quick movements weren't as easy as she was accustomed to, but she managed to step back and avoid both attacks. She swung her saber at the creature, and it deftly stepped back, easily avoiding the slash.

In her peripheral vision, Leah could see that Olorus, Lycon, Sif, and Tel were locked in similar engagements. All seemed to be discovering the same thing—that not only did these things not look like coblyns, but they didn't fight like them either. From somewhere up ahead, another daemyn blast erupted, followed by another flash of sunlight.

Leah's opponent faked to one side and jumped toward her on the other, hacking with one of the hatchets. She slashed with her slender blade to redirect the attack. She intended to follow this up with a stab at its midsection, but a blur of dark movement beside her drew her full attention. She turned in time to see another one of the creatures silently charging, a long pike leveled at her.

A sudden flash of green energy tore across the street. It ripped through the advancing pikeman, blasting him backward like a mountain sapling caught in an avalanche. Leah turned to see Itzacoatl rushing to join them, wearing no armor and lagging behind, but charging all the same. He turned and hacked at the air, and another arc of green energy sliced through the street, cutting down two coblyns at once.

Leah's foe lunged at her, clearly attempting to capitalize on the distraction. But she was ready and took her chance. She sidestepped, then stabbed her saber through the creature's hip and twice more through its torso, all before it could react. It stumbled in surprise and managed to land a hatchet strike, but the blade bounced off the shoulderplate of Leah's a'thri'ik armor. She turned the saber in her hand, redirecting the cutting edge, and swung sideways. The monster's head fell from its body, and it toppled in a heap.

"Itz!" shouted Leah. "Follow me!"

She wasn't sure if the old man heard her properly or not, but he seemed to understand her meaning well enough. She had to get him to the cythraul.

"Olorus, my friend! Go!" Sif shouted, currently trading blows with two man-sized demons at once. "We will finish up here and join you!"

"Aye!" replied Olorus, and he backed away from his foe, allowing Tel to step in and take over.

"Are you with us, Major?" Sif asked.

"To the end, Elder!" Leah heard Lycon reply from somewhere amid the fray.

Boots clanked against the cobbles as Leah, Olorus, and Itzacoatl rushed up the street toward the harbor—toward the source of the darkness.

CHAPTER 116

The sun had dipped over the horizon, but, rounding the street corner, Leah could see the harbor ahead in the double-moonlight. The masts of a hundred ships, at least, could be seen silhouetted against the ocean skyline. They appeared to be Mythaean and Castydocian in design.

But one of the ships, unlike all the rest, had its sails hoisted and unfurled. And it wasn't docked. In fact, it appeared to have rammed itself against the pier without so much as slowing.

In front of the wrecked ship stood a massive cythraul, a great sickle in its giant hand. Scorched craters marred portions of the street, and not far from where it stood, a building had been blown apart, reduced to smoking rubble.

Between their current position and the cythraul, dozens of soldiers were locked in combat with the man-sized demons, many of which wielded human weapons. Coblyns skittered about here and there.

But to Leah's relief, the humans outnumbered the demons. Many soldiers had already been making their way toward the harbor, rallied by her call to action. Armed women and men were streaming in from every side street, and before long, there would be enough of them to overwhelm the lesser demons.

It was the cythraul that was the problem.

"The demons stole a League ship," said Olorus from beside her. "They must have used it to get past the fleet and unload here at the docks."

"But for what purpose?" said Leah, looking around.

There were too few of them for this attack to be very effective. Was this just the first of many ships? Or was it a distraction meant to draw the city's collective attention away from elsewhere?

A bright light flashed ahead, shining like a lighthouse, and a beam of concentrated sunlight struck the cythraul in the face. Sparks flew from the impact zone. The demon let out a roar of anger, but it shook off the attack and stepped forward. It swung its sickle in a downward arc that produced an ear-splitting clang. Leah couldn't see the object of its attack from here but assumed it was Megara. She could only hope she'd been able to dodge that attack.

A great vine suddenly rose up like a snake preparing to strike the cythraul. Before it could, the demon's sickle lopped it in half. Gunnar was there, too, then.

Zechariah was up there somewhere, too. And Marcus. And Adonica and Hook, too, if the jailbreak had been a success. Perhaps together, and with the help of the soldiers pouring in, all of them would be enough to kill the cythraul. But who knew how many would be killed in the process?

"Itz," said Leah, turning to Itzacoatl.

The old man stood rooted to the spot, horrified by the sight of the cythraul.

"Itz!" Leah shouted, stepping in front of him.

Itzacoatl blinked, snapping out of it.

"I've seen aurym powers like yours cut down beasts like that!" Leah said. "If I get you there, can you—?"

"Watch out!" cried Olorus.

Leah had no time to react before Olorus shoved her hard. As she fell, she saw a man-sized demon form charge forward, a round shield raised.

Thanks to Olorus's shove, the shield slammed into Olorus and knocked him to the ground instead of her. Leah stumbled to her knees on the cobblestones, caught herself, and regained her feet just in time to see a coblyn come rushing at her. Her saber had been lost in the fall, so she raised her hand in a desperate attempt to defend herself. Teeth clamped down on the armplate of her a'thri'ik armor but were instantly broken out of the creature's mouth, leaving not a scratch on the armor. Still, the coblyn held on.

A blast of daemyn erupted from somewhere ahead, and she heard soldiers scream their last before being eaten up by the demonic power. Leah shook the coblyn loose from her arm. It hit the ground, and she brought her booted foot down to crush its neck.

Leah turned, searching for her saber—searching for any weapon at all to use against the coblyns, the cythraul, and whatever these man-sized demons were. A dozen yards away, Itzacoatl was hacking green energy into a swarm of coblyns threatening to push through.

Nearer to Leah's position, Olorus lay in the street. He appeared to be conscious, but for some reason, he wasn't moving. Leah couldn't see Olorus's facial expression behind his helmet, but his body language bespoke shock as he looked up at the man-demon that had struck him down.

This creature, to Leah's horror, not only wielded a shortsword and shield but was outfitted in armor. And not just any armor. The same armor she was wearing. A full set of a'thri'ik armor, minus the helmet.

No! thought Leah. *Where did demons get cat's eye armor?*

Grabbing her saber from the ground, Leah dashed forward. She saw that the demon's head had strands of thin hair clinging to its scalp, but otherwise, it was the same sort of fleshless, black skull she was used to seeing on a cythraul. She hauled back, preparing to lop the thing's head off at the shoulders.

The man-sized demon turned to face her. Whitened eyes, set within a skull-like face, stared at Leah. It raised its shield. Its mouth opened and closed as if to form words, and Leah noticed the remnants of a chinstrap of red facial hair lining its jaw.

Leah's heart grew cold. Her charge slowed involuntarily to a halt, and the saber drooped in her limp hand.

"Marcus," she breathed.

CHAPTER 117

Hook held tight to the barrel lid in one hand and his belt knife in the other. He was about to round the corner of the house when a distant roar caused him to come up short.

Cythraul, he thought.

Before he could worry about what to do next, something caught his eye inside the window of the house just beside him. A dull green light—

Hook leaped sideways. There was a loud crash and a shower of glass as his lance's tip—which glowed green only until it reached the moonlight, then faded to the color of normal steel again—came stabbing straight through the window at him.

Hook dropped the knife, grabbed the lance behind the blade, and pulled. The attacker had the presence of mind to let go of the lance, but not before his arm was within reach of Hook's hand.

Hook yanked the man bodily through the window. No easy task; he was a brute of a man with a round belly, and when Hook slammed him down onto the ground on his back, he let out a grunt. The wind was knocked out of him. It was Cadmus.

Hook would have been on top of him in an instant, but the act of pulling Cadmus through the window had jarred the crossbow bolt sticking through him. It tore one way and then the other, and the pain was enough to sit Hook down against the wall of the house, grinding his teeth and trembling with the shock of it.

Get up, he silently screamed at himself. *Get up!*

Cadmus was on his back, gasping for breath. Hook sat with his back against the house. And the lance lay between them.

Cadmus was the first to gain his feet. Hook, in spite of the pain, pushed against the wall, knowing he had to stand now or die.

But instead of lunging for the weapon, Cadmus stumbled back and fell heavily to the ground. He tried to stand again, seemed to lose his balance, and fell back down. And Hook realized that a dark pool was spreading in the grass beneath Cadmus's body.

Hook stood and looked down at Cadmus, only now noticing the long gash in the big man's arm. Blood was seeping from his wrist in a steady, rhythmic, pulsing flow, like sap from a scored tree. Taking his time, Hook grabbed the lance from the ground. The tip of its blade was coated in blood.

Lucky throw, he thought.

Cadmus had already lost a lot of blood from the cut. He tried again and failed to stand. His attempt at stabbing Hook through the window, evidently, had taken the last of his strength. He looked up at Hook, his round, cleanly shaven face ghastly white. His royal admiral's hat was missing, revealing a mostly bald scalp beneath, making the ring of scar tissue around his forehead stand out all the more.

Cadmus favored Hook with a scowl.

"Well, then," he said. "Go on and finish it, Dark-eyes. Do it for your little Fawn."

Hook stepped forward, holding the lance in both hands.

CHAPTER 118

The demon with the chinstrap of red facial hair snarled and lunged at Leah, and it was all she could do to force herself out of her stupor and swing her sword to swat aside the incoming blade.

"Marcus . . . no," she heard herself say.

Another lunge—this one aimed at her chest. Her body reacted automatically, responding to reflexes developed over years of duelist training. She redirected the attack to her right and hopped a step to her left. But she couldn't keep her eyes on the opponent's blade as she should have; she couldn't tear her gaze from the creature's blackened, mostly fleshless, yet undeniably familiar face.

Was it really Marcus Worth? Was that even possible? Or was it some trick—?

She paid for her lapse in attention with a strike that would have killed her if not for her a'thri'ik armor. The demonic version of Marcus feinted high and to the left, then spun its body in a full circle, leading with its shortsword in a horizontal chop.

The double-edged blade struck Leah with full force, directly in the sternum. She staggered back, reeling from the impact. The creature followed it up with a hack at her neck, trying to slip its sword through the gap between her armor and her helmet. She barely managed to get her saber up in time to redirect the attack, resulting in a glancing blow to her shoulder instead.

"Please, Marcus," she said. Tears ran down her cheeks inside her helmet. "It's me, Marcus. Don't do this!"

Marcus smiled at her—a smile that cracked the remnants of blackened flesh still clinging to its face, splitting open the skin so wide that Leah could see the cheekbones beneath. Its upper lip crumbled like ash. The blank, white eyes bulged in their sockets.

Leah bit back her sorrow. With one hand, she raised her saber to the proper defensive position in front of her. The other, she placed behind her, at the small of her back, in a duelist's posture.

"Don't make me do this," she said.

Marcus threw his shield to the ground, took his shortsword in both hands, and rushed at her.

C H A P T E R   1 1 9

The green nebula that had momentarily encapsulated Justin faded away before his eyes at the same moment that he felt warm water surrounding him—nearly at chest height.

He backed up in surprise. When he'd left, the water had been below his waist. Clearly, he had left at low tide, and now the tide was high. It was still nighttime—but not *still* night, of course. He knew better than that; it only happened to be nighttime again. Weeks had probably passed here during his brief absence on Earth. Looking out at the stars hanging over the ocean, he wondered how much time had passed and how he would be able to tell—

A low grumble sounded from behind Justin. He closed his eyes, recognizing the sound at the same instant that he recognized the distinctive presence, felt through the extrasensory perceptions of aurym.

Slowly, Justin turned. Standing along the shoreline were five giants with bodies made of otherworldly black bone armor, with massive, misshapen skeletal heads atop broad shoulders. Each of them held a weapon in its massive hands. One held two.

From this distance, in the light of the two moons, the monsters' individual features were not easily visible, except for the red glow that emanated from their empty eye sockets. They stood in a row, facing him, weapons at the ready.

They've been waiting for me.

Justin drew Ahlund's broken sword from the baldric hanging over his shoulders and raised his father's shield before him. He tightened his grip around the sword's hilt and called on aurym. The blade glowed red—redder than the eyes of a cythraul.

CHAPTER 120

Itzacoatl was doing his best to thin the herd of coblyns with blasts of green energy as more soldiers poured into the streets to help. Olorus had regained his feet but had been cut off from Leah and was now single-handedly fighting two of the human-sized demons.

Not human-sized, Leah realized. *They* are *humans. Or, at least, they were.*

The creature that had once been Marcus Worth advanced and swung at her in a wild chop. Leah yet again batted the blade one way as she simultaneously stepped in the opposite direction. Her opponent was thrown off-balance, and she hauled back with her saber but did not have the heart to deliver the killing blow. Instead, she stepped backward and raised her blade to the defensive position again.

Marcus raised the tip of his blade to point it at her. He bared his teeth, causing more of his lips to crumble and break away like brittle, dry leaves, then lunged. Leah kicked backward off her front foot, slapping the advancing blade aside and landing two steps back. Marcus snarled. The red light flared deep in his empty eye sockets.

Leah could taste the tears on her lips but was aware that their flow from her eyes had stopped. She narrowed her gaze on the thing that had been Marcus. She shifted her sword to a high position over her head with the tip pointed down.

"Don't make me do this, Marcus," she said again.

A noise erupted from Marcus's throat like laughter, and he shot forward in another lunge. This time, she recognized it for what it was: a badly disguised feint. So she waited. Marcus stopped himself mid-attack, redirected the sword strike, and attempted to bring his blade up and under her defenses in a raking upward slice. But he had exposed himself. And Leah had found her opening. She lined up her shot, preparing to bring her sword down through his neck like a needle—

A flash of green light. A surge of pure, overwhelming aurym power. *Justin. . . !*

Leah, deaf and blind in an instant, felt her legs go weak. The sensory overload was too much, and before she could catch herself, she staggered and dropped to her knees. There was a ringing in her ears. She raised her sword in a blind attempt to ward off Marcus's oncoming strike, but she was helpless. Defenseless.

CHAPTER 121

I should have expected this, thought Justin.

After all, how much time would have passed during his absence? A week? Five weeks, like last time? The demons had probably sensed the aurym of his departure from this world and had followed it here. Perhaps they'd been waiting most of that time for him to return.

Justin looked around. He saw no sign of Cyaxares, Kallorn, or any of the other Ru'Onorath, and their boats were nowhere to be seen. Instead, a black ship was moored off the coast a couple of hundred yards away. A demon ship. For now, Justin could only pray that his friends had made it off this island before these cythraul arrived.

Are there only five? thought Justin, reaching out with aurym to attempt to sense the presence of any other individuals nearby. *Maybe there are dozens here.*

But he didn't sense any others at the moment.

There are hundreds of islands in the Raedittean Archipelago, he reminded himself. *Cythraul are probably spread out across the Raedittean, covering as much of the area as possible, waiting for me to come back.*

With sword and shield raised and at the ready, Justin waded through the water, toward the beach, toward the five cythraul. The biggest of them exhaled sharply, sending a visible ripple outward across the surface of the water.

One of the cythraul had a great sword planted tip-down in the sand beside him, at least twelve feet long, with a blade that measured a foot across. Another held two curved scimitars. The third and fourth ones wielded double-bladed axes. And the fifth did not seem to have any weapon at all. Then Justin noticed that it was missing both of its hands. Instead of hands—whether placed there through some terrible surgery or another unknown process—were long, pointed metal claws. There were three on each wrist, like three great railroad spikes.

Others will have felt my arrival, thought Justin. *They'll be drawn here, to this island.*

As he drew nearer to the creatures, he spun Ahlund's sword in a flourish, sending a gout of flames sputtering from the end.

Got to act fast.

Suddenly, the five cythraul opened all five of their mouths at once.

"THE PLAN NEARS PERFECTION."

The voice came from all five mouths as one—like surround-sound, emitted from all five skulls all at once.

"YOUR ROLE IN THIS WORLD IS *OVER*."

A single voice, speaking through five demons as one.

The Nameless One.

"It's you," said Justin. "You are all of them."

The five cythraul spoke. "I. AM. MULTITUDES."

Justin clenched his teeth and took a defiant step forward. "What you did to my father, you will never do to me."

The cythraul made a sound together—a sort of grunt. "YOUR FATHER BEGGED FOR MERCY. LIKE A CHILD." Another grunt. "HE DID NOT KNOW THE NATURE OF *MY* MERCY."

Justin tightened his grip on Ahlund's sword. "Yet you still couldn't beat him. He escaped."

"ESCAPED," said the five cythraul as one, "OR WAS LET GO?"

Justin took another step forward, trying to mask the falter in his conviction.

"HE SERVED HIS PURPOSE," said the Nameless One through the five cythraul. "HE MADE THE WAY FOR *ANOTHER*. ONE MORE SUITABLE. HIS SON."

"I'll die before I let you turn me," said Justin.

"NO," said the cythraul, and all five slowly shook their heads. "NOT YOU."

Before Justin could respond to this, the five cythraul raised their hands—or what they had that passed for hands—and pointed them at Justin. "THE PLAN NEARS PERFECTION. *YOU* ARE NO LONGER NEEDED."

Swirling singularities of black energy appeared, hovering before the demons' hands, ringed with veins of purple electrical energy. Pure daemyn power. Justin's soul quaked at the feel of it even as his demon arm seemed to hunger for it.

CHAPTER 122

Hook looked down the length of the lance at Cadmus. His eyes wandered to the coiled whip hanging from Cadmus's belt. He still carried his row-master's whip, despite his new position as royal admiral. As if it meant more to him than its utility. As if it were a token. A trophy.

Could it be the same one, even after all these years? Had the scars on Hook's back been left by lashes from the coral-studded leather of this very whip?

And Jocasta's scars, too.

The high of adrenaline was passing, and the bolt-shot to Hook's shoulder was hurting in earnest now. The pain came in dizzying waves. Double vision caused Cadmus's face to momentarily split in two, and Hook shook his head to shrug it off.

Hook leaned over and reached into Cadmus's left-front pocket. Jocasta's bandana.

Hook pulled it out and stood back up. He caressed the fabric between his fingers. In his mind, for the thousandth time, he saw it pulled away from Jocasta's hair in his desperate attempt to catch her as she fell overboard—with one of Cadmus's crossbow bolts through her chest.

Hook set his jaw and redirected his gaze from the bandana to Cadmus.

"Guess I'm not the first man to be killed by a dog from his own kennel," Cadmus babbled, almost incoherently. "Go on and do it, slave-scum. For your little Fawn."

Yes, thought Hook. *Not for me. For her.*

Hook tightened his grip on the haft of the lance, then drove it down—sticking its tip into the blood-stained grass.

Hook bent down, took Cadmus's arm, and wrapped Jocasta's bandana around the cut where the artery had been nicked. Cadmus's blood spilled out over his fingers, soaking the bandana. He pulled the bandana as tight as he could before tying it in place, causing Cadmus to growl in pain. Hook examined his work. With any luck, it would be enough to reduce the blood loss until he could get him to a healer—

Cadmus lurched forward, swiping at Hook's face with a shard of broken window glass hidden in his hand. Hook was so delirious from his own injury that, if Cadmus hadn't already lost so much blood, the trick might have worked. But the move was slow and clumsy, and Hook easily caught him by the wrist. Cadmus thrashed against his grip. And when that didn't work, he spat into Hook's face.

Holding this defenseless man by his meaty wrist, feeling the man's saliva running down the side of his face, Hook glared into Cadmus's eyes. Pitiless, hate-filled eyes. How Hook longed for the poetic justice of using this man's own whip against him. How many times he had dreamed of the chance to split this man from bowel to jowl and dump *him* in the water—disposed of like a used tool, as *he* had done to so many men and women.

But Jocasta's words rang in Hook's head.

"Someday, you'll have to live for yourself. When you do, you'll realize that mercy is a stronger healer than revenge. And forgiveness will always win over hate."

Hook wasn't sure he believed Jocasta's theory about mercy, and he didn't think he ever would. But he was willing to try. For her.

"I'll kill you," mumbled Cadmus, still trying to pull away from Hook's grasp. "You animal. You—"

Hook squeezed Cadmus's wrist, and the shard of glass fell from his hand as he yelped in pain.

Hook's knees were weak, but he could still stand and walk, and that would be enough. Carefully, he spun Cadmus around and pulled the whip from his belt. The moonlight reflected off the black-red puddle in the grass as Hook used the whip to bind Cadmus's hands behind his back. He then pulled the lance from the ground and used the blunt end to prod Cadmus's lower back, an unspoken command for Hook's prisoner to march.

CHAPTER 123

With a series of pulses, the five daemyn blasts were released like a cannon volley—not all together, but strategically staggered to maximize their effectiveness.

The implications of the Nameless One's words threatened Justin's focus, but he pushed them away, opting instead to open himself to aurym. To embrace the peace that surpassed understanding. To surrender himself to be used by it rather than to use it.

His actions felt like second nature as he powered up Ahlund's sword, feeding aurym through it until the dancing flames became an unstable, blue-white glow. He felt the radiant heat burning his hands, but he ignored it. He would need to find some sort of protection from that in the future.

The five shots had been aimed in different places. Both he and the Nameless One knew from experience that he could absorb daemyn with his demon arm, so a blast fired straight at him would have been ineffective. The first was aimed at his body, but the others were directed at a series of points in front of him. Each would explode upon impact.

Justin swung Ahlund's sword in a chop at the first daemyn blast; the knowledge that came from outside of himself told him what would happen even before it did—the blue-white beam that extended from

Ahlund's broken sword split the daemyn blast down the middle, sending two half-spheres of dark energy flying off in wild trajectories to either side of Justin.

He then dived forward and sidelong, ducking behind his raised shield. A blast hit the ground several yards away. He felt the swirling, tearing forces of unleashed daemyn energy as it erupted, but his father's shield protected him from the electrical discharges and chunks of earth flying toward him. He quickly looped the shield over his shoulders, strapping it to his back and exposing his black, chitinous demon arm. The third blast was coming toward his new position, and he reached out for it.

The blast connected with his arm, where it altered in shape from an oblong spheroid to a swirling vortex. As purple lightning danced across the shallow tropical waters, the daemyn was sucked into Justin's hungry demon arm.

The fourth sailed over Justin's head. But before he could react, the fifth one landed a mere ten yards away from him. It swallowed up water and sand and exploded outward, and an invisible shock wave slammed into him.

Justin felt and heard his nose break. His eyeballs felt like they were being pushed into his head. His feet left the ground, and he flipped over backward.

CHAPTER 124

Justin was airborne for a moment, then landed on his back several yards away in the shallow surf. All the while, he knew that another blast would be coming, and he pushed himself to his feet just in time to meet it: a ball of concentrated night shooting toward him.

He reached his arm out toward it, intending to suck it in as he'd done before.

No, said a voice in his mind.

Justin listened.

Surrendering again to the peace from without, Justin allowed instinct to take control of his actions. He reduced the aurym power in

Ahlund's blade slightly, raised it to a defensive position, and braced himself.

The daemyn blast struck the flat of Ahlund's sword, forcing Justin to go sliding back through the surf. But it held. The blast neither broke through his defenses nor was cut in two as the previous one had been. It halted in its path and hung suspended before Justin's face.

For a moment, it was as if the scene had been frozen in time. Justin felt the radiation of daemyn and the heat of Ahlund's sword burning his skin, and he clenched his teeth against the pain. Then he let loose a war cry, and he sent aurym flooding through the sword again.

The daemyn shot backward like a rubber ball off a brick wall. Three of the five cythraul reacted in time, diving sidelong to avoid the blast. But the two at the center weren't fast enough.

The daemyn blast did not slow as it hit the two cythraul. Instead, it ate neatly through their bodies, leaving two headless half-torsos standing and gushing black ichor. Both quickly succumbed to their own sinister internal energies and violently imploded.

While the other three cythraul scrambled to recover, Justin was already charging forward, determined not to give them any time to react. Now, for the first time, he understood that he was not fighting multiple cythraul; he was fighting the Nameless One in multiple bodies. What one of them knew, all the others knew. What one saw, all the others saw.

That is why coblyns obey them, thought Justin as he ran up the beach. *Not because they are cythraul. But because they are* him.

Justin stabbed Ahlund's sword forward like a spear. An unstable beam of blue-white fire lanced up the beach and hacked a scimitar-wielding arm off one of the still-recovering cythraul. It dropped its second scimitar and clutched at its gushing shoulder socket with its remaining hand. Justin followed up with a hammer-like chop that sent a tidal wave of white flames roaring toward the spike-handed cythraul. Sand turned to glass beneath his aurym power, and the cythraul gave a single mournful wail before it was reduced to ash.

The cythraul with the twelve-foot sword, meanwhile, had fully recovered. It came charging forward to meet Justin. But Justin did not slow.

CHAPTER 125

The twelve-foot sword came at Justin in a horizontal slash. Too low for him to duck. Too high for him to jump. And too fast for him to dodge. He raised Ahlund's sword—whose aurym-powered blue-white blade now made it twice as long as it had been even before it had broken—to meet the attack.

The two blades connected in a clash of dark and fiery energies. The force knocked Justin back.

Immediately, something struck Justin across the back, causing his head to snap back with whiplash due to his change of direction, and sending him sprawling forward to the ground. He wasn't sure what had hit him, but it almost surely would have killed him if not for his father's shield strapped to his back. He rolled across the sand. A cythraul's twelve-foot sword—broken in half from the clash of their weapons, yet no less effective as a halved six-foot sword—slammed into the ground where he had been lying a split second before.

Justin's roll positioned him right in front of the cythraul with the broken sword. He saw a huge foot lift off the ground and start to come down on him. He hacked upward with Ahlund's sword, severing the leg at the thigh. Black blood fell, and he hacked again. This time, the fiery beam shot up straight through the cythraul's middle, separating its right side from its left. The pieces of its body—including portions of its fleshless skull, split in two by the attack—fell to either side of him.

Justin tried to run, but try as he might, he couldn't quite escape the residual daemyn energy as the defeated cythraul imploded on itself and then burst outward with massive force. He felt a searing pain in his side and his hand, and he was thrown into deeper water.

Justin was submerged for a moment and came up hacking out sea-water, realizing a moment too late that Ahlund's sword was gone. The blast had thrown it from his grasp. He drew Benjamin's hand-and-a-half sword and turned, trying to remember how many of the cythraul he'd killed and how many were left—

A massive hand grabbed Justin by the front of his cloak and lifted him off the ground. He flailed against the bone-armored hand as he was lifted, but it was no use. He attempted to unclasp the brooch and slip free of his cloak, but the cythraul's hand was twisting, tightening the garment around him like a noose.

The demon picked him up in the air until he was suspended high above its fleshless head—a head as wide as a truck tire. This was the cythraul whose arm he had severed at the shoulder. Black ichor still poured from the empty socket, but it no longer seemed to care. Its attention was entirely on the small human in its remaining hand.

Panic threatened to override Justin's sense of spiritual peace. Ahlund's sword was gone. Desperately, he swung his hand-and-a-half sword against the creature's wrist, but the blade bounced off, deflected against a surface as hard as a mountainside.

"THE PLAN NEARS PERFECTION," the Nameless One said for a third time, through the mouth of the cythraul looking up at Justin.

Justin felt the noxious, stinging, sulfuric breath issued from the creature's mouth. Saw the glowing energy deep within its boney throat and empty eye sockets.

How foolish he had been to come back like this, so unprepared. His new armor and shield were nothing against daemyn. Had he really thought that Ahlund's broken sword would be enough against the will of the Nameless One? He had nothing else to fight with—

Your pocket, said a voice in his head.

Dad's stone! he realized.

Hanging suspended fifteen feet in the air, Justin reached into his pocket. He wrapped his hand around the object that had been in his mother's coat pocket until a few moments ago: an aurstone red as a ruby and polished to a brilliant sheen.

"It was my strongest weapon, Justin," his father had said. "My most reliable source of power."

Beyond that, he'd refused to tell Justin anything about it.

Justin didn't know what it did—didn't even know if it would work for him. But it was all he had.

Justin willed aurym into the stone. He felt the flow of power. He was doing it—it was working.

But nothing happened.

He felt a warmth emanating from the stone. Nothing more.

"ONE LESS SON OF BENJAMIN," said the cythraul.

As the giant demon pulled him closer, Justin continued feeding aurym through the stone, silently praying that it would do something—anything.

A sound like concrete blocks grinding against one another emanated from the cythraul's face, and Justin saw the bone armor of its cheek distorting in a sneer, forming the closest thing to a smile that a fleshless skull was capable of. In an instant, Justin realized what it planned to do. It was not going to turn him fully, as he'd once feared. It was going to bite his head off at the shoulders.

The mouth opened. Double rows of blade-like teeth parted, and the Nameless One's voice roared knowingly, "BURN THE *SHEEP!*"

CHAPTER 126

When the light finally passed and Leah's senses returned, the first thing she saw was Marcus's body lying on the ground in front of her. His blackened, disfigured body lay face-down in a puddle of blood, the fletched butt of an arrow protruding from the back of his head.

Leah blinked in confusion and turned to see an a'thri'ik-armored form walking toward her on stiff legs, a bow in its hand. The armored form removed its helmet, and Sif looked down at Marcus's body. His deep, round eyes welled up with tears.

"I am so sorry," Sif choked out, "my friend."

"Marcus . . ." breathed Leah, staring down at the dead body of her friend.

The cythraul transformed him, she realized. *Just like the cythraul in the forest did to Justin's arm. Except it turned* all *of him.*

"*Leah!*" came a cry from behind.

She turned. Olorus was still locked in combat. Behind him, the coblyns Itzacoatl had been fighting were all standing stock-still. Like her, they had been momentarily stunned by the overwhelming sensation of aurym. Itz either hadn't been affected, or he had quickly recovered, as he was now cutting coblyns down as fast as his hands could move. Where Lycon had disappeared to, Leah didn't know. But Olorus, who had shouted Leah's name, was waving one hand frantically toward the ships of the harbor.

Leah gazed out over the crowd. The cythraul at the waterfront had either abandoned or lost its sickle. Clutched in one of its hands was a human-sized body—a body fully clad in a'thri'ik armor except for a hooked hand.

As Leah watched, the cythraul shrugged off a blast of sunlight from Megara. Then it grabbed the head of the armored warrior in its hand and carefully, almost gently, removed the helmet. A long, white beard spilled out from beneath.

"Zechariah!" Sif cried in alarm, charging up the street toward the cythraul.

Olorus ducked an attack and swung his sword, beheading his opponent, then turned to race with Sif to help Zechariah.

But they wouldn't get there in time. No one would.

Zechariah struggled within the cythraul's grasp. The beast let loose a roar of triumph, then brought its hand down toward the old man's head. And Leah realized what it was going to do. It would turn Zechariah, just as it had turned Marcus.

A feeling the likes of which Leah had never known before suddenly rose up within her. It was, all at once, desperation, determination, fury, and the urgency to act. Pure, unbridled rage like she had never known coursed through her body, sending fiery impulses from her chest all the way to her fingertips.

Leah ran.

Sif and Olorus had a head start of several steps. Leah passed by them as if they were standing still.

She splayed her fingers out and pumped her arms as she sprinted. She realized, mid-stride, that she didn't have her saber, but she didn't care.

She had already closed the distance to the cythraul by half when a coblyn came at her. She lowered her shoulder and barreled through it as if it were nothing. Ahead, the cythraul's open hand was held back for a moment by one of Gunnar's vines, but it wrenched itself free and reached again for Zechariah's head.

Another coblyn came at Leah. She caught it by the throat. She pulled back with her opposite fist and slammed her metal gauntlet into its face five times in half a second. Gray matter jetted from its ear. Her hand moved in a blur of motion—the speed of her strikes impossibly fast, her grip on its neck improbably tight. Filled with a rage that was pure and all-encompassing and righteous, she gave this anomaly little thought.

Leah cast the oozing abomination aside and kept running, now moving even faster than before. She was still twenty feet away from the cythraul as it brought its hand down on Zechariah's head. Instinctively, she jumped.

CHAPTER 127

Leah felt her body flying through the air. Heard the rush of air passing by her. Felt her aurym flowing through one of the aurstones plundered from the Ellenean crown, in the pouch that still hung from her belt. It was the hydstone, she understood without being told—the same stone that she'd seen a man named Innocen use to rip people's limbs from their bodies as if pulling apart a freshly baked pastry.

Leah's body spanned the twenty-foot distance between her and the cythraul in a split-second's time. Zechariah saw her coming, and his expression changed from terror to astonishment just before the cythraul's hand closed over his head.

Leah realized in mid-leap that she was too high to strike with her fist, so she bent her leg at the knee, then snapped her foot forward. She heard a boom and a crack as her a'thri'ik-armored boot connected with the side of the cythraul's head, and kept going.

Leah snapped out of her possessed reverie while still in mid-air, suddenly realizing the impossibility of what she was doing. She turned wildly in the air, flailing her arms; beyond reaching the cythraul, she hadn't planned her trajectory. Her body somersaulted and continued along its path, pulled by gravity through a long, high arc.

She landed hard on her back. Her armor clanked and scraped and sparked against the cobblestone street as she slid, bounced, and rolled end-over-end. The cobbles turned to boards, and her armor gouged long lines like claw marks across the wood as she skidded toward the edge of the docks. She would have toppled over the edge and into the water below, had a long, snakelike appendage not grabbed her by the ankle and wrenched her to a stop.

Leah looked up. A flowering vine had hold of her just above the boot. She threw her helmet off and gasped for breath. The wind had been knocked out of her by the fall, and her back and ribs flared with pain. A dozen yards away, the cythraul had dropped Zechariah. It had its hands in shock. The cythraul's fleshless skull had been partially separated from its shoulders and now hung at a grotesque, lopsided angle. Black blood was seeping from its mouth and eyes. Leah had kicked its head off.

Leah saw Megara step forward and raise her gauntleted hand. A flash of concentrated sunlight shot forth, knocking the cythraul to its knees. Beside her, Gunnar threw his hand sideways as if in orchestration, and a large, woody vine grew upward and wrapped itself around the cythraul's head. It pulled hard. But it needn't have. Only soft tissues were holding the skull to the body—the inner structures had been shattered and severed, and the head came away from the shoulders as easily as a pulled weed.

Leah raised her hand to protect her face from the resulting daemyn blast as the defeated cythraul imploded, eaten from the inside by its own internal energies. Her other hand came to rest almost unconsciously on the satchel at her belt and the aurstones within.

Experimentally, Leah fed her aurym into it and felt the hydstone eagerly accept, channeling her power.

Leah's vision lost focus. Darkness consumed the corners of her vision, rapidly telescoping inward until all she could see was her own armored hand in front of her face. And then nothing. She felt her head fall back against the dock, and she knew no more.

CHAPTER 128

The last of Justin's resolve broke. He felt himself trembling like a child as he stared into the gaping, bladed mouth of the cythraul about to close around his head.

A flash of orange light. A cloud of peripheral flames.

The cythraul's fleshless skull, which had been smiling a few moments before, morphed into an expression of shock and despair. Its mouth closed, and it redirected its head to look down. Justin followed the gaze.

The cythraul's bone-armored, barrel chest was glowing orange, like an ingot steadily being melted from the inside. As Justin watched, a hole opened in the middle, its chest collapsed inward, and flames leaped up from within.

The cythraul looked back up at Justin. It opened its mouth and brought him down toward its gaping jaws, determined even now to finish the task.

Another flash of orange light erupted, and the center of the cythraul's chest split violently open. Despite the demon's resolve, its head flailed back in pain. The chest opened further outward, revealing burning hot coals and flames licking across the surface within.

The hand holding Justin let loose involuntarily, and Justin dropped.

He landed awkwardly in the shallows but immediately scrambled, trying to relocate Ahlund's sword. But he couldn't find it.

He wheeled back to face the cythraul and held his father's stone out toward it, continuing to feed aurym through it. The ruby-colored stone had changed in color and was glowing pale blue. Whatever was happening to the cythraul, his father's stone seemed to be responsible.

The one-armed cythraul stumbled forward onto its knees, staring in shock and disbelief at the fires raging inside its split-open chest. No sooner had it dropped to its knees than another bright orange flash came from behind.

Ahlund's sword, Justin realized, a moment before the broken blade came swinging at the cythraul from behind.

The flaming sword cut partway through the cythraul's neck, gagging its roar. A set of hands—human hands—wiggled the sword free, reared back, and swung again, this time chopping all the way through.

The cythraul's head dropped to the sand. An explosion of daemyn erupted as the cythraul's dying energies consumed it. All the while, Justin watched with wide eyes, struggling to catch a glimpse of the figure behind the cythraul—the figure holding Ahlund's sword.

The blast left a crater in the ground. Thick smoke rolled, obscuring the man-shaped figure that held Ahlund's sword.

"Justin," said a hard, gravelly voice.

This time, there was no mistaking it for the voice of aurym, his father, or anyone else.

The figure stepped forward through the smoke, and Justin stared.

Standing before him, in the form of a translucent blue silhouette, was Ahlund. His broken sword, the one Justin had dropped, was clutched in his half-transparent hand, flames dancing from the blade.

C H A P T E R 1 2 9

He looked not as he last had in life, but rather, as Justin best remembered him: in travel-worn clothes, standing tall and impassive, looking as immovable in body as he was in spirit. His hair and facial hair were as scraggly as ever but seemed cleaner than Justin could ever remember seeing it. He bore none of the mutilating wounds that had killed him—no cuts across his back or stomach, no hole in his chest. There was no sign of the daemyn-touch that burned into his face and forehead and caused his hair to fall from his scalp. In fact, he appeared entirely unharmed. He stood in the form of a partially transparent silhouette. His figure seemed to be made of blue-black space dotted with stars. From his belt hung a sheath. It was empty.

Ahlund took a few steps forward through the shallow water, and Justin noticed that the water lapped against his boots the same as it did against his own. Ahlund stopped a few feet away from Justin, looked curiously at his burning sword in his hand, and reduced the flames until the blade looked like normal steel again.

Justin couldn't speak.

Ahlund stood quietly, just watching him for a moment. Then his hard, transparent blue eyes shifted to look past him, into the distance, to where the starry horizon met the sea. He squinted as if he could just faintly see something out there on the sea.

"I'm out there," he said. His voice echoed richly. "Aren't I?"

For a moment, the shock of it all caused Justin to lose focus. The aurym flowing through him—through the stone in his hand, which his father had given him—faltered a bit. In response, Ahlund's blue shade dimmed and almost disappeared into nothingness, and the broken sword fell through his grasp as if his hand were made of smoke.

Justin caught himself in time and fed his power back into the stone. Ahlund's form regained substance.

For a moment, Ahlund stared at where his sword had fallen. He reached down and picked it back up. He stepped forward and held it out to Justin. Dumbly, Justin reached out and accepted it.

"I don't understand," said Justin. "What's going on?"

Ahlund looked down at his empty, ethereal hand. He flexed the fingers into a fist, then back into an open hand again. "Good question," he said.

Justin looked at the stone in his hand. But then something caught his eye. Behind Ahlund, scattered across the beach, there were others.

Half a dozen bluish, starry silhouettes of humans stood on the beach or at the edge of the jungle. Back in the jungles of Esthean, Justin had been able to see the aurym-glow of the blue tiger and other animals and life forces. Even in the darkness, even when he'd closed his eyes, he'd sensed their life forces so clearly that he'd been able to see their aurym as distinct silhouettes. The images he saw now were just like that.

Except, this was something different. These were the silhouettes of people who weren't there.

Justin stared at the apparitions. One of them, up the beach, was standing still and appeared to be looking up at the stars. Others were walking about as if looking for something. And two seemed to be in conversation with one another.

Was he seeing the past? Was that how his father had conquered so many lands? With knowledge gained from observing others via this stone?

But as Justin watched, the half-dozen glowing blue figures suddenly seemed to realize that they were not alone. One by one, they all stopped what they were doing and turned to look directly at Justin.

"Did I just," breathed Justin, "raise the dead?"

Ahlund looked around. "I don't think so," he said in his echoing, gravelly voice. "But you have found a way to bother us, it seems."

"But you *are* dead," said Justin.

"Obviously," said Ahlund.

"So . . . how is this happening?"

"Use your head," said Ahlund. "Look around you. There are others here like me, but not very many. Why?"

"I don't—"

"Think," Ahlund commanded before Justin could say more.

Justin had to suppress the old urge to bristle at Ahlund's bluntness. He considered for a moment.

"You must be here," said Justin, "because this is the last place your body was." He looked around at the other blue shadows, all still watching him from a distance. "Maybe I'm seeing other people who died here."

"Yes," said Ahlund.

"And this stone lets me see you," said Justin. "So you're stuck here, haunting this place, and this stone lets me—?"

"Of course not," said Ahlund. "I've never seen this place before. Until a moment ago, I was somewhere else. Your stone brought me here."

"Somewhere else?" said Justin.

"Somewhere else," agreed Ahlund. "I can't remember where. Wherever it was, I wasn't in this form while I was there. I wasn't *Ahlund* as you know him."

Justin looked hard at the starry, bluish specter of Ahlund. "But you're dead," he said. "How could you use your sword?"

"Why couldn't I?" said Ahlund.

Ahlund's seven-foot frame stepped forward until he was less than a foot away from Justin. There, he paused, raised his arm, and shoved Justin in the shoulder so hard that Justin stumbled and fell backward, landing on his rear end with a splash.

"Hey!" Justin protested.

"Do you not remember anything I taught you?" said Ahlund, glaring down at him.

"What are you talking about—?"

"*What* is aurym?" Ahlund demanded in a growl.

"Aurym is. . . ." said Justin. He began the sentence feeling confident but quickly realized that he wasn't sure how to answer.

"Life," Justin finally finished. "Aurym is life."

"No," said Ahlund. "But life is aurym."

Justin made a face. In response, Ahlund rolled his eyes and sighed, then extended a hand to help Justin up.

Justin reached out toward Ahlund's glowing blue, transparent hand. In spite of everything he'd already seen, he still expected his hand to travel through Ahlund's grasp. Instead, Ahlund's fingers closed around his hand, and he hauled Justin to his feet.

"I told you," said Ahlund, "the human spirit is made of aurym. It may not always be visible, but it's real. It's not some mystical feeling, and it isn't incorporeal. It has physical properties. If it didn't, it wouldn't be able to take physical form—like the fire from my sword."

Justin thought about this for a second.

"Death occurs," said Ahlund, "when the physical body is no longer a suitable dwelling place for aurym, and it is forced to move elsewhere."

"So, if the human spirit is made of aurym . . ." said Justin. He looked down at the stone in his hand. "This stone must have the ability to call on the aurym that has left people's bodies. To . . . bring those people back, sort of."

"Which is why I have physical properties," said Ahlund. "I can use my sword because *I am here*. That stone appears to have drawn back together the parts of aurym that were me, causing it to recoalesce into this form again."

Justin surprised himself by laughing. He stared at his friend. "Ahlund!" he said. "It's really you! This is so strange—I never thought I would talk to you again!"

Ahlund stared at Justin. "How do you think I feel?"

CHAPTER 130

Leah did not wake up gradually. Instead, her eyelids shot open.

For a few moments, she stared at the starry sky above. She felt the wooden boards beneath her body. Heard the gentle breeze as it ruffled her hair. Listened for the quiet voice of aurym, which she could have sworn had been speaking to her a few moments prior.

"She's awake!" someone shouted. "Over here!"

There came the sound of hurried footfalls. Leah tried to turn her head toward the source of the sound, but her neck was sore and stiff. She closed her eyes and groaned. Her entire body hurt. Especially her back and her ribs.

When she opened her eyes again, a series of faces had appeared above her. Lycon and Megara were there first. Then Olorus. Then Hook.

"Hook!" Leah said, relief flooding through her.

She started to sit up and reach a hand for her old friend, but Lycon put a hand on her shoulder to stop her. Only now did she realize that she wasn't in her armor. She was mostly undressed, lying beneath a blanket. She wasn't, as she had at first assumed, lying on the dock where she'd fallen. Rather, she was on a ship that was swaying back and forth with the motion of the sea.

"Wait, My Lady," said Lycon. "Try not to move just yet. I haven't been able to see to all of your injuries. I wasn't sure about your neck, so it took forever to get you out of that armor without risking further injury."

Leah relented and allowed herself to be placed on her back. Beneath the blanket, she held a hand to her side and probed with her fingers, hissing in pain as she did.

"Three broken ribs," she reported. "One separated, I think. Neck's only bruised. Back, too."

"I was glad to see you at the docks," Hook signed. *"But do you mind me asking how you did that?"*

"Yes!" Olorus cried, smiling broadly. "And why you have never seen fit to do so before!"

"It was one of the stones," said Leah, gasping a bit through the pain in her side. "One of the ones you brought back, Hook."

She was about to say more. Then she noticed the thick, dark blood-stains down the front of Hook's clothing.

"Do not worry about me," signed Hook. *"Lycon has dealt with the worst of it. The rest, he will see to after he has healed you."*

Leah nodded. She let her head drop back to the deck, and she shut her eyes. A coldness filled her heart as the details of the battle came flooding back to her.

"We lost Marcus," she said to no one in particular.

Part of her hoped that it had all just been a bad dream. No one voiced a reply—confirmation that it had been all too real.

"With your permission, My Lady?" said Lycon, touching the edge of the blanket.

"For the love of aurym, would you just call me Leah?" she said, opening her eyes again. "Yes, go ahead, please. And try not to lose any pieces this time."

Lycon winced, glancing at Leah's half-missing ear, but when he saw by her face that she was jesting, he blushed a bit and smiled. He started to pull back the blanket to begin the healing process, but Megara rested a hand on his shoulder and shot a look at the rest of the men.

"We'll give you some privacy," said Olorus. "Take good care of her, Major."

"Wait," said Leah. "What's happened? Where are we? Zechariah—is he all right? And Sif—?"

"They are around here somewhere," signed Hook. *"And doing fine."*

"Our exit did not proceed quite as we had anticipated," said Olorus. "But we made it out, nonetheless. We are at sea, sailing northeast as planned. Castydociana is hours behind us."

Leah hesitated. She was almost afraid to ask.

"Did anyone come with us?" she finally said.

Hook grinned. Megara laughed and smiled wide enough to show her missing canine tooth.

"Did *anyone* come with us?" repeated Olorus, incredulous. "Why—"

Hook raised a hand to stop him. *"Let her see for herself,"* he signed.

"Yes," agreed Megara. *"Incentive for her to get up and moving."*

Leah snorted a laugh. *"Asses,"* she signed.

CHAPTER 131

Hook lay alone on a bunk below deck, his arms folded behind his head. Above him, a simple oil lantern hung from the ceiling, swinging back and forth with the swaying of the ship. It was so familiar—that swaying feeling. So hauntingly familiar. He imagined it would take a long time to wear away at the negative associations that it brought. Maybe he would never get over it. But he would certainly have plenty of time to try.

Hook raised one hand to run a finger over the bare scar tissue on his forehead, which was no longer covered by Jocasta's bandana. The flesh ached beneath the surface; it had never healed properly, and it always ached, every moment of every day. A constant reminder of everything he'd lost. And everything, against all odds, that he'd gained.

A gentle knock came from the door. As a reply, he knocked once against the wall beside him.

The door opened, and Adonica stepped in. She was clothed in her usual soldier's gear—with the addition of a wide-brimmed feathered hat atop her head.

Hook cocked an eyebrow at her. *"Shouldn't you be aboard your ship, Captain Lor?"*

"Decided to make a quick transfer trip over to see how Major Belesys was holding up," she said.

"And?"

"Same old Lycon," she said. She pointed to her hat. "The stuffy bastard *saluted* me."

Hook grinned.

Adonica hesitated, then stepped further into the room. "I wanted to give you something," she said.

Hook sat up on his bed as she came closer. She reached into her pocket and brought out a long strip of cloth.

"I cut it from the flag of the *Naiad*," she said. "All of us are doing it. Cutting down our flags, I mean. It's supposed to be symbolic of our new status as an army that belongs to no nation. Makes sense, I guess. Everyone's a sucker for a meaningful gesture, right?"

Hook accepted the strip of cloth. He rubbed the fabric between his fingers.

"Lycon told me what you did," said Adonica.

Hook looked up at her.

"He said you came to him with an injured prisoner to be healed up," Adonica continued. "Said you asked that he be taken to be kept with Wulder and the others, if he was well enough. A big fella. With his hands bound in the coil of a slave driver's whip and a long scar across his forehead. And a strip of cloth binding what would have been a mortal wound."

Hook looked away, still seated on the bed, still rubbing the cloth between his fingers.

"She meant everything to you, didn't she?"

Hook looked up at her, blinking in surprise.

Adonica shrugged with her hands. "A girl can tell, you know."

Hook gave a small laugh through his nose.

"I lost someone close to me, too," said Adonica. "He was a good man. Made me a better person." She sucked at her teeth. "Wounds like that never heal fully. And anybody who tells you they *do* is full of it. There's no moving on. But you can go forward. One step at a time."

Hook looked into her eyes. Eyes that were so much like Jocasta's. Yet somehow completely different, in a way that was not altogether unpleasant.

"Whoever she was," said Adonica, "if you ever want to tell me about her, I'm all ears." She made a face, then quickly signed, *"So to speak—you know what I mean."*

Maybe Hook would have told her about Jocasta right then. Maybe he would have asked her to stay for a while. Maybe longer than a while. But Adonica reached down and patted him hard but amiably across the cheek—allowing one finger to linger a moment on the side of his jaw before she turned and left the room.

Hook looked down at the strip of cloth. He caressed it between his fingers. Then he raised it to his head, fitted it over his scar, and tied it in place.

CHAPTER 132

Leah held her hand to her side as she crossed the deck of the ship. So eager was she to get a glimpse that she hadn't bothered to get fully dressed and instead walked with the blanket draped around her shoulders to cover herself. She stopped at the railing and looked back at a fleet of ships, their masts lit blue-white beneath the twin moons high above the sea.

Her mouth dropped open.

She started trying to count them, then realized that they extended so far back that she couldn't see that far. Her vessel, a large double-masted sailing ship, was in the lead, and the fleet expanded behind it in an arrow-shaped formation. A few rows back, the formation reached ten ships wide. Even from here, thanks to the full moons, she could see that the ships continued backward through at least twenty ranks.

"You made some powerful enemies tonight," said a voice.

She turned to see Gunnar standing behind her, his long black locks swinging in the ocean breeze. "And I ought to know," he added.

"That's partly how I know I was right," said Leah. She tilted her head toward the procession of ships behind them. "How many are there?"

The admiral came forward to stand beside her, resting his arms against the railing. "Your guess is as good as mine," he said. "Zechariah and I procured several vessels to carry the number of soldiers we *thought* would be joining us. Then we helped ourselves to the city's stockpiles and loaded a few ships with rations. Only what we needed, of course, though I may have helped myself to some of their finest vintages—they won't miss 'em anyway.

"I thought we'd have a couple dozen ships following us, at most, and that would be it. But even as we were setting off into open water, more soldiers kept arriving, asking to join the 'Queen's Crusade.' When we finally set sail, they were still coming, with no end in sight." He shrugged. "There are only so many boats in Castydociana, you know. Hopefully enough to accommodate everyone who wished to volunteer. *Aaand* hopefully enough that Wulder and his new admiral will have a couple left when somebody finally lets them out of that barn."

Leah's face fell. "I just hope we have enough food to feed everyone who came with us."

"Oh, give me a *break*!" Gunnar objected, making a disgusted face. "Did you *hear* what I just told you? You have so many ships and people following you that you literally may have cleared out the whole League! I swear, Princess, you can create a problem out of anything."

"Queen," she corrected.

Gunnar ran an exasperated hand over his brow and massaged his temples.

"Cap'n! Cap'n!"

Gunnar turned to find Borris and Pool rushing toward him.

"Ha-*haaa*! There you are, lads!" Gunnar roared, rushing toward them. "By the seas, I have been longing for some proper drinking company!" He raised his voice even louder as he shouted, "Anyone else care to mend their woes by partaking in some of Castydociana's choicest spirits?"

Across the deck, Megara's hand went up.

The three men erupted in cheers and were carrying on loudly as they made their way down below decks with Megara close behind.

In their wake, three other men crossed the ship. These three, however, were far more sullen.

Sif, Itzcoatl, and Tel approached quietly, and Leah thought back to her final glimpse of Marcus Worth's body, lying with the fletched butt of an arrow sticking out of the back of his blackened head.

Before Sif could say a word, Leah crossed the deck and wrapped her arms around him. She felt him lower his head shamefully, resting his chin on her shoulder.

"There was nothing else you could have done," she said. "He wasn't himself."

Sif sniffed, returned the embrace halfheartedly, and then backed away. Leah could see it on his face; he didn't believe that he deserved any such kindness.

"He didn't want to do it, Elder Leah," offered Tel. "But we saw you fall to your knees, defenseless. And Marcus had his sword raised. It appeared he was about to kill you, and Sif had his bow—"

"I know," said Leah. "Sif, you were entirely in the right. That *thing* wasn't Marcus. Not anymore. The cythraul did something to those people. If I had known they were capable of such things. . . . I suspect that your arrow graced the man we once knew with a merciful end. My only regret is that I didn't do it myself when I had the chance—so that you wouldn't have had to."

Sif nodded, apparently grateful for her words.

"My Queen," said Itzcoatl. "I had heard you speak of demons. And I have encountered coblyns before, as a younger man. But those things. . . . I was not prepared for such a sight."

"Neither was I, Itz," said Leah. She favored each of them with a smile. "It's been a long few days for all of us. Get some rest. There's no telling what we may face between here and Erum."

And there's no guarantee, Leah reminded herself, *that Wulder's forces—or others—won't come after us once they have recovered from our betrayal.*

"Thank you, Elder Leah," said Tel.

Sif still said not a word as Tel and Itz led him away.

CHAPTER 133

Leah gave the fleet of ships one last look, then turned to cross the deck to the other end of the ship. She passed the helm, where the woman at the wheel saluted smartly and Leah returned it. A moment later, she was standing alone on the bow, looking out toward the empty, open ocean in front of them.

She sensed his approach but did not turn to meet him. There was something about him that she had begun to realize that she could sense, when he was near, even without seeing him. Something to do with aurym, probably.

"Justin came back," said Leah.

"You felt it, too," said Zechariah from behind her.

"Felt it?" she said. "It nearly knocked me out."

"Me, too," said Zechariah. He walked up and stood beside her at the bow, looking out over the ocean. "That was how I found myself in such a compromised position. I daresay that if you hadn't acted when you had. . . . Thank you."

Leah nodded.

"I hope you don't mind, but I took the liberty of setting it for you," said Zechariah.

Leah turned to find Zechariah holding a necklace out to her.

Hesitantly, Leah took the necklace in her hand. For a moment, she looked at it as if it were a snake that might strike her at any moment. Then she rubbed her thumb over the smooth facets of the hydstone. Even now, she could feel the stone's willingness to accept her aurym. Zechariah had sent Gunnar, Hook, and Adonica to look for this thing, all in the hope that someone among their numbers might be capable of using it. She hadn't expected that someone to be her.

"The cythraul and those coblyns," said Leah. "How did they get into the city?"

"While Marcus and I were loading up, an unmarked ship sailed into the harbor and rammed itself against the pier," said Zechariah. "Out from it came the demons."

"Including those half-human things?" said Leah.

"Yes," said Zechariah. "Gunnar and Megara arrived just in time to help us fend them off, while Adonica helped your friends—the elderly chap and the little girl—get to safety."

Leah stared out over the ocean. "Those half-humans. Did you know that a cythraul could do that to a person?"

"Yes," said Zechariah.

Leah chewed on her tongue, holding back tears. "Did you see it happen to Marcus?"

Zechariah sighed. "Yes."

A long silence passed. So long that Leah, listening to the ocean waves and feeling the wind in her hair, nearly forgot that Zechariah was there.

"Where do you think he is now?" Leah finally asked. "Justin, I mean."

Zechariah made a thoughtful noise in his throat. "Now what makes you think of such a thing like that, at a time like this?"

Because I love him, thought Leah.

"Because I'm worried about him," she said. "Do you think we'll ever see him again?"

"I think so," said Zechariah. "I hope so, at any rate. He and Ahlund are probably out there somewhere even as we speak. Will we see them again? In some form or another, I am quite sure."

"I hope you're right," she said.

"Until then," said Zechariah. "We sail. To war."

Leah slipped the necklace over her head and stared out over the ocean. "To war," she agreed.

CHAPTER 134

Long into the night, Justin spoke, and Ahlund listened.

They sat across from one another in the sand, and Justin told him what had happened. How he'd escaped with Cyaxares and the rest of the Guardians. How they'd come to this island. And how he'd traveled back to his world.

He shared much of what he had learned from his father. And although he left his suspicions about Avagad's true origins unspoken, the look on Ahlund's face said that he, too, was mentally connecting the dots.

"Dad told me to take this," said Justin, looking at the glossy stone, glowing pale blue in his hand. "But he wouldn't tell me what it did. He said he used it to build his empire."

"I have never heard of an aurstone like this one before," said Ahlund. "Perhaps, like a gauge stone, normal individuals can only use it in a more basic application. But the power of an ethoul can make it do something entirely different."

"But how could he build an empire by talking to the dead?" said Justin.

Ahlund looked around, and Justin followed his gaze to take in the other six spirits on the island. They had continued to keep their distance so far, but they also continued to stare at Justin and Ahlund.

"Imagine," said Ahlund, "being able to stand on a ravaged battlefield and call back, in physical form, every ally who had fallen that day. If the wielder could select which individuals came back and which did not, then the enemy would have to face the same army a second time. Or a third time. Perhaps there is a limit to how many times such a thing could be done. Or perhaps not."

"An immortal army," said Justin. His gaze went distant. "Fighting, dying, then being called back to fight and die again? That sounds like torture. Repetitive, unending torment."

Ahlund was silent for a moment, then said, "Yes. It does."

Justin shivered, thinking back to his father's words: *If I told you about what it could do, only for you to have it fail. . . . I think it would frustrate you.*

Dad, thought Justin. *To do something like that to your friends, you must have been farther gone than I thought.*

"Does it . . . hurt?" asked Justin. "To be called back like this?"

Ahlund stroked his jaw. "It is a bit uncomfortable. It's like I was a waterfall one moment, and I was suppressed into a thimble the next. But it does not pain me."

Justin lowered his head. "Ahlund. I'm sorry. *I* got you killed. It was all my fault."

"I allowed myself to be killed," said Ahlund, "so that you could escape. The only apologies necessary would be if you had failed. But you did not."

"You said," said Justin, "that before I called you here, you were in another *form*?"

"Yes."

"Are you in, like, an afterlife or something?"

Ahlund hesitated. "I can't remember. And I would suspect that as long as I am here, in *this* form, something prevents me from remembering such things. Perhaps it works the opposite way as well. Perhaps in the other form, I cannot remember things that happened to me in this one. I hope so. It would be a welcome reprieve. As close to paradise as I can imagine."

Justin looked down at the stone in his hand, considering the significance of its location. In the pocket of his mother's green jacket. The one that had been hanging on the coat rack since the day she died.

"Cyaxares and the Guardians have moved on, I see," said Ahlund. He gestured over his shoulder toward the black demon ship anchored off the coast of the island. "A wise choice, given that your departure drew the demons here."

Justin nodded. "And me coming back here will have alerted them again. I don't think they can tell *exactly* where I am when I use my power. If they could, there would have been fifty cythraul here instead of five. But the Nameless One knows everything they know. He knows exactly where I am now."

Justin blinked hard and shook his head. The constant focus required of him to power the stone for this long was making him weary.

"So what are you going to do now?" said Ahlund.

Justin looked toward the demon ship. "Get off this island, for a start." He pulled some of the folded sheets of parchment from his pocket—the maps he had copied from Avagad's tower. He found the one he was looking for and handed it to Ahlund, pointing to the mark on the far-eastern continent. "Then, I'm going here."

"Is this where you think Avagad is?" asked Ahlund.

"For all I know, you killed Avagad back at Esthean," said Justin. "And anyway, I don't think he's the leader of the demons. At least, not the way we initially thought he was. But, judging by his maps, this location is important for some reason. It could be the demons' center of power. Maybe if I can disrupt them there, the rest of the demons throughout the Oikoumene will be easier to take out."

"So, we are sailing," said Ahlund.

"*We*?" said Justin.

"Do *you* know how to sail?" said Ahlund.

Justin made a face. "Well, no."

"Then we sail," said Ahlund.

Again, Justin blinked to clear the mental fog. He could feel sweat beading on his forehead.

"I can't keep this stone going forever," he said. "I don't even know how it really works. What if you can't come with me—what if you can't leave this island?"

"If I am beyond your reach, then things will be no different for you than they were a few minutes ago. We will have to learn as we go."

Without another word, Ahlund stood and started walking toward the demon ship.

Justin stood up. "Ahlund, wait."

The blue silhouette turned to face him, and Justin tossed the broken sword through the air. Ahlund caught it by the hilt. His cheek twitched with the slightest hint of a smile as he closed his fingers around it, savoring the feel. He spun it once, then slid it home in the ghostly sheath at his side. Justin could see the half-sword, visible inside the semitransparent sheath. For a moment, it almost looked as if the blade were whole again.

"You just can't catch a break, can you?" said Justin. "Even after you're dead, somebody still wants your help."

"Just get on the boat," said Ahlund.

CHAPTER 135

He stepped forward to face the seven cythraul. Alone.

The monsters looked down at him from empty eye sockets—glowing pits in the fleshless, black, oversized skulls atop their massive bodies. They were literal giants in comparison to human beings. Even more so, when compared to a man of below-average height like himself.

He had no armor. He carried no weapon. He wore only a simple hessian tunic. And he stared up at the seven cythraul, unafraid. The beasts stepped aside, and he walked between them, not bothering to look back, carrying a wooden chest propped on his shoulder.

The castle was ancient but had been kept mostly up to date. The entryway was anything but spartan; Darsidan royalty were, after all, notorious for their pretension and gaudy tastes. The decor might have struck him as intolerable on a normal day. But in its current state—with the floors and walls painted in swaths and splatters of dried blood and puddles of gore no one had yet bothered to clean up—Innocen almost liked it.

Ahead of him was a single staircase. He took it one step at a time, favoring the leg that had been wounded during the battle in Nolia. It had healed, but it still gave him a bit of trouble—a nagging reminder of his failure. A plan that had taken him weeks of reconnaissance and infiltration, and should have culminated in the abduction of the young princess of Nolia, had been ruined by a single, brief moment of carelessness. He'd managed to escape, but they knew his face now. It would be difficult to get that close again.

He regretted the setback but refused to dwell on it. The only path forward was to learn. And adapt.

In a trial by fire, the weak burn and die, Innocen reminded himself. *The strong are burned, too. The difference is that the flames only make* them *stronger.*

Innocen adjusted his grip on the wooden chest propped on his shoulder. His footsteps echoed up through the stone and marble spire as he ascended. The walls of the staircase were decorated with hanging tapestries, mounted pieces of armor that were presumably of historical significance, and framed paintings. Presently, he trod over a dried, rust-red stain coating the stairs and noticed that the face in the portrait hanging on the wall above it wore a red splatter across her chin, looking a bit like a child at table who had forgotten to use a napkin. Innocen glanced at the portrait's face, licked his lips, and kept climbing.

The door at the top of the stairs hung open. He had expected to find more cythraul waiting for him here. Or perhaps some soldiers. But there were none. Just a single man standing in the room at the top of the spire, staring out at the spectacular view of the sea—a sea dotted with hundreds of black sails.

The man stood with his back to Innocen and did not react, even though he had surely heard him enter. Innocen could see a band of silver wrapped around the back of the man's head—a crown, he suspected. A purple cape hung from his shoulders, only partially covering the ornate, snow-white armor. The white shoulderplates curled upward like two ivory tusks, and Innocen found himself wondering what kind of material that armor was made of. He'd never seen anything like it.

"I *knew* you were still alive," said Innocen. "There were conflicting reports, of course, but I knew better than to count you out until I had seen your corpse with my own eyes."

Avagad continued staring out at the black ships on the sea. He said nothing.

"I suffered a similar setback," said Innocen. "In Nolia. I had planned to kidnap Princess Anavion and use her to lure the ethoul out of hiding. But I—"

Avagad still did not turn to face Innocen as he said in a low mumble, "What is it you want?"

"Nothing," said Innocen. "Less than nothing. I come bearing gifts."

When Avagad offered no reply, Innocen tossed the wooden chest down in front of him. It shattered on the floor, spilling out hundreds of aurstones, ranging from rough-looking pebbles to precious stones. It must have taken the old man a lifetime to collect them all.

Innocen folded his hands together, got down on one knee, and bowed his head toward Avagad's back. "This is a peace offering, My Lord. I've had a change of heart, and I have come before you in humble supplication."

There was silence for a moment. Then Avagad mumbled, "Really?"

"The ethoul has returned," said Innocen. "Surely you felt it, too, as I did. In the past, I rejected your proposal—rejected your master's call. We have both fallen short of capturing the ethoul, but I now see that together, we could do marvelous things."

Avagad still said nothing.

Despite his resolve, Innocen found himself fighting a sense of unease. So far, there was no way to tell if the man with the crown was buying his act.

"I was a fool not to have seen the wisdom of an alliance before," said Innocen. His head was still bowed, his gaze to the floor, but he sensed Avagad finally turning to face him. He looked up. "For my shortsightedness, My Lord, I humbly beg your mercy—"

A bolt of purple energy flashed from Avagad's outstretched hand, striking Innocen in the chest.

Innocen felt his heart stop—an interesting sensation—then start back up again. He felt the momentary halt of his blood flow, felt it from the tips of his toes to the top of his scalp.

His head struck the ground, though he could not remember falling, and for a moment, he could only lie there, spasming on the floor, trying to make his muscles work. He willed aurym into his hydstone, but another purple flash arced through his vision and struck him where he lay. He gasped for breath and saw sparks dance through his vision as the pain expanded from his chest, outward through his arms, down into his stomach, groin, legs, and feet. He heard himself screaming. Smelled his skin burning.

When the sparks and the burning pain finally stopped, Innocen tried again to call on aurym to activate his hydstone—to leap up from the floor and make his escape. But before he could make a move, he felt a stabbing pain in his forearm. He looked down. A crystal-clear icicle several inches in diameter had been driven through his wrist, pinning him to the floor. Blood oozed from the wound but froze instantly as the ice expanded, growing outward, encapsulating his hand, wrist, and arm. It formed a block of ice that held him pinned to the floor.

Innocen raised his free hand to claw at the icy restraint when a shadow fell across him. He looked up.

The last time Innocen had seen Avagad—through the Kharon, when this man had attempted to recruit him to the Nameless One's cause—he'd been a clean-cut, immaculately groomed man. A sharp jaw. Full lips. Smooth skin that was devoid of wrinkles in spite of his improbable age—several thousand years, if the rumors were correct. But the face that looked down at Innocen now was very different.

His cheeks were masses of web-like scar tissue. His left eye was an empty socket—a divot of pink flesh—and his right eye looked as if it had only just barely been spared the same fate. He had no lips, only rounded flaps of flesh bordering a small, fish-like mouth. Where his nose should have been was a gaping hole in the front of his head. The soft structures visible within reminded Innocen of the shell of a walnut.

Innocen was speechless, partially from the pain, partially from the appearance of the man standing over him. The only parts of Avagad's face to have escaped whatever disaster had caused this were his right eye and the right side of his forehead, where his hairline was still perfectly shaped. The left side of his head hadn't been so fortunate. The crown that sat atop his brow had been partially melted. The silver was mis-shapen like a frozen stream merged deep into his flesh—like a tree root in shallow earth.

Avagad pushed back his purple cape. Beneath it, Innocen could see that even his ceremonial white armor had suffered from the effects of this catastrophic injury; the breastplate was scorched black, warped, twisted, and melted inward so badly that Innocen was certain it, like the crown, also must have melted into the flesh beneath.

Off-center, not far from Avagad's heart, was a split in the armor. A shard of steel—what Innocen assumed to be a broken blade—pro-truded a bit from the place where it had been rammed into him.

By now, the growing block of ice had spread all the way to Innocen's armpit. The skin beneath felt like it was burning.

"I came h—here—" Innocen stammered through the pain. "To pro-pose a *partnership*!"

Avagad looked down at him with one eye. Idly, he reached beneath his purple cape and drew forth a long sword—a two-hander, claymore-style weapon with forward-sloping quillons. He drew a firm grip on the hilt, and the blade erupted with blinding green light. The voice that came from Avagad's lipless mouth was devoid of passion.

"A partnership," he said, his badly scarred mouth forcing him to speak in a lisping sort of mumble. "Yes. My master had the same idea."

The cythraul had to duck to enter the room through the oversized doorway. A moment too late, Innocen realized what was about to hap-pen to him.

Innocen sent a surge of power through his hydstone and struggled so hard against the anchor of ice that he felt several of the bones in his hand pull apart. But Avagad continued the onslaught, pouring ice over him, holding him down.

The cythraul's hand clamped down over Innocen's head.

"No!" Innocen screamed.

Searing pain filled him as something entered through his flesh. He felt it burning him, eating through his scalp. A darkness filling his mind.

"*No!*" he screamed again, and his voice sounded strange in his ears. "Please! *Mercy!*"

He felt the tickle of loose hairs as they dropped from his head. Felt the darkness traveling across his face, down his spine, burning, electrifying, and decaying every nerve as it progressed.

No, Innocen thought.

"YES," Innocen said.

But it wasn't he who said it. It was another. Speaking through him.

The agony of the darkness was unrelenting. He felt it enter his lips, slide down his throat and enter him. His vision faded to blackness as he felt his eyes shrivel, then melt.

"*Mercy*, he says," Innocen heard Avagad mumble. "What a concept."

The blackness of Innocen's vision changed, and suddenly, despite the loss of his eyes, he could see again—in a strange, shadowy, reversed-color image. He saw Avagad standing over him. Visible waves of aurym power emanated from the man. Innocen hungered for it.

Innocen felt his arm break free from the case of ice. He felt his body standing, no longer under his command.

Innocen was no longer in control of himself. He was controlled by another. But the pain did not end. It intensified. He felt the tiny part of himself that was still him being compressed, shoved into a corner. Shackled, helpless, immobile.

"Now for a test," Avagad mumbled. He gestured toward the pile of aurstones spilled on the floor. "Demonstrate your abilities, please."

Innocen's half-human, half-demon body moved toward the pile beside the broken chest. He stooped and gathered up a handful of the aurstones. Under no control of his own, he felt aurym flow through the hydstone implanted in his body—inserted deep in his stomach by the skilled hand of his Hyd master long ago.

The hydstone flared, flooding his muscles with aurym power like coal to a hungry furnace. His hand closed around the aurstones and crushed them to dust.

"Good," said Avagad, using a purple handkerchief to dab at the spittle that had accumulated at the corner of his lipless mouth. "Sometimes aurym abilities are lost during the transformation process. I am glad to see yours have been retained. This, I believe, will be a fine partnership indeed."

No! Innocen tried to scream. Instead, a voice that was not his own spoke through his mouth. It said, "The plan nears perfection. It is time . . . to burn the sheep."

The story continues in
CHILDREN OF THE FALLEN

NOTE FROM THE AUTHOR

My name is Corey McCullough. I'm the author of the book you just read, and I just want to take a moment to say, from the bottom of my heart, thank you for checking it out.

I've had the privelege of meeting a lot of readers over the course of my author journey so far. As a group, readers are fascinatingly diverse, but I've found that they all share a few things in common: they tend to be passionate, empathetic, and altogether awesome. And, being the genuinely awesome people they are, they often want to know the best way they can support their favorite authors, so I've come up with **five easy ways** you can help your favorite author keep the dream alive. To make it simple, I've listed them in order of easiest-to-do to most difficult.

1. **Contact the author** to let them know you finished the book. (This is not a promotional thing, it's just encouraging for an author to learn that someone has read their story, and a simple reach-out can go a long way toward helping them stay motivated.) For me, you can do so by texting me at (814) 499-1311.
2. **Follow the author** on your favorite social media platform.
3. Share a **picture of the book** on social media.
4. Leave an **honest customer review**. Positive *or* negative, ratings and reviews help by providing legitimacy to products.
5. Subscribe to the author's mailing list so you don't miss their next book. For mine, go to **coreymccullough.com/signup** (I'm always giving away freebies and bonuses to my subscribers, so I hope to see you there).

There are so many stories yet to be told, so many worlds yet unseen. Please take a minute to do one or two of the items listed above for your favorite author. You could change the fate of an entire universe.

Thanks again for reading,

Corey

ACKNOWLEDGMENTS

Thank you to my wife and kids. Your ceaseless support and patience make all these stories possible.

Thank you to my parents. You always believed in my dream to be an author.

Thank you to my proofreaders, Kyle and Roxana.

Special thanks to my advance readers, Stef, Kyle, and Ryan, for their invaluable feedback.

But most of all, my gratitude goes to you, the reader. The book you just read was written and self-published by an independent author. The choice to self-publish my books was motivated by a desire to retain total ownership and complete creative control of my work. This choice, as you can imagine, comes at the cost of many of the resources available through major publishing houses. But, by reading this book, you have made it possible for me to continue to share stories that entertain and delight. Thank you.

You can be a champion of independent art by spreading the word about artwork, music, games, and books by indie creators.

ABOUT THE AUTHOR

COREY MCCULLOUGH has worked as a ghostwriter, copy editor, proofreader, and archaeological field technician. He lives in western Pennsylvania with his wife Vanessa and their four children. His favorite pastimes are reading, writing, spending time with his best friend (Vanessa), and, most of all, being a dad.

www.coreymccullough.com
Instagram @core.author
Facebook.com/core.author
X (Twitter) @core_author
TikTok @core.author
Text (814) 499-1311

Visit **patreon.com/coreymccullough** to download full novels, read short stories available nowhere else, gain early access to Corey's new work, and receive other exclusive content.

Limited-time offer: Get 3 FREE audiobooks

For a limited time, you can download or stream these 3 full, unabridged audiobooks by Corey McCullough.

Go to **coreymccullough.com/audiodeal** to get yours.

www.ingramcontent.com/pod-product-compliance
Lightning Source LLC
Chambersburg PA
CBHW060242030726
47493CB00025B/1575